BAL
CHA

CUT & RUN SERIES BOOK 8

BY ABIGAIL ROUX

RIPTIDE
PUBLISHING

Riptide Publishing
PO Box 6652
Hillsborough, NJ 08844
www.riptidepublishing.com

Ball & Chain (Cut & Run, #8)

Cover Art by L.C. Chase, lcchase.com/design.htm
Editor: Rachel Haimowitz
Layout: L.C. Chase, lcchase.com/design.htm

ISBN: 978-1-62649-107-6

First edition
March, 2014

Also available in ebook:
ISBN: 978-1-62649-106-9

BALL & CHAIN

CUT & RUN SERIES BOOK 8

BY ABIGAIL ROUX

RIPTIDE PUBLISHING

TABLE OF
CONTENTS

CHAPTER 1

Kelly stood at Zane's side behind a barrier at the bus depot of Camp Lejeune. Zane didn't know him well enough to read him, and he wasn't interested in trying. He couldn't get past his own butterflies to analyze his companion's state of mind.

It had been six months since they'd watched Sidewinder walk down the gangway to their plane. Six long, lonely months of confusing feelings and dread whenever the phone rang. Zane had woken every morning expecting to hear horrible news about the men he considered friends, and not a day had passed that Ty hadn't been on his mind.

The call Zane had lived in fear of receiving had never come, thank God. In fact he'd only received a single satellite call from Ty in all the time he'd been gone, the one telling him when they'd be coming home. It had been like a drop of water to a dying man, and coming just weeks before Christmas, the best present Zane could have asked for.

Kelly had admitted to much the same type of existence as they'd driven there from the airport. Every day a struggle to keep his mind on something besides the fact that he wasn't there to help protect them.

"You nervous?" Zane asked him.

Kelly took a deep breath, nodding. "I've never been on this side of it."

"Is it any easier on the other side?"

Kelly glanced up at Zane, shrugging. "Not really. You sit there with all your buddies, men who've been your world for months, years. You think about the people at home, wonder if they've missed you. *Pray* they've missed you. Your mind cycles through everything that could have changed, and the nerves start building. Even the smallest thing can hit you like a hammer when you come out. I've seen guys break down and cry because their wives got a haircut."

"That why you made me shave?"

Kelly grinned and nodded as the first buses began to pull in. Nerves skittered through Zane as tired Marines in rumpled uniforms began to trickle into the tented areas where family awaited. Kelly inhaled sharply. Zane's hand began to tremble. "God," he said under his breath.

"The first ship holds seventeen hundred men. We might be here awhile," Kelly warned.

And they were. An hour and a half later, they were still standing behind the roped-off area, witnessing reunions, waiting. Zane was watching a man embrace two blonde toddlers when Kelly slapped his arm to get his attention. Zane scanned the crowd almost frantically, searching for whomever Kelly had caught sight of.

He only saw one familiar face, and it wasn't the one he was desperate to lay eyes on. "I thought they'd be out together," Zane mumbled. He glanced to his side, but Kelly was gone. He'd bolted and hopped the barrier, taking off at a dead sprint through the celebratory crowd.

Zane laughed as Kelly cut a swath toward the unsuspecting Marine. Nick was striding through the crowd of young sailors and Marines, nodding as they saluted him in passing. He looked long and lean in his uniform, hair shorn close and face clean shaven. He had more stripes on his arm than Zane remembered seeing in photos, and he walked with a change in his gait, like he might have been hiding a limp.

Zane hustled after Kelly, but he couldn't keep up. People parted for Kelly, sliding out of his way like they knew he wasn't going to let them slow him down just to be polite. He pushed off a few people receiving hugs, hopped around a few children too tiny to get out of the way. It was probably those erratic movements that caused Nick to spot him in the crowd.

A smile graced Nick's tanned face, and he braced himself at the last minute as Kelly leapt at him and tackled him to the ground. They disappeared from Zane's sight briefly, and Zane hurried to join them.

Kelly didn't seem to care who saw them, or what anyone thought of his lack of decorum, or even what Nick thought. He hugged Nick hard. Nick flailed under him, trapped between Kelly and the seabag still on his back. He finally wrapped his arms around Kelly and stopped struggling, laughing instead.

"Jesus Christ, if that's the welcome wagon, I think I'll walk home," Digger said as he approached. He shook Zane's hand and patted him on the shoulder. Then he dumped his seabag at Zane's feet and threw himself on top of Kelly.

A moment later, Owen appeared from the sea of faces and launched himself at the other three, wrapping his arms around all of them as they formed a dog pile in the middle of the crowd. Zane almost felt sorry for Nick being on the bottom. Almost.

He glanced up, scanning the crowd for the only person he desperately needed to see. He was searching so hard that he almost skipped right over him, standing just a few yards away and gazing at Zane with a smile.

Zane's breath caught. "Ty."

"Hi," Ty said with a bigger grin. He was tanned and bearded, which was why Zane hadn't immediately recognized him. His hair was longer than when he'd left too, obvious even under the hat he wore, and he was far leaner. But his hazel eyes still glinted like they always did.

Zane started toward him, not caring who might see or what the consequences would be. Ty jogged the rest of the distance and threw himself into Zane's arms. Zane buried his face in Ty's neck, relishing the warmth and solidity of the man. He breathed in his scent, even though it wasn't the one Zane usually associated with Ty. It was still him.

"Oh my God," Zane gasped finally. He tightened his arms around Ty, clutching at his uniform.

"I missed you," Ty whispered in his ear. His hands gripped at Zane's hair, and he stood on the toes of his boots so they could cling tighter to each other.

The thought of a kiss never entered Zane's mind. He didn't even think about stepping back so he could look at Ty's face, the face he'd seen in his dreams and forced himself to remember every night as he lay awake. He just squeezed his eyes closed and held on to Ty like he might be taken away again, clutched at him as he would grasp for his very soul in a pit of a thousand reaching hands.

Ty held to him the same way.

"Can't breathe!" a pitiful voice finally called out, interrupting the joyous reunion.

Ty pulled back only enough for him and Zane to glance over at the tangle of limbs and laughter that were their friends. Nick was trying to extricate himself from the bottom, with little luck.

Ty shook his head. "Don't care," he muttered as he finally looked Zane in the eyes and grinned widely. He took Zane's face in his hands. "Hello, beautiful."

Zane returned the smile, only to have it ruined as Ty pressed their mouths together, kissing him for all the months they'd missed. It was usually at this stage of a dream that Zane would wake up, alone and so heartsick he thought he might cry. But the kiss lingered on. Ty's hands on his face were still warm and solid. His beard was scratchy at Zane's cheek. He was real. This was real, and Zane wasn't about to let it slip away.

He grabbed Ty and dipped him backward, kissing him for all he was worth. He heard the distant snap of a few cameras, the tears of joy from other reunions, tiny voices welcoming their mothers and fathers home, the muffled gripes from Nick to let him the fuck off the ground so he could at least try to be dignified about coming home. He felt Ty smiling against his lips and holding on to his neck so he wouldn't fall.

It was the most satisfying rush of emotion Zane had ever experienced. Better than any high.

When he finally stood them back up and let go of Ty, they were both breathless and laughing. Zane couldn't keep his hands off Ty, wanting to maintain contact, wanting to reassure himself that this wasn't a dream.

Ty took his hand and didn't let go. "You look amazing," he said as he leered at Zane.

"So do you." Zane ran a hand over Ty's shoulder and the new insignia there. "Captain Grady, huh?"

"Captain." Ty nodded, his beard almost hiding his smile. "They gave us all a bump in rank equivalent to the time we would have served if we'd stayed in the Corps. Owen and I got kicked over to officers."

"Captain Grady," Zane repeated. He shook his head and swiped his fingers across Ty's chin. "Nope. You'll always be Staff Sergeant to me. What's with the beard?"

"Special forces. Don't worry, it's coming off."

"No, I like it. Keep it for a while."

Ty grinned. "Whatever you want."

Zane pulled him into another hug. He was peripherally aware of the rest of Sidewinder picking themselves up off the ground and trying to straighten their uniforms, and he finally let Ty go long enough to turn toward them.

They were all grinning from ear to ear, hugging Kelly repeatedly, unable to stop laughing long enough to speak. Kelly began poking fun at their new titles.

"Mother fucking Master Sergeant O'Flaherty," he said with a pluck at Nick's sleeve.

Nick brushed himself off, retrieving his hat from the ground with a grunt.

"Why the new ranks?" Zane asked Ty. He did a double take, unable to keep his eyes off the only man he'd been waiting to see.

"It's not as good a deal as it sounds," Ty said. "The ranks came with some pretty steep responsibilities. It was the reason we were called back. That's . . . that's pretty much all I can say."

"Are you out now?" Zane asked. "Is it . . . is this it?"

"Yeah, this is it," Ty answered. "I'm out."

"Me too," Digger said, almost singing the words. He bent to pick up his seabag and slung it over his shoulder.

Owen laughed ruefully. "They asked me to stay on. But, uh . . . I told them to stick it. It's back to the private sector for me."

Zane snorted, glancing at Nick. He was looking at his feet, and Kelly was watching him with narrowed eyes.

"Nick?" Kelly asked. "Did they ask you to re-up?"

"Yeah, they did," Nick answered without looking up.

"You didn't," Kelly whispered.

Nick cleared his throat. "They asked me to stay on as a drill instructor."

"Oh, good casting," Ty mumbled. Zane glanced at him, and Ty mouthed, "He's scary."

"I told them no." Nick smiled at Kelly, then looked around before picking up his seabag again. "I'm done with carrying a gun."

He walked off. The others stared, looking stunned and confused. After a few seconds, Kelly jogged after him.

Zane finally found his voice and turned back to Ty. "What the hell happened to you guys?"

Ty was still watching Nick make his way through the crowd, his mouth hanging open. He had to tear his attention away to meet Zane's eyes.

Owen grunted and smacked Digger in the chest. "Let's go get a fucking milkshake."

"Milkshake?" Zane echoed.

Owen nodded and grabbed up his bag. "And meat."

"Oh, meat!" Digger practically skipped after the others, leaving Ty and Zane alone.

Ty was still staring after them, frowning. "There's something wrong with him."

"Digger? Hasn't he always been like that?"

Ty shook his head. "Nick. There's something wrong with Nick." He turned to Zane and wrapped his arms around his neck. "I missed you."

Zane pressed his face to Ty's neck and closed his eyes. He laughed. "Can we skip milkshakes and just go home?"

"Nope. Bad luck." Ty kissed his cheek, then took his hand and began leading him through the celebratory crowd.

When Ty walked into the federal building in Baltimore, it caused quite a fuss. Zane hadn't told anyone he was coming home because he hadn't wanted to deal with all the teasing from his coworkers. But also because he'd wanted to walk out of the elevator and see all their faces when they realized Ty was with him.

The commotion started with their old team. Clancy saw them and screamed and flailed, which caused Alston to duck and cover like he was used to her smacking him. She came running over and threw herself into Ty's arms, hugging him around the neck and letting her feet dangle. Ty was wearing a red Santa hat with a white fluffball on the end, and the fluffball hit Clancy in the head when they hugged, but she didn't seem to care.

Alston, Perrimore, and Lassiter swiftly joined her, giving Ty hugs and handshakes. Others came over to welcome Ty home, and it didn't take five minutes for the teasing and ribbing to start. Everyone in the office, including Zane, had had six months to get used to the idea of Ty and Zane being a couple. Zane had endured a great deal of good-natured banter, with a side helping of nasty comments and uninformed opinions. For the most part, though, it had become old news. People had gotten over it and accepted it, then mostly forgotten it the longer Ty had been away.

For Ty, though, it was all new. And from the look in his eyes, it was scary.

The uproar in the office gained the attention of the Special Agent in Charge. McCoy stepped out of his office and started to shout at them, but he caught himself when he saw Ty at the center of the group.

"Grady!" he shouted. The group broke apart and people turned to look at their boss. Everyone was silent as they waited for McCoy to continue. He pointed at Ty and then Zane. "You two, in my office."

He disappeared back into his office.

Ty and Zane shared a glance, and Zane grinned.

"Like being home again," Ty said as they obediently headed for the office.

McCoy was digging in his desk drawer when they came in. "I've got something for you," he told Ty. He pulled Ty's service weapon and badge out of his drawer and set them on the desk.

Ty stared at it for a moment, a smile playing at his lips. "Don't I have to pass certification again first?"

"You've been living in certification," McCoy countered. He glanced at Zane, but his smile was hesitant and a little sad. He lowered his head. "It's good to see you back safe, Grady."

"Thank you, sir."

"Have a seat. I'm afraid I don't have good news from the home front."

Zane groaned. "Please tell me you're not putting him back on desk duty. You remember what happened last time."

McCoy turned his chair so he could rest his elbow on the desk and prop his chin in his hand. He didn't seem amused. In fact, he seemed downright solemn.

After a long moment of silence, he breathed in deeply. "Gentlemen," he said as he examined a file on his desk. He tapped it as if trying to decide what else to say. "During the course of Grady's leave of absence, a few things came to light that . . . I would have preferred to remain in the dark. Unfortunately . . ." He trailed off and shook his head.

Zane's good humor drained away as he watched their boss through narrowed eyes. He caught himself turning to Ty and stopped.

Ty leaned back in his chair, slumping and scratching at his forehead. He pulled the Santa hat off. He'd gone pale, and his knee was bouncing. They both knew what was coming.

McCoy looked up at Ty from under lowered brows, and then his gaze shifted to Zane.

Ty held his trembling fingers over his brows, as if shielding himself from the sun.

"I need to know one thing from you both before I continue," McCoy said grimly. "Are you now or have you ever been involved . . . romantically?"

Ty closed his eyes as the rest of the color drained from his face. Zane blinked hard over McCoy's question and had no idea what to say. How could they reply when McCoy already knew the answer, but the truth would probably separate them?

McCoy watched them silently. Ty finally moved, sitting straighter in the seat. "Yes," he answered, the sound barely even a recognizable word.

McCoy slammed his hand onto his desk. "Dammit, Grady! All the times you've lied to me over the years, and you pick *now* to be honest?"

There wasn't anything Zane could add. Not really. He wasn't ashamed of being in love with Ty. He watched his partner as Ty met McCoy's eyes. He looked ill, but Zane knew why. They were well and truly out now. For better or worse. Ty was handling it better than expected, really.

McCoy propped both elbows on the desk and massaged his temples. Finally he leaned back and shook his head at them both. "Now, I want it made very clear that the Federal Bureau of Investigation does not give a good goddamn about *who* you fuck." He kept rubbing his fingers over his chin and mouth in a nervous habit that rarely manifested. "Heterosexual, homosexual, bisexual, omnisexual, transsexual . . . we don't give a damn. As long as you conduct yourself in a manner that is dignified and discreet, you do whatever you want. We will not tell you who or who *not* to be involved with. That having been said, my concern here, and that of my superiors, is how your relationship impacts your job performance and those around you."

"Romantically involved or not, we were one of the best goddamned teams you had," Zane said.

"And now you're his superior." McCoy shook his head and covered his mouth again. He met Zane's eyes; then his gaze flickered to Ty. "Gentlemen, if I could snuff this out, I would do it in a heartbeat. But you made a very public display before Grady left. While it's not against any specific Bureau policies, it's frowned upon, and it's been dealt with the same way across the board in the past."

"By sending one of us to North Carolina?" Zane asked with a bitter laugh.

"By separating you, yes."

"This is bullshit," Ty said.

"This is precedent," McCoy snapped. "You're both good agents, but neither of you have ever been above reproach. We can't afford to have your integrity come into question in the future because you're fucking. Especially now that Garrett is essentially your boss."

Zane grunted. "We're no longer partners, there's nothing to separate."

McCoy looked at him with true regret and sighed heavily. "You're management now, Garrett. There's no going back. And you can't have your . . . your boyfriend working under you."

Ty opened his mouth, and McCoy held up his hand. "If you make a joke, I'll shoot you."

"Yes, sir," Ty mumbled, slumping further into his chair.

"I have to reassign one of you."

Zane stared, appalled by this sudden obstacle thrown in their path. A reassignment could mean any number of things—different shifts, different departments—most of them not so conducive to him and Ty seeing each other regularly. There was no way McCoy could have any idea how serious their relationship was. He seemed to simply think they were sleeping together. Zane glanced over at Ty, who was sitting stock still and watching McCoy intently.

"We have several options," McCoy told them, obviously uncomfortable. "One of you will be transferred to another field office. DC or Philly would be relatively close. Even Newark. Unless you're willing to end your relationship to stay where you are?"

"No," Ty answered immediately, his voice low and firm. Zane shook his head. He wouldn't give up Ty now that he'd just gotten him back.

McCoy nodded as if he'd anticipated that reaction. "Well," he said slowly. "Which one of you will it be? Grady, we could send you to Philadelphia, closer to family. Garrett, you're already familiar with DC. You could easily go back there, where there are more chances to advance."

Zane dropped his gaze to his hands. Yes, he'd expected them to be separated. But he'd been anticipating them working different shifts, not this.

DC was a good choice. When he'd lived there when they'd first been partnered, Ty had driven back and forth from Baltimore. But it had only been for a matter of weeks. Zane drew a slow breath, trying not to resent McCoy for what he was making them do.

Before he could speak, though, Ty reached between their chairs and brushed his fingertips across Zane's elbow, eyes still on McCoy. Ty didn't appear angry or upset. In fact, Zane's usually temperamental partner looked downright composed as he pushed to his feet. He lowered his head as he reached under the lapel of his suit coat and pulled out his badge—the badge he'd just gotten back. He laid it on the desk in front of McCoy, followed by his Bureau-issued sidearm, still in its holster.

When McCoy looked up at him, his eyes were wide and his lips were parted.

Ty merely shook his head. "Nobody's moving."

Zane distantly wondered what the thundering noise was until he realized it was his heartbeat in his ears. He stared at Ty, unable to look away. He knew how much Ty loved and lived for his work. He was afraid to speak for fear of what would come out.

"Grady, think about this, would you?" McCoy said patiently. "I understand, okay? It's a shitty situation, and if I could sweep it under the rug, I would. I tried."

Ty was shaking his head, gently pushing the badge on the desk around in circles with his finger. "I know, Mac. But being separated is not an option." Zane's gut clenched as Ty used the one finger to push his badge closer to McCoy. "Garrett can stay where he is. Consider this my resignation."

"No, no," Zane finally managed to say. He stood and snatched Ty's badge from the desk. "No, I can't let you do that."

Ty turned to face him.

"You'll go insane if you're not working, Ty," Zane whispered. "I'm two years from retirement. Let me take the bullet on this one."

"Exactly, you're *two years* from retirement," Ty hissed. "Two years and it's over."

"Gentlemen." McCoy sighed. "If the Bureau loses either of you right now, it's my ass they'll come for. I can't let either of you resign, goddamn it. That's not a solution."

Ty shook his head and gave him a small smirk. "It's my way or the highway, Mac."

McCoy began to massage the bridge of his nose.

Ty reached for Zane's hand and gently removed the badge Zane was clutching. He set it on McCoy's desk and pushed it toward their boss, his eyes never leaving Zane's. Then the smirk turned into a smile—the same beautiful grin Zane had always loved. The laugh lines at his eyes appeared. His nose scrunched. But there was no light in his eyes, the sparkle that said he was enjoying life. That light hadn't been there since he'd gotten home.

"I've got a rubber band ball to retrieve from my desk," Ty said. He patted Zane's arm. "I'll see you at home."

He walked out, leaving Zane and McCoy staring after him with their mouths hanging open.

"I can't believe he just did that," McCoy finally said.

Zane shook his head. "Give me time before you file his paperwork, okay?"

"You're the Assistant Special Agent in Charge," McCoy said, and he stuffed Ty's badge and gun into a desk drawer. "*You* file his damn paperwork. Get out of my office."

Ty spent the next two weeks reacclimating to civilian life. He got up early to run, relearning his old route and taking note of everything that had changed. Buildings being redone, neighbors being gone, a florist where a dive bar used to be, a martini bar where the Fosters used to live.

It all felt the same, but it was different. A car would backfire and Ty would drop and roll. A baby would cry and Ty would reach for a gun he no longer carried. Zane would knock into him in the middle of the night and Ty would grab him and roll him off the bed.

Okay, that had been kind of funny after the fact.

But it was taking Ty longer to get used to being in his own skin again than he would have liked. He didn't hear much from the other guys, either. He supposed they were all suffering through the same sense of vertigo as he was. Sometimes it was easier to get used to real life again if they didn't speak for a while. They'd discovered that years ago. The only person Ty had expected to hear from already was Nick, but he hadn't even received a text message from the man. That in itself was strange, and it felt like something was missing from each day.

Not working was also disconcerting. He'd never in his life been without a job. It was driving him a little crazy already, and he knew he would have to find something else soon. A city cop position like Nick had taken up, or even private security somewhere, because as far as he was concerned, guns were the only thing he did well. But all he had to do now was work on the old Mustang in the backyard, and pore over the scraps of evidence Zane brought him about their mole.

Since their ordeal in New Orleans with Liam Bell resurfacing and the uncanny knowledge both he and the Vega cartel possessed about Ty and Zane's movements, Ty was just as sure as Zane was that a mole had infiltrated the Baltimore office. Burns had confirmed it the day Ty'd received his orders from the Marine Corps. Someone was relaying information to the Vega cartel, and God knew who else. Enemies who would kill Ty or Zane without a blink.

The danger had always been at the back of Ty's mind, knowing Zane was home, alone, with no one he could trust to watch his six. Kelly had spent a great deal of time in Baltimore getting to know Zane, keeping an eye on things for Ty, but Ty hadn't known that when he'd been away, so he'd fretted at night, worried himself sick when he had the free time to do it. Nick had attempted to distract him at first, but even he had given up on trying to keep Ty's mind off the very real threat.

Coming home and finding Zane happy and healthy, smiling and beautiful, had very nearly erased the worry from Ty's mind. But walking out of the office the day he'd quit, the realization had come tumbling down on him again that there was still a traitor in their midst, and now he'd removed himself from the game.

So he searched. He pored over news articles and police reports about the cartel. He tried to find connections between the events of New Orleans and any of their cases, delving into everything he had at hand that wouldn't tip off the mole. But his resources were minuscule, and there was so little to go on.

All he found were dead ends, and so more often than not he found himself just like he was now, on his back on a modified mechanics creeper—really just a plywood board he'd reinforced and put wheels on—beneath the Mustang.

He was humming along to the radio, trying to keep his mind clear as he worked, when someone grabbed him by both exposed ankles and yanked. He closed his eyes and tensed his entire body as the creeper shot out from under the Mustang, shocked he didn't catch his head on any protruding parts. When he cleared the undercarriage, he had his gun in hand, and was shielding his eyes from the winter sun with his wrench, even though he was pretty sure he knew who his assailant was.

"Let's go inside," Zane said, the mischief quite clear in his voice. He didn't even bother helping Ty off the ground, nor did he seem fazed that a twitchy war veteran had just pulled a gun on him. He headed for the door, already yanking at his tie and shrugging out of his jacket.

"What did you do?" Ty called after him.

Zane laughed, and Ty hurried to follow. He was pretty sure that whatever it was, he didn't want to miss it.

Zane jumped Ty before he could even say hello or wipe his greasy hands off on his jeans. He dragged him through the door and slammed him against the wall, leaving Ty's radio playing and all his tools laying out in the yard as snowflakes began to drift down.

The next kiss made Ty think he could buy new tools if they got stolen or rusted. Zane pulled at his jeans and shoved at his heavy wool shirt, growling at him to take everything off.

"Jesus Christ, what happened to you?" Ty gasped.

"I was sitting at my desk, wanting to shoot myself," Zane said as he kissed his way down Ty's neck. "And I remembered that you were at home, just sitting around doing nothing."

Ty made an insulted noise, but he couldn't even argue because it was true.

Zane kissed him again, shoving Ty's jeans down his hips and sliding his fingers against Ty's bare skin. Then he stopped and met Ty's eyes with a smile that crinkled his laugh lines. "And I couldn't fucking wait to get home."

Ty moaned when Zane sank to his knees.

The first touch of Zane's tongue to the soft, sensitive skin at the crease of Ty's thigh and groin made his entire body shudder. Zane's bristly cheek glanced along the side of Ty's cock as Zane paused to suck hard on a patch of skin just inside the curve of Ty's hipbone.

Ty gripped the back of Zane's neck as he tried to catch his breath. This was the kind of '70s porn situation he had played over and over in his mind while he'd been gone. This was why he'd continued to fight when they'd been outnumbered, continued to duck when bullets flew. Not the sex, though that was certainly a bonus. But coming home to this, to Zane.

Zane's reply was a drawn-out hum, and he didn't stop until he'd placed a kiss at the base of Ty's cock.

"Jesus, Zane," Ty gritted out as his fingers tightened in Zane's hair. He didn't know whether to pull Zane's head back and ask him what the hell he was up to or hold his head there until he finished what he'd started. Because like it or not, Zane did not often come home from work ready to go at it against the kitchen wall. Ty missed working with him, missed seeing him at all hours of the day. And he hated, absolutely loathed, being out of the loop like this, wondering what the hell Zane was up to when he made advances.

Ty didn't care what his motives were once Zane licked all the way up his cock to the sensitive head.

He called out wordlessly and grabbed at Zane's shoulders with both hands, his back bumping against the brick of the kitchen wall.

He tried to push his hips forward but couldn't, instead settled for watching Zane. It wasn't messy or hurried; Zane was taking his own sweet time, tonguing and kissing and tasting and rubbing every millimeter of skin his lips met. Thoroughly and repeatedly. Just the sight of his lips on Ty's cock was enough to get Ty's blood pumping. Ty held his breath, his entire body thrumming with anticipation and teasing jolts of pleasure.

Then Zane took Ty into his mouth and sucked gently, and tipped his head back enough to look up at Ty. Ty couldn't take his eyes off him. "Don't think because your mouth is full you're not expected to explain."

Zane pulled off Ty long enough to press a kiss to his belly. He smirked up at him, then picked up where he left off, sucking carefully but with more strength while the fingers of his free hand curled into the muscles of Ty's hamstring.

Ty sucked in a breath and let his head fall back as his dirty fingers flattened against the rough brick behind him, and when he looked back down, the urge to sink his fingers into Zane's dark curls was almost overwhelming. It left him grasping for anything else to hold on to because he knew what he'd do to Zane if he got a handle on him.

"Zane!" he gasped again as his knees began to go weak. He wasn't even close enough to the stairs to grip the railing.

Zane's answer wasn't verbal; he simply gripped Ty's hips and pinned him to the wall as he continued his slow and methodical approach. Ty had to give Zane points for attention to detail. Classic Garrett.

"Fuck," Ty groaned plaintively. He banged his head back against the wall. Then somewhere close, amidst the pile of clothing Zane had yanked off him, his cell phone began to ring. He distantly recognized his brother's ringtone. "Christ, not again."

"Do you need to answer that?"

Ty shivered all over and shook his head. No way in hell could Deuce have *anything* to say to him that was more important than Zane on his knees with his mouth on Ty's dick.

"Are you sure?" Zane drawled before licking from Ty's balls all the way to the head of his erect cock in one wet swath. "Might be important."

Ty's eyes fluttered shut, and he groaned desperately. "Damn you," he gritted out. He reached for Zane's hair and yanked at his head so he could step away from the wall and pounce on the jeans that had been tossed aside. He grabbed at the phone, then turned back to Zane with every intention of continuing what they'd started without further unnecessary delay.

Apparently Zane was thinking the same thing, because he latched onto Ty's hips and pushed him back against the wall. *Damn*, he was determined.

Ty hung his head and panted for a few frantic breaths, trying to regain control before he answered the phone. He rested one hand on top of Zane's head, his fingers automatically curling as he answered with a curt, "Call me back in ten minutes."

Zane's tongue flicked over the head of his cock, and Ty bit his lip against a moan.

"Oh God. You're either having sex or being shot at, aren't you?" Deuce asked with dread. "*Why* do you answer the phone?"

"Got to go," Ty grunted as he swiped the phone off and tossed it into his pile of clothes, letting his hand join the other one in Zane's hair.

Muffled laughter sent vibrations through Ty's groin, and Zane pulled back, sucking all the way until Ty's erection popped free and rubbed through the whiskers on his chin. "Who was it?"

"My asshole brother," Ty answered tightly.

Zane bit his lip, peering up at Ty and waiting.

"Please, Zane," Ty begged, shameless. He slid his palm against Zane's cheek, his fingers digging into the back of his neck. Zane nodded slightly before leaning forward, taking Ty in on his tongue. He couldn't fit all of Ty's erect cock into his mouth, but it didn't matter. He wasn't teasing anymore; he was focusing on the endgame.

Ty did his best to keep his eyes open, watching as he disappeared between Zane's lips. He wanted nothing more than to come down Zane's throat. It was barely a matter of minutes with the visual stimulation, and Ty was soon gasping and tugging at Zane's hair in warning.

Zane pulled off, wrapped his fingers around Ty to pump him hard, and leaned his forehead against Ty's belly to kiss the warm skin.

Ty gritted out Zane's name as he came hard, watching lasciviously as it splattered onto Zane's throat and chest, onto his pressed dress shirt. As if on cue, his phone began to ring again. Zane jacked him through his orgasm, obviously not caring about how damn debauched he looked.

Ty's hand moved to Zane's shoulder and squeezed harder as his legs went weak and he began to sink toward the floor. Zane slid his arm around Ty's waist, and Ty wound up on his knees, panting hard as they kissed. The phone continued to ring, ruining the afterglow with its obnoxious tune. Ty ignored it for as long as his conscience would allow. Zane hugged him close for a long moment before he nipped at his lower lip, then he reached for the phone.

"Hello?"

Ty grunted at him and flopped to his back on the hardwood floor, unashamed. He could hear the tinny sound of his brother's voice through the phone. "Push the speaker button," he said to Zane.

Zane laughed at something Deuce said before jabbing the button and holding the phone out between them. "How's it going, Deuce?" Zane asked warmly. He wiped at his mouth and chin with the back of one hand.

"I hope he at least buys you dinner before you do that," Deuce said to Zane.

"I don't have to bribe my bedmates," Ty shouted at the phone. His brother laughed heartily. Ty couldn't help but smile. He looked at Zane and winked.

"I called to ask you a favor, Ty," Deuce said.

"Shoot," Ty said lazily, still lying on the floor and enjoying the post-orgasm high.

"I want you to be my best man."

Zane grinned. "You're getting married, finally?"

"Yep, we settled on the details."

Ty sat up, suddenly wishing he was wearing pants. "I better damn well be your best man," he muttered as he crawled closer to his jeans and lay back down to slide them on.

"Calm yourself." Deuce sounded very pleased with himself. "Zane? I expect you to be a groomsman as well. We're keeping the guest list small, and frankly, I don't know that many people I like."

"Sounds like a circus," Zane teased. "You know we'll be there for whatever you need." When Ty glanced up, Zane raised a brow in question and leaned to tug at Ty's jeans leg, trying to dissuade him from putting them on.

Ty narrowed his eyes in warning. "I need pants on to talk about this," he whispered.

"You know I can hear you, right?" Deuce said, voice wavering with laughter.

"Then you shouldn't call when we're in the middle of things! When's this thing going to be?"

"Well . . . it's next week."

"Next week?" Ty blurted. "What's the rush, man, you already knocked her up once!"

Zane smacked Ty in the head before he could duck.

"We're getting married in Scotland. And we thought, what better time to do it than Christmas?"

"Scotland?" Zane echoed, perking up. "Does that mean Ty has to wear a kilt?"

"Christmas in Scotland sounds . . . cold," Ty added.

"Get a hold of yourself," Deuce said. "A week away, all expenses paid. I'll email you the info."

Zane looked positively gleeful. He offered Ty the phone as he shifted to get up. Ty watched him walk away, then pressed the speaker button again and put the phone to his ear. "Deacon," he said softly.

"Beaumont," Deuce replied in a low voice.

"Are you happy?"

"Very much so," Deuce said. The answer would have been clear in his voice regardless.

Ty smiled. "Good."

"I have another favor to ask you," Deuce said quickly, his voice losing its enthusiasm.

Ty's brow furrowed. "Anything."

"Can you bring someone with you to the wedding?"

"What do you mean?"

"One of your Recon buddies."

Ty sat up, his unbuttoned jeans forgotten. "What? Why?"

"Short version? Livi's dad is concerned about safety. His company's been getting threats, apparently. That's why we're rushing it. He's got his own private bodyguards, but I'd feel a lot better if we had someone there who could put all his attention on the baby girl if anything goes wrong."

"You want a bodyguard for the baby at your wedding?" Ty frowned harder. He glanced up when Zane came back into the kitchen, shrugging at the questioning look Zane gave him, and Zane turned to head back into the living room. Ty's eyes lingered on his ass as he walked away.

"I know it sounds overboard, but I swear man, the way her dad talks, it makes me paranoid. And I don't want to have to worry on my wedding day."

"Yeah, no," Ty said quickly. "I got it. I'll call someone."

"I'll make him a groomsman so he'll have access to all the crap we're going to have to go through. Pay his way, everything. And give him a guest. It's only fair. All on us."

"Got it."

"Thanks, bro."

Ty nodded, grinning. "Now, if you ever call me again while I'm getting head, I'll kill you."

"Understood," Deuce said with a laugh, and the phone clicked off in Ty's ear.

Ty smirked, looking down at the phone for a moment before clambering to his feet. "Garrett!"

"What?" Zane called back.

Ty found Zane in the bathroom, shirt off, wiping himself down with a hand towel. "I'm not done with you. We have to celebrate."

Zane smiled indulgently. "Celebrate Deuce's engagement by *engaging* in copious amounts of hot sex?"

Ty spread his arms and cocked his head with a grin. "Sounds like a plan, right?"

Zane left the towel in the sink and moved until they stood chest to chest. He placed his hands on Ty's hips, his thumbs stroking the skin bared by Ty's unfastened jeans. "You know what that wedding means, don't you? A whole week. The two of us. On vaca—"

Ty tapped Zane's lips with two fingers, shushing him. "Don't finish that thought."

Zane blinked at him, smirking. "What else did he need?"

"Later," Ty grunted, determined to get back to business. "There was an inappropriate celebration we were getting to, remember?"

Zane chuckled, a low rumble in his chest. "You can't distract me that easily."

"Watch me," Ty growled.

It took Nick a long time to talk himself into climbing the front steps of the triple-decker he'd grown up in. He glanced at the upstairs window as he stood on the sidewalk. His father was laid up in bed there, dying from all the poison he'd put into his body in the last sixty or so years. He wanted to see all his children before he passed, wanted to make peace with them.

At least, that was what Nick's mother had told them. Nick knew there was something more going on, though. It had taken his mother two weeks to contact him after he'd returned home, and the first words from her mouth hadn't been to say she was glad he was home safe. Just that his father needed to see him.

He climbed the front steps and knocked before he could decide against it. His mother answered the door, her smile strained and her hug stiff when she greeted him.

"I'm glad you're here," she said, voice quiet. "You look good, Nicholas. Your father's been asking for you."

Nick merely nodded, resisting the urge to glance up or in the direction of his father's study. He was closer to forty than four, but he still felt that flash of anxiety and outright fear when he thought of walking down that hallway.

They stood in awkward silence, not really looking at each other, not really wanting to. This was the first time Nick had been in his childhood home since he'd told his parents he was bi. He hadn't been welcome after that.

Nick cleared his throat.

"Katherine and Erin are here," his mother said finally. "They've been waiting for you to get here before they go up to see him."

Nick nodded again, shrugging out of his snow-covered coat. He and Kat and Erin shared memories the younger siblings hadn't been subjected to.

"They're down—"

"I know where they are," Nick murmured, and headed for the creaky old door to the cellar.

The light at the top of the staircase didn't turn anything on, but then, it hadn't since Nick had gotten old enough to figure out how to cut the wires inside the switch. He descended in darkness, hoping his memory of the stairwell would keep him from breaking his damn neck. His footfalls were silent on the concrete steps. When he reached the bottom, a pool of weak light emitted from the corner, where old room dividers and screens and large concrete pillars partitioned off a piece of the cellar.

His two sisters were together on an old sofa in the corner. A battered coffee table with a duct-taped leg, braced with a broken hockey stick, sat before them. A lamp on a milk crate gave off the only light. They were flipping through a photo book, both alternately sniffling and laughing.

Nick shoved his hands into his pockets as he approached them, trying for a smile. He stood on the other side of the coffee table. "I thought I'd find you two down here."

Kat smiled weakly and cleared her throat. "Do you remember when he'd come home drunk and you'd gather all of us together and bring us down here?"

Nick fought to swallow past the tightening in his throat. "I remember."

"You'd tell us stories and we'd play board games or listen to the Sox play until we heard him go to sleep." Kat wiped at her eyes.

Nick stepped around the table, and they both moved over so he could sit between them. He spread his arms on the back of the couch, and both women leaned into him.

Kat's voice quivered when she spoke again. "I was never afraid when we were down here. Not when you were with us."

"Neither was I," Erin whispered. She hugged Nick close. "We knew you would protect us. You always did."

Nick closed his eyes, his arms tightening around them.

The three of them had met for dinner the day after he'd returned to Boston, catching up after he had been gone for so long. But this was something they never talked about.

Kat began to cry softly. She shoved the picture book away and pressed her face against Nick's chest. "These pictures . . . we never realized how young you were. My God, Nick, you were just a baby. You were younger than Patrick is now." Her oldest son. He'd just turned ten last week. "Who stood in front of you?"

"It's okay," Nick whispered.

They sat in silence, listening to the house creak, to their mother moving around upstairs, to the occasional voice of one of their two youngest sisters asking where the hell they were. The young ones didn't remember the basement, didn't remember Nick and Kat carrying them down here in bundles of blankets and setting them in stacks of pillows or beanbag chairs and singing them to sleep so they'd be safe. They didn't remember to look for their older siblings down here when the thought of facing their father was too much for them.

"Nicholas!" their mother called from the top of the steps. "Your father's awake. He's asking to see you."

Nick took a deep breath. The three of them shared a glance. Both his sisters looked like they wanted to hang on to him for dear life, just like they'd done when they were little.

"Let's go to tell him to kiss our asses," Erin said as she stood.

Nick stared at the rectangle of light near the bottom of the steps. He had so many memories of sitting on this couch, his arms around Kat and Erin, their baby sisters asleep on their laps, listening to the sound of their mother crying upstairs. And waiting. He remembered the terror of watching the silhouette of his father appear in that frame of light, hoping the man would try to storm down the steps Nick had booby-trapped with his sports equipment, praying he'd just trip and break his neck on the concrete floor when he landed.

He'd never grabbed one of those sticks or bats on his way up the steps after being summoned, though. He'd always left them where they were, knowing the veritable minefield would keep his sisters safe.

That didn't mean he'd never dreamed about taking that hockey stick and watching it crack his father's skull. He'd grabbed a baseball bat one time, the day before leaving for Basic. It had been the last time his father raised a hand to any of them.

A shadow appeared on the floor, different than the one that haunted him. "Nick?"

"Coming," Nick called. Kat and Erin trailed behind him as he made his way up the two flights to his father's bedroom.

He stood in the doorway, Kat and Erin still behind him. His two youngest sisters, Alana and Nessa, sat in chairs beside the bed, where Brian O'Flaherty lay propped amongst several pillows, jaundiced and weak. All three of them looked at the doorway when they realized Nick was standing there.

"Son," his father said. He pushed himself up, trying to sit straighter. He didn't quite make it.

Nick moved toward the bed. Nessa stood and gave him a stiff hug. Nick held onto her, flooded by memories of running down the hall and gathering her out of her bassinet, wrapping her up in her blankets and hugging her to his chest as he and Kat scrambled to get down to the cellar before their father hit the front door.

He let her go, and she and Alana moved to let him sit beside the bed. His father's eyes stayed on him, and Nick didn't look away. Eye contact had always been something he'd fought for. When he'd been little, it had pissed his dad off. He'd seen it as a challenge, like a fucking junkyard dog.

It had been worth a backhand to meet the man's eyes.

"You're home safe," his dad finally said. "That's good."

Nick nodded.

"You didn't even tell us you were leaving. We'd have come to see you off."

Nick snorted. "You hadn't spoken to me in over a year. You said I was going to hell."

Brian's eyes hardened. "I'm too sick to fight, Nicholas."

"That's a first," Nick said through gritted teeth.

"Nick, he can't handle stress right now, why don't you try to be civil," Alana spat. She was standing by the door, leaning against the wall with her arms crossed.

"Why don't you shut your mouth," Kat snapped.

Nick glanced over his shoulder at them, then back to his father. "I'm not here so you can say a tender good-bye. What do you want?"

"I want to make my peace with you, son. We had a rough road. But now I'm dying. And I'm scared."

Nick narrowed his eyes. He knew what sort of changes the thought of impending death could bring on a person. He'd suffered through them himself. But he knew his dad, too. The man wasn't seeking retribution or forgiveness. He wanted something, something only Nick could give him. And it wasn't peace.

"Cut to it. What do you want from me?"

Brian took a deep, rattling breath. "Without a new liver, I'll be dead in three to six months."

One of Nick's sisters sniffed. Nick didn't look away from his father.

"You're close enough to my size you could be a match, son. You're the only one who might be. You got that O blood type."

Nick sat back and closed his eyes.

"You've got to be shitting me!" Erin shouted.

"Erin!" their mother cried. "Your language!"

"Stuff it, Mom!" Kat waved a hand at Nick. "How the hell can either of you ask him to do this?"

"Dad is dying," Nessa said, her voice small and scared. "Even you can't be so selfish you wouldn't help him if you could. Even Nick's not *that* selfish."

Nick glanced over in time to recognize the warning signs of Kat and Erin about to blow a collective gasket.

"Everybody get out," he said softly.

"Nick!" Kat started.

"Kat, stay calm, okay? Give us a few minutes."

Kat held her breath but nodded. She ushered everyone out of the room and closed the door behind them, leaving Nick and his father alone.

"Temperamental women," Brian mumbled. "They run in the family. Got to keep the reins tight."

"The only person in this family who should be tied down is you," Nick snapped.

They stared at each other for several long moments, neither willing to look away. Brian swallowed hard and licked his lips. Nick hated that he enjoyed seeing his father scared. He hated the fact that he wanted revenge for all the terror and pain of his childhood. But he did. He'd have to live with the kind of person that made him.

"I know you hate me, Nick, and you got the right. But do you think I'm such a horrible man I deserve a death sentence?"

Nick narrowed his eyes. "You probably don't want me to answer that."

"Will you consider it before you say no? For your sisters? And your mother?"

Nick began to smile. "Tell me something, Dad. How fucking terrified were you when they told you I was the only one who could save you?"

What little color there was drained from Brian's face. "Nicholas," he tried.

"I've got somewhere to be," Nick said, and stood.

"Son, please. I'll die without your help."

"Probably should have thought about that thirty-seven years and fifteen broken bones ago," Nick said as he headed for the door.

His father called after him, his voice a pale echo of the shouts that used to ring through this house.

Nick ignored him. He stalked down the hallway to the stairs, beginning to fume as he thumped down the steps. The man had no right to ask that of him. He had no right to put that decision in Nick's hands. How many times had Nick prayed for his father's demise over the years? And now it seemed the only way it would happen was if Nick pulled the trigger on him. It wasn't fucking fair.

The rest of the family was gathered in the kitchen. Nick's mother was hunched over the kitchen table, Alana and Nessa sitting on either side of her. Kat and Erin were stalking back and forth like hungry lionesses, and they pounced on him when they heard him coming.

"What did he say?" Erin demanded.

"You're not going to do it, are you?" Kat added. "You don't owe him shit."

Nick's phone began to ring before he could answer. He glanced around at the five women as he dug in his back pocket. Nessa and Alana were watching him, their expressions full of hope and fear and pain. How many times had Nick seen those eyes—frightened but not sure why, trusting him to protect them.

His mother stood. "Nick, please," she whispered.

Nick tore his eyes away from them to look down at his phone. "I have to take this." He grabbed up his coat and turned toward the front door without another word, leaving his family behind to step out into the freezing air. His hands were shaking and he felt like he might throw up in the bushes. The cold air helped to calm him, and he began making his way to the brand-new Range Rover parked at the curb.

"O'Flaherty," he answered, his voice choked.

"Hey, Irish, you okay?" Ty asked. "You sound like shit."

Nick cleared his throat and glanced at the house behind him when he got to his car. "Yeah, you just did me a solid, man. Got me out of a tight spot. What's going on?"

"Well, long story short, you want to be one of Deacon's groomsmen? All expenses paid."

"When?"

"Next week."

"Where?"

"Scotland."

"Scotland?"

"Scotland."

Nick stared at the window above him, pursing his lips. "Yeah, okay."

"Bring a date."

Nick closed his eyes and smiled. "Okay."

"And a gun."

Nick opened his eyes. "Wait, what?"

Ty's laughter was all the answer Nick got.

CHAPTER 2

"There's not a single town name here I can pronounce," Zane said as he peered at a map inset of the Scottish highlands and Inner Hebrides. He kept pronouncing Hebrides wrong on purpose, and it was driving Ty crazy.

Ty tossed his arm over Zane's shoulders, leaning back in his chair. His feet were propped on a suitcase. They'd flown into Glasgow via a hellish eighteen-hour layover in Iceland, and now they were waiting at baggage claim for Nick and his date to join them. They were a little behind the rest of the Grady family, who'd chosen to take Theodore Stanton up on his offer to fly in his private jet. Zane hadn't been able to get off work in time to do it or Ty would have been all over it.

"You don't need to pronounce it," Ty said. "Apparently the Stantons own the entire fucking island."

Zane shook his head. "Private jet, private island, private security force. I'm starting to think Deuce is in way over his head."

Ty grunted, and a sense of unease fluttered through him again. "I wish I'd been able to talk to him a little more before he left Philly. Nick's going to be pissed that I don't know more about what's going on."

Zane hummed.

"No, seriously. Nick's going to kill me."

Zane began to chuckle. "Maybe this date he's bringing will make him behave."

"Or at least keep him distracted," Ty mumbled.

A few minutes later, Ty caught sight of Nick making his way through the crowd. He stood to go meet him, but stopped short when he recognized the man walking with Nick.

"Doc!" he cried, and wrapped Kelly up in a hug when they got closer. "What the hell are you doing here?"

"You said to bring a date and a gun," Nick said with a crooked smile. "So I brought a date *with* a gun."

Ty laughed and stepped in to give Nick a hug as well. Zane shook both their hands. "How was your flight?"

"Flight was good. Security was rough," Kelly said.

Ty frowned. If Nick and Kelly hadn't been able to bring their weapons along, their trip had been for naught. "They give you shit about your gear?"

Nick shook his head.

"No, no, no," Kelly said before Nick could answer. "The guns and knives and fucking night vision goggles or whatever he has in there, those permits went through fine. It was *him* they wouldn't let go through."

Zane began to laugh despite obviously trying not to. "Why not?"

"The way the new machines are? They take a picture when you stand there, right?" Nick said, raising his arms above his head. "The fucking shrapnel in my thigh makes it look like I have something sharp in my pocket. They kept telling me to empty my pockets, and I was like, 'I can't!'"

Kelly began to laugh. "They made him drop his pants. He got whistled at."

"By you!" Nick shouted.

Kelly laughed harder. Nick rolled his eyes as Ty and Zane snickered.

"Anyway," Nick said. "How long a drive do we have to this place?"

Ty slung his arm around Nick's shoulders. "Couple hours. You feel like driving it?"

"I'd rather me do it than you."

Ty snickered, and Kelly jabbed his elbow into Zane's ribs. "Never let him drive in a country with left-hand driving."

"Okay?" Zane said with a raised eyebrow at Ty.

Ty shrugged and winked at him. Nick and Kelly headed for the luggage conveyors to retrieve their suitcases, and Ty slid closer to Zane. "They're right, never let me drive here."

"Noted." Zane's grin was a warm one. "I can't believe O'Flaherty brought Doc instead of a real date."

"The thought of a week at a wedding with a real date probably flat gave him a panic attack." Ty gave Zane a spontaneous squeeze around the waist.

They gathered their luggage, and Nick and Kelly joined them to head for the rental car counters. Ty told Nick to go to the counter and handle the rental because he knew Nick's luck. The man was fucking blessed when it came to traveling. He'd been Sidewinder's "acquisitions specialist," and he'd been damn good at it. But even beyond skill came luck, and Nick had that in spades.

They'd booked a compact car, but sure enough, Nick came back with a "free upgrade" to a brand new Audi A4 and the counter girl's phone number. He handed the number to Kelly and the receipt to Ty, then waved the keys as he headed for the door to the parking lot.

"How the hell does he do that?" Zane asked. Kelly merely laughed as they trailed after Nick with their luggage.

Ty and Kelly both fell asleep in the back of the sedan as Nick made the three-hour drive to the little town where they were to catch a very private boat to the Stantons' very private island. Ty woke whenever they took an especially sharp curve or slowed for a trekking biker, and each time he did, Nick and Zane were talking companionably. Several times their laughter roused him.

Halfway through their deployment, Nick had been sent home for forty-eight hours. Ty knew he'd been sent to Maryland to deliver a message to Naval Intelligence because Ty had specifically chosen him for the mission. When he'd returned, Nick had told him that he'd dropped in on Zane and brought a letter back with him, the only communication Ty and Zane had been able to have during those six months.

From what Ty had observed since landing in Scotland, Zane and Nick had come to an understanding during that visit. He might even call them friends. The level of relief he felt at that was astronomical, given their rocky start.

The next time Ty woke, Kelly was using his lap as a pillow, and they were making their way through a tiny, crowded coastal town. Ty stretched and patted Kelly's chest as he peered out the window. The quaint shops seemed to lean toward them as they drove past, and the cars on the wrong side of the road came way too close to the car for his comfort. He was glad Nick was driving because the roads in the UK made him twitchy.

They could see sailboats in the harbor and a great expanse of deep blue water beyond. In the far distance, the tops of gently rolling mountains were visible.

The Stantons' private island was somewhere out there in the wilds of the Inner Hebrides, two hours away. It didn't have a name on the map.

Ty shook Kelly awake as Nick found a tiny parking spot and turned the car off. They all climbed out, stretching and groaning. Nick rolled his neck and Kelly took hold of his shoulders, massaging them to loosen him up. It made Ty smile. It had been odd being deployed without Sanchez, without Kelly. Seeing Kelly and Nick together was like a balm on an open wound he hadn't realized was there.

They gathered their luggage and began making their way to the private dock tucked into the picturesque seaside near the larger ferry landing. Kelly and Nick pulled ahead of them, heads bowed as they talked.

Zane took Ty's arm and slowed him. "Is there something going on with them?"

"What do you mean?"

"They're kind of . . . touchy-feely."

Ty laughed. "Nick and Kelly have always been like that. Either one of them would cuddle *you* if they had the chance."

Ty picked up the pace again to catch up with their companions. Zane trailed behind for a few steps.

"Huh," Zane finally said.

When Zane climbed out of the craft, the sun was trying desperately to shine through the afternoon cloud cover. The dock seemed to be out in the middle of nowhere, with a winding dirt pathway that supposedly led up to the mansion that inhabited the small island. There were patches of snow in the shade, and the wind was frigid. The crew began to unload mail and packages from the boat, and two men piled them into a small electric vehicle.

"You're the brother, then?" a man asked him.

Zane turned to him, eyebrows raised. The man was short and stocky, with a wild gray beard and even wilder eyebrows. He was wearing a wool skullcap and small, round glasses. His cardigan was torn and tattered, and so were his fingers, which were wrapped around a wooden oar he was leaning on like a cane.

"You're the brother?" he said again.

"Oh! No, I'm . . . I'm the brother's partner." Zane took a step closer and offered his hand. "Zane."

"Call me Mackie," the man said. His Scottish brogue was so thick, Zane had a hard time deciphering what he'd said. "In charge of the docks. You need something to float, you come calling."

Zane grinned and nodded. "I'll keep that in mind."

Mackie left him to go supervise the loading of the packages. Zane glanced over the island, whistling under his breath. Talk about getting away from it all. This tiny island on the brittle northwestern coast of Scotland was about as far away as you could get. He shook his head and looked behind him. Ty was straddling the boat and the concrete steps that were built down into the sea off the dock. Nick was handing suitcases up to him, and Kelly was standing on the boat, giving them cheeky directions, no doubt to annoy them both.

Zane grinned at them.

Ty glanced up as he balanced on the edge of the boat, several wardrobe bags over his shoulder. "Give me a hand, huh?" he grunted. He raised up one of the bulky bags that carried the tuxedos they'd brought from Baltimore.

Zane took the garment bag and laid it over one arm before accepting the next satchel Ty shoved at him. "You make a good pack mule."

"Shut up," Ty grunted. He tossed Zane's luggage unceremoniously onto the dock. Kelly laughed and held onto his side, using Nick's shoulder and Ty's hand to get onto the steps.

Ty helped Nick with the last two suitcases, then gave his surroundings a once-over, taking in the crimson ribbons tied to the dock and the hint of ancient ruins in the distance. "Poor Deacon."

Zane stifled a laugh. "It's not that bad."

Ty was scowling, obviously not in agreement.

Nick found his feet and gave the island his own once-over, looking grim. "I'm going to die in Scotland," he muttered.

Kelly barked a laugh. Nick reached out and grasped his forearm to pull him onto the dock.

"Let's get this over with then," Ty said as he bent to pick up his bags.

Zane chose the better part of valor and stayed quiet. Ty and Nick both had gotten crankier and crankier as the trip went on, but then, hours of layovers, car rides, and a choppy boat trip to an island that may or may not have power would have tried the biggest of travel lovers, especially since they were mere weeks off six months of deployment.

Zane slung a satchel over both shoulders, being careful of the tuxedo bag. When they made it to the dirt path, a golf cart broke the rise ahead and trundled their way, three familiar figures riding in it.

Ty grinned widely at the sight of his brother. He dropped the heavy bags he was lugging and jogged toward the golf cart, which stopped several yards off. Livi put Amelia on the ground, and she bounded toward Ty, who knelt and held his arms out for a hug. Amelia bypassed him, though, running right under his outstretched hand to leap into Zane's arms. She giggled as Zane twirled her around. Ty's shoulders drooped, and he trudged back over to them.

"That was the most epic rejection I've ever seen," Kelly said, snickering behind his hand.

Amelia was only fifteen months old, but between the auburn hair and eyes the same unusual hazel green as Ty's, she was going to be one killer little lady when she grew up. She wore nothing but dresses, the frillier the better, and she insisted that her shoes match her ribbons. And she was apparently the only child Ty had ever met who would have none of his charms.

Her parents had spent most of her life showing her pictures of Ty, telling her he was her uncle who loved her very much, and Zane had taught her several tricks under Ty's strict instructions. But none of it had convinced her to give Ty the time of day yet.

Zane squeezed her close, and nodded at Livi, who gave them a wave and smiled brilliantly. She was quite lovely in a robin's egg sheath dress that matched her eyes and a wool coat that matched her dress, even though the wind plucked at her silvery blonde hair and gave her a disheveled appearance. Zane was amused to see that she was wearing galoshes. No unwieldy heels for this one, fashion be damned.

Nick whistled when he stopped next to Zane. "Damn. Hate to say it Zane, but Deacon won this round."

Zane gave that a hearty laugh.

"That's not very nice," Kelly muttered. "Zane could pull off that dress."

"Not really my color."

Nick and Kelly both chuckled.

Deuce gave Ty a long, tight hug, squeezing him until he started to struggle for freedom. When Deuce finally released Ty, he offered his hand to Zane. "Agent Garrett," he said, mockingly formal.

Zane rolled his eyes as he propped Amelia on one hip. "Dr. Grady," he drawled, shaking his hand heartily.

Deuce turned to Nick, shaking his hand as well and smirking. "Snakebite, been a while. Good to see you back on your feet."

Nick sighed heavily. "Never going to live it down, am I?"

Deuce practically giggled.

"Snakebite?" Kelly asked.

Nick shook his head, but Zane cackled when he realized what Deuce was talking about. "Oh my God, you're the one who went hiking and got bit by the snake?"

Nick turned a glare on him.

"Dad told you not to poke it," Deuce said.

"I had to poke it, it was in my sleeping bag!"

Kelly chuckled. "When was this?"

"When we were young and stupid," Nick told him.

"Some of us more so than others," Deuce added. He turned to Kelly, offering his hand. "I recognize you."

"Kelly Abbott, I was the Navy doc for Sidewinder."

"I'm sure we've met before, but it's nice to meet you again."

"Likewise."

"Thank you both for coming on such short notice. I know you're probably wanting some answers about why Ty asked you to come. I figured we'd let you rest a little and then sit down and talk tonight, if that's okay."

"Sounds good," Nick said. Zane was a little more ready to demand answers faster, but Nick and Kelly were both the epitome of hassle-free.

Ty was gallantly helping Livi out of the golf cart, and he offered her his arm as they rejoined Zane and the others. She introduced herself to Nick and Kelly, thanking them for coming just as Deacon had. She seemed sedate for a bride-to-be. She gave Zane a hug and kissed him on the cheek, and then Ty put an arm around her and kept it there as Zane introduced Amelia to the others.

"Can you say hello?" he asked.

"Hello," Amelia echoed.

Zane lifted her a little higher, holding out his fist to show her. "Can you give Nick a fist bump?"

Nick gave Ty a wary sideways glance, but he held his fist up to the little girl. Her eyes were shining when she punched her fist to his, but it didn't end there. She pulled her hand back and spread her fingers, making an exploding sound as she did so, and then she came back for a second bump.

Nick and Kelly laughed raucously as Zane hugged her tight. "That's my girl!"

"How in the hell did you become the favorite?" Ty grumbled. He looked genuinely upset, and Zane gave him an apologetic smile. He'd actually spent more time with Ty's niece than Ty had because of the deployment, and he'd overcome his awkwardness with children to become quite comfortable with her. He carried her over to the golf cart, leaving Ty to gather the rest of Zane's bags for him.

Ty and Nick piled the bags onto the cage on top of the cart. Nick and Kelly took the rear seat, facing backward, and Zane set Amelia between himself and Ty as Deacon guided them toward the main house.

"Pretty swank, Deuce," Ty said, leaning forward so he wouldn't have to yell.

"Oh my God, wait until you see the house," Deuce said, laughing.

"My granddaddy had a flair for the dramatic," Livi told them. "I mean, the place was pretty dramatic to start with from what I understand, but he completely gutted and redid it when he inherited it.

"How long's the island been in your family?" Zane asked.

"A little over a century. When the steel boom started and the robber baron era came along, my great-great-grandfather bought the island and built the mansion as a way to escape public outcry when his dealings went shady."

Zane raised both eyebrows, impressed with her candid handling of her family's not-so-stellar history. "Wow."

"I'm going to die in Scotland," Nick said under his breath. "In a kilt."

Zane coughed to cover his laugh.

"The castle ruins on the lee side of the island are from the sixteenth century. But the main house was built in the late 1800s," Livi continued. "The island was produced by an extinct volcano, so it's riddled with caves, lava tubes, and cliffs. The house is built near the highest cliff, actually. You guys should have plenty of territory to explore."

Nick turned around, putting his arm over Ty's shoulder and leaning closer to hear. "Did she say lava?"

Ty shook his head. "You're not going to die in Scotland."

Livi smiled sympathetically at him. "Deacon tells me you and Kelly are both members of Ty's Recon team."

"Yes ma'am," Nick answered.

"Sidewinder, right?"

Nick and Kelly both nodded.

"So do all of you make a habit of being bitten by snakes, or was that like a personal journey of discovery for you?"

Deuce and Ty burst out laughing, and Livi covered her mouth like she was embarrassed for making fun. Amelia giggled, even though she didn't know why. Zane glanced sideways to see Nick pursing his lips and nodding like he was trying to hide a smile.

"Everyone's a comedian," he finally muttered, turning back around and shaking his head.

"I still love you, babe," Kelly said to him, patting him on the knee.

"Shut up."

Livi finally got control of her laughter and continued talking. "I have to apologize, when Ty told us you were bringing a date, we just assumed . . . the room you have has one queen-sized bed."

"That's fine," Nick said. "We've shared before."

"You're sure? We could probably do some creative switching, maybe find you two twins."

"No, we're good," Kelly insisted. "Thank you, though. He brought me for a free week in Scotland. Least I can do is put out."

"You damn right you will," Nick said. They both laughed.

It took another few minutes to reach the house, and even Zane's eyes widened at the sight of the place. It was a Gothic revival mansion, with spires and gables and ancient windowpanes that sparkled in the weak sunlight, all of it made of aged stone and dark brick.

They sat and stared at it as Deuce and Livi clambered out of the cart. Kelly leaned forward to peer up at the structure, then turned to Nick grimly. "You're going to die in Scotland."

Nick just nodded, his mouth gaping open.

"Jesus Christ," Ty whispered.

Four porters appeared to retrieve their luggage, leaving them free to gawk at the house as Livi led them toward the intimidating front entry. Zane instinctively clutched Amelia closer as they stepped under the front archway and through the massive wooden door.

The inside of the house was pleasantly light and airy, though, with none of the doom and gloom of the exterior. The wooden floors were a light gray color, covered with cream-colored fiber rugs to soften their appearance. The walls had all been plastered over and painted in cool colors, with the exception of the occasional artful patch of stone showing through to remind visitors of the age of the stately home. The light fixtures were all glittering centerpieces hanging high above their heads, illuminating surprisingly modern décor with comfortable-looking furniture and family photos dotted throughout, rather than deer heads or family crests like Zane had half expected.

Livi stood in the foyer, extending her arms. "Welcome to Stanton Hall. I can give you the grand tour now, take you right to the kitchen for some snacks, or show you where your rooms are so you can rest."

Kelly and Nick both raised their hands, and said almost in unison, "Rest, please."

Livi laughed and nodded. She took Amelia from Zane, rubbing her nose against the baby's cheek. "I'll show you to your room."

Nick and Kelly trailed after her, still checking out the massive house as they climbed the grand staircase.

"I wouldn't mind a bite to eat," Zane said. "Maybe some coffee."

Ty took a step and craned his head, watching Nick and Kelly as they disappeared onto the second level. "I'd like a tour."

Deuce took Ty's arm in his to lean on him as he walked. "I'll lead Zane to the kitchen and give you a halfass tour, how about that?"

"Where is everyone?" Zane asked.

"Guests won't arrive until the day of the ceremony. Until then, it's just family and the wedding party."

"Jesus, Deacon, what the hell have you gotten yourself into?" Ty hissed.

Deuce lowered his voice, trying not to laugh. "I was just going for the hot yoga girl, okay?"

Zane cackled as he followed after them.

Deuce led them through the great hall, pointing out different rooms as they passed. There was a gentleman's study and a billiards room, a living room and a parlor, an office with the door closed, a sitting room, a morning room and a dining room, and a hallway that led off toward even more rooms, which Deuce claimed included a pool and a theater.

The kitchen was located at the bottom of a flight of curved stairs. Zane had to duck.

A white-haired, cherubic little woman was bustling around the kitchen, humming softly as she prepared what looked like a simple, huge dinner. She stopped and smiled when she noticed them.

"Gentlemen, this is Mrs. Aileen Boyd. Stanton Hall's cook," Deuce told them. "Mrs. Boyd, this is my brother Ty and his partner Zane."

Aileen came over to greet them. She had a splotch of flour on her cheek. She was holding a large knife in one rubber-gloved hand. Ty discreetly leaned away from it. "Lovely to meet you both," she said, her smile genuine and warm. "You've come for food, have you?"

Zane glanced around the kitchen and shook his head. "You're so busy here, we wouldn't dare bother you."

"Oh, don't be silly!" Aileen said with a wave of her hand that coated Ty in a fine mist of flour. "You've been traveling, and big boys need big food. Here, you just take whatever you need." She headed back to her work station, offering up the entirety of the kitchen to them.

Ty gave Deuce a hesitant glance, and Deuce shrugged. They made themselves small plates of food to tide them over until dinner. Zane found himself admiring the pristine kitchen. There were four ovens, two glass-fronted refrigerators, a large stainless steel walk-in freezer, and what seemed like miles of counter space full of pots, pans, appliances, and food. The walls were made of stone, decorated with carved figures. It seemed supremely odd that a kitchen would be covered with carved angels, but he swiftly realized a subterranean room this expansive could only have begun life as one thing: a chapel.

"We'll get out of your hair now, Mrs. Boyd," Deuce called. She waved cheerily, and they took their plates with them and headed back up the winding stairwell to the main hall.

Deuce led them toward what he called the morning room, and there they found several small tables set up for dining. At one of them, a man was polishing a brass candlestick with a blue cloth. He startled when they appeared, then put a hand to his chest and smiled at them. "Gave me a bit of a jump."

"I'm sorry, Hamish," Deuce offered. "I'm giving my brother and his partner a little tour. Guys, this is Hamish Boyd, the house manager. Hamish, this is Ty and Zane."

"Boyd?" Ty asked. "Did we just meet your wife?"

"Indeed, if you were exploring the kitchen." Hamish finished his polishing and set the candlestick back in its rightful spot. "Would you like anything?"

"No, Hamish, thank you," Deuce answered.

Hamish gave a nod and picked up another candlestick to polish. Ty turned until he was staring at Deuce, a smirk curling his lips.

"What?" Deuce asked.

"You have a butler. I'm judging you so hard right now," Ty said under his breath.

Zane tried desperately to muffle his laughter as the tour continued.

Nick and Kelly followed Livi into the suite she had designated as theirs. The room was modern, with silver-toned floors and ebony-stained furniture. A four-poster bed with sparkling, gray netting sat opposite an intricate fireplace, complete with an ornate mirror and corbels carved into angels. A silver chandelier cast gentle light on sumptuous gray-toned linens.

On the outside of the door was a little wooden sign with their names carved in it, a stylized ampersand between, hung with a red ribbon. Livi blushed as Nick looked it over.

"I'm really sorry, I completely misunderstood when Ty called and told me the name of your guest," she said. "I can have another placard made for you."

Nick laughed and jerked his thumb at Kelly. "Blame the doc, he's the one with the girl name."

Kelly jabbed him in the ribs. "Don't worry about us. I'm sure you're up to your ears in things to deal with, so you can mark us right off your list. We're happy."

Nick nodded in agreement, still trying to catch his breath. The little girl kept grinning at Nick, reaching her hand out to him, but Nick wasn't comfortable responding. He didn't handle children well.

Livi smiled, her shoulders slumping in relief. She hitched Amelia higher on her hip. "Thank you both. For so many things. I can't even begin."

Nick managed a weak smile at Amelia before meeting Livi's eyes again. He could see the strain around her eyes and mouth, the worry she was trying to hide behind the task of being a hostess. This was not the way a blushing bride was supposed to feel. For the first time, Nick truly began to worry.

"Well, I'll leave you to rest up," Livi said. "There's a welcome dinner tonight at seven on the back patio. After that, Deacon and I will try to fill you guys in on what's going on."

"Sounds good," Nick said, keeping his voice gentle.

Kelly held his fist up as Livi passed, and Amelia gave him a fist bump over her mother's shoulder. She giggled as Livi carried her out. Kelly chuckled and pushed the heavy door shut after them, leaving him and Nick alone for the first time in almost twenty-four hours.

They stared at each other for a few seconds, and just as Nick was about to step closer, Kelly smiled slyly and moved away. He peered at the fireplace, walking with his hands in his pockets. Nick trailed after him, watching the way Kelly's shoulders moved, the way he cocked his head and exposed his neck.

"Kels," Nick whispered.

Kelly turned to grin at him. "When are we going to tell them?"

"If we tell Ty now, he'll go ballistic, and we'll ruin that poor girl's wedding. And you know it."

Kelly laughed. "So . . . the plane ride home so he can't be armed?"

"Agreed," Nick growled. He took a last step and grabbed Kelly by his upper arms, shoving him against the paneled wall beside the fireplace. He pressed their bodies together and kissed Kelly hungrily.

Kelly flailed, reaching out to grab at the closest thing for leverage. His hand fell on one of the angel corbels, the one whose bent wing was attached to the fireplace by a dainty ball and chain. Something clinked inside the fireplace, and before they could break the kiss, the wall gave way behind Kelly's back and they both went tumbling into a hollow space behind it.

Nick tried to catch himself on the edge of the new opening, but Kelly didn't let go of him and they crashed gracelessly to the floor. They were both laughing before the dust settled.

"Ow," Kelly groaned, still giggling. "What the hell happened?"

Nick pushed himself up, looking around. The walls were hollow, with at least two or three feet of space between the thick stone and plaster of each room. The passageway came to a dead end where the hallway was, but in the other direction it seemed to turn a corner on the outer wall. Shafts of light pierced the darkness in odd places, highlighting cobwebs and floating dust motes.

"This place just gets creepier and creepier," Nick muttered. He shoved up, helping Kelly off the floor and dusting both of them off. They peered at the bend in the passageway, then met each other's eyes.

"Want to see where it goes?" Kelly asked, his eyes sparkling.

"Hell, yeah."

They got out their phones, turning on the flashlight apps. Kelly took the lead, Nick's hand on the small of his back as they moved together with practiced ease in the small space. When they got to the bend in the passageway, it stretched off in both directions like Nick had suspected, but it also presented them with a narrow set of stone spiral stairs. They each aimed their lights in opposite directions. Several feet off, the wall came down so low they would have to crawl to get under it. Nick assumed that was the window casing.

"Up or down?" Kelly asked.

Nick put his lips against Kelly's ear, smiling. "Down."

Kelly shivered, leaning back into Nick's hand briefly. They managed not to give in to temptation just then and instead headed down the steps to see where they'd end up. The steps were so narrow Nick's foot didn't fit on them even if he turned it sideways. His shoulders brushed both sides of the staircase. He was glad he wasn't claustrophobic because it felt a little like getting stuck in a hole as they descended.

Kelly looked at him once the staircase was so tight that he had to turn to get down it. "Guess this rules out showing Ty this shit."

Nick nodded. Ty would go into a full-fledged panic trying to get down these things.

At the base of the staircase it opened up again. There were more shafts of light that Nick guessed were peepholes into rooms. He also assumed there were more ways in and out, but he saw no indications along the walls. Kelly went to the first peephole and peered through, then made room for Nick to look.

The room beyond was the gentleman's study, decorated with heavy, rich materials rather than light, modern ones like the other rooms they'd seen. Green medallion carpeting, heavy wood, leather seating. The walls were paneled in leather, and the scent of expensive cigars lingered even over the smell of ancient wood inside the passage.

Deuce and Zane were sitting in leather club chairs near the fireplace, and Ty was perched on the arm of Zane's chair as they talked.

Deuce was in the middle of speaking to Ty. "The Stantons are very . . . please don't wave any weaponry or kill anything in their presence."

Ty held up his hand. "Promise."

"That's the Girl Scout pledge, Ty," Deuce observed, deadpan.

Ty looked at the fingers he'd raised and then sneered at Deuce.

"You're not really expecting us to need weaponry, are you, Deuce?" Zane asked.

"He never needs an excuse," Deuce's reply was as long-suffering as his gesture at Ty. They laughed, but then Deuce grew serious once more. "The truth is, I don't know. When we sit down tonight with Theodore, I think we'll all learn a little more about it."

Ty and Zane both gave worried nods.

"Thanks for bringing your friends," Deuce added. He sounded weary.

"Always." Ty glanced up and around the study, like he was sensing something off. He visibly shivered. "This place gives me the creeps, man."

Deuce laughed.

"No, seriously, I feel eyes on me in here."

Kelly snorted. Nick quickly clapped a hand over his mouth and nose, biting his own lip so he wouldn't laugh as well.

Ty's head whipped around and his eyes darted back and forth over the section of wall they were behind. His sharp hearing had picked up on them, and the display of his predatory senses made the hairs on the back of Nick's neck stand up. He gripped Kelly tighter, and they both held their breath.

"Did you hear that?" Ty asked.

Deuce laughed harder.

"Yeah, Ty, the walls are talking to you," Zane teased.

"I heard something."

"You two go get some rest before dinner," Deuce urged, still snickering. "Before Ty opens up some sort of paranormal investigation."

"That's not funny," Ty insisted as his piercing eyes raked over their hiding spot one last time. Nick wondered how in the hell the peepholes were concealed if Ty couldn't spot it. Ty turned to follow Deuce and Zane out, but Nick could tell he was on the alert now just by the way he carried himself. His voice trailed off as they left the room. "This place is creepy, Deacon."

Nick and Kelly barely held in their laughter.

Kelly grinned widely. "This could be fun. Want to see where else it leads?"

Nick was grinning and nodding. "Want to go get naked first?"

"Yeah." He took Nick's hand and tugged him toward the stone steps.

Ty could hear Nick and Kelly arguing as he and Zane approached their room. Nick and Kelly were in the next room over from them, with a cute little wooden placard with their names carved on it. Ty laughed and pointed it out to Zane. Though the way Nick and Kelly were, it was likely neither of them cared. They'd probably be fighting over who'd get to take it home by the end of the week.

He stood at their door and cocked his head to listen, but he couldn't make out the words of the argument. They were interspersed with laughter, though, so Ty wasn't all too concerned about it being a real fight. He gave the door a knock, then tested the knob to see if it was unlocked and shoved it open.

He stopped short when he encountered Nick and Kelly on the queen-sized bed they were sharing. Nick was reclining against the headboard in nothing but his boxers and a worn-out Red Sox T-shirt, and Kelly was kneeling beside him holding a small tube of something.

"Was that really fucking necessary?" Nick demanded as he wiped a runny white substance off his calf.

Kelly was laughing hard. "I'm sorry, it just shot out!"

Both men glanced up when they noticed Ty and Zane in the doorway.

"Hey," Nick said.

"What the fuck are you doing?" Ty asked in horror.

Kelly held up the tube. "First aid."

"He's making a goddamn mess is what he's doing," Nick corrected. He scratched at his calf.

"He's scratching himself bloody, I was trying to put this hydrocortisone cream on him while I had him immobile," Kelly explained. "But the plane ride must have made it separate or something, 'cause . . . I've never seen this shit do that."

Nick laughed.

Kelly shoved at his knee to make him turn onto his side, and then he put the tip of the tube at his calf where the skin had been scratched red. When he squeezed it, though, another thin stream of opaque liquid shot out instead of the thick cream it was supposed to be.

"That's obscene," Zane muttered.

Kelly laughed harder and wiped at Nick's leg before it could drip to the sheets.

"Oh my God!" Nick shouted. "What kind of janky fucking medic are you?"

"I'm sorry!"

"It's a tube of cream, how hard is this exactly?"

"It's separated!"

"You're sleeping in the wet spot tonight!"

"No, it's not my fault!"

Zane finally lost it at that. Laughing, he strolled into the room and sat on the end of the bed.

"Jesus Christ," Ty said, moving closer. "You don't want to know what I thought was going on in here."

Nick glanced up, scowling as he scratched at his calf.

"I don't understand why you're still itching, there's no bite or anything there," Kelly grumbled.

"You're not even allergic to anything," Ty added. "Where have you been?"

"I don't know, but I'm itchy," Nick grumbled. "I think this place knows I'm Irish."

Kelly barked a laugh. He placed the cap on the tube and shook it vigorously. The same persistent liquid shot out from under the tightened cap, hitting Nick in the face.

Nick howled and flopped to his side, covering his face and laughing raucously. Kelly pitched forward, cackling so hard he had to rest his head on Nick's hip. Zane practically guffawed.

"You got it in my mouth!" Nick finally cried. He rolled to his back, pawing at his face.

Kelly was hooting and snorting and wheezing too hard to answer. He buried his face against Nick's stomach and shook his head, holding the dripping tube of cream up.

"In my mouth! Is this shit poisonous? Am I going to *die*?" Nick fumbled on the bedside table for his water bottle, gulped it down and wiped at his face frantically with a pillow.

Kelly brought the tube of cortisone cream up again, and when Nick caught sight of it he rolled out of bed and thumped to the hardwood floor. "Don't fucking come near me with that shit! I'd rather be itchy!"

Kelly tried to argue, but he still couldn't catch his breath.

"I'm taking a shower," Nick cried, distraught. He pulled his shirt off and wiped his face with it, then disappeared into the bathroom and slammed the door.

Zane was holding his stomach, trying to sit up and laugh at the same time. Kelly chuckled. He quickly capped the tube then tossed it toward the trash can. He looked around for something to wipe his hands off on and Ty backed away from him.

"There were so many things wrong with that," Ty told him, close to giggling.

Kelly snorted. "What did you guys need?"

Ty shook his head. "I don't even fucking remember."

Zane cackled. "I feel like I just watched free porn."

"Oh, look at this shit we found earlier," Kelly said, grinning like a little boy as he hopped past Ty toward the fireplace. He reached up to one of the carved angels on its knees with its hands clasped. A chain ran through its broken wing and attached to a ball higher up the corbel. He pulled the angel's head.

Nothing happened.

Ty and Zane shared a glance, and Ty put two fingers to his lips to indicate Kelly may have been toking earlier rather than resting. Zane snorted.

"That's weird," Kelly said. He tried again, tugging at the angel's head. Again, nothing happened. He glanced over his shoulder at them. "I swear to God this thing opened a door earlier."

Ty snickered.

Kelly looked it over with a deep frown, pushing on the wall next to the fireplace. "No, seriously."

"We believe you, Doc," Zane said kindly.

"No! There was a door here! The walls are hollow, and there are stairs and everything," Kelly insisted. He glanced at the bathroom door. "Nick!"

"No!" Nick called from the bathroom. The water shut off. "No, no, no."

Zane began to laugh again.

Kelly put his shoulder into the wall, leaning against it. He reached up to tug the angel's head again. "Damn it!"

Nick came out of the bathroom, a towel wrapped around his waist. He watched Kelly for a few seconds before saying, "Pull its wing."

Kelly glanced at him, then up at the carving. He pulled the fragile-looking wing and something clicked within the fireplace. The wall gave way against Kelly's shoulder, and he stumbled sideways before catching himself.

Zane stood, and Ty took a step forward, eyes widening.

"That's so cool!" Zane cried.

Ty took another step, peering into the dark passageway. "How the hell did you find that?"

Kelly glanced at Nick, opening his mouth and closing it like a fish.

"He, uh," Nick said quickly. "He tripped over the wood holder down there. Grabbed at it when he fell."

"Did you follow it?" Zane asked, his brown eyes gleaming.

Ty was struck speechless for a moment, just staring at him. Good Lord, the man was beautiful. He didn't know if it was because he'd just missed Zane so much, but he was pretty sure Zane had grown even more attractive while he'd been deployed. The sprinkling of silver in the hair at his temples had increased, and the light in his eyes was there more often than not. He'd slimmed down, losing a little of the bulk in his muscles, but he was still trim, and his suits seemed to fit just a little better than they had. There was a weightlessness to him now as well that hadn't been there before, like the burden of his past had finally been shed.

Not lifted, no. No one had lifted Zane's burden for him; he had shed it himself, like a caterpillar unfolding its wings to become a butterfly. Ty would never tell Zane he thought of him like a butterfly, of course.

"We followed it a little way," Nick answered, reminding Ty that no one else in the room was smitten and they were still talking. "Down to the study. We saw you two in there with Deacon."

Ty pointed a finger in his face. "I knew someone was watching me!"

Nick and Kelly laughed.

"You let me think I was being stalked by a ghost, you fuck nuts!"

Kelly laughed harder. He pushed at the angel's wing, and the opening in the wall creaked closed.

"Are there more doorways?" Zane asked.

Kelly shrugged. Ty grumbled at Nick and shoved him lightly, and Nick swatted at him.

"We can go back in later and explore," Kelly said, grinning like the Cheshire Cat.

"I think something in there made me itchy," Nick said.

"But you're not allergic to anything," Kelly argued.

"I know, but I showered and I'm not itchy anymore."

"You got groped by a ghost," Ty teased.

"Shut up."

"A ghost gave you crabs," Ty added as he hopped toward the door.

"Shut up!" Nick was looking around for something to throw, and Ty darted for the door. He and Zane made their escape as Kelly peered at the wall and the angel who was chained to the fireplace and Nick hunted for a projectile.

CHAPTER 3

Zane and Ty had just enough time to shower and wind down, and that was what they did. Together. When the water started running cold, they turned it off and stayed in the shower for several more minutes, until it got cold enough to drive them into the bed and under the covers. They fell asleep wrapped up in each other.

When Zane woke, he slipped out of Ty's arms and pulled on a robe. He headed for the doors to the balcony and stood leaning against the frame, gazing out at the gardens, the cliffs, and the choppy ocean beyond.

The bed creaked, and he turned. Ty was sitting on the edge, wearing only his sweatpants, watching him. "What do you think?" he asked after another moment of silence.

"It's gorgeous. I didn't figure it would be so fucking beautiful. But it's . . . rugged and captivating."

Ty's eyes strayed to the pristine vista behind Zane, then back to Zane. He smiled slowly.

"Kind of like someone else I know," Zane added. He raised an eyebrow. "I sense mischief brewing."

Ty stood and joined Zane by the doors. Zane turned, and Ty stopped in the doorway, facing him with the same crooked smile still on his lips. It felt like he had something important to say, but the surroundings seemed to be outdoing him. Beyond the manicured gardens below, a sheer cliff stretched in either direction, ushering the angry sea along its way.

"Ty?"

Ty took a deep breath and grasped Zane's hand.

"What are you up to now?" Zane asked, even more suspicious.

"Marry me, Zane."

Zane's breath caught. His hand involuntarily tightened on Ty's, and all he could do was stare into Ty's eyes. He'd never dreamed he'd hear Ty say those words, especially not so soon after returning home. He'd never dreamed he'd experience half the things Ty had offered him. He brought Ty's hand to his lips and kissed his fingers, inhaling deeply to calm everything that was suddenly churning inside him.

Zane did want to marry Ty. But he didn't want it yet, not when they still had so much to learn about themselves and each other.

"No," he breathed.

"No?"

"No," Zane repeated shakily. Ty huffed. Thank God he looked bemused instead of upset, one eyebrow cocked and a gentle smile on his lips.

"You're not even going to think about it?"

"No," Zane repeated, more confident this time. He was relieved Ty didn't appear to be hurt, but he also knew how well Ty could hide his feelings. He took Ty's face in his hands, hurrying to explain. "I know you, Ty. And I know the thought probably *just* popped into your mind. You haven't thought it through. You haven't looked at it from any angle other than the one we can see from our balcony."

"That doesn't make it any less sincere," Ty said, frowning.

"I know, doll." Zane took a deep breath, wishing he had the words to explain just what Ty meant to him, how much he really did want what Ty was asking. The time just wasn't right. It didn't feel right saying yes, not after they'd been apart for so long, not after all that had happened to them. Not after they'd both changed so much. Nothing seemed like an adequate explanation, though, not when so much of him wanted to just say yes. Instead he sighed. "Let's . . . let's get to know each other again first. And you give it as much thought as I do everything. And if you can convince me you've done that, then when you ask me, I'll answer as fast as you always do."

Ty's lips quirked up, and he didn't take his eyes off Zane's when he leaned back. "You're saying no?"

Zane stepped closer and kissed him. His lips moved against Ty's when he murmured, "I'm saying no for now."

Ty cupped his cheek, his fingers playing with the tips of Zane's curls. "I'm going to keep asking until you say yes."

"I look forward to it." Zane grinned, drawling when he added, "Try to be creative next time, huh?"

Ty kissed him one last time, then shoved at his chest and patted his cheek hard. "Asshole," he grunted before turning away.

Zane reached past Ty on both sides to grasp the doorframe, trapping him in place. "Don't be mad," he growled.

Ty smirked, jutting his chin out for a kiss. Just before their lips brushed, there was a loud rap on the door.

Zane pulled back, and Ty huffed in irritation. "And so it begins."

Zane chuckled and let Ty loose, going to his suitcase to unpack and to find clothes for dinner. When Ty opened the door, Mara Grady threw herself into his arms and hugged him tightly.

He laughed in surprise and returned the hug. "Hey, Ma."

"Don't you 'Hey, Ma,' me! Why the hell didn't you come see me as soon as you got here? Gone a year—"

"Less than six months."

"—and can't come see his mother," she scolded, holding him by his broad shoulders and shaking him. Then she hugged him again, pressing her cheek against his chest and patting his back.

"Missed you too, Ma."

Zane chuckled and moved closer.

Mara released Ty and practically shoved him aside as she stalked into the room. "Don't you think you can hide from me," she told Zane. "Get over here and give me a hug."

"Yes, ma'am," Zane said, and the smile on his face was honest when he hugged her.

"You boys both look so handsome!" Mara said, even though Zane was still wearing his robe and Ty was in a ratty pair of sweatpants.

Ty laughed, rubbing a hand over his chin as he closed the door. "Where's Dad?"

"Still trying to convince your grandfather that we did *not* just hit the shore of Guadalcanal and he should *not* hit anyone on the head with that shovel." Mara released Zane and put her hands on her hips.

Ty was biting his lip hard as he tried not to smile. "Did you come for reinforcements?"

"Well, no," Mara said thoughtfully. "Might not be a bad idea."

"Did he really bring the shovel? On the plane?" Zane asked, not suppressing his laughter very well.

Mara shrugged. "He wouldn't come otherwise."

"He should make an impression on the in-laws anyway," Ty said under his breath. "Do you know where your room is, Ma?"

"We're in the other wing. Old farts and married folks are over there. Young troublemakers are shacked up on this side."

Zane laughed before he could stop himself.

"Speaking of troublemakers, where's Nicholas? I've got a hug for him, too."

"He and Doc are in the next room," Ty answered.

"Doc? Which one was that?"

"The one who lost his parents when he was young. I brought him home for Thanksgiving one time. You told him you wanted to wrap him up and bake him in a pie and he never came back."

"Oh, that one! Oh, he's a cutie. Little skittish. Well, make sure Nick comes to say hello to me and your daddy, got it? Earl was asking after him."

"Yes, ma'am."

"Okay. I just wanted to come get a hug before you got into trouble," she told them as she headed for the door.

"Why does everyone assume I'm going to get into trouble?" Ty asked, his brow creasing with frown lines.

"Because we know you, baby," Mara told him. She walked by him, patting his cheek. "See you boys at dinner."

After shutting the door, Ty shot Zane an evil grin that damn near caused them to be late. Thankfully, it was a casual affair, or they never would have gotten ready in time. As it was, Ty was still tucking his shirt in and fixing his tie as they made their way to the back patio of the massive house.

Someone whistled from behind them as they were hustling down the stairs. Zane glanced over his shoulder to find Nick and Kelly, both looking well rested and more relaxed than they had been. It was also the first time Zane had ever seen either man in a suit.

"You dirty whores," Nick drawled quietly.

"Shut up," Ty mumbled, still fussing with his tie.

Zane just smiled and gave Nick a cheeky wink. They headed for the party with a handful of other guests. Zane didn't know the numbers, but he estimated there were roughly thirty people on the island, with another hundred due to show up the day of the ceremony.

Not a large wedding for such a prominent family. It was just family and friends, perhaps, but no business associates. Zane knew how these affairs went, and he found that particularly odd.

He glanced at Ty, his body warming all over. Ty had asked him to marry him. He'd been entirely sincere, too, in the way only Ty could be when he thought of something spur of the moment. It brought a smile unbidden to Zane's lips, and he quickly schooled his expression to something a little less giddy as they joined the crowd.

The patio was full of outdoor heaters and covered with a large party tent with plastic windows and ties to keep the doors closed against the wind. The tent protected parts of the garden, too, giving the space an outdoor feel without the outdoor frostbite to accompany it.

While Ty and Zane had been placed at the table of honor with Deuce and Livi, Nick and Kelly were at the next table over with the other members of the wedding party. They split off and took their seats just in time, beating Deuce and Livi by mere seconds.

Zane knew everyone at their table except the older couple he assumed were the Stantons, and a younger man who was probably Livi's brother. They didn't have time for introductions before a man approached the table to say hello. Ty and Deuce both stood abruptly, and it startled Zane and the Stantons into flinching when they did it. Zane glanced up to see Assistant Director Richard Burns standing there.

Ty reached out to shake Burns's hand. "Sir."

"Tyler. Deacon," Burns said as he shook Ty's and then Deuce's hands. He turned to Ty's father, Earl, who was in the process of pushing back his chair to stand. They embraced warmly.

Livi cleared her throat. "Mama, Daddy, this is Director Richard Burns, a dear friend of the Grady family."

The tall, white-haired man stood and offered a hand to Burns. "Theodore Stanton. Pleased to meet you, Director. This is my wife, Susan."

As they exchanged greetings, Livi continued. "And this is Tyler Grady, Deacon's brother. And Special Agent Zane Garrett, Ty's partner."

"Pleased to meet you all," Zane said, standing and shaking Stanton's hand when it was offered, just as Ty had done.

Burns took Livi's hand in a dainty, formal greeting. "Congratulations, my dear, you look lovely."

"Thank you, Director, that's very kind of you."

Burns nodded to them all, then gave Earl a wink and patted his lapel pocket as he turned away. "Earl, I'll find you later."

Ty's hand sought out Zane's under the table, squeezing. Then his thumb stroked over Zane's palm, and any anger or resentment aimed toward the director that had been bubbling inside Zane began to fade. He glanced at Ty to find the man watching him.

Ty mouthed a silent, "I love you."

Zane couldn't help but smile.

They engaged in only a couple minutes of small talk before Deuce and Livi stood and Deuce tapped his crystal glass with a knife. The room quickly went quiet, all eyes turning toward them.

"Good evening everyone," Deuce said, just loud enough to reach all the tables. He possessed a certain presence, like a man accustomed to speaking to large crowds or being in the spotlight. He smiled as he spoke. "You are our nearest and dearest, and we want to thank you all for making this journey to be here with us."

He waited a beat, and Livi took over. "Deacon and I decided that we wanted our families and friends to enjoy this as much as we will, which is why you were all invited to stay for the entire week with us." She turned a loving smile up to Deacon. He hugged her around her slim waist. "Rehearsals and planning are being kept to a bare minimum."

"Just enough to make sure we don't make fools of ourselves," Deuce assured everyone, drawing laughter.

"And so we can all get the most out of this experience. We ask you to please enjoy yourselves this week as our most beloved guests."

"And if you partake of the open bar, please stay away from the cliffs."

More laughter arose from the crowd, and as Deuce held his glass up to toast, it was followed by applause.

Waitstaff appeared to man the buffet. Zane stayed in his seat and watched as others got in line. He smiled when Deuce hugged Livi and kissed her forehead. He tried to remember what he'd felt like before his wedding, but he couldn't recall much of anything beyond nerves. Deuce and Livi looked anything but nervous, despite whatever trouble was apparently brewing.

They were a good couple, and Zane was genuinely happy for them.

When his eyes met Ty's, he found his partner relaxed in his seat and watching him with a small smile. Ty winked at him, flushing Zane's body with the same convictions he'd experienced the first time that wink had hit him. He lifted his water glass and toasted Ty before pushing out of his chair to join the buffet line.

As soon as dinner wound down and people moved on to drinks and dancing, Deuce stood and tilted his head at Ty to indicate they should go inside.

Ty turned to seek out Nick or Kelly, and immediately found Nick's sharp eyes on him. He waved at him to follow, and Nick nodded.

At the doorway to the study, a man was standing with a metal-detecting wand. Ty stopped and spread his legs, holding his hands out. Zane did the same as he followed Ty into the study. Ty was still glancing around the room when a commotion arose behind him.

"Why am I being wanded?" Kelly asked.

"Just stand still," the guard ordered.

"I am standing still," Kelly said. "What, does that thing not work when I'm talking? It gets distracted? It's a metal detector with ADD?"

"Jesus Christ, Kels, just let him wand you," Nick said, rubbing his eyes as he stood behind Kelly, waiting for his turn.

"I usually get dinner first. No, that's a lie," Kelly said as the man waved the wand over his chest.

Kelly cleared his throat and nodded, but his eyes were sparkling when he stepped into the room. Nick stood obediently and let the man wand him, but just as Ty knew it would, the wand went off at Nick's thigh near his pocket.

"Do you have a weapon on you, sir?" the guard asked him.

"No." Nick unbuttoned his jacket and turned his suit pocket inside out. "It's shrapnel in my thigh. There are certain frequencies it sets off."

The man patted Nick's thigh down, then wanded him again after finding nothing in his pocket. Nick narrowed his eyes. When the man looked up at him, Nick shook his head.

"Not taking my pants off, man."

The security guy snorted and waved him past.

They were joined in the study by Livi's father, Theodore Stanton, and her brother, whose name had escaped Ty. Two other men followed along and positioned themselves at the door of the study, not being discreet at all about the fact that they were Stanton's private security. They called each other English and Hardin. Ty had pegged them as ex-military as soon as he'd seen them, and he guessed the others had as well.

One more man joined them. Despite the casual evening, he was wearing a suit and vest. His movements were fast and nervous, and his forehead glistened with sweat. He carried a smooth worry stone in his hand, and he was almost continuously rubbing his thumb over it. Stanton introduced him as Ernest Milton, the company's head of operations. He seemed pretty young for such a prestigious position, which probably explained his obvious stress-related issues.

"Gentlemen," Stanton said as he poured himself a drink and took a thick cigar out of a humidor on a desk in the corner of the room. "I understand Deacon asked you to come here as added security."

Ty raised an eyebrow. He glanced over his shoulder at Nick and Kelly, who were both frowning hard but not yet looking defensive.

Stanton took a deep breath and looked at his daughter, his expression softening. "I've always believed in too much rather than too little, so thank you. And welcome."

That surprised Ty, and out of the corner of his eye he saw Nick's shoulders relax. They'd been expecting a little resistance.

Stanton continued. "My family has always received threats. That's the way of the business, I'm afraid. But when news of Amelia's birth got out, some of those threats turned their attention to her."

"How so?" Ty practically growled.

"To be perfectly blunt: as leverage."

Ty and Zane both turned to Deuce. He'd gone considerably paler. He met Ty's eyes and nodded. "Kidnapping her and using her to force Theodore to make decisions for the company."

Ty's blood began to boil at the mere thought. These people had no fucking idea what kind of fire they were playing with if they came after Amelia.

"I'm sorry," Kelly said. "But what do you do that's so important to your competitors to warrant threats of that magnitude?"

"Two years ago, we bid on a defense contract. It was awarded to us over four other companies. There are some . . . sensitive projects being undertaken."

"Has it escalated since then?" Nick asked.

"We received several specific threats regarding the wedding, yes," Deuce said, his voice hoarse. "Not just to Amelia, but to Livi, myself, and Theodore and Susan. That's why we moved the timetable and cut the guest list down to bare essentials."

"So at its core, this is a corporate espionage issue," Kelly muttered. He and Nick shared a look. "You should have asked Owen to be your date."

Nick gave him a solemn nod. "But at least you put out."

Ty glanced back at them with a frown. Neither man was laughing.

Zane was sitting on the edge of the couch, resting his elbows on his knees. He'd been quiet so far, but he finally took the opportunity to speak. "Were there any specifics? Any indication of how they intended to strike or what they were after?"

"I brought the communications for you to look at," Deuce said, and headed for the desk to retrieve a flash drive. He held it up, looking guilty. "I'm sorry, I know you're not on the job right now. I feel bad putting this on you."

"You're talking about my niece, Deacon, fuck the job," Ty growled. He stood and took the flash drive, then handed it to Zane.

The nervous head of operations, Milton, finally spoke up. "Our security is well prepared for any eventuality. We don't anticipate a problem. Everyone here, with the exception of these two," he added, gesturing to Nick and Kelly, "has been vetted with background checks."

Ty looked up in time to see Kelly narrow his eyes and Nick bristle. Ty cleared his throat. "Your company's security clearance isn't high enough to check their backgrounds, so don't bother."

The man sniffed, dismissing Ty's words with a wave of his hand.

"These are people I trust to protect my daughter," Deuce said, his voice going hard. He examined the two bodyguards. "All due respect for your preparedness, of course."

"Bottom line, gentlemen, we don't expect trouble," Stanton announced before more words could be exchanged. "But if trouble comes, we intend to deal with it in-house." He nodded toward the two bodyguards at the door.

"We have five men on the island, with constant patrols," the man called English said. His eyes went from Ty to Nick and Kelly. "Our files indicate you're Marines, is that right?"

"That's right," Ty answered. He surveyed the man up and down. He was huge, with biceps the circumference of small trees, and a chest that looked more like a barrel of ale and produced a deep, echoing voice. His head was shaved clean, and his brown eyes were sharp and observant.

"Green Beret?" Nick asked out of the blue. Ty had to quickly look down at his hand to hide a smile.

English stiffened. He nodded, his jaw tightening. He obviously didn't like that someone could peg him without the benefit of a file. "Force Recon team Sidewinder. Now defunct."

The other bodyguard, Hardin, grinned, showing his crooked teeth. "Sidewinder. Like the snake." The room was silent, waiting for his point. "You know what they used to call the Green Berets when we were active?"

Ty tried hard not to roll his eyes. Behind him, Kelly answered wryly, "Snake Eaters."

Both security men chuckled. "Best watch out, Sidewinders. Don't want to get eaten."

Nick barked a laugh. "I appreciate the offer, Hoss, but I got someone taking care of me already."

Hardin squared his shoulders, his face growing ruddy.

"Don't worry, you'll find that someone special," Kelly assured him, his voice sincere.

Zane turned to Ty, grumbling under his breath. "They're going to get us killed."

Ty knocked his knee against Zane's and fought desperately not to laugh.

"I think we're done here," Stanton said to Deuce.

"No, wait a minute," Zane said. "You're telling us you don't anticipate trouble, but every move you've made so far has been in anticipation of trouble. I get the feeling we're getting the runaround here. I'd like the whole story."

Nick and Kelly both made sounds of agreement.

"Like we've said," Milton grunted. "We've got it taken care of. Just enjoy your brother's wedding and leave the heavy lifting to the professionals."

"That's enough," Stanton said, his voice soft but stern. His expression was completely unreadable. "I understand what you men are capable of, and I appreciate your dedication to your family, and to mine. The fact is, we don't know what to expect. My men will handle the perimeter defense of the activities if the four of you will concentrate on the safety of my daughter and granddaughter." He gave Livi a fond smile.

Ty and Zane shared a glance. "Sir, we'd be honored if you trusted us with that task," Ty said.

Stanton came closer and shook his hand. His grip was firm and curt, and he made eye contact and kept it. He then shook the hands of the other three, thanking them for understanding. He left the room, his two bodyguards and Milton trailing after him.

Livi sat down hard, sighing audibly. "Thank you for keeping it mostly civil with Daddy's guys."

Deuce rolled his eyes and limped to the wet bar to make himself a drink.

"Where is Amelia now?" Ty asked Livi. "Does she have a nanny or babysitter or something?"

"Not usually, but the island employs a full-time nanny, her name is Maisie. Amelia took to her immediately, they've been inseparable ever since."

"You trust her?"

"Her mother was our nanny when we were young." Livi waved at her brother. "I'm sorry, I don't think I introduced any of you. This is Theo, my older brother. Theo, this is Zane, Ty, Nick, and Kelly."

Theo raised his glass to them. "Pleasure." His tone wasn't convincing.

"Don't get *too* excited, bud," Kelly said.

Livi cleared her throat and stood, smoothing her hands down her skirt. "Well. I guess we should get back to the party."

Ty sat in a chair around an unlit fire pit on the edge of the garden, far enough away from the heaters for it to be a little chilly, nursing his drink and watching the few remaining people mill about the dining area.

Amelia had long ago been tucked safe in her bed, along with all her cousins. Nick and Kelly had, of course, landed at a table with three of the bridesmaids, including Ty's baby cousin, Emma. She was a beautiful young woman with a personality to match. Ty would have to remember to threaten both men if they even thought about making a move on her. Nick was the most obvious danger, but Kelly had a way of slipping through the defenses before you noticed him there.

Deuce and Livi were making the rounds to the last trickle of guests, saying good-night. Zane was standing at the end of the bar, water glass in hand, stuck talking to another of the groomsmen. He finally made his escape as Ty watched. He had to smirk when Zane strolled toward him, one hand in a pocket, his shoulders thrown back and relaxed. He'd taken his tie off and loosened the top few buttons of his shirt, and he cut an impressive figure.

Ty bit his lip. "Indeed," he said under his breath. Zane saw his expression and smiled as he came closer.

Soon the patio was empty enough for Deuce and Livi to retreat into the darkness of the gardens and sit with Ty. They both looked exhausted. Ty held his glass up and tapped it against Livi's.

"To the lovely bride," he said.

"To my future brother," she replied, grinning. "God help me."

"You mind if I smoke?" Deuce asked as he dug into his jacket.

"Only if you share," Livi answered wryly.

It wasn't a cigarette Deuce pulled from his pocket, though. Ty laughed in exasperation. "How did you get that through airport security?"

"Private plane, man. What, you thought I was marrying her for her personality?"

Livi snorted. Zane materialized out of the shadows and settled in next to Ty, who set his glass on the ground and wrapped an arm around Zane's shoulders. Zane leaned into him, and they shared a kiss before he propped his feet on the fire pit.

Just as Deuce was getting ready to light up, they noticed Nick, Kelly, and Emma heading their way. Deuce glanced at Ty. "Nick still a cop?"

"Sort of. Little far from his jurisdiction."

"Did he go hardass? Like . . . forget-who-his-friends-are kind of cop?"

Ty frowned. "What are you talking about?"

"*I'm* more likely to arrest you than he is," Zane told Deuce.

Nick and Kelly came strolling over, Emma between them with one arm hooked through each of theirs. She was a natural blonde with hints of strawberry and darker tones in her long hair, and it was split into two messy ties just behind her ears. She was tan and fit with an athletic, curvy build and delicate features, and her eyes were a deep green. She'd always been a pretty girl with a mischievous personality, just the type Nick and Kelly both would probably be drawn to. Ty gave her skimpy cocktail dress a disapproving once-over.

"Did they forget to sell you the rest of that dress, sweetheart?" Ty asked her.

"I got it half-price," she answered with an unconcerned shrug. Ty laughed and stood to hug her. She let go of Nick and Kelly and threw her arms around Ty's neck, hugging him so hard that he staggered backward.

"I thought you had better taste than these two," Ty finally grunted with a nod at his friends.

She stepped back and smacked Ty in the side of the head. "I haven't heard from you in forever!" She turned to Zane and stuck out her hand. "You're Zane, right?"

"Yes ma'am."

"Nice to meet you, Zane. I'm Emma, Ty's poor, neglected cousin."

"Quit bitching, I called you on your birthday. Last year," Ty said as he sat back down.

Emma gave them both a big grin. "Mara told me you two were cute together," she said, completely devoid of any tact, just like Ty and the rest of the family.

Zane seemed to struggle with that piece of news. "She did?"

"It's not supposed to still be a secret, is it?" she asked worriedly. Ty shook his head. She rolled her eyes in relief. "That's good, 'cause everyone knows."

"Awesome," Ty grunted. He'd known his extended family would all find out sooner rather than later because that was how his mother rolled, but it still caused butterflies. He winced at Emma. "Good or bad?"

"I'd say mostly good. Pretty much nobody gives a shit because they all expected you to be dead by thirty. Actually, Elliot won like three hundred bucks on a bet he made with Tag back in high school that you were gay, so Tag's still kind of pissed at you."

Ty barked a laugh.

Zane shrugged and smiled at Ty. "Hell, your opinion's the only one that matters anyway."

"Aw, that's sweet," Emma said as she looked Zane up and down. She glanced at Ty. "Yeah, they're going to eat him alive."

"I know," Ty agreed with a long-suffering nod. "And seriously, where's the rest of your dress?"

"Shut up, I'm flaunting it while I've got it."

Nick sat in the chair next to Ty, holding a glass of champagne he'd been nursing. He put his feet up on the fire pit, setting them next to Zane's. "Emma was telling us about what she does. I still haven't decided if she's messing with us or not."

Emma laughed. "I'm not messing with you."

Kelly repositioned the last stray chair next to Nick and sat down, and Emma perched on his knee for lack of anywhere else to sit. Ty narrowed his eyes at them.

"Emma has a degree in underwater archaeology," Deuce provided.

"That sounds like it'd be interesting. What do you do with that?" Zane asked her.

"Not what most people do. I'm a member of a team of researchers who investigate cryptozoological anomalies, historical mysteries, and natural phenomenon."

"Cryptozoological?" Zane repeated incredulously. "That's . . . animals that aren't scientifically recognized, right?"

"Like Bigfoot and the Loch Ness monster?" Livi asked.

Emma laughed. "Among others, yes."

"Seriously?" Zane asked.

Emma laughed harder.

"I think it's fucking cool, man," Kelly said, peering through the darkness at Nick. Nick raised both eyebrows but chose to take another sip of champagne rather than comment.

"The team's sort of on hiatus right now," Emma admitted. "Marley, our camera specialist, came with me to film the wedding. We're going to make a side trip and see if we can head over to Loch Ness after."

Ty frowned. "Why are you on hiatus?"

Emma sighed. "Our expedition leader had a little disagreement with the producers of the show they're trying to get off the ground, and then he went on strike. They're trying to find someone to replace him so they won't have to deal with him."

"So you're without a team leader?"

"Pretty much. And those are some weird resume requirements, know what I mean? Not only did he have the skills to keep us from getting maimed in the Amazon, but he also had the degrees to qualify as an expert in the fields of history and anthropology. He filled two posts despite being kind of an arrogant asshole. Then our medic went and got pregnant, so we're down by three spots."

"Kelly's a medic," Ty told her. "And Nick's currently being a jobless bum, plus he knows everything about history there is to know. He could lead your expeditions."

Nick grunted.

"Really? You were both Recon like Ty, right?"

Nick shook his head, but Kelly's eyes lit up. "What kind of expeditions are we talking about?"

"The kind with really big snakes to poke," Emma answered, glancing sideways at Nick.

They all laughed, and Nick shook his head harder.

"I've been getting a little restless where I am," Kelly admitted. "I wouldn't mind finding out more about this."

Ty chuckled as Emma sank her teeth in and started talking up the open positions on her team. He could see Kelly fitting in with a bunch of adventuring whackos like Emma and her crew. Nick would go nuts, though.

Deuce brought the blunt out again, leaning forward to light it. He was able to take a long drag on it before Nick reached over the fire pit and plucked it out of his mouth.

Livi laughed. "You're being oppressed by the Man."

"Damn it."

Nick gave the blunt a sniff. "Medical grade?"

Deuce smirked and shrugged. "I have a bad leg."

Nick laughed, and to Ty's surprise he took a short hit before handing it over to Kelly. "That's better than your other stuff," he told Deuce.

"Tell me about it," Deuce said, chuckling.

"How do you know about his other stuff?" Ty demanded.

Nick and Deuce both laughed at him.

"Please, you think I sucked snake venom out of his leg because he's a nice guy?" Deuce asked. "I'm just glad he hasn't turned over any new leaves since then."

Ty gaped at Nick, who was snickering and sipping his champagne. "Like I don't even know you," Ty said to him.

Nick merely shrugged.

They passed the blunt around, Ty and Zane both refraining. Ty didn't really have any objections to marijuana, but if he didn't like the way a contact high felt, he knew he wouldn't like anything stronger. He'd never tried it and didn't intend to.

Emma passed the blunt back to Deuce and turned to Livi, her eyes shining. "I want to see your dress tomorrow. I can't stand waiting any longer!"

Livi's laugh was light and carefree. "I haven't gotten to show it off to anyone yet, so I'd love that. Bring your bridesmaid dress so I can see if it's horrible!"

"Oh, fun! I will!"

Because of the restricted guest numbers, Deuce and Livi had filled in the ranks of their wedding party with family. Livi's brother Theo was a groomsman, and Emma was one of Livi's bridesmaids, even though the two had never met before this week.

As they continued talking about the wedding colors and the cakes and the dresses, Kelly groaned and rubbed at his eyes.

Livi settled into the crook of Deuce's arm, smiling kindly at Kelly. "You've been through this, huh?"

"I have. I'm sure this won't be as big a disaster as mine was," Kelly assured her.

Nick and Ty both made noises of agreement. They'd barely gotten Kelly to that wedding alive, much less gotten him out of the marriage.

"I remember the tales of that bachelor party," Deuce said. "Which is one reason I'm not letting Ty plan mine."

Ty grunted. "Hey, that wasn't me. I was an innocent victim. Mostly. Sort of innocent."

"It was me," Nick confessed.

"I woke up the morning of my wedding on the front lawn of the church, tied up, with my tux covered in sequins they'd taken from stripper outfits."

Nick grinned. "We Bedazzled him."

"The minister told me I was the shiniest groom he'd ever seen."

Nick burst out laughing, slumping further in his chair.

"It took a long damn time to collect those sequins, too," Ty added. "We had to beg every dancer in Jacksonville."

"Why didn't you just buy a bag of sequins from a craft store?" Zane asked.

Ty and Nick shared a look, both of them frowning. Nick took a drink as Ty muttered, "Wow, that would have been easier."

"Not near as fun, though," Nick added.

"Have any of the rest of you ever been married?" Livi asked.

Zane raised his hand. Nick shook his head and took another sip of his champagne, but Ty was already snickering and pointing at him. Nick narrowed his eyes as he swallowed.

"Nick's been married," Ty drawled.

"What are you talking about?" Kelly asked. Then his eyes widened. "Oh! Oh my God, I'd forgotten about that!"

"There's nothing to forget," Nick insisted. He glared hard at Ty. "Why the hell would you bring that up?"

Ty laughed harder.

"O'Flaherty, you've been married?" Zane blurted.

"Not . . . no. Sort of," Nick stuttered. "Not like *they're* getting married, though."

"Hitched is hitched, man," Ty said.

"Shut up! I can't believe you're bringing this shit up!"

"The ten-year statute of limitations has passed."

Nick made an insulted sound that came out squeaky.

Deuce leaned forward. "Did you get drunkenly married in Vegas?"

Nick rolled his eyes and slumped in his chair. "Yeah."

"Interesting."

Zane threw his head back and laughed. Ty pulled him closer. He loved it when Zane got loose and started enjoying himself.

Ty reached out to pat Nick's shoulder. Nick shoved him away and shook his head. "Don't touch me, traitor."

"What happened?" Deuce asked.

"We were on leave before deployment," Nick answered. "We headed to Vegas because none of us had ever been before."

"The six of you?" Zane asked.

Ty grinned and nodded. "We had two days. And we all thought we were going to die on our next deployment, so we went all out."

"I remember that," Deuce said. "You told Ma and Dad you were going through extra training or some shit."

"Yeah, and if you tell them different, I'll ruin your wedding."

"Hey!" Livi cried.

Ty shrugged, completely unapologetic. "Nick went on this craps run. I've never seen anything like it. Just roll after roll of winners. He won over five hundred thousand dollars in like three hours."

"At craps?" Zane asked, impressed.

Nick nodded and took a long drink. "Pure luck, no skill."

"Casino security frisked him three times looking for loaded dice," Kelly added.

"The next morning we all woke up in the honeymoon suite with six women we didn't remember meeting," Nick said. "Heart-shaped bed, champagne, confetti everywhere. Digger was wearing this powder-blue tux with tails, and Johns had nothing on but a cummerbund and a fuzzy tiara that said 'bride' on it."

Ty began to giggle uncontrollably. "It was instant mass panic."

Nick tried to add something, but he was laughing too hard to speak. Zane was shaking beside Ty, and Ty could barely breathe as he remembered the scene of that morning. Each man had been trained to deal with life-or-death situations; they were all cool as could be when on the battlefield. But faced with the prospect of one of them having married someone the night before, they had all panicked like a bunch of new recruits tossed into a hot zone.

Ty and Nick were both laughing so hard they couldn't breathe. Kelly had to continue the story for them. "We started checking our fingers for rings. It was like the scariest game of drawing straws ever."

"And I had this beautiful engraved gold ring on my finger," Nick said bitterly. He held up his hand to look at his ring finger as if the memory lingered with him. Knowing his fear of commitment like Ty did, he could imagine Nick literally having nightmares about that morning.

"He started cussing and kicking things," Kelly wheezed. "I mean, just months before this, he'd helped me salvage all my shit from my crazy ex-wife, so it was doubly traumatic for him."

"Hey," Nick grunted. "Marriage is just a word for some people, but for others it's a fucking sentence, okay?"

Zane was holding his side. "Oh my God, marriage puns! Oh my God . . ."

Nick was trying not to grin, but he finally couldn't help himself. "Once we established I was the victim, then we had to find a girl with a ring on *her* finger to figure out which one I'd fucking married."

Ty leaned against Zane's arm, laughing so hard he could no longer sit up straight. "The look on his face!"

"He made a marriage pun," Zane gasped.

"So we're mostly sober," Nick continued, getting more agitated the harder the others laughed at him. "And I tell the girl, look, we need to get this thing annulled fast. Clock's ticking." He tapped his watch. "And the chick said no!"

Ty and Kelly both howled, and Nick glanced at each of them with renewed indignation.

"She wouldn't give you an annulment?" Livi asked.

"No! She refused, said she liked *soldiers*. I told her we were Marines, and she said, 'Same thing!'"

Ty snorted. "We had to hold Digger back."

"Never call a Marine a soldier," Kelly said seriously.

"Then she fucking asked me what her new last name was."

"So wait, did you have to get a divorce?" Zane asked.

"No, I gave her half of what was left of my winnings from the night before, and carried her ass down to the courthouse to sign the annulment."

"You paid a woman *not* to be married to you?" Deuce asked.

Nick nodded solemnly. "Worth every penny." He raised his champagne glass to Livi. "No offense."

She giggled and shook her head.

Zane hid his face behind his hand as Ty finally wound down from his fit. "How much did freedom end up costing you?" Zane asked.

Nick threw back the rest of his champagne. "Close to fifty thousand dollars."

The rest of them howled with laughter, but Deuce was shaking his head. "Wow," he finally said. "Those are some impressive commitment issues you have going."

"Please."

"We'll talk," Deuce promised.

The blunt was gone and the night was growing colder. Deuce wrapped his coat around Livi's shoulders, and they both stood. Livi slid her arm around Deuce's waist as they said their good-nights and headed inside. He leaned on her, his arm around her. Ty smiled at them. They made a good pair, and his brother was happy. That was all that mattered to him.

"What a gentleman," Emma cooed. "Okay, whose coat do I get? 'Cause I'm freezing."

"Maybe you should go find the rest of your dress," Ty said.

"You're the only one complaining!"

"'Cause I'm your cousin! Go put some clothes on!"

Emma stood, freeing Kelly's lap. She did a little turn, showing off the backless dress. It left very little to the imagination. She shimmied her hips for good measure. Nick and Kelly both tilted their heads like puppies as they watched her. Ty growled at all of them.

"I don't know, Tyler, I think it's a nice dress," Nick drawled. He uncrossed his ankles, standing and shrugging out of his suit jacket.

"I don't think it's the dress," Kelly said. Nick helped Emma into his coat, wrapping it around her shoulders with all the delicacy of handling a Ming vase. She thanked him and then sat on the bench Deuce and Livi had vacated.

"I hate all of you," Ty grumbled.

They ignored him, and Emma started talking about the open spots on her team again, trying to convince Kelly to think about joining.

Zane slid his hand down Ty's shoulder. "You're feeling no pain," he whispered against Ty's ear.

Ty's cheeks were flushed, and he couldn't feel the tips of his fingers. It was probably from the cold, but whatever they'd been serving had been quality stuff, and he'd had too much of it. He turned his face into Zane's and kissed him.

Zane chuckled, then pushed himself to stand. "C'mon, we'll take a walk, then head back to our room."

"If I fall over when I stand up, you're going to catch me, right?"

"Of course I'll catch you."

Ty took Zane's hand and hefted himself up. He wavered closer to him and gave him a gentle kiss.

"That's cute," Emma said fondly.

Ty blushed in the darkness, and Nick and Kelly whistled. He pointed at both of them. "Either of you touch my baby cousin, I'll kill you."

They both gave him obedient, if slightly sloppy, salutes.

Ty pointed again. "I'll kill you."

Zane slid an arm around his shoulders and turned him toward the flap in the tent that led out into the gardens. Ty slid his hand into Zane's as they walked.

"You having fun yet?" he asked.

"Maybe not fun, but it's been nice so far," Zane said as he laced their fingers together. "I actually had a casual conversation with Burns earlier. It was a little bizarre, but . . . getting there."

"Try having him over for Thanksgiving dinner," Ty said wryly. They hit the rocky ground that indicated the cliffs were near, and walked until there was nothing but moonlight to light their way.

It was quiet, and the wind smelled of salt and snow, and Ty was happy. It was easy to forget how lucky he was to be able to hold Zane's hand, to kiss him, talk to him whenever he wanted. He'd told himself every night of his deployment that if he made it home, he'd never take that ability for granted again.

The path angled down, taking them away from the cliffs until they were on the level with the surf. The sand beneath their feet became softer, and the crash of the waves intruded on all other sound. It was much colder down here, the wind whipping in off the waves.

Ty came to a sudden stop, pulling Zane closer to him. Zane hummed appreciatively and let his free hand fall to Ty's hip as their chests bumped. Ty ran his nose up the side of Zane's cold cheek, finally taking the proper kiss he'd been wanting all night.

When he heard a noise above the surf, his entire body tensed, and Zane leaned away from him.

Even here, remote and safe, he couldn't seem to force his mind to relax. He wondered if he'd ever be able to. He cleared his throat and squeezed Zane's hand, refusing to let his fingers slip away.

"Who the hell thinks walking on the beach in the freaking dark is romantic?" a woman asked breathlessly as the two figures came close enough to be heard over the surf.

"Maybe it's romantic if you're being carried," a man suggested.

"My calves are killing me!"

Ty and Zane both chuckled, exchanging quiet greetings as they passed the two people in the dark. The couple waved as they walked by, angling away from Ty and Zane and heading toward the mansion path rather than trying to be sociable. Ty glanced down the beach at the cottages on the end of the shoreline, where the staff were housed. They were all dark and silent.

A crash of thunder sounded not far off, and the thrashing sea was lit up by a bolt of lightning. Ty and Zane both stared at the dark ocean, struck momentarily dumb by the violent storm that seemed to be closing in with so little warning. Zane tugged on Ty's arm. "Come on. Nice, private room waiting."

"I'm with them," Ty told Zane as he allowed himself to be turned toward the mansion. "We used to run with all our equipment in the sand until we threw up. Never really saw a beach as romantic."

"I was going to suggest a run in the morning, but maybe not," Zane said as he guided Ty along with a hand on his elbow. "And I'm probably the last person to ask about what's romantic."

Ty pointed a finger. "I will run in the late-morning to early-afternoon time frame. Otherwise I intend to be hungover." He waited a beat before glancing sideways at Zane. "Where were you married?"

"Church wedding in Austin." There was a note of curiosity in Zane's voice.

"Was it nice?" Ty asked carefully.

Zane snorted. "It was way overdone. My mom did the whole thing because we were living in Dallas at the time. But I guess it was okay. I don't really remember much about it." Zane made a noise in his throat.

"What, too much bachelor party?"

"No, it's just . . ." Zane waved his hand around. "You stand there in this important ceremony, nervous as hell because everyone's watching you and you don't want to trip on the steps, and then it's over and you don't remember a single thing and it seems like such a waste of all that time."

Ty snorted and shook his head. They walked hand in hand down the beach, the cold waves lapping at the rocky sand near their feet, the lightning highlighting whitecaps on the water.

"Care for another waltz in the rain?" Zane asked, his voice gone lower.

"Always."

Zane stopped him as the thunder rolled, and pulled Ty to him. They began a slow box step, taking note of the rocks and their footing.

"Have you ever done the sex-on-the-beach thing?" Ty asked as his fingertips played over Zane's palm. Zane shivered.

"Yeah. Once. I kind of enjoyed it, but she was complaining about sand in weird places for days afterward."

Ty gave a surprised laugh.

"I always thought it sounded sort of uncomfortable, when you got down to the logistics of it," Ty mused. He began to hum as they danced. The skies rumbled and lightning flashed almost on top of the sound, meaning the storm was almost upon them.

Ty gazed up at Zane, his stomach fluttering. Rather than illuminating the warm brown of Zane's eyes, the night seemed to sap all the color from him, leaving them a luminescent gray. He couldn't help but stare at his lover, wondering how Zane just got more and more attractive to him as the days went by.

"You're the only person I've ever been with who made me want to try things like that."

Zane grinned, and their dance slowed to a stop. "I make you want to roll around in the sand?"

Ty shook his head. "That came out wrong."

"No, it didn't," Zane murmured, still grinning as he ran his hand up Ty's arm.

"I just mean . . ." Ty held a pent-up breath as he met Zane's eyes again. Zane's face was so sincere, looking at Ty in that way that always made Ty feel warm and loved. "I mean that all the experiences I've ever heard of in life . . . I want to have them with you."

Zane's smile grew more tender. He ran his knuckles down Ty's cheek. "Ty—"

"Marry me, Zane."

He could feel Zane's heartbeat quicken. Every part of him tingled where Zane touched him. He held his breath.

"Nope," Zane whispered.

Ty grinned, laughing silently. Leave it to Zane to reject him and make him laugh at the same time. "You don't want to at least consider for a minute this time? Run the numbers a little?"

"Ty, shut up," Zane murmured, and pressed his lips to Ty's, wrapping around him in a passionate embrace and kissing him for all he was worth.

Ty's arms tightened on him, fingers gripping. The sound of the tide and the approaching rain became a backdrop to the sound of Ty's heart pounding in his chest. He wanted Zane to know he'd thought this through, that he wanted them to spend the rest of their lives together. But he also kind of liked the idea of Zane making him ask until he got it right, making him work for it. Ty needed to work for it. They could play this game because in the end, Ty knew Zane would say yes. He just had to find the perfect time, the perfect place, the perfect way.

"I love you," Ty whispered against Zane's lips.

Zane smiled and pressed his nose against Ty's cheek. "I love you, too."

"I'm going to keep asking until you say yes."

Zane smiled against his cheek. "I know."

Zane took his hand and began to lead him toward the path again. Ty glanced up at the lights ahead of them and squinted. "Please tell me you know which freaking haunted room in the freaking haunted mansion is ours."

"Yes, I know which one is ours," Zane assured him. The thunder crashed behind them and they quickened their pace. "This is nice, that Deuce and Livi get to do something like this. Wedding and honeymoon all in one, stretch it out and take their time. I would have gone tropical maybe, but still."

"Yeah, well, Deuce is terrified of airplanes, so I'm guessing he only had enough tranquilizers for one trip," Ty said. "You didn't get to do the honeymoon thing?"

"We were both working, and neither of us wanted to take time off right then." He didn't sound put out about it. "That stuff wasn't really our kind of thing."

Ty just nodded. They walked in silence for a while. When they came closer to the house, they hit a stone walkway and Ty stumbled on the unexpectedly hard ground.

True to his word, Zane caught him around the middle and steadied him. Ty snorted as he wrapped an arm around Zane's neck. Zane squeezed Ty close as they started up the stairs. Flickering hurricane lamps lit the hallway, though Ty suspected they were electric. But it was dark inside their room, with just the moonlight filtering in the ancient windowpanes. Muffled sounds of laughter came from Nick and Kelly's room. It kind of sounded like someone was getting laid in there, and Ty idly wondered which one had gotten lucky with which bridesmaid and which one was sleeping on some sofa downstairs.

He stood motionless near the doorway to his and Zane's room, letting his eyes adjust and knowing he would wind up face-planting onto the floor if he tried to walk. The thought made him snicker quietly, and he clapped a hand over his mouth. Then Zane's arms slid around his waist from behind, followed by his warm, hard body.

Ty tilted his head to the side, biting his lip in an attempt to stop the laughter. He calmed briefly, but then another fit overtook him as Zane's stubble tickled at his neck. He closed his eyes and shook silently at the absurdity of the romantic location. He and Zane were definitely more of a backseat-of-the-Mustang kind of couple. The thunder rumbled outside.

"All right, funny guy," Zane said. He smacked Ty on the hip. "You're clearly entertained without my help."

Ty reached out for his wrist. He pulled Zane toward him in the dark. "No, don't. I'll be good."

"You being good isn't a problem," Zane growled. "Focused, yes. Good, no."

Ty nodded determinedly and cleared his throat. "I'll be focused."

Zane leaned forward, his lips skimming from the corner of Ty's mouth, along his cheekbone, and to his ear. "Don't make promises you can't keep."

Ty tried to meet Zane's lips with his own, but Zane moved away too quickly for a kiss. Ty wrapped his arms around Zane's shoulders. "I think you should do something I'll be ashamed of in the morning."

Zane gripped his hips and pushed their groins together. He hummed thoughtfully. "What could I do that would make you blush if you thought about it tomorrow?"

"If I don't get a kiss soon, I'm going to hit critical mass, understand?"

Ty barely got the last word out before Zane's mouth was on his, hot and hungry. He groaned and let Zane take control of it, hoping his lover knew which way the bed was. Zane ran one hand up his back to cup his head as he deepened the kiss, his other hand moving between them to pull at Ty's shirt, drawing him into the darkness.

"So, how embarrassed would you be if Nick and Kelly mention hearing screaming through the wall tomorrow?" Zane drawled.

"Just tell them I saw a ghost; no one will ask questions."

Zane pulled his shirt over his head, and then he was right there again, all defined muscles and warm skin. After another long kiss, Zane asked, "What's your pleasure, doll?"

"You know exactly what I want," Ty answered breathlessly. He pushed Zane toward the bed. They could see it when lightning struck outside, the pale gray bedcover practically glowing blue as their eyes adjusted to the darkness. Ty pulled Zane closer to kiss him as he fell back onto the soft mattress.

It wasn't until it was too late that he remembered the gauzy rings of decorative netting that hung from the four-poster bed. The clingy material wrapped around them as they fell into it, getting caught up between them and around their limbs and tightening as their weight pulled the netting.

"Hell." Zane pushed off Ty and batted at the netting, trying to find his way out of it. "Shit, I can't see. Quit moving!"

Ty shook his head and broke down all over again. He held his hands up obediently, trying not to move. But he was hopelessly encased in netting. He laughed harder, until he could barely catch his breath, and the sound went from loud and ringing off the rock walls of the suite to nearly silent as he tried and failed to pull in air. Zane's cursing and struggling just made it funnier.

Finally Zane got loose and rolled away.

"Get some rest," Zane said quietly as he moved around the dark room and out of Ty's visual range. He sounded disgruntled. "You don't want too much of a hangover tomorrow."

"Wait, Zane, don't go." Ty tried to go after him but wound up tangled even more in the netting. "It's not funny, I swear," he tried, even as he snickered.

He heard Zane snort from the foot of the bed. "Be careful."

"You're seriously leaving me here?" Ty asked, his voice a higher pitch than it usually was.

Zane was quiet for a long minute. He finally sighed. "No." He moved, and a light flipped on, blindingly bright.

Ty winced away from it and tried to cover his eyes, but that only served to tangle him further, which was for some reason wildly funny.

Zane threw up his hands. "I am not even dealing with this," he said, his voice trembling with amusement. He turned the light back off. "You're a mess."

"No, Zane! Don't leave me here!" Ty said in the most pitiful voice he could muster, which was ruined by the continuing peals of laughter he just couldn't stop.

"Good night, Ty." The bed dipped as Zane got in on the other side.

After long moments of trying desperately to calm down, Ty finally managed it and came to terms with the fact that Zane probably wasn't going to fuck him tonight. He probably wasn't even going to untangle him, and Ty was much too drunk and pleasantly sleepy to try to do it himself.

"Well," he sighed, his movements accompanied by the creaking of the canopy above him. "This was not what I had in mind when I told you I wanted to be ashamed of myself in the morning."

CHAPTER 4

Zane watched the sun rise out of the distant horizon and shimmer on the water from where he lay sprawled on the bed. He'd slept some as the storm raged through the night, although not as well as he would have while holding Ty, who was still encased in a protective roll of netting. And if he were honest, he'd been a little too edgy to sleep deeply after the discussion they'd had with the Stantons. Expecting trouble or not, Zane felt like it was around the corner.

He'd also spent much of the night thinking about Ty. He knew Ty had meant every word of it when he'd asked Zane to marry him. And Zane might be wrong, Ty may have thought about it every night while he was gone and played through every possibility in his mind before he asked the first time. But Zane knew Ty pretty damn well, and he wanted him to think about it again and again. And again. Then one last time, just to be sure.

He also knew he had made some pretty drastic changes to himself. He wanted Ty to see those, to know those changes were permanent and to make sure he was still what Ty really wanted. Ty hadn't come back the same person. The more time they spent together, the clearer that was to Zane. He smiled less, he joked less, he was quicker to strike. Zane was almost afraid Ty's proposal was just another quick strike. They just needed time.

The canopy above the bed creaked as Ty moved within the netting. He groaned and rolled, only to have his progress halted by the gauzy, tangled material. He stopped, one hand actually suspended above the mattress by the netting as he lay flat on his back. He mumbled something in a language that may or may not have been foreign and tried to move again.

Zane half wanted to laugh, but waking Ty up that way might kick him into a full-blown, flashback-induced panic attack.

The bed groaned, and Ty shot up with a gasp, still wrapped in netting.

Zane rolled off the bed, out of reach. "Ty," he said carefully. Sometimes even when Ty's eyes were open, it didn't mean he was there with you.

Ty responded with a nearly panicked few words in Farsi, but he wasn't flailing or fighting. Not yet. He spoke again, rapid fire as he gave his arm a good yank. "Where's O'Flaherty?"

"Ty, you're awake and you're okay." Zane moved into Ty's line of sight. "Nick's asleep next door. He's okay too. Everyone's okay, doll. Let me help you."

Ty watched him, his breathing slowing as reality seemed to soak through to his brain. His hands still shook with adrenaline and probably an ounce or two of fear, but he was silent and still as he let Zane untangle him.

"Worst morning after ever," Ty said, almost calm enough to fool Zane into thinking he was okay with waking up to a full-fledged flashback.

Almost. Zane continued to untangle the netting, trying to move Ty's arms without holding or clasping them. He got one loose, but the other hand was really caught up. How had he even done this to himself? "I can cut it loose, doll."

Ty shook his head. "It's okay."

He began using the hand Zane had freed to disentangle his other leg, taking long, slow breaths to try to calm himself. As soon as Zane managed to free his other hand, Ty clambered out of the bed like it was on fire. He used Zane to pull himself out, practically climbing up and over him to get away from the netting. Zane sighed and let him do it; to try to hang on to him or stop him would have been a mistake.

"Thanks, Zane," Ty whispered, rubbing at his chest.

Zane's heart swelled with a confusing mix of love and pity and anger for the things Ty had been put through. He knelt on the mattress and reached out, brushing Ty's cheek with the tips of his fingers. He smiled wryly when Ty met his eyes. "At your service."

Ty managed a weak smile. "My hero."

Zane flattened his palm against Ty's cheek. "Come here."

Ty promptly stripped off the clothing Zane hadn't gotten off him last night and crawled back into the bed beside Zane. Zane scooted and laid himself out, reaching for him. Ty pulled the covers over both their heads and Zane gathered him up to hold him.

"Sorry I ruined the night," Ty offered. "I'm really sorry."

"We'll laugh about it later," Zane said, skimming one hand through Ty's hair.

Ty snorted. "Don't be nice to me when I'm hungover."

"Quit being an ass." Zane poked him hard in the side, and Ty chuckled against his chest. Zane hugged him tighter before loosening his grip again. He'd learned that at times like these, Ty wanted to be held but sometimes couldn't tolerate it, so Zane let him decide. Ty rested his head on Zane's shoulder, his fingers playing with the hair on Zane's chest.

Zane was desperate to know what Sidewinder had gone through to make Ty's nightmares so devastating, to make Digger and Owen walk away from the Marine Corps, and to make Nick look positively haunted when he thought no one was watching. But the only thing Zane could do was offer his shoulder. Literally.

Zane tapped under Ty's chin and got him to raise his head, then leaned in to steal a kiss. "You okay?"

Ty wrapped his arms around him and threw a leg over him to pull him closer. Zane closed his eyes, his chest aching. It was moments like this that made dealing with the shit of their pasts worthwhile, that made their future seem possible.

He pressed his lips to Ty's temple. "Love you," he whispered.

Ty smiled and snorted against his neck. "I know."

They were both silent, soaking in the peace and quiet. Then Ty narrowed his eyes at Zane. "I proposed on a moonlit beach in Scotland. How do you just say 'Nope!' to that?"

Zane laughed. "I'm surprised you remember it."

Ty muttered some more as he cuddled back down. Zane began to relax again, allowing Ty's weight to push him into the bed. They were both almost asleep when something thumped from the room next door, followed by boisterous laughter.

"Assholes," Ty said. He raised his head and banged on the wall above the short headboard. "Assholes!"

A few seconds later, someone banged back. If they said anything, the thick walls drowned it out.

"What the hell are they doing up this early?" Zane asked.

"Screw early, what the hell are they doing, period?"

"Sounded like someone fell out of the bed. I'm putting money on it being Kelly."

"Me too. Nick shares a bed well, but Kelly spreads like a fucking puddle of Jell-O. Forces you to fight back." More laughter came from the other side of the wall. Ty rested his elbow against Zane's chest. "Want to make some noise on our side?"

Zane slid his fingers down Ty's defined arm, stroking the marred face of the bulldog tattoo. A bullet had ripped through the ink and formed a jagged scar, but that just made it look tougher. Zane tore his eyes away from it to look up into Ty's. "What'd you have in mind?"

"The kind of noise that you have to hold on to the headboard for."

Zane's body was instantly interested in this new proposition, and the predatory look in Ty's eyes said he knew it.

Ty leaned down and gave him a slow, sensual kiss. Zane dragged his hands up Ty's arms, over his shoulders, and down his back to hold on to his trim waist as they kissed. Ty smiled against his lips and climbed over him, staying on his knees and straddling Zane's thighs, putting both hands on Zane's shoulders. Zane tipped his head back, more than happy to give in to Ty's attentions.

Ty's hands plunged into his hair, and his scruff scratched at Zane's chin and lips. It stirred the warmth inside Zane, and his skin heated with each stroke of Ty's tongue against his. When their mouths parted, Zane whispered, "Let's make some fucking noise."

Ty's breathing was harsh when he nodded. Zane dragged his hands down Ty's body to grasp his ass. Ty responded, his muscles bunching, his cock stirring against Zane's groin, kicking up a wicked feedback loop between the two of them as they rubbed against each other and grew more and more aroused.

Ty halted it before they could get too far ahead of themselves, throwing the covers off and rolling out of bed.

"Ty," Zane said, deadpan. "Wasn't finished over here."

"Do you have any idea how many times I dreamed about you?" Ty asked, going to the massive fireplace. It was cold in the room, which while perfect for sleeping wasn't as conducive to other activities. He turned on the gas logs, grinning mischievously at Zane. "Every night."

Zane followed that come-hither look, giving up on the idea of grabbing the headboard in favor of being laid out on that rug in front of the fire. Ty was obviously thinking the same thing.

Zane took their bottle of lubricant from the bedside table and dropped it to the floor at Ty's feet. He pulled his T-shirt over his head, tossed it to the side, and joined Ty on the thick rug in front of the fireplace.

Ty gripped his chin and kissed him, slowly maneuvering them both until they were stretched out on the plush rug. He immediately laid Zane out, settling between his legs, gathering up Zane's wrists to hold him and kiss him soundly. "Every night," he repeated in a whisper.

Zane relaxed into the rug as Ty's weight bore down on him, and as Ty's hands closed around his wrists, he gave a gentle moan. The thought of Ty taking control and holding him down sent a shudder through him. It was something Ty hadn't done since getting home, something Zane had sorely missed. Zane couldn't help but wonder how much of Ty would never be the same again after this past year. So many things were still missing. Every time Ty seemed to regain something, even something as trivial as wanting to overpower Zane and screw him into the ground, it was like a weight being lifted from Zane's mind.

"Please," Zane whispered.

Ty was already mostly hard, and he rubbed himself against Zane's hip. He gathered Zane's wrists into one hand, grip tightening, and the kiss became more demanding as Ty responded to his plea.

Ty's free hand slid down Zane's body, fingers digging in possessively as they dragged along his chest and then his ribs to his hip. Ty pushed up to give himself room to rut into Zane as he licked and bit and sucked at his lips.

Zane groaned and pulled at Ty's hands, testing his grip. Ty grunted at him, using the weight of his body to hold Zane down. He pushed at Zane's thigh with his knee, shoving his legs further apart and stealing any leverage Zane might have found. His hard cock pushed against Zane's hip as Ty straddled one thigh. He rocked against him as he sucked on Zane's tongue, slowly but surely draining Zane's control.

Zane was hard, too, straining against his boxers. He whimpered, desperate for more. It wasn't often that Zane wanted this from Ty—needed it, begged for it—but when he did, Ty would nearly eat him alive before getting him off.

Zane so desperately wanted to be eaten alive right now, just to reaffirm that everything would be normal again, that Ty would return to his irascible self and still be able to make Zane's knees weak with a smirk. That one day Ty would ask him to marry him again and Zane would say yes without a second thought.

Ty pushed at Zane's boxers, rising up just enough to shove them down Zane's hips before plunging his hand into Zane's hair. Zane had let it grow a little longer, and Ty seemed to love it. He gripped Zane hard, holding him still as he took his fill of the kiss. Then he yanked Zane's head back and ducked to kiss at the tender skin of his neck.

Arching under him, Zane bared his throat. He moaned when Ty bit him. He knew what Ty was going to do to him just by the way he kissed him, by the tense energy already emanating from Ty's body. "Yes . . . please."

Ty kissed him again, covering the words with his mouth and licking at Zane's tongue before working his way over Zane's chin, down his neck, and across his chest to bite at the hard muscle of his shoulder. With every movement, Ty's hand tightened in his hair. Each tug drew a soft groan, and each groan caused Ty to come back for another kiss. If Ty continued this way, he was never going to reach his goal, and Zane was going to come long before he got close.

Finally, Ty let go of Zane's hair and slid both hands under Zane's shoulders instead, jerking him against the floor as he kissed and bit along his chest. He sucked a nipple between his lips, flicking his tongue over it.

The moans tearing out of Zane were growing steadily louder. He was vocal anytime he was enjoying himself with his lover; he saw no reason to hold it back, especially when Ty loved to hear it so damn much. He didn't care if everyone in the mansion heard them. They no longer had to hide, not from anyone.

Ty couldn't seem to keep himself from Zane's mouth, and he pushed up to kiss Zane again, mumbling to him between the harsh kisses. His beard scratched at Zane's tender skin. His grip was hard enough to make Zane squirm. His muscles bunched under Zane's fingers. He felt like a wild animal in Zane's arms, barely under control.

Then he was back to trailing down Zane's body as Zane shifted under him. Ty's hands slid underneath him as he finally got to Zane's hip and bit him, just hard enough to leave a red mark. It drew a cry of pleasure out of Zane. Ty sat up and yanked Zane's boxers off, then propped the back of Zane's thigh against his shoulder before bending over him and licking the head of his cock.

"Oh God, I love it when you do this."

Ty wrapped his arm around Zane's thigh. For some reason it made Zane feel vulnerable, propping that leg up on Ty's solid shoulder, watching him insinuate himself between Zane's legs to take his cock into his mouth. It made him feel vulnerable, and he loved it. It turned him on because Ty was the only person who'd ever made him feel that.

He shuddered and clutched at the rug as he thrust his hips toward Ty's sinful mouth. "Oh God, please," he whispered. "Baby, please."

He would beg, plead, and grovel if he needed to. He'd never done that for anyone before, but he was irrevocably addicted to Ty's touch, to the way Ty made him feel. And he loved the way his begging spurred Ty on.

Ty's fingers dug into the front of Zane's hip as he held him in place and went down on him. It took him a few attempts, but he finally got the head of Zane's cock to the back of his throat and swallowed around it. A strangled yell from Zane echoed off the stone walls around them, and he strained uselessly to snap his hips up for more. The hot slide of Ty's tongue all over him was irresistible.

Someone banged on the wall, followed by a taunting whoop from their audience next door. It was a far cry from the fear Ty must have lived with all his life of being exposed, to have his friends catcall him as he fucked his boyfriend.

Ty continued on, seemingly devoted to making Zane lose it. But then he stopped abruptly, pulling off Zane's cock with one last lick from balls to head.

"No, no, please," Zane gasped, reaching for Ty desperately. "Please, don't stop, baby."

Ty let Zane's leg slide off his shoulder and knelt between Zane's knees. Zane's pleas ceased when he saw the look in Ty's eyes. Ty slid both palms up Zane's torso, his fingers dragging against the muscles, ending up at Zane's shoulders and pushing him into the floor. He kissed him passionately, practically devouring him as he rutted against Zane's thigh. Zane moaned against his mouth, offering up complete control of his body and mind. Hell, his soul if Ty wanted it.

It was times like this, times when Ty gave in to utter passion, that his true strength revealed itself. It was a heady feeling, being completely under his control. Zane loved to imagine sometimes what it would be like to meet Ty in battle, to be at the mercy of this sort of power. Ty's hands moved all over Zane's body, alternately holding him down and pulling him up off the floor to suit whatever whims Ty had. It took a lot of muscle to manhandle someone Zane's size so effortlessly.

Finally, he reached for the bottle of lubricant, then found one of Zane's hands without breaking their kiss and squeezed some into his palm. Dazed, Zane dragged open his eyes as he panted and shivered under Ty, wondering what he was going to tell him to do. Zane would do anything right now to please him. To please them both.

"Get me ready," Ty growled.

He groaned as soon as Zane touched him, bowing his back to bite at Zane's lip. Their foreheads pressed together, their gasps mingling, and Ty whispered "I love you" between each kiss.

Zane spread his legs farther apart as he jacked Ty. "Fuck me, baby," he rasped. "I need it."

Ty's harsh breaths gusted across Zane's cheek and ear as he kissed toward Zane's neck and bit him right beneath his earlobe. He pulled at Zane's hair, jerking his head to the side, dropping little nips that left enough sting for Zane to want more. And Zane begged for them with broken sounds and soft cries.

Ty put his lips to Zane's ear. "Louder."

Zane fought to swallow. His cock jumped against Ty's hip.

"Louder, Zane," Ty ordered, voice going sharper. It *was* an order, just like the ones he gave in the field to Marines who hopped to obey his every command. Like he was finally declaring to the world, to anyone who would listen, that Zane was his.

With his other hand, Ty pulled Zane's leg up and sideways until Zane lay on his side, leg tucked up to his chest. He grabbed Zane's wrist and slammed it to the ground beside Zane's head, pinning him, twisting him, then scraped his teeth over Zane's ribs as he flexed his hips, going for the spot that was most exposed, that felt the most vulnerable. Zane tried to curl and couldn't.

Zane's desperate half growl tore out of him as he writhed under Ty, body twisted, so turned on that it hurt, jolted by sweet agony every time Ty almost entered him.

"Ty . . . Ty, oh fucking God, please," he whimpered, his entire body shaking. "Please . . ."

Ty pushed at his head to turn him into another brutal kiss. "Louder," he snarled.

"Please!"

Ty's hands tightened almost painfully, and he flexed his hips, and the angle of Zane's twisted body was just right to let him push the head of his cock inside. He rocked there several times, forcing Zane apart, causing him to cry out again, then he shoved in harder, rocking Zane's body against the thick carpet.

Zane's shout of pleasure and pain echoed off the walls. His gasps were caught between Ty's lips, and it was a near-impossible struggle to stay still as Ty rocked into him, to keep his hips at that perfect angle, one leg straight between Ty's knees and one drawn up to his chest as Ty took him from above. He needed to move, to ease the ache of invasion, to intensify the brutal pressure. God, he loved it, Ty forcing his way in, laying claim to Zane's body.

He was on the edge of completely falling apart. Thank Christ Ty was there to keep him together, just like he'd always been. His cries turned to wails. "Please!"

Ty finally loosened his hold, and his hands began to roam again as he started a slow, steady rhythm. "Move, baby."

"Oh *fuck,* thank you," Zane gasped, turning to angle his hips as Ty pushed into him. He squeezed his eyes shut and then opened them to see Ty over his shoulder.

"You're so fucking beautiful like this," Ty panted. He pulled at Zane's leg, turning him again to laying him out flat, belly to the rug, hips off the floor, and drove into him mercilessly.

Zane's shouts became louder and more frequent. He looked over his shoulder so he could see Ty fucking him, see him losing control.

Ty pressed his cheek against Zane's shoulder as he picked up his pace, his panting breaths harsh in Zane's ear and sweat dripping from his temples. Zane loved the sensation of Ty's hips flexing against his ass, his knees pushing at Zane's with each thrust, his fingers digging into Zane's shoulders as Ty used his body for leverage.

Zane couldn't have stopped his cries if he'd wanted to. The pleasure was overwhelming, and not even the pain of his own need for release could distract him.

Ty slowed and pushed himself up, trailing gentle fingers over Zane's shoulder blades. His hips were still thrusting into Zane, and his entire body was gleaming with sweat from his efforts and the heat of the fire just feet away. The change in momentum drove another husky wail out of Zane. His back arched almost painfully, and he threw a hand out, his fingers again digging helplessly for some sort of leverage from the rug.

"You better wait for me, you hear me?" Ty warned. He snapped his hips forward, driving deep into Zane with a growl of pleasure, forcing another shout.

Ty had been so close to the edge since he'd been home, fighting so hard to stay in control. Maybe what he needed was just to simply let it go.

"Don't stop."

Ty returned to the same punishing rhythm he'd started with, obviously not caring that Zane was trying to prolong it. Then he pulled back until the head of his cock was forcing the tight muscles of Zane's ass to spread and spasm, and made Zane roll his body again, one leg up as Ty drove hard into him.

Their eyes met, neither of them blinking or looking away as Ty thrust into him over and over.

Ty couldn't keep up the punishing rhythm for much longer, even though Zane begged him to continue. He pushed his face against Zane's neck and cried out Zane's name. Zane dragged his blunt fingernails down Ty's back, pleading with him not to come yet, begging him to keep fucking him, hard and merciless. Ty's answer was another agonized shout of Zane's name as he emptied himself deep inside him.

Zane soaked it all in, quivering uncontrollably. Ty was solid and warm in his hands, and he didn't let go while Ty kept moving inside him. He would never get enough of that feeling.

Ty's hips continued to rock as he laid himself down over Zane. He moaned, the sound tortured and exhausted. "Jesus Christ, you're fun to fuck," he rumbled as he pressed his lips to Zane's neck.

Zane groaned and shivered hard, turning his chin to give Ty all the access to his neck he wanted. That scruffy beard scraping across his skin was indescribably sexy. Whatever the reason Ty had grown it while he'd been gone, Zane was damn glad he'd kept it. Ty kissed under his jaw one last time before pulling out of him with a plaintive moan. He was damp, and his body glistened in the light of the fire and the morning sun.

Zane moved to take himself in hand, but Ty reached for him instead. He wrapped talented fingers around Zane's cock and stroked him lazily as they kissed. Then he scooted down and took Zane's cock in his mouth. It wasn't long, maybe a minute or two, and Zane was shouting helplessly as his entire body seized, muscles cramping, fingers digging into Ty's hair, hips jutting upward. He choked out a last moan and came so hard his vision sparkled, each thin stream coating Ty's tongue as he sucked Zane through it, driving his moans louder and louder into a pained yell and then a begging sob.

Ty sucked and pumped him until Zane had spent every last drop of himself, then pulled off and kissed Zane's hip. He rolled to his back and sprawled out on the rug, eyes closed and chest heaving.

The gust of air from Ty's movement sent another shudder through Zane. He could still feel Ty all over him: smarting bite marks, the whisker burn on his throat and shoulders, rug burn on his chest, elbows, and knees, sore spots from Ty's fingers digging in, and best of all, Ty's cum sliding down his leg. He felt absolutely mauled.

Eyes still shut, he reached out to his side and his fingers met Ty's hip. He stroked the heated, damp skin. A moment later, Ty's fingers tangled with his, lacing together. Ty didn't say anything. They were content to hold hands as they lay on the floor together, soaking in the warmth of the fire and the morning sun stretching toward them.

Once their breathing calmed and the ringing in Zane's ears faded, he heard the muffled sound of Nick and Kelly in their bedroom, catcalling and applauding. Ty must have heard it as well, because they both began to laugh at the same time.

"Is it wrong that I'm turned on by the idea of forcing your friends to listen to us having sex?" Zane asked with a frown.

Ty laughed harder. "Just don't tell Nick that. He'll offer to critique your performance. Or worse, join us."

"Can't have that." Zane dragged Ty closer, snuggling him even though they were both still sweating and kind of gross. "Did you see the note in the bathroom about saving water since the island is run on a self-sufficient energy system?"

Ty smiled against Zane's lips. "Must have missed that."

"Means we should probably shower together again, don't you think?"

Ty was already nodding. "For nature."

"Obviously."

Ty chuckled and they shared a languid kiss. Ty was smirking when they parted. "Marry me, Zane," he whispered.

Zane burst out laughing and sat up. These weren't exactly the ideal conditions for a proposal they needed to be telling to family. "Nuh uh."

"Oh, come on!" Ty called after him as he ducked into the bathroom. "Lying naked on a rug in front of a fireplace in a fucking castle?"

"Nope." Zane caught himself grinning in the mirror, but he didn't even try to wipe it off when Ty joined him.

Ty shoved him against the sink to kiss him. He mumbled against his lips. "You might have to lower your standards."

Zane hummed. "How about you . . . up yours?"

"Is that . . . is that a pun?"

Zane held to Ty as he tried to pull away.

Ty rolled his eyes. "Jackass."

Ty and Zane were some of the first people down to breakfast, beaten only by Chester, Ty's parents, and Nick and Kelly. The five of them were sitting at a table together, talking.

Ty glanced around the morning room, surprised by the nerves he felt when he saw Nick with his family. He gave Zane's shirtsleeve a tug at the doorway, stopping him from entering the room before the others saw them. Zane let him draw him to the side, out of sight.

Ty hesitated and peered around the door again. Earl and Nick were carrying on what appeared to be a pleasant conversation. Earl was laughing, and Nick looked like he might be telling a story. Ty turned to Zane. "How much do you know about Nick's father?"

Zane raised both eyebrows, obviously confused. "Nothing?"

Ty sighed. "Okay. Well, Nick's dad used to beat the hell out of him. I mean legitimately should have spent time in jail for what he did. When we graduated from Basic, our parents all came down for the ceremony and they took us out for dinner that night. They got into an argument, and Nick's dad started in on him and then walked out when Nick stood up for himself. Let's just say Dad took offense and basically adopted Nick after that."

Zane nodded, still frowning in confusion. "I thought Earl didn't even remember Nick's name from the snake incident."

Ty shook his head. "He was just messing with you, trying to make you nervous about hiking. Nick spent practically every leave with us after that. Ma and Dad are pretty close to him. I'm telling you this so . . . just don't let Nick know how Dad reacted when Grandpa outed us, okay?"

Understanding finally dawned on Zane's face, and anger swiftly followed.

"Please?" Ty tried. "Dad can handle himself, he deserves what he gets, but Nick . . . Nick sees my parents as his own."

Zane schooled his initial emotions, merely nodding instead. "I promise. For Nick, not for Earl."

"Thanks, Zane," Ty whispered, and he slipped his arm around Zane's waist as they headed into the breakfast room.

They were greeted by the others with good mornings from Earl and Mara, and knowing smirks from Nick and Kelly.

Ty plopped down in the seat next to Kelly and peered over at his friends. "What the hell happened to you two this morning?"

Nick began to snicker and Kelly rolled his eyes as he took a sip of coffee. "I fell out of the bed."

"Fell?" Zane asked. "Or you were pushed?"

"Legit fell. Rolled right out of that thing and took the covers with me. I dreamt I was being attacked by a giant squid and woke up thinking I was drowning."

"I woke up cold and very confused," Nick added.

Ty couldn't help but laugh.

Kelly smiled slyly. "What happened to *you* this morning?"

"I wasn't attacked by a giant squid, if that's what you're asking," Ty drawled. He glanced toward the end of the table at his grandfather, giving him a smart salute. "Gramps, how's it going?"

Chester grumbled over his bacon and eggs, piling them all together onto a piece of bread to make a sandwich. He glanced up at Ty and Zane, narrowing his eyes before turning his attention to Nick, who was sitting next to him and minding his own business.

Chester pointed his fork at Nick's face. "When I was your age, sonny, they used to say redheads was relations of Satan."

Kelly choked on his breakfast, but Nick just gave Chester an enigmatic smile.

"What do they say about you now?" Chester asked him.

Nick gave an easy shrug. "They say we have no soul."

Chester pursed his lips, nodding thoughtfully as he patted one gnarled hand against Nick's shoulder. "Eh. True enough."

Nick raised both eyebrows, but then he held up his orange juice and Chester toasted him by tapping his coffee to the glass. Kelly was still coughing, trying to swallow and laugh at the same time. He finally had to excuse himself and stumbled out of the room to go find somewhere to spit it out.

Ty glanced at Zane and found the man hiding his face with both hands, laughing silently. At least now he knew it wasn't just him Chester spoke to that way. But Nick had always taken Chester's eccentricities in stride, probably even better than Ty and Deuce did because Nick just never gave a fuck.

Nick was still smiling, shaking his head as he ate. From the first time Ty had brought him home, he'd fit into the Grady family shockingly well. Earl had taken a special interest in him after the scene Nick's father had made at their graduation. Whether Nick's father would have tried to hit Nick in front of them all was questionable, because men like him usually worked behind closed doors, but Ty had known immediately that he was going to have to pull his father off Nick's if a punch was thrown.

Ty realized he was staring at Nick, frowning with the memories. Something about Nick had been off ever since they'd been deployed, and it had gotten worse once they'd returned home, but Ty couldn't put his finger on it. Something just felt . . . wrong. Nick was keeping something to himself, something that was troubling him. Ty told himself to find some time alone with his best friend to see if he needed to talk.

Zane jabbed him in the ribs. "You okay?" he whispered in Ty's ear.

Ty tore his eyes away from Nick and nodded, realizing belatedly that Earl had been speaking to him. "I'm sorry, what?"

"I asked how your night went, but I guess I know," Earl said with a short laugh.

Chester began to cackle at the end of the table. "I'm the only Grady didn't get lucky last night!"

Nick dropped his fork and put his hand over his eyes.

Chester grabbed his arm and shook him. "You want to bang something too, sonny, you can borrow my shovel!"

They were still laughing when Kelly came jogging back into the room. He looked flustered. "Guys, there's something wrong outside."

Ty shoved back from the table, Nick and Zane on his heels as they followed Kelly to the front door. Several other early risers were milling around, looking worried or confused. Kelly cut a swath through them and shoved through the door, pointing toward the staff cottages near the shore. Another small group of people was gathered down there.

Ty took Kelly's arm. "Doc, will you go to Deacon's room and make sure they're safe?"

"Aye," Kelly said, then darted back into the house.

Ty and Zane took off at a run toward the commotion, with Nick hesitating briefly and then following them instead of Kelly. When they reached the crowd of roughly half a dozen people, Zane immediately took control of the situation, trying to discern what was happening in a loud, commanding voice. They received a cacophony of confused answers, but the prevailing words seemed to be "dead" and "murdered."

A redheaded man with a hawk-like nose and a ruddy tan finally broke away from the other staff and came up to Zane. "Jockie Fraser," he said in a Scottish accent, offering his hand. His fingers were stained dark and he was wearing a pair of heavy-duty overalls. "I'm the groundskeeper. I was on my way to the docks when I heard Maisie scream and I came running. Found her hyperventilating and found him like this." He led them over to the scene, wringing his hat in his hands.

The body was facedown in the sand, just yards away from the encroaching surf. The shoreline around him was completely trampled.

Nick cursed under his breath. The homicide detective in him must have been pulling the pin on a grenade inside his head just looking at this messy scene.

Zane made his way carefully to the body to check for a pulse. He found none, as he'd probably expected, and he stood and backed away in his own footsteps. "We need to secure the scene and call the local authorities," he said to them.

Ty pulled his phone out of his pocket, but soon found he had no service. He glanced at Nick, who was shaking his head at his own phone.

"We got nothing," Ty muttered.

They asked the staff about their cell service, since they were locals, and were told the island's service was spotty and only found in the highest of places. They were too remote.

Zane singled out one of the onlookers to go to the mansion and have someone contact the mainland. The girl ran off, and Ty and Zane stood staring at each other for long moments. How did this always happen to them? Every single time. Another vacation, another psychopath.

Nick smacked Ty on the back, bringing his attention back to the present. "You recognize that vest, man?"

Ty took a closer look at the victim's muddy vest. Burgundy with a gold-stitched fox-and-hound scene repeated over and over. His stomach sank. It was the head of operations, the man who'd insisted the island was safe. "Milton."

"What do you mean we can't contact the mainland?" Ty hissed to his brother's future father-in-law.

The man had ridden down from the mansion when he'd heard the news, accompanied by his two bodyguards and Deuce. Nick assumed Kelly had remained behind with Livi and Amelia to watch over them, but his eyes kept straying to try to catch sight of him.

Stanton's voice was strained when he answered Ty. "The house telephones aren't operating properly, there's too much static on the line. Hamish believes there's water in the lines. But we're not getting a radio signal either."

The larger of his two bodyguards, the overeager leader of the Snake Eaters they all called English, took his sunglasses off and stepped forward. "It could be the work of a signal jammer."

Stanton sighed in annoyance. "That is one possibility, perhaps. There's also a massive storm cell all around us, the same one that passed over last night. That's why we moved tomorrow night's rehearsal ceremony inside. Communications are disrupted like this two, three times a week during the stormy seasons. It's no real reason for concern."

"I'd say it's reason for *him* to be concerned," Ty said with a point to the dead man.

"Of course," Stanton said, staying impressively calm. "I'm merely saying the lack of communications is not unusual. It could be a coincidence."

"What about a sat phone?" Zane asked.

"Do you have one?" Stanton asked, his tone one of hope rather than sarcasm.

Zane shook his head.

"Neither does anyone else. My personal one has gone missing."

"That's a little bit of an alarm, there, boss," Ty grunted.

"Amelia was playing with it at dinner on the first night. Maisie was trying to retrieve it from her, but I haven't seen it since. There's no telling where it is."

"Great."

"I'll have the staff begin a quiet inquiry for anyone else who has one, but we're trying not to alarm anyone."

"Even the radios on the boats are out?" Nick asked.

"I've not yet got word back from the man I sent to the dock. I don't have high hopes. Even the staff's walkie-talkies are on the fritz."

"Storms usually do that?" Zane asked.

"Not that I've seen, no."

Nick gritted his teeth in frustration. This was kind of like being in the Marines all over again and trying to communicate with cans and string.

"What about the ferry?" Ty tried. "When will they notice they've lost contact with us?"

"The day of the wedding is the next arranged landing if the weather is fair. After that, next week. Next month. Maybe. There's no real schedule for the ferry because the island is private."

Nick scratched at his eyebrow, looking over at Ty with a shrug. "We'll send someone in one of the island's boats, then. The authorities have to be notified of this, we can't just wait until *nature* lets us call."

Stanton turned to one of the groundskeepers. "Will you please send word to the dock to have one of the smaller launches prepared for the crossing? And see what's keeping them so long with the radios."

Once the man had gone and the rest of the staff had begun to disperse for their daily responsibilities, Stanton drew closer to Ty and Zane, lowering his voice. "Is this . . . was this an accident?" he asked, obviously more rattled than he had been letting on.

Ty and Zane shared a look. "We don't know. We haven't touched the scene other than to clear it."

Nick moved closer, keeping the two Snake Eaters in his peripheral vision because they both annoyed the shit out of him. "If help is going to take a long time in getting here, we need to look at that body," he told the others. "Evidence is disappearing as we stand here, and there's more rain coming. And we can't leave the body like this for much longer. The tide will come in. We'll have to document the scene as best we can and then move him somewhere to preserve whatever's on him."

Ty nodded, still frowning.

"And Ty. If he was murdered . . ."

"There's probably a murderer on the island with us, yeah." Ty nodded, his frown growing even deeper. "Do it."

Nick raised both eyebrows, opening his mouth in surprise. He clutched his right hand to his thigh, making a fist with it. "Me?"

"You're the homicide detective, right?"

"Not anymore."

"Irish, just look at the fucking body and see if you think it's a murder or an accident, okay?" Ty snapped.

Nick grunted in annoyance. "Aye, aye, Captain."

"I'm sorry." Ty swiped a hand over his forehead, closing his eyes. "Please."

Nick huffed and brushed past him, stepping carefully in Zane's footprints to kneel next to the body. There were no defensive wounds on the parts of his arms that were visible, but the dead man's watch was cracked. Nick cocked his head to read the time. It had stopped at 3:48 am.

"Possible time of death here," he said without looking up. He pressed his fingers to the man's neck. He was cold. He tried to articulate the dead man's fingers and they moved without resistance. Nick frowned. If he'd died just four hours ago, he would still be in rigor. The cold night could have sped up the cooling of the body, but the evidence was saying different things about when the man had died.

He looked around for pieces of the glass watch face, finally finding them in the mud next to a rock a foot away from the man's head. The beach was littered with rocks and boulders, some smooth, some jagged. It was possible he'd slipped while walking and hit his head. Nick reached for one of the shards of glass, but his fingers were trembling again. He clutched his hand into a fist and pulled it back, swiping it across his thigh instead. He'd need someone to take photos of the glass shards anyway, so he left them there.

Footprints were impossible to decipher. The sand was too loose, and too many people had passed this way. He leaned far over the dead man, trying to see his face without disturbing the scene any more than it had been. What he found was a gaping wound at his hairline, so deep he could see bone and brain matter. The blood had mingled with the ocean and soaked into the sand. The absence of a blood pool made the brutal wound a shock to find.

"His skull's been caved in," he announced.

"Could it be from a fall?" Zane called to him.

Nick shook his head before he even gave the question real thought. "Wound like this, there was some real leverage behind it. Looks like someone brained him with a rock. Never saw it coming. Didn't put up a fight."

"He *was* murdered," Stanton said under his breath, covering his mouth with his palm.

There was a shout from the pathway, and when Nick stood to peer past the others, he saw a man guiding one of the golf carts up the path, waving at them frantically as he swerved the cart all over. When he got closer he hopped out and sprinted toward them, leaving the golf cart to roll by itself down the incline. People shouted and hustled for it before it could hit the cliff and sail over the edge, but the driver didn't notice.

"What the hell," Ty said.

"They're gone," the man blurted as he ran toward them.

"What's gone, Gillis?" Stanton demanded.

"The boats!" the young man named Gillis gasped out when he finally skidded to a stop in front of Stanton. "All of them. They're all gone from the dock. Even the rowboats and kayaks. Mackie says the boathouse was hit by a tree and they're all gone."

"Gone," Stanton echoed.

"You can see them, little dots out floating in the water." The kid was still breathless. He waved his arm around. "The storm set them all afloat. The ones not still floating sank at the docks."

Stanton's eyes were wide when he turned back to Nick and the others. Nick felt his stomach drop as the realization sank in. They were trapped on the island with no way to communicate with the outside world, possibly for days. And there could very well be a murderer among them.

He took a deep breath and let it out, grumbling to himself. "I'm going to fucking die in Scotland."

Zane sat quietly in an office chair through a brief debate over whether the wedding festivities should carry on as planned, or if the guests should be told of the murder and the loss of the island's launches. Ty and Nick argued first with the Snake Eaters and then with each other over which avenue would be most expedient for keeping everyone safe. Kelly was still with Livi and Amelia, or Zane was sure Kelly would have been able to keep things calmer. As it was, Zane just hung back.

Ty insisted keeping the guests in the dark would, at least for a little while, prevent a mass panic and allow them to try to find a solution in relative peace. Nick was adamant that people in danger deserved to know they were in danger, and steps could be taken to protect them and convince them to cooperate.

Zane felt like he was witnessing the core of why Ty and Nick had always made a good team. They were very yin and yang.

Finally, Nick pointed out that word would get around despite their attempts to keep it quiet because most of the island's staff had seen the body. "Rumors are always worse than truth, and once they start, we won't be able to get people to trust us when we try to start sharing truth with them."

Ty and the Snake Eaters all grunted in unison, but none of them could come up with a counterargument to that.

Someone knocked on the door to the study, and a moment later they opened the door to see Kelly standing there. The bodyguards let him in and locked the door behind him.

"Is it true someone got stabbed in the ear with a broken seashell?" Kelly asked incredulously.

Nick held his hand out to Kelly, eyes on Ty. "See?"

Ty was massaging his temples, nodding. "Okay, you were right."

"We make an announcement," Zane said, smiling fondly at Ty.

Stanton didn't look amused, though. "Agreed. I'll make a call for all the guests and employees to assemble in the great hall. We can address the situation there. Who is with Amelia?"

"Korean dude who doesn't talk," Kelly answered.

"We need to set an investigation in motion in the absence of proper authorities," one of the Snake Eaters told Stanton. It was the large leader of the private security force, a man named John English. He struck Zane as a little too cocky, but he seemed efficient and mostly sensible.

"How are you going to do that?" Zane asked him. "We have no authority to question these people, or detain them, or search for evidence."

English shrugged his huge shoulders. "They don't know that."

"Which will be handy later on," Ty added.

Zane grunted, beginning to grow annoyed with the attitude of the Snake Eater crew. It was disturbing to him on several levels how easily Ty fit in with them. He often wondered how close Ty had been to taking the mercenary road. He definitely set foot on it here and there.

Stanton started to pace, chewing on a cigar. "We'll make it clear it's an informal inquiry, being performed merely to keep everyone safe. There is a murderer roaming the island, after all, people deserve protection. Anyone who wishes not to participate will be . . . locked in their room for the safety of others."

"Still not really legal," Zane advised.

"Neither is murder," Theo Stanton snapped. They were the first words Livi's brother had uttered since the meeting had started.

"These are extraordinary circumstances, I'm afraid." Stanton turned to Nick, cheeks pale and eyes drawn. "Rick, isn't it? You're a police detective? You'll do the investigation."

"Excuse me?" Nick said, not even bothering to correct his name.

"You have no blood connection to either family, nor to the business. You're as neutral a party as we'll find and you're trained to do the job."

Nick glanced around at all of them, looking like he wanted to argue, but the logic was sound. Zane nodded encouragingly when Nick met his eyes. Nick sighed and jerked his head to the side.

"If I can have the doc assisting me, then I guess I don't have any objection."

"Whatever you need," Stanton agreed. He shook Nick's hand distractedly. "What *do* you need?"

Nick hesitated before shrugging one shoulder. "Well, it's an unusual situation in that our pool of suspects is static, so gathering alibis would be the first step. But that's something we'd need to organize everyone for. If I tried to do it quietly, word would get around and people would be able to coordinate their stories. It would make it pointless. So we tell people we're trying to discern a timeline, to see if anyone out of place was on the island."

Stanton nodded and absently handed his cigar to Nick, who took it and looked at it like he'd just been handed a unicorn as Stanton walked away. Nick glanced at Kelly, who was biting his lip and trying not to smile.

"We don't have any way of telling time of death, though," Theo argued.

"Without definitive evidence, we'll have to go by his broken watch," Zane provided.

Nick shook his head, turning to Kelly. "I need you to confirm it for me."

"Confirm it . . . how?" Kelly asked.

Nick winced. "With a turkey thermometer probably."

"Oh gross, Nick."

"I'm serious."

"I know, that's why it's gross!"

Even Zane was a little disgusted at the thought, but Nick was probably right. It was much more accurate to check the body's temperature by measuring the liver temp than assuming the watch had been broken in the fight that ultimately killed him.

Nick handed the cigar to Kelly and began writing down the information he would need to estimate the time of death from the body's temperature, indicating that roughly every two and a half degrees it had dropped meant he'd been dead an hour. "Give or take a little because of the cold. I don't trust the watch as time of death." He ripped the page off the notebook and handed it to Kelly. "You have to hurry before he hits ambient temp, okay? And I need you to do it before we put the body in cold storage. Like, right now, as soon as we're done here."

Kelly nodded and took the slip of paper, nose curled in distaste. Stanton was still pacing, and Kelly held the cigar out for him to take as he walked by. Stanton plucked it from Kelly's fingers and put it in his mouth without even seeming to realize he'd ever given it up. Zane found himself fighting back a laugh.

"If the temp puts time of death in range, we'll assume the watch is correct," Nick told them. There wasn't much point in arguing with what little they had to go on.

"If the body and the watch are saying different things, is it possible he was killed elsewhere?" Zane asked Nick. He was the only one who'd been close enough to the body to see.

Nick was shaking his head before Zane could finish. "No. There were no signs on the body that it'd been moved."

"You sure?" Zane asked.

Nick gave him a brief glare, then nodded. "Been doing this a long time, Garrett, I don't need my hand held."

Zane held up both hands and shrugged. He didn't want problems with Nick, not now.

"If this is the first step in an escalation against the company, then we have motive," Ty added. "That could narrow down the first wave of interviews, at least."

"I'd like to search his room," Nick told Stanton. "Get a hold of his laptop, phone, any papers. If we could lock that down ASAP to keep anyone from getting in there. In fact, Grady and Garrett could handle that while I'm interviewing people."

"I'll get you the key, but Grady and Garrett will be watching Amelia while you're doing that, thank you," Stanton promised. He headed for the door, gesturing for his men to follow him. "I'll meet you gentlemen on the patio in ten minutes for the announcement. We'll serve brunch and allow you to do your interviews while people are eating. Will that work?"

All eyes turned back to Nick, who was watching Stanton with a frown. When he realized the man was actually waiting for a response, he nodded, obviously flustered. "Yes, sir, thank you."

Stanton nodded and left the room. The door clicked behind Theo, leaving the four of them alone in stunned silence.

Kelly sat on the back of the couch where Nick was leaning, brushing their shoulders together. "Is this what traveling with you guys is usually like?"

"Yes," Ty and Zane both groaned.

"No," Nick said with a sorrowful shake of his head.

Kelly wrapped an arm around his shoulders, hugging him. "It's okay, Rick."

Nick snorted. Zane chuckled, even though he felt guilty for laughing. Nick looked so distraught to have been singled out for the job, Zane had to wonder why. He'd been a detective in Boston for at least seven years, and from what Ty said about him, he was good at his job.

Ty sat on Nick's other side and patted his knee. "You okay to do this?"

"Does it matter?" Nick asked.

"We got your six, man," Kelly said.

Zane nodded immediately. "Piece of cake."

Nick rubbed his fingers over his eyes. The very tips of his fingers trembled, barely noticeable. But Zane noticed it. He'd noticed it outside, too, when Nick had made to reach for something in the sand but then stopped. He'd noticed it last night at dinner when Nick had switched his fork from his right hand to his left and then clutched his right hand into a fist before hiding it in his lap. Nick was a lefty, so using his left instead of his right wasn't unusual, but it had caught Zane's attention nonetheless. The tremor in his right hand was the same type Zane had developed when he was coming off everything in rehab.

Combined with the other things Zane had noticed—his uncharacteristically sedate behavior, his shorter temper, refusing to go back to a job everyone said he'd loved, the haunted look in his eyes—Zane was almost positive Nick was either using or trying to stop.

"I guess we should get out there," Ty finally said. As they all stood to file out of the room, Ty grumbled under his breath, "We have a fucking murderer to find at my brother's wedding."

"I hope it's one of those asshole security guys," Kelly said from behind Zane.

"Maybe the butler did it," Nick offered. Kelly answered with a groan.

When they reached the great hall where people were already gathering, Ty went straight over to his parents, whispering to them about the situation. Mara had a hand over her mouth and her eyes were wide, but Earl merely nodded grimly. Burns was sitting with them, and he didn't show much surprise either. It seemed they'd already gotten wind of the news. From the low murmurs throughout the room, a lot of other guests had as well.

Zane stood watching people assemble for a few seconds before he decided that now might be the best time to pull Nick aside. When this was over, they'd be in the center of an investigation, no matter how unofficial. He approached Nick with a hint of trepidation and caught him trailing after Kelly through the crowd to head back out into the hall. He took his elbow to stop him.

Nick turned to him with a confused smile. "Garrett? They moved the body to the kitchen to store it, we're heading down there. Might want to order vegetarian tonight."

Zane snorted and glanced around them. "Can I talk to you first?"

Nick's smile fell. Kelly had stopped to wait for him, and now he stood frowning a few feet away. Nick looked around just like Zane had done to see if anyone else was paying attention to them, then nodded. "Sure. What's up?"

"Somewhere private. I'd prefer if Ty didn't see us talking."

Nick's confusion and sudden apprehension were painfully clear, but he turned to Kelly anyway. "I'll catch up with you, Kels."

"Okay," Kelly said, frowning at them but turning to head off to the kitchen on his own.

Nick left the great hall with Zane, but he didn't ask questions, and Zane was grateful for it. He led Nick into the hallway and found a quiet nook to duck into. He turned to Nick and glanced at the doorway behind them.

"What's going on, Garrett?" Nick seemed to be losing his patience with the cloak-and-dagger stuff.

"Look, I want to help you, okay?" Zane said in a rush.

Nick raised both eyebrows and leaned a little closer. "Aren't you pretty much already signed up for that?"

"Not with that. I saw your hand shaking out there. And I saw you popping pills yesterday in the car when you thought I was asleep." Zane reached for Nick's right hand and brought it up, then released it. There was a tremor to his fingers as Nick tried to hold it steady. Zane nodded grimly. "I've been there."

Nick looked at his hand, then gave an exhausted, almost relieved laugh as he dropped it to his side. He glanced away for a moment, then met Zane's eyes again. "Propranolol."

Zane's brow creased. "What?"

"That's what I was taking in the car. I take it every morning."

"Never heard of it."

"It's not a narcotic," Nick said wryly. "It's prescribed. One a day."

Zane took a moment to let that settle in, but it didn't alleviate his concern. In fact, it only served to double it. His stomach tumbled. "Are you sick, O'Flaherty?"

Nick lowered his head, sighing and turning away. He ran a hand through his hair.

Zane glanced over his shoulder to make sure they were still alone, then took a step after Nick. "What's it for?"

Nick flopped his hands against his thighs. "I have a tremor. That's what it's for."

Zane's gaze drifted down to Nick's right hand, which was clutched at his side. "From what?"

Nick shrugged. "Doctors did tests. No one knows. But the medicine keeps my hand from trembling, so I take it. If I forget, I shake like fucking San Francisco in an earthquake."

Zane laughed before he could stop himself. He put his hand over his mouth. "I'm sorry."

Nick smiled. He ran his fingers over his forehead. "It gets worse if I'm tired. Like the muscles can't work hard enough to keep me steady."

"What do they think is causing it?" Zane asked.

"The original diagnosis was something called essential tremor. Basically, just bad luck genetics. Then the prevailing theory with the military docs was PTSD. That's pretty much what they call everything they can't pinpoint, though. All I know for sure is it's not MS or Parkinson's Disease. They checked for those. Twice."

Zane's body flushed with ice for the briefest of moments. "Jesus."

"If it's PTSD, who knows what'll happen. It might get better, I don't know. But if it's the essential tremor thing, it won't go away. And even though the medicine controls it, it'll probably get worse as I get older."

"That's why you didn't go back to Boston PD, isn't it?" Zane asked softly.

Nick winced and shrugged. "What was I supposed to do? If I miss those pills a few days in a row, I can barely hit a target. When it started the first time, my hand completely locked up, my captain thought I was having a seizure and they called an ambulance."

"When was that?"

Nick licked his lips, stalling. Then he sighed and looked away. "Right before New Orleans. That's why I had the time to go. They would have taken me back when I got home, they wanted to. And with the meds, I would have been okay. Maybe. But hell, if it *is* a side effect of PTSD, I'm just a huge fucking trembling liability. I couldn't ask a partner to depend on me knowing that."

"You don't really believe that, do you?"

"I'm a sniper with a tremor, Garrett. It's like a bad joke."

He laughed, and it made Zane chuckle along with him even though there wasn't a damn thing funny about it. Nick held up his hand, frowning at it like it had betrayed him.

"O'Flaherty," Zane whispered, but he was unable to follow up with any words of comfort. He cleared his throat, feeling stupid for thinking what he had. "I'm sorry I thought you—"

"Don't worry about it. I probably would have thought the same thing."

"Okay, so if it's PTSD, what do you think started it?"

Nick shrugged, not meeting Zane's eyes.

"It was the thing with Cross and the CIA, wasn't it?" Zane asked. "We led them right to you. They came at you on your boat."

"Sure they did, Garrett, but people have been trying to kill me every day since I was eighteen. Hell, even before that if you want to count being tossed down the stairs, so who the fuck knows. Got real bad a few months ago, though; they almost sent me home. I had to convince them to keep me deployed until the others were let go, too."

Zane waited a few beats. "You haven't told anyone?"

"Kelly knows. He has for a while."

"But not Ty?"

Nick laughed bitterly. "Yeah, there's a couple things Ty doesn't know. I've been waiting for a good time to talk to him. You know how Ty is."

Zane nodded sadly. Ty would freak the fuck out at the first *hint* of Nick being sick. "Yeah."

"I mean . . . how do you tell your best friend that you're sick and no one knows why?"

Zane shook his head, at a loss. An awkward silence began to creep in as they stood in the hallway staring at each other. Zane thought maybe Nick was holding his breath, and he suddenly realized why. "If he asks me directly if I know anything, I'll tell him to talk to you. Otherwise, it's none of my business to tell him, right? You'll do it when you're ready."

"Thanks, Garrett."

Zane nodded and made to step away, but Nick reached for his arm and stopped him.

"And . . . thank you for being concerned and ready to help. I know it's not easy to come up to someone like that. That's solid."

"I'm just glad I didn't have to give you my rehab speech."

Nick barked a laugh. He put his arm around Zane's shoulder, patting his back and steering him toward the great hall. He let him go before they reached the door, and they rejoined Ty and Kelly just before Stanton addressed the crowd.

They set Nick up in the game room. A billiard table and a long shuffleboard table sat along one wall, and a disconcerting stag head glared from over the fireplace. Nick pulled a stool behind the wet bar and laid out a notepad, several pens, and his iPad, feeling vastly unprepared for the task ahead of him.

After Stanton's announcement, people had been edgy and nervous, but no one had outright objected to the questioning. Nick was expecting some hostility, though, and it was going to be awkward as hell when he started interviewing people he knew. He also felt naked without his badge.

Susan Stanton was nearly inconsolable during her interview. "Ernest was a good man, he didn't deserve to die like that. Oh my God." She put her fingers to her lips and closed her eyes. "Poor, poor man. He wasn't even supposed to be here! He and Theodore had some last-minute things to work on so he came on the plane with us."

Theodore Stanton was less flustered when Nick interviewed him. "We were working on a project, yes. He insisted he come along so it could be finished. He was like a bulldog when it came to the government work."

Livi Stanton cried through her entire interview. "If it hadn't been for Mr. Milton, Deacon and I would never have met, did you know that? He went to Deacon for his stress problems, and he noticed Deacon's limp. He gave him my card and told him to try it." She broke down into tears again, and Nick was forced to call Deuce to come get her. He didn't comfort crying women unless they were gutshot.

"Yeah, you know I'd forgotten that," Deuce admitted. "He did give me her card. Jesus, now I feel kind of bad. I mean I felt bad anyway, you know, but now I feel worse. I mean I feel bad that he died at my wedding, not because I killed him or anything. Why are you looking at me like that? Why are you writing that down? Oh my God, Deacon, stop talking."

Mara Grady babbled through her entire interview just like her youngest son. "What was he doing out on that beach at night? That's so dangerous, you know he wasn't down there for anything good. Nicholas, dear, you look tired. You need some coffee."

When Earl Grady entered the room, he was carrying a plate and a steaming mug. "The wife said to bring you this," he said as he placed them at Nick's elbow. "I saw the dead man at dinner. He kept checking his watch like he had somewhere to be. And he was on his cell phone the whole time. Figured it was a sat phone since everyone seems to have shit for service out here."

"There isn't a damn bar of service on this stupid island," the maid of honor told him. She was a pretty woman with copper-colored hair. Her eyes were drawn to Nick's notepad. "Oh, I'm sorry. I'm Nikki Webb. I hate being here, okay? My entire body itches and I can't get it to stop, and my hair is frizzy as hell because of all the rain, and I can't even have phone sex with my boyfriend because we're out in the middle of damn nowhere. I mean I love Livi, but so help me God this marriage better last *forever*."

Nick had already met one of the bridesmaids, Catalina Cruz, at the dinner last night. She was a looker, and she had the kind of fire that Nick enjoyed. He'd spent a while talking with her, and if not for Kelly, they probably would have been each other's alibis last night. "Let me guess, Nikki spent ten minutes complaining about the phone service? I'm rooming with her. She spent at least an hour last night wandering the halls, desperate for a bar of service. She almost fell over the balcony railing holding it up to the sky. No one should get that wrapped up in a guy, you know what I mean?"

The next bridesmaid to sit across from him spelled her name for him. "Miyoko Mason." She was tall and possibly too thin to be healthy, with an exotic look that spoke of an Asian ancestry. "I talked to him for a while. He could quote Sun Tzu. That's *The Art of War*, in case you didn't know. He was very smooth, like a spy in some novel. He kept saying he had to meet with someone and checking his watch. He didn't say who."

The groomsmen weren't as impressed with Milton. Christian Orr, Deuce's oldest friend, was tall and lanky, and his handshake was firm. "Yeah, I saw him at the party. He was pulling some sort of spy con on two of the bridesmaids. It was kind of funny to watch. I didn't see him after he left the party. Thought he got lucky, but . . . guess I was wrong. I switched rooms when Matt hooked up with that brunette bridesmaid. I spent the night with the Asian chick, Miyoko? Read her a fucking poem and she's yours, man."

"I mean, how do you pretend you're some sort of damn secret agent at a wedding for a psychiatrist and a yogi?" Matthew Ferguson asked Nick. He was short and athletic, with dark hair and a playful smile. "I spent most of the party with Ashlee. Have you seen her yet?

Ashlee Knight? I mean, God*damn*. I was with her until around four this morning. She woke me up when she left my room."

Nick had started out making a chart of who had been sleeping where and with whom, but it had begun to look like a spider's web. He shouldn't have been surprised by that, but the bedroom machinations of the staff caught him more off guard.

"Well . . . it's a small island," Maisie Ross told him. "Jockie and I grew up together, so of course we've been together. There are only a handful of year-round staff, and I'm one of them, even if I am just the nanny when the family's here. I work as a housekeeper as well, and I help Jockie with the gardening. But when Amelia's on the island, she's my only job. I was with her that night, asleep. I have to sleep when she does or she runs me ragged."

Most of the staff and wedding guests were cooperative. Others were so nervous they could barely remember their names when Nick asked, and a select few were irritable or downright combative about being there. The Snake Eaters, especially, were irate when they were questioned.

Nick put the latter guests in a special list, which included all five of the Snake Eaters, to question them again. Just to irritate them.

"My men wouldn't kill someone by bashing their head in with a rock," John English insisted. "That's just insulting."

"You're damn right it's insulting," Lenny Hardin sneered. He was around Nick's size, with dark hair and a receding hairline he tried to hide by keeping his head nearly shaved. "If I was going to kill some snot-nosed little bitch like that Milton guy, I sure as damn hell wouldn't use a *rock*. Come on. I bet even you Recon bitches know how to snap someone's neck."

Solomon Frost was one of the Snake Eaters Nick actually liked. He was lanky and laid-back, with close-cropped blond hair and a hard face that seemed at odds when he smiled. "I was doing my rounds. The beach wasn't part of our territory; we stuck close to the house. I'm just here to do a job. Are you getting paid for this shit? Because you should be."

The one female Snake Eater, Avery Kline, was even more irritated at being questioned than the others had been. "Do you know what it's like being the only woman on a team like this? I have to work twice as hard to prove myself, and I still get the shitty assignments. They kept me inside the house the entire night, said it would make the female guests feel more comfortable. Do you know how much bullshit that is? Half those girls weren't even in their own beds most of the night anyway!"

Riddle Park, the silent Korean Snake Eater, had nothing to say about the night before. Nick was searching his memory for the few bits and pieces of Korean he had learned to ask if the man spoke English when Park leaned closer to him and peered over the sunglasses he wore. One eye was a milky-white color. "I saw nothing," he said, and then got up to leave.

Hours into the day, after over thirty questionings, a picture of everyone on the island in his iPad, and an entire notepad full of notes, charts, and scribbles, Nick was ready to bash himself in the head with a pool cue.

He glanced up when the door clicked shut, and he sighed in relief when he saw that his next interview was Kelly.

"Good afternoon, Detective," Kelly drawled. He pulled up the stool opposite Nick and sat.

"This is fucking exhausting," Nick said. "Anyone out there look nervous?"

"Everyone out there looks nervous. What the hell are you doing to people in here?"

Nick shrugged helplessly.

"On the plus side, no one else has shown up dead."

Nick rubbed at his eyes, fighting the throbbing that had started up about an hour ago.

"You okay?" Kelly asked, his voice going softer.

Nick met Kelly's multicolored eyes, and warmth spread through him, easing the stress. He reached across the bar top and took Kelly's hand in his, kissing his palm without a word.

"Aren't you going to take my picture for your records and ask me where I was last night?" Kelly teased.

Nick responded with a low rumble, because he damn well remembered every last second of where Kelly had been last night. They were both silent for a few moments, their hands clasped. Kelly finally picked up Nick's iPad and took his own picture, making a face when he clicked it. Nick chuckled and took it away from him, setting it aside.

"You remember anything from last night that was off?"

Kelly shook his head. "I've been trying, but I can't think of anything."

Nick nodded. That was the answer he'd been getting all day.

Kelly stood and walked around the end of the bar, coming up to Nick and sliding his arms around his shoulders. Nick rested his cheek against Kelly's chest and closed his eyes as Kelly rested his chin on Nick's head. He wrapped his arms around Kelly's waist and Kelly slid closer, holding him tight. They stayed that way for long minutes, giving Nick a break, soaking in each other's presence.

"Ty is waiting for the next interview," Kelly finally said, his voice suddenly tense.

Nick groaned, closing his eyes and burying his face in Kelly's chest. After interviewing Ty, they would have to switch and Ty would interrogate him. This was not the way he had envisioned telling Ty about himself and Kelly, but he supposed there was no choice now. It was his alibi, after all.

"It'll be okay," Kelly told him. He patted Nick's cheek and stepped back. Nick's hands fell away as Kelly headed for the door. "Scream if he tries to kill you."

"That's not funny."

"It's a little funny."

Nick grunted as Kelly slid out of the room, and before the door closed, Ty had stepped in.

"You look rough, buddy," Ty said with a smirk. He set a bottle of water down at Nick's elbow, along with a couple of aspirin, then took the stool across from him.

"Thanks." Nick stared at the bottle, feeling like his entire body was tumbling with nerves.

"Anyone stand out?"

Nick forced himself to meet Ty's eyes. "Not anything glaring. I've been starting with the party and having them walk me through to four this morning. Most of the answers I'm getting are alcohol or someone else's bed."

"Not surprised," Ty said with a huff. "Why the party? Why so early?"

"Doc's temp check said eight hours at least. Even accounting for the night being cold, that puts us around midnight, give or take an hour. The watch is wrong."

Ty frowned hard, leaning his elbows on the bar. "So he . . . he probably left the party and then bought it. How'd his watch break at three something?"

Nick raised an eyebrow and nodded. He'd been asking himself the same thing. "I have no clue. I have two theories, though. Want to hear them?"

"Yeah."

"A few people have said they noticed he was messing with his watch all night. It could have been broken, frozen at that time."

"Huh. What's the other theory?"

Nick shrugged. "Someone killed him knowing time of death would be tricky way out here, so they wound the watch to a later time and smashed it. Made it an easy TOD. Made sure someone saw them hours later for the alibi."

Ty narrowed his eyes, cocking his head.

"That's what I'd do, anyway. In a pinch. Hope no one would bring out the turkey thermometer."

"You'd make a really scary serial killer, Irish."

Nick tapped his pen on his pad of paper, staring until Ty shifted uneasily. "Okay. Walk me through the party."

"Well. We ate. We had the meeting with Stanton. I think I left the patio twice over the course of the night to go take a piss. Then we wound up in the garden watching you smoke a joint with my brother."

"We'll leave that out of the notes," Nick grumbled as he wrote the rest down. "Did you see the victim at the party?"

"Not after the meeting in the study."

Nick added Ty to the list of people who *hadn't* seen Milton after the time of that meeting. He'd obviously not returned to the patio that night, and that gave them roughly a ten-hour window for the crime.

"Did you see anyone leave the party after the meeting, anyone who struck you as behaving oddly?"

Ty gave it some real thought before shaking his head. "Honestly, I was more concerned with you and Doc chatting up my baby cousin than watching anyone else."

Nick tried hard not laugh. "Where did you go after you left the party?"

"We took a walk toward the beach. I asked Zane to marry me. He turned me down. Then we headed back to the room."

Nick stared at his best friend for a few beats before saying, "What?"

Ty slammed his hand on the bar top. "He said no! Twice!"

"Ty." Nick sighed, rubbing his temple as he recognized the warning signs of Ty winding up.

"No, no. Three times! Three times he's turned me down!"

Nick reached for the aspirin Ty had brought him.

"Three times!"

"Tyler, listen, I'm really sorry about the . . . three times, but you seem to be handling it pretty well this far, and this isn't one of those instances where I need to talk you off the edge, so could we maybe save this until after I eat?"

"Look, a beautiful beach in Scotland? Nope. Castle? Nuh uh. Rug in front of a fire?"

"Oh God, stop. Ty, please," Nick said quickly. He put his head in his hands. "That's . . . no."

Ty cleared his throat and nodded. "Sorry."

Nick watched him for a few seconds, still covering half his face with one hand. Ty looked absolutely miserable. He might have seemed like he was handling the rejections well, but Nick could see underneath the mask just like he'd always been able to. "Condolences on getting shot down. Repeatedly."

Ty didn't even glare at him. He looked like a kicked puppy, and it made Nick want to slam his face into the wet bar. "You need to talk about it, babe?"

"Please. I'm going fucking insane trying not to give him . . . puppy eyes and beg him to rethink it."

"Well, you can quit giving *me* puppy eyes. You've asked him *three* times?" Nick asked, hating himself for giving in and feeling sorry for Ty instead of feeling sorry for himself right now.

Ty nodded. "He said I hadn't thought it through yet."

"He's probably right."

"You're supposed to be on my side, here," Ty grunted.

"I'm on the side of the righteous, babe; means I'm *rarely* on your side."

Ty barked a laugh.

"What kind of time span are we talking here?"

"I asked him the night we got here," Ty said as he began to play with one of Nick's extra pens. "Before the dinner."

"You've asked him to marry you three times in thirty-six hours?"

Ty smacked his hand on the bar again. "If I had you on the balcony of a castle with the motherfucking wilds of fucking Scotland out the window and I asked you to marry me, wouldn't you say yes?"

Nick shook his head. "No."

"Damn it!"

"It's not the location that'll reel Zane in, Ty."

Ty looked almost desperate when he realized Nick was willing to give him advice. He leaned forward. "What do I do?"

"Well . . . he said you hadn't thought it through. So think it the fuck through for him. Let him know you're serious and you're thinking about life instead of just wearing a ring. You know him. I mean, think about it, how would you propose to me?"

Ty waited a beat, then said, "Season tickets at Fenway and a ring in your beer during the seventh inning."

Nick waved a hand. "And I'm yours." They both laughed. Nick was still smiling when he dropped his voice to a more serious note. "What are *Zane's* season tickets? What's the thing that will tell him you're in it for the long haul and you want him there with you? It's sure as hell not a beach in Scotland."

Ty nodded, his gaze losing focus. Nick let him ruminate for a few seconds, until Ty finally snapped out of it. "Thanks, Irish."

"He'll say yes eventually." Nick looked back down at his notes, trying to remember where they'd been in the interview. "Okay, so you were on the beach getting shot down by the love of your life."

Ty grumbled wordlessly.

Nick smirked and fought to recover a straight face. "Did you see anyone else while you were out there?"

"Yeah, there were two people walking. Guy and a girl. We passed them."

Nick frowned at his notes. He paged through them. "What time was this?"

"Maybe . . . half past midnight."

Nick pulled out every page of interview notes with a woman. No one, man or woman, had mentioned being out on the beach for a walk. "What'd they look like?"

"I don't know."

Nick glanced up, eyes going wider. "You don't know?"

"I didn't . . . look at them. I don't know. The girl was wearing a dress."

"Ty, every woman on the island was wearing a dress last night."

"I'm sorry, I didn't pay attention to them."

"Were they young, old? Flustered, composed? Hair color, height? Were they hot, not? Were they bloody and carrying a very large rock?"

"I don't know!"

"Tyler!" Nick dropped his pen and rubbed his hands over his face. "Do you realize you may have seen the killers and you can't even tell me what fucking color their hair was?"

"I'm sorry! I guess I don't check people out like I used to."

Nick groaned. "I'll be sure to inform Garrett that your eyes don't wander. Did he see them as well?"

"Yeah."

Nick shook his head in disgust, glaring at Ty. "You're the worst witness ever."

"I know."

Nick grunted and picked up his pen again. "Anything else you *didn't* see?"

"No, but you don't have to be snippy about it."

Nick fumed for a second. "What time did you return to your room?"

"One, maybe."

"And who was with you?"

Ty sighed.

"Ty, just answer the fucking questions, okay?"

Ty rolled his eyes. "Zane was with me."

"And you remained there?"

"Yes. I got tied up in the curtains."

Nick squeezed his eyes closed. "Why would you tell me that?"

"No, I mean I literally got tied up in the curtains. I got stuck. Zane left me there."

Nick glanced up, frowning.

Ty rolled his eyes, blushing a little. "I got tangled in the curtains and I couldn't stop laughing, so Zane left me there and I fell asleep."

"You mean you passed out drunk."

"If that's what they call 'sleeping' in Boston, sure."

"So . . . could Zane have left the room at any point?"

Ty frowned, shifting on his stool. "I guess."

Nick gave a curt nod and jotted it down.

"Did you just write that down?" Ty asked with an accusatory point.

"Yes."

"Why?"

"Because I'm writing everything down, Ty."

"You didn't write down that you and Deacon were getting high in the garden!"

"Because it wasn't pertinent to the murder."

"Neither is Zane leaving me passed out drunk in the curtains!"

"I thought you said you weren't drunk."

"Don't try to confuse me to get a confession, damn you!"

"Tyler, come on!"

"This is police brutality!"

"I swear to God, Beaumont . . ."

Ty glowered for a moment. "Okay, so is that all?"

"Yeah."

"Your turn?"

Nick's stomach tangled up, but he nodded and slid the pad across the bar top. "Go for it."

Ty ran through the same questions Nick had been asking all morning. With every answer, Nick got more and more nervous. He'd probably fail a fucking lie detector test at this point.

"What time did you return to your room?" Ty asked.

"Just after midnight."

"And you were there the remainder of the night?"

"I was." Nick watched as Ty's pen moved across the pad. He swiped his palms across his knees, trying to steel himself for what was coming.

"What did you do in your room the remainder of the night?"

Nick swallowed hard. "I was in bed."

Ty raised his head. "You were *in bed* or you were sleeping?"

Nick stared at him, holding his breath. "I was in bed."

Ty's eyebrows shot up, and he straightened. He almost looked like he'd been expecting the answer, like maybe he'd heard enough through the wall last night to know Nick hadn't been sleeping, but he still seemed perturbed by it. "I gather you weren't alone."

"No, I wasn't," Nick answered. He took a deep, shaky breath. "Look, Ty, this is not the way I wanted to tell you about this. We were waiting until after the wedding stuff died down so you wouldn't freak out and go nuclear when you're already under stress."

Ty narrowed his eyes. He placed the pen on his pad of paper, the movement briefly drawing Nick's eyes. "Who?" Ty asked, his voice going low and dangerous.

"Oh, Ty, don't freak out."

"Who were you with, O'Flaherty?"

Nick couldn't get enough air to take a breath to steady himself, much less extract a promise from Ty to remain calm. "I was with Kelly," he said in a rush.

Ty stared, his brow furrowing and the tension seeping out of his shoulders. "Kelly who?"

Nick frowned. "Kelly. Our Kelly. Doc."

Ty was still staring like he didn't understand, his head cocked like a puppy hearing a new sound. He glanced at the door, then at Nick again. "You were fucking Kelly?"

"Yes."

Ty was silent for several more seconds, then barked out a laugh. "I thought you were talking about Emma!"

Nick sighed in relief. This was not the reaction he'd expected, but he'd take it.

Ty laughed harder, but soon he wound down and then stood up. "Wait, you were boning *Kelly*? How fucking high were you two last night?"

"That's not . . . it's not just last night."

"What does that mean?" Ty demanded.

"I mean it wasn't the first time. I didn't just bring him because he has a gun."

"What the fuck, man, how did that happen?"

"It's a really long story."

"I have time," Ty growled. "How long has it been going on?"

"It started after New Orleans, when we got to Colorado."

"That was . . . that was months ago! Why the hell am I just finding this out now?"

Nick stood so he would be on the same level as Ty. He was glad the wet bar was between them. "It kind of caught us both by surprise. Then I got deployed before we could figure anything out. Ty, we didn't even know what the hell there was between us. We kept it quiet because we wanted to know it was serious before we said anything."

"Bullshit, you could have told me any— Wait, what do you mean *serious*?"

Nick found himself snickering again. He couldn't seem to stop, and the more he laughed the more agitated Ty got. He put out a hand to try to calm Ty. "It's serious."

"How serious?" Ty asked, still looking scandalized. Nick half expected him to hold his hand to his heart any second now, maybe clutch a string of pearls. Nick howled, doubling over and holding his stomach as Ty glared at him.

"What is so funny?" Ty shouted. "I feel like I need bleach for my ear holes!"

"You," Nick gasped. He pointed at Ty and shook his head, trying for enough breath to speak. He finally got himself under control and straightened his shoulders to meet Ty's eyes. He smiled almost serenely. "I love him."

Ty blinked at that, his mouth falling open.

"I love him, Ty."

Ty stared at him, then looked down at the bar top for a long few seconds, then back up at Nick with narrowed eyes. "Are we talking with the heart love or with the dick love?" he asked, echoing Nick's words from so long ago.

Nick merely grinned.

"Good," Ty said softly.

"What?"

"Good," Ty repeated. He came around the end of the wet bar, beginning to smile, then pulled Nick into a hug, holding him and patting him on the back. "He'll treat you right and you deserve that. That's good."

Nick gasped as the relief hit him. He squeezed Ty tightly. "You're not pissed?"

Ty shook his head. He stepped back, meeting Nick's eyes. "Not pissed. Maybe a little confused, but . . . it kind of makes sense, the two of you. You fit. And to be honest, I'm relieved."

"Relieved?"

"I thought you were mad at me, man. You didn't call, you didn't write." He patted Nick hard on the cheek before turning away. "You dog, you."

Nick found himself gaping as Ty strolled to the door.

Ty said over his shoulder, "I'll send Zane in so he can tell you what those people looked like."

Ty came out of the game room with a huge smirk on his face. It immediately put Zane on edge.

"What?" he asked, almost afraid to get an answer.

"I'll tell you after," Ty promised with a passing pat to Zane's stomach.

Zane gave him a sideways glance as he headed for the door. Ty made his way to the lounge area where Kelly was sitting with the four other children who were on the island for the wedding, all kids of Ty's cousins. Amelia was on Kelly's knee. Kelly and Ty had been entertaining them during the interviews, telling them campfire stories and doing magic tricks. Both men were exceptionally good with the young ones, but then Kelly should be since he worked at a camp for at-risk youth.

When Zane stepped into the game room, he was nervous for some reason. As soon as he saw Nick, though, the nerves vanished. He was sitting on a stool behind the wet bar, his nose and forehead pressed to the polished wood, his hands flattened to the bar top like he'd just bashed his face into it.

Zane smiled, understanding Ty's smirk now. Nick picked his head up and stared at him.

"I'm sorry," Zane said immediately. He sat opposite Nick.

"I've never had to interrogate him before. Only ever seen it from the other side."

Zane bit his lip. "I can't imagine."

"He accused me of police brutality."

Zane finally gave in and chuckled.

Nick just shook his head.

"Do you want to take a break?"

"No, you're one of the last five on my list," Nick said. He was flipping through his notes, looking for a blank page. He started talking before he landed on one. "Do you remember seeing anyone on the beach last night during your walk?"

"Yeah, we passed a couple walking, a guy and a girl."

"Would you recognize them?"

Zane shrugged. "Maybe. I didn't, though."

"They weren't any of the guests or staff?" Nick asked.

"Not that I've seen, no. But I haven't seen everyone."

Nick handed him the iPad and brought up pictures he'd taken of each person he'd questioned. He tapped the screen. "Start flipping through those for me, see if you recognize anyone."

Zane took the iPad.

"What can you tell me about them?" Nick asked.

Zane shrugged and began to flip through the photos. "They were both still dressed up from the party. Both fairly young. The guy was possibly blond, the girl maybe had dark hair, it was hard to tell because there was no moon. The girl had an accent."

Nick raised an eyebrow at that, looking hopeful for the first time. "What kind?"

Zane winced. "I'm not sure. It sounded sort of like a mix, or maybe like she had a problem with her palate. Ty could probably tell you."

Nick smiled wryly. He rubbed his eyes with the heels of his palms, then nodded like he was giving himself a pep talk to continue. "Did they say anything to you?"

"Not directly, no. They were talking about walking on the beach not being romantic because it made their calves hurt."

Nick stopped writing and simply peered at Zane for a few moments, letting the silence stretch. Zane fought not to shift in his seat. Finally, he couldn't handle the scrutiny any longer and said, "What?"

"You should probably know," Nick started, sounding uncertain. "Ty couldn't tell me a damn thing about these people."

Zane frowned, confused.

"Couldn't even tell me what color hair they had. Didn't mention the accent. Didn't give either man or woman a second glance."

Zane smiled when he realized Nick's point. Ty had always had straying eyes, and that had never bothered Zane. Hell, he did too sometimes. There was nothing wrong with looking at a beautiful person. But out there last night, holding Zane's hand on the beach, Ty hadn't noticed a thing about two possibly attractive people other than the fact that they were walking by.

"Yeah, grin all you want, but these two people might be our doers."

"Seriously?"

Nick tapped his notes. "None of the other statements account for them. Did you leave your room last night, after Ty fell asleep?"

Zane frowned at the sudden change in questioning, but he nodded. "Well, not the room. I went out on the balcony at one point. I couldn't sleep."

"What time was that?"

"Anywhere from four to just before the sun came up. I'm not sure."

Nick's expression remained neutral. "Did you see or hear anything? Notice anything unusual?"

"I don't think so. The storm was going pretty hard at that point."

Nick gave a curt nod and lowered his head. He stared at his notes for a few more seconds, and then glanced back up, narrowing his eyes. His voice was lower when he spoke. "The storm was going?"

Zane raised both eyebrows. The more he saw of Nick's professional façade, the more impressed he was. As a rule, federal agents didn't often get along with police detectives. Their turf war had been turned into something of almost mythical proportions, and was often furthered by strutting and bragging and bickering when they were forced to collaborate. Rookies bought into the rivalry and perpetuated it. Zane had worked with quite a few detectives he enjoyed, but he'd also been forced to deal with more he absolutely hated.

He kind of wondered what it would have been like to have met Nick on a job rather than through Ty.

Nick put his pen down, staring at Zane.

"What?" Zane finally asked.

"Where'd you get your time from?"

"What?"

"You said it was after four," Nick reminded him. "How can you be sure if you didn't know the exact time?"

Zane shrugged, beginning to blush. "I . . . you can't tell Ty this."

Nick nodded solemnly.

"I remember rolling over at one point and looking at the clock. It was 4:20. I found it funny."

Nick blinked rapidly, his mouth going harder.

Zane sniffed. "Are you laughing at me?"

Nick rubbed his fingertips over his lips and shook his head, but when he glanced back up he was sniggering softly. He cleared his throat and schooled his features. "Okay. So it was after 4:20."

"Yes," Zane grunted. He crossed his arms, blushing harder.

"How bad was the storm when you went out there?"

Zane exhaled slowly, rubbing at his neck. "It was bad. I'm not surprised a tree took out the boathouse. I mean, it was raining sideways and the wind was howling. It was, um . . . it was beautiful."

Nick sat motionless, his green eyes on Zane, his face expressionless. Finally, his gaze drifted upward and he seemed to be staring at the ceiling over Zane's shoulder.

"O'Flaherty?"

"How did that broken watch make it through a storm like that?" Nick asked.

They sat in silence, staring at each other, both stumped by the question. Nick rested his chin in his palm, tapping his lower lip with his finger. "It couldn't have."

Zane shook his head. "The pieces would have been washed away for sure. The gears probably inundated."

"Someone killed him around midnight, then went back after the storm was gone and smashed that watch. Why?"

Zane sat frowning at Nick, trying to come up with a reason why someone would do that. "I've got nothing," he finally admitted.

"We need to look at that watch again."

Zane nodded. "I'll go with you as soon we're done."

"Yeah."

Nick shook off the mystery of the broken watch and proceeded to ask Zane a few questions about the party, approaching several things from different angles in an attempt to jog details loose from Zane's memory. He seemed tired, though, and Zane could see his fingers trembling almost imperceptibly.

Nick was almost done with his questioning when the door burst open and Kelly barged into the room. Nick and Zane both stood.

"Sorry, just be a second," Kelly said to Zane, and he made a beeline for Nick behind the bar. He grabbed him before Nick could say anything, and kissed him.

Zane's mouth fell open, and he sat back down hard as he watched. Kelly pulled away from the kiss, leaving Nick wide-eyed and speechless. "Ty told me what you said. Love you, too." He kissed him one more time for good measure, then turned with a nod to Zane and left the room.

The door shut with a muffled click.

Nick stared at the door as Zane stared at him. When Nick finally glanced at him, still looking stunned, Zane pointed a finger at him and shouted, "I knew it!"

CHAPTER 6

Nick emerged from the game room after half a day of interviews, looking ragged and irritable. Ty felt badly for him.

The wedding party and staff had mostly dispersed, the latter going back to work, the former enjoying what was apparently a rare sunny day on the island. There was a pool in one of the wings Ty hadn't explored yet, a sulfur spring somewhere on the island, and he'd heard people talking about badminton and croquet. There were rumors of a movie room somewhere, too, and tonight's big event included a screening of something. Ty had a feeling he'd be skipping that in favor of other endeavors.

Amelia and the other Grady kids had all been carted off to the pool by the grandparents and one very disgruntled Snake Eater. Ty and several of the others were loitering around one of the many lounge areas in the great hall. Zane and Marley King, Emma's cameraman, were involved in a pretty hefty game of chess. Livi and Emma were playing some sort of game they both had on their iPhones, competing for high scores and alternately trash-talking each other and giggling. Deuce and Kelly had drifted away, their heads bent together in a conversation Ty was pretty sure someone should arrest them for having. Take Deuce's medical-grade weed and grow it with Kelly's homemade mountain blend, and they could probably occupy small countries with it.

Two of the Snake Eater bodyguards, a Korean of very few words named Riddle Park and a wiry blond named Solomon Frost who never seemed flustered by anything, had been drawn to the crowd, too. Ty had sat talking with them about their adventures for a while. They were essentially mercenaries, but they were interesting men and they'd led interesting lives. By the time the interviews were all over, Park and Frost were trying to recruit Ty into their company, and they were giving it a pretty good sell.

At one time, Ty would have made a perfect mercenary.

When Nick approached, they all halted their activities and watched him expectantly. Deuce and Kelly wandered back over, and everyone was silent, watching Nick.

"So," Ty finally said after the silence had grown awkward. "Do we talk about your findings and suspects, or do we talk about the more important matter of you and Kelly banging?"

Nick pointed his notepad at Ty. "And there it is."

The others laughed, and Kelly came over to wrap his arm around Nick's waist. Nick pulled him closer to hug him. Ty couldn't help but grin. He was a little thrown by it, he would admit. And he had decided to deal with the horrifying realization that two of his closest friends were now fucking each other by just not ever accepting the fact that they were. Problem solved. But that aside, Nick and Kelly had always been affectionate with each other, and had always loved each other. This wasn't so huge a step.

As long as Ty didn't think about them fucking, it was all good.

There was a clatter from the side table where Zane and Marley were playing chess, and Ty glanced over at them.

Zane was peering under the table. "Shit, sorry. I didn't realize it was under there."

"Don't worry about it, man, it's a tough old bastard," Marley said as he bent to pick something up. Marley was an easygoing guy with the beginnings of dreadlocks and a perpetual smile. He was wiry and athletic, with the long, lean body type Ty associated with surfers. The flip-flops, cargo pants, and graphic tees he always wore reinforced the image, and his pockets seemed to be loaded down with all kinds of tools and miscellaneous bits. Plus, he was kicking Zane's ass at chess. Ty liked him.

He sat back up cradling a large camera, patting its side like a baby. "You're okay."

Zane was smiling, but as Ty watched, he saw an idea strike Zane like it had physically hit him. Zane leaned forward and pointed at the camera. "Have you been filming with that?"

"Yeah, I got most of the party last night. Little bit of scenery this morning. I was going to go through it tonight, put some B roll together."

Zane turned to Ty, his eyes wide.

Marley glanced between them, frowning. Then it dawned on him why Zane would be interested, and his face split into a huge grin. "Maybe it recorded something important, right?"

"Wow, if we'd thought of that five hours ago that would have been nice," Nick grumbled.

Emma hopped up from the couch. "We're on it!" she said, tapping Marley on the shoulder. "Want us to look for anyone who looks like a rock-bashing psychopath, right?"

"Ideally, yeah," Ty told her. "Find anything of Milton you can so we can track his movements."

"There's a movie room," Livi told them. She stood as well. "I think you can attach your camera to the equipment and watch the footage on the big screen. I'll show you where it is."

The three of them headed off, Marley lugging the camera on his shoulder.

"What are the odds he caught the murder on camera while he was eating or something and we can all go back to being common wedding guests?" Zane asked under his breath.

Park and Frost both shook their heads. "Nope," Frost said.

They all turned their attention back to Nick. He looked exhausted and frustrated.

"Hey, Irish, you want to get some real food before we powwow on this?" Ty asked him.

"Yeah. I also wanted to take one more look at the body, see if we can pull something off that watch, so I'll just head for the kitchen."

Kelly smacked his ass. "We'll come with."

Zane snorted and stood. They said good-bye to the two Snake Eaters, who had to go take their shifts, and left Deuce to retrieve Amelia from her nanny. The four of them headed for the kitchen.

They were halfway down the winding steps to the kitchen when Nick stopped abruptly and Ty bowled into him from behind. They barely caught themselves from tumbling down the steps.

"What the hell, man?"

"That smell," Nick whispered. He backed up a step, reaching wildly. His hand landed on Ty's stomach and he clutched at Ty's shirt.

His other hand grabbed for the gun he had tucked in the small of his back. Ty hadn't even known Nick was carrying.

He immediately recognized the panic in the other man, and he knew what happened when Nick panicked. Going for the gun himself would've gotten Ty killed, so he grabbed Nick from behind, wrapping him up so he couldn't get it either. Ty felt like he'd just grabbed a tiger by the tail.

"It's okay, it's okay," he said urgently. He pulled Nick backward, lifting him and swinging him up the steps, away from the kitchen. Nick kicked against the stone stairwell wall, slamming Ty against the opposite wall. His breath left him in a rush and he saw stars.

They struggled silently for several more seconds, until Nick was hyperventilating and Ty had given up on getting him up the steps. Zane and Kelly crowded closer.

Ty fell to his back on the steps, using the weight of his own body to drag Nick down. Kelly reached for them and Nick lashed out at him.

"What the hell triggered it?" Kelly asked. "When did he start doing this shit?"

"I don't know. I've never seen this!" Ty answered, voice strained.

"I'm okay," Nick gasped.

Ty could feel Zane hovering behind him, obviously at a loss. Zane had become well versed in how to handle Ty's flashbacks and panic attacks, but he'd never seen Ty react like Nick just had. Ty's instinct when the memories got too close was to freeze and curl up and wait for them to pass.

But Nick's instinct had always been to stand and fight. He'd go on the offensive before he could be hurt. He'd expose himself to whatever triggered him until it no longer caused a reaction. And if he got lost enough in a flashback, he could be downright dangerous to anyone and everyone near him. He'd once nearly taken out an entire med bay on ship before he was sedated.

"I'm sorry," Nick offered, voice hoarse and weak. "I'm okay."

"Like hell you're okay," Kelly said softly. He shook his head at Ty. "He's done. I'm pulling medic rank. No more of this shit today."

Ty nodded. Kelly would find no argument from him.

"No!" Nick grunted. He took a deep breath. His entire body was trembling, though, and he couldn't even look toward the bottom of the stairs. "We have to go down there."

"I'm going to vote no on that one," Zane said under his breath.

"You have to," Nick insisted. He twisted in Ty's arms, his muscles flexing. Ty loosened his grip, and Nick instantly began to relax. "The smell . . ."

"What was the smell?" Ty asked.

"Copper. Blood." He reached to the small of his back and brought out his Glock, handing it to Ty. "It's blood, Ty. Get down there."

Ty left Nick and Kelly on the steps, and he and Zane hustled to the kitchen. He led with the weapon, clearing the kitchen silently as Zane remained in the stairwell, then signaled for Zane to join him.

Zane stood over the pool of deep dark blood spreading across the pristine white tile of the gourmet kitchen. The copper scent was almost overwhelming.

"He's got one hell of a nose on him," Zane said.

Ty nodded, taking in the gruesome scene. The cook lay sprawled on the floor, the blood still trickling from a wound in her back. One of her expensive knives was protruding from her spine, and her fine white hair was caked with blood. Ty bent to check her pulse. She was still warm, but there was no heartbeat and far too much blood on the floor for her to have lived long.

"Doc!" Ty called out anyway.

Ty turned when he heard the scuff of a shoe on the stairs. Kelly stood there, face pinched in concern. "Blood?" he asked.

"Lots of it," Ty answered. "Don't let Nick down here, okay?"

Kelly shook his head, but a second later Nick appeared at his side, peering into the kitchen. He was pale and shaken, and he was holding his shirt over his nose to prevent another bout of scent-induced panic. But he was there and he looked determined to stay.

"Victim?" he asked, his voice muffled.

"Cook's dead. Knife to the back," Ty answered.

Kelly moved toward them and bent to check her regardless.

Ty was watching Nick, though. "Irish, you don't need to be here."

The apprehension in Nick's eyes said he completely agreed, but he shook his head. "Where's Milton's body?"

Ty glanced around for the walk-in freezer, making his way carefully over to it. There were no signs of a struggle in the kitchen, nothing out of place or messy. He covered his hand with his sleeve when he opened the freezer door to prevent his fingerprints from contaminating the scene. Not like they could fingerprint anything, but still.

He peered into the freezer and was immediately knocked back by what he found inside. He turned his head away from the sight, gagging and covering his face with his sleeve as he shoved his shoulder into the door to close it.

"Oh God," he managed to groan.

"What is it?" Zane asked, voice laced with dread.

"He's been gutted. He's hanging from a meat hook." Ty squeezed his eyes closed, trying to erase that visual from the databanks.

"That seems so unnecessary," Kelly muttered.

"And hard," Zane added. "Took at least two people. Or one very big one."

"Need to find that big Snake Eater," Ty said.

Kelly came closer, joining Ty at the freezer to crack the door open and look inside for himself. He didn't have the reaction Ty'd had, but then, Kelly had always been able to compartmentalize with wounds and death and gore.

Nick sat on the bottom step and lowered his head between his knees. Ty knew why the smell of blood threw Nick back into a moment of terror. He was surprised Nick was managing to hold it together at all right now.

"He's been disemboweled," Kelly told them, then stepped into the freezer.

"Oh, please, no," Ty whimpered as Kelly disappeared. "Please come back. Kelly. Kelly! Doc! I'm not coming in there! I'm not."

Kelly's voice echoed from inside the freezer. "They cut him open good. Looks like they were looking for something."

"Looking for something?" Zane asked. "*Inside* him?"

"Means whatever it is, it's small enough to swallow," Nick offered. He sounded positively ill. "Is his watch still on him?"

"No, it's gone. O, get out of here," Ty said, almost as desperate to have Nick leave as Nick probably was. When Nick raised his head, Ty hardened his expression. "Consider that an order if you must."

Rather than getting pissy about Ty pulling rank on him, Nick gave him a grateful nod and retreated up the stairs.

Kelly stepped out of the freezer wearing a pair of black butcher's gloves that went up to his elbows. He was holding a section of Milton's insides. He showed it to Ty and Zane with a frown, then squeezed it between his fingers. Ty backed away from him, covering his lower face with his arm. Zane coughed and put a hand over his mouth.

"I don't think they found what they were after," Kelly concluded with another experimental squeeze. It made a wet, squishing sound.

"What is wrong with you?" Ty cried. "Put that down! Jesus Christ!"

Kelly looked from him to the gore in his hand. "What? I'm wearing gloves."

Ty gagged and had to turn away. "I can't," he said pitifully, and made his way to the stairs to follow Nick's retreat.

"Why don't you think they found what they were looking for?" Zane asked Kelly as soon as they reached the top of the stairs.

"They cut open his stomach, which is probably where anything he swallowed in the last day would still be. Then they started on his intestines. But I can tell you right now, it wouldn't have made it that far. I think they stopped because they were interrupted by the cook, not because they found anything."

Zane curled his lip in disgust.

"Unless we're dealing with a straight-up psychopath who likes playing with people's insides," Kelly added. "I mean, low probability, but it is you and Ty, so anything's poss—"

Zane held up a hand to get Kelly to stop talking.

Kelly patted his shoulder in sympathy.

After Ty and Nick had both vacated the kitchen, Zane sent Kelly to go find Stanton. Night was falling, they now had two bodies on their hands, and one of those was the wife of the head butler. Deuce had been forced to sedate the man when he'd been told. The staff was a shambles, the members of the wedding party had all locked themselves in their rooms for the night, and the Stanton family was beginning to eye the Gradys like this was all somehow their fault. The Gradys, for the most part, were carrying on like it was business as usual. Two dead bodies at a family get-together hadn't caused many of them to blink.

One thing he knew with certainty was that this would continue to spiral and more people would get hurt if they didn't figure out how to get to the mainland somehow. He wasn't even sure that getting to the bottom of it and finding out the whys and hows would help at this point.

Until they could get help from the mainland, though, they would have to handle this on their own. Zane asked Marley to video the scene, and the blond Snake Eater Ty had gotten friendly with, Frost, was taking photos. Every inch of the kitchen from top to bottom was being recorded as John English supervised. He had a solid alibi—he'd been watching Amelia and the other kids swim—and he was the only man on the island who could have lifted Milton's body onto that hook alone. Zane wasn't sure he necessarily liked the big Snake Eater, but he was an effective leader and his team all seemed to respect him. That said a lot about a person.

English was now treating Zane like his counterpart: the leader of the Grady/Sidewinder band. Zane wasn't sure how that had happened, but he supposed with Nick and Ty both upstairs throwing up, and Kelly more interested in blood-spatter patterns than motive, Zane was the only one left.

He was fairly certain they'd lost Nick as the lead on the investigation, and he would probably have to take it over now. He'd have to sit down with Nick and find out what he'd learned, but it wasn't his first priority right now. None of this was his first priority.

"Nick going to be okay?" he asked Kelly.

Kelly shrugged. "That was a new one for me. He's never reacted like that to blood, not in front of me. Means whatever that was happened while they were gone this time. I don't know. I'm beginning to understand why he refused to go back to work, though, and it wasn't because he has a fucking tremor in his hand."

"Ty's been doing the same thing. Not to that extent, but . . . what happened to them over there?" Zane asked, voice hushed and edging toward desperate.

Kelly stopped walking and peered through the glass doors of the back patio, where Ty and Nick were both sitting on a bench in the garden. Nick had his head down, holding it in both hands. Ty sat with his hand on Nick's back, rocking to and fro.

"I have no idea," Kelly answered. He stared at them for a few moments longer. Then he squared his shoulders, and his lips moved like he was giving himself a silent pep talk. Then he nodded and marched toward the patio doors.

Zane took a deep breath to bolster himself, then followed. They made their way to the bench in the garden where Ty and Nick were sitting. Zane wasn't sure how to handle this, because he knew Ty always seemed embarrassed after he panicked. He covered it with jokes, making fun of himself and hoping anyone who'd witnessed it would simply pretend it had never happened. Zane had a feeling Nick would handle it a bit differently.

Ty and Nick raised their heads at their approach. Ty looked grim, the lines around his mouth tight and his brow furrowed. Nick, on the other hand, struck Zane as simply being humiliated. He returned his gaze to the ground. Kelly sat on his other side, their shoulders brushing. He waited a beat before gently resting his hand on Nick's back. Ty removed his hand, letting Kelly take over. When Nick didn't protest, Kelly slid his arm around him and hugged him.

"You okay?" Kelly asked.

"Caught me off guard, is all," Nick whispered.

"I want to give you something to knock you out for the rest of the night," Kelly said to Nick. "You've pushed yourself too far with all this."

"Give him something?" Zane asked. He winced, remembering the one time he'd tried that tactic with Ty. It hadn't gone well, but then Nick and Kelly had a lot more history and trust behind them than Zane and Ty'd had at that point. And Kelly was asking first instead of just slipping it into Nick's drink.

Kelly glanced up at him. "Yeah, I have my kit with me. And I bet Deacon has something with him if I don't. Whatever he used on the butler, if he has enough to put Nick out. I kind of doubt he does." He looked back to Nick, who was watching him. They sat staring at each other in silence for a few seconds before Nick nodded.

Kelly patted Nick's knee and stood. "I'm going to go see what I can find."

The rest of them remained where they were as Kelly jogged off into the house. Zane turned his attention back to Ty and Nick.

"What now?"

Nick sat back, taking a deep breath. "Everyone has a shaky alibi. The couple you two saw on the beach are the only anomaly, and I can't figure out who the fuck they could be."

"No one fits?"

"A *lot* of people fit. That's the problem. Then there's the broken watch, which is wrong every way we look at it. Whoever came back and cut him open, they took that watch, so it's got to be important for some reason."

"Do you have the pictures you took?" Zane asked.

Nick nodded and pulled his iPad out of a pocket inside his jacket. He handed it over.

Zane looked at the iPad with a frown, brushing his fingers along the edge of it. Nick had been carrying it with him since this morning, but the screen was spotless. Maybe Nick cleaned obsessively like Ty did when he was bothered by something. Zane glanced at the two of them again, sitting side by side like two little boys who'd been sent out of class for misbehaving. Nick's head was down, his shoulders slumped. Ty was staring off into the horizon, watching the last rays of the sun disappear.

"I think we should call it a night. Let you two recover," Zane said.

Ty nodded in agreement. He absently raised his hand to Nick's back again. Zane didn't know if Ty did it to comfort Nick or himself.

"These islands have a reputation for being hit with rogue waves," Nick said without raising his head.

Ty and Zane locked eyes, both of them frowning in confusion. They both looked back to Nick, waiting for him to connect rogue waves to *anything* that had happened today. Nick raised his head, glancing at them both. Then his eyes fixed on the cliff not far off.

"Ships would dock at these remote islands where nothing but lighthouses stood and find them completely deserted. Food still on the plates. Fires nothing but embers. Clocks not wound for weeks.

Everyone on the island vanished. They called them the Ghost Isles, no one would go near them because they were cursed."

Ty began to run his hand over Nick's back in slow circles. "Nick," he whispered.

"The theory of anyone who didn't believe in curses was rogue waves. Ninety, sometimes a hundred-feet high or more, just sweeping in out of the blue and taking everything on the island with it."

"Nick," Ty said a little more forcefully. "You're not going to die in Scotland."

Nick turned to meet his eyes, and they sat there simply staring at each other for several moments. Zane shifted his weight, realizing he was a little unnerved by the monotone of Nick's voice. He was seriously beginning to wonder just how messed up Nick's mind was, but then Nick leaned closer to Ty, narrowing his eyes.

"How many places do you think we swept through, leaving people to wonder where the rogue wave came from?"

Ty blinked rapidly, obviously taken aback by the direction Nick had gone. "What?"

Nick glanced at Zane, then stared out at the cliffs again. "Nobody's safe on this island as long we're out of touch with the mainland. *Everyone's* going to die in Scotland if we don't stop this."

Ty couldn't seem to tear his eyes away from Nick, but Zane turned and glanced into the house. "Where the hell is Kelly with those fucking sedatives?" he said under his breath. Nick was starting to make even him nervous; he didn't need Ty losing his shit, too.

"Irish, you have to look at this as just another case, okay? Just another murder. That's all it is," Ty was saying, keeping his voice low as he leaned closer to Nick. "You have to take the island and the boats and the phones out of the equation."

"Why?" Nick asked pointedly.

Ty opened his mouth to respond, but then snapped it shut again.

"Why would you discount all that? Why, when it makes for the perfect backdrop to wipe out a company with defense contracts? To take out a team of mercenaries? Target a family whose wealth fuels Philadelphia? Why would you think that storm destroyed those boats when it could just as easily have been a person?"

Ty was left with a frown of consternation, and Zane was left even more unsettled than he'd been.

Nick was still shaking his head when Kelly returned, a canvas bag with a red cross sewn onto it slung over his shoulder. Nick stood and waved him off. "We don't need that," he mumbled. "I've got stronger shit in my suitcase."

He walked off toward the house, shoulders hunched and head down. Kelly gave Ty and Zane a mystified glance before turning on his heel to follow.

"He's insane," Zane finally said to Ty once they were alone, horrified by the realization. He'd always been under the impression that Nick was the sane one, the *only* sane one, the one who kept the others all in line, the one who kept Ty from going for rides on the loco coaster. Now it looked like Nick was driving the damn thing.

Ty nodded. "He always has been. He controls it well. It's part of his charm. The hell of it is, he's right, too."

"Right about what? Rogue waves and dying in Scotland? I mean, I'm no goddamn psychiatrist, but even I can see he's under way too much stress. He's rambling, Ty. He's cracking."

"So what if he is?" Ty said heatedly, standing to face Zane. "He deserves to after what happened! How many times have you seen me crack and you still listened to what I was saying, even if it sounded like I was losing my mind?"

Zane sighed and squeezed Ty's arm to calm him. "You're right."

Ty stared at him like he'd been expecting him to argue.

Zane pulled him closer, tightening his grip on Ty's arm. "What the hell happened to you guys?" he whispered. "Whatever it was, it's driving you both over the edge."

Ty blinked and licked his lips, trying to speak and failing. He finally swallowed and managed to say, "You know I can't tell you that."

"You need to tell someone," Zane said gently. "You both do. Before it eats you up inside."

The haunted look in Ty's eyes returned briefly before he turned away. "Can we just deal with one thing at a time here?"

Zane nodded. He knew when to stop pushing Ty, and he'd reached his limit. "There's not much else we can do tonight. Let's go to bed."

Ty shook his head, glancing up at the house. "Nick was right. We didn't even look at the boathouse. I want to go down to the dock."

"Now? Ty, it's dark, what do you expect to find?"

"I don't know," Ty said with a frustrated shrug. "But it's time we start looking at this as the perfect location to massacre a group of people instead of a few freak accidents."

Zane had been looking at it that way all along, but he realized he'd also been looking at it as strictly Not His Problem. This wasn't their jurisdiction. The victims were strangers to them. And since no one Zane cared about had been accused of the murders, he'd simply been shrugging his way through, waiting until help came from the mainland. Ty had, too, to an extent, until Nick's words had sparked something.

"If that boathouse was taken out on purpose, it means someone intends to have his way with this island and everyone on it," Ty hissed. "We've been looking at it as a murder. What if it was a shot across the bow instead?"

Zane sighed. "I was so hoping this would be a normal vacation."

Ty smacked him on the side of the head. "Don't use bad words," he said as he walked off.

They followed the cliff path, taking an indirect route to the boathouse and dock so no one would see them heading off and wonder where they were going. The way to the dock was wooded and kind of creepy at night. It was also a long walk in the cold, something they should have realized since they'd ridden in the golf cart when they'd arrived.

"Did you bring a flashlight?" Zane asked as he glanced up at the trees reaching over them, their skeletal branches silhouetted in the moonlight.

"I admit I didn't think this through," Ty mumbled. He dug in his pocket and extracted his phone. "This is all I have."

"Me too."

"Awesome."

They carried on in the darkness, using the spotty moonlight to show their way for as long as they could. When they broke the edge of the woods and came up to the rise in the path just before the docks, they both stopped at the same time. There was a light moving around the ruins of the boathouse, playing over broken boards and twisted rope. Everything else was dark. As they stood watching, disjointed voices drifted toward them, two or three people speaking quietly.

They both crouched and moved closer, silent on the dirt path. When they got close enough to the docks to hear the words being said, they moved off the path and knelt behind a pile of broken and battered canoes.

"What brings you boys out the night?" a voice asked. Zane recognized the barely understandable Scottish brogue of Lachlan Mackie, the ferryman who'd met them on the docks the afternoon they arrived. He held a lantern, its weak glow not quite reaching the two figures he was addressing.

"We came to see you, Mackie," one of the men responded.

Ty gasped when he recognized the voice.

Zane smacked him in the shoulder. "It's Kelly," he hissed.

Ty put his hand on Zane's head. "I know, shut up."

"I recognize a kindred soul when I see one," Kelly continued. The light continued to play over the wrecked boathouse. Zane assumed Nick had the flashlight. "See, we had to go through airport security to get here, left our hands a little empty."

"Ah, I see," Mackie said with a chuckle. "I think I can show you some hospitality."

"Are they here buying weed?" Zane whispered in Ty's ear. "We walked half a mile through the creepy woods to watch them buy weed?"

Ty shushed him, shaking his head.

"Do you stay out here, Mackie?" Nick asked.

"Aye. I make quarters up yonder the path." Mackie was doing something with his hands, probably pulling out or rolling a blunt, if Zane were to guess.

"Must have been one hell of a racket when the storm hit," Nick commented carelessly. He took the rolled cigarette Mackie handed him.

"Aye, that it was. It was pelting down. I got out here in time to see the tree falling. Stood right where you are. Wasn't until the lightning strike I saw the dock was gone, the boats all with it."

Nick stepped closer, and Mackie lit the blunt for him.

"Must've been hard, watching all your boats head out to sea without you," Kelly said.

"Wasn't the first time, won't be the last."

"Really?"

Mackie nodded. "These islands, they weren't meant to be lived on. That old castle on the hill, she'll tell you some stories. The house will, too. Even the caves in the cliffs, they'll sing to you about death. The island likes to be left alone."

Nick and Kelly stood side by side as Mackie turned and headed back up the path, using an old wooden oar as a cane. Smoke rose as one of them took a hit.

"You boys have a good night."

Ty and Zane crouched lower as Mackie passed by. There was no reason to reveal their presence, not until the old ferryman was gone.

"Dude's kind of creepy," Nick said after he was out of sight.

"That's you in twenty years."

Nick jabbed Kelly hard in the stomach, making him double over with a bark of laughter.

Ty sighed heavily, shaking his head. In the moonlight, Zane could see Kelly quietly poking fun at Nick as he lit the blunt again. But Nick was staring over Kelly's head, looking in their direction.

"He spotted us," Ty whispered dejectedly.

"Grady?" Nick called out. Kelly turned to peer into the darkness.

Ty and Zane both stood, coming out of their hiding spot. "What gave us away?" Zane asked.

"I saw you come over the rise," Nick admitted, smirking. He waved his flashlight as they made their way toward them. "Did you hear?"

"Most of it," Ty answered.

"Sounds like I was wrong, it really was an accident. Unless Mackie set the boats loose himself."

"That means the murderer is stuck here just like we are," Zane surmised.

Kelly nodded. "And probably really pissed about it."

Nick glared and took the marijuana from him, shaking his head. Zane narrowed his eyes when Nick stuffed the blunt in his pocket. Kelly clapped a hand over his mouth, trying not to laugh.

"How'd you two get here so fucking fast?" Ty demanded. He swiped at Nick, smacking him in the arm. "And how do you go from full-fledge meltdown to out here investigating? Rambling about rogue waves and scaring the shit out of us! You had me all freaked out!"

"We rode," Nick answered, gesturing toward the darkness up the coast. He let out a whistle, and there was a gentle nicker in response. Hooves stomped the wet ground.

Ty glanced around. "Rode what?"

"Horses. We went to the stables."

"There are stables?" Zane asked, his mood lightening at the mere mention of it.

"Nope," Ty said.

"Did you two walk through the Sleepy Hollow woods in the dark?" Kelly asked.

"Yes, and it was scary!" Ty shouted. "Why are there horses?"

Nick and Kelly both laughed. "Do you want one of our horses for the way back?" Nick asked.

"Yes," Zane answered at the same time as Ty's emphatic, "No!"

Nick flicked on his flashlight again, pointing it at the sound of clopping hooves. The two horses came closer, and Kelly moved toward them, talking to them in gentle tones. Both Nick and Kelly seemed comfortable and knowledgeable around the animals. One of them nudged Nick's shoulder and he patted the horse's neck, then took the reins.

"Here," he said, handing them over to Zane. "They know the path, so their footing's sound in the dark. You don't even have to lead them."

"Thanks."

"I'm not getting on that thing," Ty insisted. They watched Kelly mount, his movements natural and easy. Zane recognized a man who'd worked with horses a great deal. Kelly offered Nick his hand, and Nick pulled himself into the saddle behind him.

Zane glanced at Ty, smiling widely. He hefted himself into the saddle easily, making himself comfortable on the large horse. "Come on, doll, go for a ride with me."

Ty glared at each of them, including the horses. "I hate you all," he said before reaching for Zane's hand.

Ty held tightly to his waist, refusing to release him even after the horse had settled into an easy trot. They came abreast of Kelly and Nick, the horses tossing their heads at each other. It was nearly impossible to see under the cover of the trees. Nick's flashlight was the only light.

"What made you two decide to come down here tonight?" Zane asked them, raising his voice over the clopping of the horses' hooves.

"Same as you," Nick answered. "I just needed to know what we were dealing with." He pulled his flashlight, turning it into a small lantern that he held out between them. His other hand was on Kelly's waist, resting there. He wasn't gripping Kelly like Ty was gripping Zane, and he seemed pretty at ease with the whole horse thing even though he wasn't in control of the animal.

"How does a city boy from Boston get to know horses?" Zane asked.

Nick looked from Zane to Ty, both eyebrows jumping. "Ty never told you?"

Zane glanced over his shoulder. Ty shook his head.

"We were some of the first into Helmand Province," Nick explained. "The mission was to clear Marja, and we were part of the advance team sent in for recon. But there were no roads. No equipment had even been floated in yet. Nothing but what we could hump in on our backs. The only way to get from one point to another was by horse. We probably spent six weeks on horseback altogether."

"Oh Jesus, Digger on a horse," Kelly said. "He kept threatening to make his horse into stew."

"He *named* his horse Stu," Nick added.

"And Ty's kept biting him. I even switched with him after a few days," Kelly continued. "But then it would gallop to catch up to him just so it could bite him."

Nick and Kelly both laughed. Their horse shied to the side, and Kelly glanced off into the woods.

"It wasn't funny," Ty grumbled into Zane's ear.

Somewhere in the woods to their right, a tree branch snapped, the sound so loud it startled the horses. A moment later there was a thump and another crack, and Zane would have sworn it sounded like silenced gunshots.

The horses both reared, neighing in terror. Ty's grip on Zane's waist tightened, and they both managed to stay in the saddle. Out of the corner of his eye, Zane saw Nick hit the ground. The lantern in his hand went rolling with him, casting garish shadows on the trees around them before it disappeared into the ditch along the side of the path and extinguished, throwing everything into complete darkness. Kelly's horse bolted, and Zane's galloped off after it.

Zane fought with the reins, trying to turn the horse, to stop it. They heard shots behind them, not silenced this time, but booming through the wet night. Kelly struggled with his horse, trying to force it to turn back for Nick, but it was too spooked by the gunfire. Zane finally got his horse to stop in the middle of the path. Ty pushed off him, dismounting and hitting the ground with a grunt.

"Go get him!" he shouted.

Zane turned the horse, spurring it to a gallop into the inky darkness.

Nick lay in the middle of the road, staring at the moon through the creepy, bare branches of the trees. He had his gun in his hands, still pointed at the trees on the side of the path. He hadn't emptied his revolver, even though that had been his first instinct. He had two shots left.

He heard the pounding hooves seconds before he felt the vibrations beneath his shoulders. The fall had nearly knocked the sense out of him, and he didn't think he could move. That horse was probably going to trample him, and he still couldn't find the ability to scramble off the path. Instead he raised one hand, aiming his gun into the night sky like he could hit Orion's Belt. He waited until he could see the outline of the charging animal and then fired into the air.

The horse reared, bucking and trying to retreat, and Zane cursed, trying to calm it.

"O'Flaherty!" Zane shouted.

"Don't let that thing step on me," Nick called back.

The horse sidestepped toward him, still nervous but calming as Zane cooed to it. Zane hit the ground just feet away, and then knelt beside him, keeping the horse between them and the woods.

"Are you hit?"

"Stag," Nick said to him.

"What?"

"It was a stag. I shot it."

Zane looked over his shoulder into the woods. "It wasn't shots fired?"

"Nope. Bigass deer. Help me up, huh?"

Zane pulled him up to sit, giving him a moment to make sure nothing was broken before dragging him to his feet. He stretched and shook himself out, managing not to whimper. "I think I broke my ass bone," he said, and they both grinned.

The other horse trotted up, Kelly and Ty in the saddle. "Are you okay?" Kelly cried.

"I shot dinner," Nick said.

Kelly snorted. "Look, Hannibal, you can shoot back if they're shooting at you, but it's still not okay to eat them afterward."

Zane retrieved the light, converting it back into a flashlight and holding it up so they could see into the woods. The stag Nick had shot was lying a few yards away, the bullet holes right at its heart, steaming in the night.

"Nice shot," Zane murmured.

"It was a deer?" Ty asked. "Goddamn, I would have sworn those were shots."

Nick squinted into the woods, shrugging. That was why he'd started firing back, but he supposed the wet pop of the underbrush with the weight of a deer that size would be as loud as what they'd heard. If not, they'd probably all still be taking fire.

"Let's get the fuck out of here," Zane said as he stood. He took the reins and pulled himself into the saddle, then held his hand out to Nick. "You okay to ride?"

Nick gave him a disgruntled nod and hefted himself onto the horse behind Zane. He groaned when he got up, resting his forehead on the back of Zane's shoulder. "Corpsman up," he said pitifully.

"Did you break your coccyx?" Kelly asked, just barely keeping the laughter out of his voice.

"You can check it for me tonight," Nick said wryly.

Ty made an offended sound and followed it with a simple, "Nope!" before spurring the horse into the darkness.

CHAPTER

"**I**t bothers you, doesn't it?" Zane asked as Ty paced in front of the fireplace in their room. Ty hadn't even shed his dirty clothes yet; he'd been too busy thinking about what Nick and Kelly were probably doing next door.

"No," Ty insisted. He winced, realizing the lie in his answer. He turned to Zane almost desperately. "Yes. A little. Should it? I feel like it shouldn't."

"I don't know, Ty," Zane answered. He was sitting at the little desk, booting his laptop up. He still had the flash drive Deuce had given them, and it was the first chance they'd had to look at it.

Ty stopped and ran his hands over his face. "I thought I was okay with it, but it's *weird*!"

Zane simply smiled and shook his head. "No, it's not."

"Maybe not for you. But they've known each other for fifteen years, and suddenly they're all . . . and it's . . ." He waved his hand helplessly at the wall.

"It's not the fact that they're fucking," Zane told him.

Ty pointed at the wall. "That is exactly what they're doing!"

Zane smiled, nodding. "Ty. You're upset because you know there's something else going on with Nick, and he hasn't talked to you about it."

"How could he not fucking tell me about them?"

Zane raised both eyebrows. "Maybe he was afraid you'd react like this?"

"Well, I didn't do it in front of him!"

"And now that you know they're together?" Zane continued. "You're pretty sure he's told Kelly what's bothering him, and not you. He's talked about things with the doc that he used to reserve for you and that upsets you."

Ty swallowed hard. "When you put it that way, it makes me sound like an asshole."

Zane chuckled. He was silent for a moment, then cursed quietly. "My laptop's been fried!" Zane cried. "Son of a bitch!"

"How'd that happen?"

"I don't know, looks like it didn't like the trip here; it's completely dead. I think Nick was right, these islands are cursed."

"Told you to buy a Mac."

Zane slammed the lid of the laptop closed and turned away from the desk, coming over to the bed.

Ty watched him, feeling out of sync and a little desperate to understand why.

Zane took pity on him and ran a hand over his head. "He's your best friend, Ty. It hurts when you feel like your friends are pulling away, I know. I lost every one of mine, but none of them were like Nick is to you, you know? He's not replacing you with anything. Trust him."

Ty slumped his shoulders, his brow furrowing as he looked down at the USMC signet ring on his finger. He twisted it, trying to find the truth in Zane's words. Aside from Deuce, Nick was the most consistent, oldest friend Ty had. They had been through everything together, shared everything together. They'd lived in the same room in some fashion for almost seven years; in some ways they were closer than brothers, and they had no secrets.

Or they hadn't, until the last few years. Ty shook his head. No, it was earlier than that. It was when he'd signed on for the FBI, for Burns's work. Ty had been so angry that Nick wouldn't come with him, he'd just shut him off entirely. He supposed that had been the beginning of the secrets. The beginning of where they were now. They'd reconciled, but their friendship had felt different ever since. There had been times during their deployment when Ty had been sitting in the canteen and seen Nick walk in, but Nick hadn't come over to sit and talk. A few times Nick had even acknowledged him, but gathered his food and left anyway. There had been moments they'd passed each other in camp and Nick had saluted and been on his way without even a knowing smirk at the oddity of Ty's rank.

Ty groaned and threw himself onto the bed, staring up at the high ceiling. "I feel like I lost him somewhere."

Zane stretched out next to him, lying on his side so he was facing Ty. "Did you ever think maybe he feels the same way?"

When Ty glanced at him, Zane was smiling.

"What?"

Zane shrugged. "Out of all the problems we could be lingering on tonight, I think it's kind of sweet that you're moping about your best friend."

Ty rolled his eyes. He finally snorted and swiped his hand over his face.

"You want to shower?" Zane asked, lowering his voice suggestively.

"Yeah," Ty whispered.

"You want to get dirty first?"

Ty raised one eyebrow in a show of detached interest, trying to hide his smirk. He turned his head, looking Zane up and down.

Zane grinned, his eyes warming. He rested his hand on Ty's chest, pushing the buttons apart to get to skin.

"Let's go to the hot spring," he suggested, the warmth in his eyes turning into outright fire.

"But it's all the way down there," Ty protested, pointing toward the balcony.

"It's in its own little area . . . secluded . . . steamy."

Ty began to smile, but he held his ground, shaking his head. "You kinky little exhibitionist, you."

"I'm just suggesting that a hot soak would feel *really* good for aching muscles."

"I do have some aching muscles."

Zane hummed and scooted closer, nudging his nose against Ty's chin.

Ty closed his eyes and smiled, sliding his hand up Zane's back. "You were sexy as hell on that horse tonight. Riding to the rescue."

Zane stole a kiss. "I can think of someone else I'd like to see riding something."

Ty bit his lip, loath to admit that he enjoyed Zane's cheesy come-ons. He wrapped his arms around Zane and brushed the tip of his nose against his lover's. "Whatever makes you happy, Lone Star."

Zane chuckled. "Come on, Captain. It's late. No one else will be out there."

"I thought you said I need rest for the vapors. Thought you said you were tired."

"I was until I thought about you and me in that damn hot spring."

Ty hummed as his body responded favorably to the idea. Zane's playful smile was another reason to say yes. No matter what had happened to Ty and the rest of Sidewinder while they'd been deployed, Zane had definitely benefited from those six months. He seemed unburdened now, more willing to simply grab onto life and go for a ride. Ty brushed his fingers through Zane's hair with an affectionate grin.

"You know if we get out there, I'm just going to ask you to marry me again."

Zane's grin widened further. "I'll risk it."

Ty wasn't even sure where the damn hot spring was, so Zane led him through the quiet mansion, out the back patio to the path that curved its way into the interior of the island.

Ty squeezed his hand and pulled him closer, enjoying such a simple thing as walking along the dark path with their fingers entwined. This particular path was lit by dim, boxed solar lights set low to the ground. Zane didn't hurry. He purposely brushed their arms together as they walked.

The warmth Ty had noticed whenever Zane was near him began to spread further, making the touch of Zane's fingers like traces of fire, and a sort of unfettered giddiness crept in. They so rarely had these moments, but tonight Ty could make himself believe they were normal.

Zane didn't let go of his hand when they reached the spring area. It was deserted, just like Zane had guessed it would be. It was also unlit.

"This way," Zane said, moving along the pathway to the spring edge.

Ty looked down at the water as they passed by. Only the moon and the eerily glowing mineral water of the hot spring showed them the way.

Zane pulled his shirt over his head and dropped it to the grass at the edge of the spring. Then his hands dropped to the button on his jeans, and he stopped. Ty hung back, watching him as deep breaths became harder to manage. He didn't think this thrill of anticipation would ever get old. Zane raised one eyebrow—a clear dare—and unfastened his jeans, letting them slide down his hips and thighs to fall to the dirt path.

Ty popped the button on his pants and dropped them, pulling out of his shirt without bothering to unbutton it. He kicked his clothing off to the side and moved toward Zane and the swirling water. The night was fucking freezing. Zane descended into the spring, down the carved-out steps into the bottom, and the water hit right at his chest as he turned in place to leer at Ty and hold out a hand.

"It's warm."

Ty's lips twitched at the chivalrous gesture. Sometimes Zane just couldn't help himself. Ty got in slowly, enjoying the heat as it lapped at his cold skin.

"We're both going to catch pneumonia on the way back in," Ty griped.

He took Zane's hand, pulling himself closer until their bodies just barely touched in the bubbling water. Zane curled their hands together while taking a step back, tugging gently for Ty to follow. They were, for all intents and purposes, out of sight unless someone walked around the path to look directly at the spring. It was also insane for anyone to be out when it was this cold. The knowledge didn't keep the butterflies out of Ty's stomach, though.

He followed Zane regardless, willing to risk getting caught.

Zane sat on the bench molded from the rock under the water, drawing Ty down next to him. Then he sighed happily, leaning back in the steaming water. "Now *this* is nice."

Ty settled into the water beside Zane, acknowledging the tease. He eased over and let their shoulders press together as he leaned his head back. He hooked his leg over Zane's knee, resting it there so their calves pressed together and he could slide his toes against Zane's ankle. Zane slid his palm against Ty's thigh, stroking idly under the water, then shifted a little, sliding his arm behind Ty's back and angling himself so Ty was leaning against him. He settled his hand on Ty's hip, rubbing the skin under his fingertips.

Ty closed his eyes and turned his head toward Zane, adjusting so that more of their skin touched. He was content to sit like this, comfortable and intimate. It was a gentler foreplay then they were used to, and it was doing some very interesting things to Ty's mind and body. It seemed like he was tingling all over, and it wasn't from the minerals in the hot spring. He rested his head on Zane's arm, letting the water and the promise of his lover's caresses warm him.

Zane seemed just as content to remain like that, their bodies brushing, teasing, relaxing into each other. The hot water swirled around them. It was some time before Zane even turned his head and leaned forward enough to nuzzle at Ty's ear.

Ty turned to meet his lips, nipping at him languidly as he moved his palm across Zane's hard abs. Zane growled and chased Ty's lips, making it a game while his free hand glided over Ty's belly under the water. Ty grinned and nipped at him again, backing away playfully and pushing himself out into the center of the spring. His leg stayed hooked over Zane's as he let himself float.

Zane laughed quietly and grabbed for his hips, leaning against the wall of the spring to watch. Ty smiled and closed his eyes, floating for a few moments with nothing but the sound of the spring in his ears and the feeling of Zane's hands on his hips to keep him there. It was the anchor he'd been missing for the last year, the one thing that could ground him every time he began to drift. Finally, he bent his knees and sat up, pulling himself to Zane and ending up straddling one of his thighs. He slowly slid his knee over Zane's other leg, skin gliding against skin, until he sat astride him, kneeling on the underwater bench. Zane's hands had remained on his hips. He sat gazing up at Ty in the moonlight, unabashed devotion written all over his face.

Ty rested his arms on Zane's shoulders and kissed him soundly. The warmth that had never dissipated began to churn inside him, love and desire warring for his attention. He groaned and delved his tongue between Zane's lips, seeking something more. Zane pulled him close as they kissed, responding to Ty's fervor with calm, consuming focus.

Ty smiled against his lips and finally forced himself to pull away. Zane's face was shadowed, but Ty knew every feature by heart. The laugh lines that mingled with frown lines, the curve from his broken nose, the hints of gray feathered at his temples. His warm brown eyes that could go hard as obsidian in a blink.

He slid his hand down the side of Zane's face. "Marry me," he whispered.

Zane grinned, biting his tongue as he narrowed his eyes like he was considering it. Then he shook his head once. "No, thank you."

Ty snorted. "So polite this time." They were both grinning when they kissed again, but the disappointment was sharper for Ty than he'd expected. He was going to keep asking until he got it right, until Zane had forgiven him and was ready. Knowing Zane loved him didn't mean it wouldn't hurt though.

Zane's hands slid along his skin under the water. They were crouched low, trying to keep their shoulders under water so the cold air wouldn't bite at them. Ty could feel Zane growing harder. He adjusted the way he was sitting, rubbing against Zane to elicit a moan or two.

"Ty," Zane finally whispered against his lips. His fingers dug into the muscles of Ty's thighs.

"I can't believe you convinced me to come out here with you," Ty said between kisses. He lifted up onto his knees, letting Zane guide him back down. The head of Zane's cock pushed at him demandingly. After the last several weeks of getting reacquainted, it would have been an easy entry. Ty lifted his face up to the sky, humming and sighing.

"Can we do this without lube?" Zane asked. His voice was strained, and every muscle in his body was hard and tight, no longer relaxed by the waters of the hot spring. "More importantly, should we do this in a mineral spring?"

"Fine time to ask now," Ty grunted. He lowered himself back into Zane's lap, dragging his own cock against Zane's as he sat. "What's wrong with mineral springs?"

"Don't some of them have bacteria in them?"

"I'm getting out!" Ty shouted, trying to sound dismayed, but laughing too hard to pull it off.

Zane grabbed at him as he moved away, tackling him. They both managed to keep their heads above water, but Ty lost his footing. He wrapped around Zane to stay afloat, and he kissed him hungrily to combat Zane's next attack. Zane shoved him toward the other side of the spring, slamming him against the rock wall and holding him pinned there as their kiss turned devouring, consuming.

Ty wrapped his legs around Zane, groaning as Zane's hard cock threatened to breach him again. He flailed, reaching out for a handhold. He fingers fell on cool skin.

He jerked away, gasping and shoving Zane away from their kiss. "Jesus Christ!" he shouted.

"What?" Zane cried. He pushed away, obviously thinking he'd hurt Ty or something had triggered a flashback.

But Ty's eyes had mostly adjusted in the moonlight, and he could make out the pale skin of a leg and bare foot against the dark underbrush. When Zane saw it, he scrambled toward their clothing, probably trying to reach one of their phones for the flashlight app. Ty pushed himself up onto the lip of the edge of the hot spring and reached for the foot again, tugging at it. He would have prayed it was a drunk bridesmaid, but he already knew he would be wrong about that.

When Zane got the light and shone it on the bushes, Ty realized he'd been half-right. It was definitely a bridesmaid.

Ty hesitated to knock on Nick and Kelly's door for so long that Zane reached up and knocked for him. Ty glared at him until he heard the lock thrown and the door creaked open.

Kelly's face was puffy from sleep. He was wearing just a pair of sleep bottoms, no shirt, and he had Nick's gun in his hand. He wasn't even trying to hide it.

"What?" he croaked.

"Another body's shown up," Ty said quietly.

Kelly merely stared at him, then stepped aside and gestured for him to come in.

A lamp beside the bed gave off a dim glow, and Nick sat up in bed, rubbing his eyes with one hand.

Kelly crawled back in beside him, leaving Ty and Zane standing awkwardly at the foot of the bed with nowhere to sit. Nick waved a hand at them, and Zane shrugged and crawled onto the end of the bed, sitting cross-legged like they were at a slumber party. Ty followed suit because he was past the stage of giving a fuck.

Ty showed his phone with the picture of the victim to Nick. "You recognize her?"

Nick took the phone, nodding and frowning. "That's the maid of honor."

Ty's stomach dropped. He was going to have to tell Livi that her best friend had been murdered at her wedding.

"Her name was Nikki . . . something. Webb. West. No, it's Webb." Nick still sounded half-asleep. Ty had little doubt that Kelly had given him something to make him rest.

Ty glanced up at him, then down at the photo again, feeling sick. Notifying family of victims wasn't normally a part of his job. Notifying his *own* family of deaths definitely wasn't in his resume.

"Do you want me to tell them?" Nick asked softly. "I've got some practice with it."

Ty glanced around at the three of them. All of them were frowning sympathetically at him. "No," he said with difficulty. "Thanks, but . . . no, I'll do it."

Nick nodded. He and Kelly shared a worried scowl, then Kelly nodded. They were communicating silently, and it bothered Ty. Kelly and Nick had always been able to do that, though, which told Ty that he just needed to get a fucking grip here. Nick took a deep breath. "We've got another problem."

"A bigger problem than a dead maid of honor?" Zane asked, incredulous and full of dread.

Nick shrugged. "Debatable, but . . . yeah, probably."

"When we got back from the Creepy Hollow woods, I was cleaning Nick's back up," Kelly started.

Ty raised a hand. "If this is a sex story, I'd like to take a pass."

"It's not," Nick assured him. There was no humor in his voice. "I thought I'd hit something sharp in the path when I fell, but when Doc got a look at it, we realized . . . well, take a look," he said. Then he pulled his shirt up, twisting so Ty and Zane could see his back.

A long, narrow welt covered him from side to side, starting around chest height and then streaking over his shoulder blade and the Celtic cross tattoo along his spine to disappear into the large eagle, globe, and anchor tattoo on his shoulder.

Zane cupped a hand over his mouth, leaning his arm on his knee. Kelly's foot kicked Ty from under the covers, and he murmured an apology as he tried to get comfortable. Ty barely heard him. "That's a graze," he blurted.

Nick nodded.

"Nick, that's a bullet graze."

"Yes," Nick said, voice calm. He turned and let his shirt loose, shaking his shoulders so the material would settle. "We were right. Those *were* silenced shots we heard."

CHAPTER 8

Breakfast the next morning was late in coming, mostly because no one had thought to prepare it.

Mara took over, heading down to see what she could do to cook for thirty people. As soon as she'd announced she was going to the kitchen, Zane and Nick both hustled after her, claiming they would help.

Ty knew they were going more to protect her than to use their considerable combined culinary skills. He appreciated that both men had taken responsibility for protecting his mother just as quickly as he would have.

Ty spent the morning in Deuce and Livi's room, bouncing Amelia on his knee and breaking the news of Nikki Webb's murder.

Deuce sat with his head in his hands, not even trying to be stoic anymore. Livi took the news a little better than Ty had expected, though. Her eyes were tearing over, but Ty had seen her sob over Milton's demise as well. Livi was a tenderer heart than Ty was used to dealing with.

"This is awful," Livi said. "I didn't even know her that well. I don't know how to get in touch with her family."

Ty frowned, and the bouncing stopped for a second. "What do you mean?"

Amelia cooed to him, complaining about the halt in her ride. He began the bouncing again, smiling down at her.

"I mean I didn't really know her well," Livi said again. "I met her a few months ago when she took one of my classes. I have three really close friends, and . . . frankly I was dreading choosing one of them. I don't have any sisters or cousins. So when I found out Nikki was a party planner, it just clicked. She became the maid of honor, she planned all the pre-wedding stuff, and I didn't have to choose between my closer friends."

Ty nodded, still a little confused. He was relieved, though, because he'd been absolutely terrified of making Livi cry.

Amelia latched onto his nose and giggled. Ty tried to pull his face away, but couldn't get out of her grasp. Livi laughed shakily, still wiping at her eyes.

"Ty, what's going on here?" Deuce asked. He sounded desperate. "Is this your shit following you around, or is this entirely new shit?"

"I'm pretty sure it's new shit," Ty answered, his voice nasal as Amelia held on to his nose. He almost wished he could say it was his fault, that this was about his past. But he wouldn't lie to Deuce just to make him feel better. He was done with lies.

"But what did Nikki have to do with Mr. Milton?" Livi asked. "I understand that Mrs. Boyd was in the wrong place at the wrong time, but why kill Nikki?"

"That's a good question. I intend to find out."

Deuce and Livi both nodded, wearing almost identical frowns.

Amelia squeezed Ty's nose, and he made a honking sound that set her giggling.

"Do you want to take her for a while, Ty?" Deuce asked.

Ty glanced at him, raising an eyebrow.

"I mean, when you're not investigating the series of murders at my wedding," Deuce said wryly. "You've barely seen her. I know she's safe with you. And Maisie is running late, so we're sort of in need of a babysitter anyway."

"Maisie's the girl who found Milton's body," Ty said with a frown. "Why is she late?"

"She wasn't feeling well," Livi answered. "She's not handling all of this . . ."

Ty gave that another nod and a deeper frown. He sometimes forgot that normal people *didn't* handle finding dead bodies well. He looked down at Amelia, who was reaching for the compass pendant around his neck. Her little tongue was stuck out of her mouth as she concentrated. Ty grinned. "Yeah, I'll take her for a while."

Deuce tossed him a tattered gray lamb. "Don't leave home without it."

Zane actually had a good morning, working down in the kitchen with Mara and Nick trying to get enough food prepared to feed anyone who still had an appetite. He was able to show off some of the things he'd learned to Mara, who seemed to be thrilled that "another one of her boys" had finally learned to feed himself.

He also learned a few things from Nick, who gave Zane the tip to fold his fingers in when he was cutting so he could feel the knife with his knuckles and didn't have to look at what he was doing. He shrugged it off when Zane asked where he'd learned, saying it was nothing more than spatial recognition and the need to hurry when he'd been learning to cook. He seemed to be in an unusually evil mood, so Zane mostly left him alone.

After breakfast, Zane sat in a secluded alcove off the great hall and began flipping through the photos on Nick's iPad, reading his notes, trying to follow the jumps in logic and make sense of the scribbles Nick obviously hadn't felt the need to connect when he'd been taking them.

Zane could tell which interviews had been first and which had been last because, while the questions remained thorough, Nick's notes became less legible and the scribbles devolved into pleas for someone to kill him.

Zane snorted as he read them.

He glanced up when he saw movement out of the corner of his eye. Ty was striding across the great hall, Amelia riding on his shoulders and gripping his hair like the reins of a horse. He had Amelia's favorite stuffed animal stuck in the back pocket of his jeans.

Zane lowered the iPad and notebook, relaxing his shoulders and watching his lover. Ty would take a few steps, then stop and weave to the side, then stop again, making a sound like brakes screeching, and then he'd veer in another direction. Zane realized that he was letting Amelia steer him by pulling on his hair.

They were never going to get wherever Ty was heading if they kept on like that. Zane gathered his things and stood, coming up beside them and putting a roadblock in their path.

"Uh oh!" Ty said to Amelia. "Brake!"

Amelia was laughing, her tiny fingers clutched in his hair.

"Brake!" Ty called out again.

She leaned forward instead, and Ty walked into Zane, making the sound of a nasty crash when they collided. Amelia howled with laughter and crawled over Ty's head, sliding into Zane's arms. Ty gave Zane a quick kiss, still grinning.

"How'd you wind up with this?" Zane asked, tossing Amelia up and turning her upside down to hold her by her feet. She squealed in delight.

"I don't know. I'm easily duped, I guess." Ty took her back from Zane, turning her right side up. "The nanny isn't doing too well with finding that body; she's MIA. I took Amelia so they could have an hour to get stuff done."

"Makes sense. Poor girl. You missed breakfast, by the way."

Ty grinned. "Was there venison involved?"

"Actually, yeah."

"Gross. Are those Nick's notes?"

Zane nodded. "I'm still trying to make sense of them without asking him what they mean."

"Where is he?"

"Probably curled up in a corner hissing at people as they pass by."

Ty's laugh was a surprised one. "Bad mood, huh?"

"Very. Last I saw him, he was still in the kitchen cleaning up."

"Let's go find him. I want to sit down and hear what we all know, see if we can connect some dots." Ty headed off, carrying Amelia under his arm like a sack of potatoes. Her giggles echoed off the ceiling of the great hall.

Zane hurried to catch up. "Wait, Ty, you want to do that with her with us?"

"She's a year old. She won't understand death and destruction for at least another year."

"If we ever decide to adopt, you're a mute in any interviews."

"Understood."

They found Nick and Kelly outside, sitting on the patio with Emma and Marley. Kelly had a stick in his hand, and he seemed to be drawing things in the dusty brick. Nick had his sunglasses on even though the day was overcast, and he was sipping from a glass that Zane doubted was tea. Emma and Marley were talking animatedly, but Zane couldn't tell if either Nick or Kelly was listening, much less responding.

Emma glanced up when she noticed Ty and Zane there, and her face transformed into a bright smile. "My baby!" she cried, and she held her hands out for Amelia.

"No!" Amelia shouted, clinging to Ty's shirt.

"What did you bribe her with?" Emma asked him.

"Unicorns and rainbows and *fun*," Ty said with a grin. "What are you guys doing?"

"We were pregaming the next murder," Nick said before taking a sip of his drink. Emma and Marley both raised their own glasses and drank with him.

Kelly glanced up. "I over-drugged him last night. He may be a little cranky."

"A little," Emma agreed, snorting.

Nick lowered his sunglasses, squinting at Zane. He looked like he was completely done with everything on this island. "Any new leads?"

"That's why we came out here, actually. It's time for all of us to sit down and figure out what we know." He pointed at Emma and Marley. "You too."

Nick gave that a curt nod. He pushed his sunglasses back up and hefted himself out of his chair. Amelia immediately lunged for him and grabbed his sunglasses. Nick held on to them, and after the ensuing tug of war he somehow wound up with Amelia in his arms, wearing his sunglasses on her little round face.

"What am I supposed to do with this?" he asked.

"Do what it says, no one gets hurt," Ty said, putting her lamb on top of Nick's head before going to retrieve more chairs.

"Ty, you know I don't do well with kids!"

Kelly stood to take Amelia from him, but the little girl clung to him just as she had to Ty. Nick rolled his eyes and sat back down with her.

They gathered more chairs and circled them on the patio. It was pretty wide open, but Zane trusted it more than any of the rooms in the house since there were passages and peepholes in the walls. They leaned close so their voices wouldn't carry to anyone nearby.

"What'd you two find on the videos?" Zane asked Emma and Marley.

"Nada," Marley answered. "That dude avoided the lens like a vampire. In total, I found seven frames with him in them. Frames. That's like less than half a second of video."

"And we didn't find anyone that screamed 'I'm a killer' either," Emma added. "Nothing really suspicious. Although, the dead girl was on her phone in almost every single frame she's in, and I thought it was weird because there's no service here."

"Nikki Webb," Nick provided. "She mentioned looking for service to text her boyfriend. Her roommate said she was up half the night trying to get a signal. And several witnesses stated they saw Milton on his phone. That's pretty much the only thing I know the two victims had in common."

"Hell," Kelly said as he propped his feet on Nick's knees. "I've seen every person here wander around looking for a signal at least once."

"Livi told me Nikki showed up around two months ago, took one of her classes. That's how they met," Ty told everyone.

"How'd she earn maid of honor?" Nick asked.

Ty shrugged. "She was a party planner. Livi didn't have to choose between her better friends. It's chick logic."

Emma snorted derisively. "If that girl was a party planner, I'll eat my boots."

Ty frowned at his cousin, looking troubled. He glanced at Nick and then met Zane's eyes.

Zane nodded, knowing exactly what Ty was thinking. "Sounds like Nikki Webb was a plant."

Nick sat forward, shifting Amelia onto his shoulder. She had fallen asleep on him, and she clutched at his shirt as she snored, resting her head on his shoulder. "Livi told me Milton was the reason she and your brother met. He steered Deacon toward her class."

Ty brushed a hand over his chin. "Livi's a friendly girl. It'd be easy to strike up a conversation at her class, make contact with her as a mark. She's the least sheltered member of the family, the easiest way into the company. But why plant Deacon with her?"

Nick shrugged. "I'm just telling you what I know. What really bothers me is that watch."

"What really bothers *me* is getting shot at," Kelly spat.

"You guys got shot at?" Emma blurted.

"Last night, in the woods," Ty answered. "We were checking to make sure the boats really were taken out by the storm. On the way back, a few shots were exchanged. I had Fraser, the groundskeeper, do a sweep of the woods. He didn't find any trace of anyone being hit. No casings, nothing."

"Come on," Kelly said in annoyance. "We know those were silenced shots, and we all know who would have silencers on this island. Those Snake Eaters are part of this."

"Kels, those Snake Eaters are ex–special forces," Nick said in exasperation. It sounded like they'd had this conversation a few times already. "If they'd fired at us last night, they would have hit us."

"They *did* hit you," Kelly snapped without looking back at Nick.

Nick closed his eyes and rubbed his fingers over his nose.

"There are way too many weapons on this island," Emma said.

Zane found himself nodding. Not only were the Snake Eaters all heavily armed, but there was a room devoted to nothing but hunting and stalking, lined with rifles. Not to mention all the gear they had brought with them.

"We could try to round it all up," Kelly suggested.

"That should go over well," Ty said. "Worth a try, though."

"What good is that going to do?" Nick asked. "Anyone intending to use their weapon isn't going to give it up voluntarily. And you don't need a gun to kill someone, even without training. What are you going to do, play Mr. Green and Colonel Mustard and round up all the candlesticks and lead pipes, too?"

Kelly set his stick down and glared at him.

Nick raised both eyebrows in a silent challenge. "You're not getting *my* gun."

"Quit being a dick," Kelly grunted. He pushed himself to his feet. "I'm going to go get some Advil for the dick."

Nick grumbled to himself as Kelly walked away.

"You two had a fun night," Ty said.

"Shut up, Tyler."

Zane was flipping through the pictures Nick had taken as the rest of them spoke. Ty leaned forward to look over his shoulder. When they reached the photo of the broken wristwatch Nick had fixated on, Zane zoomed in on it, cocking his head. There wasn't anything special about it, but it did look familiar somehow.

Ty patted his shoulder. "I had one like that."

Zane raised his head. "You did," he said as the realization hit him. "The one we smashed in Gettysburg. It had a tracker in it."

"You wore a tracker in your watch?" Emma asked, sounding bemused.

"Dick gave it to me."

"Burns?" Nick asked, his voice going hard. "Asshole."

Zane nodded. Why would someone first smash the watch, then come back and take it? Was it possible that Ernest Milton had been one of Burns's misfit ops men? "We need to talk to Burns," he said.

"What? Why?" Ty asked.

Nick leaned forward. "You think Milton was his?"

Zane nodded.

"It's a common watch," Ty argued.

Zane clambered to his feet. "Common or not, I'm going to ask Burns about it."

Ty frowned at him.

Zane sighed heavily. "You don't have to come. But I'm going."

"I'll come," Nick said eagerly, and stood. He handed Amelia off to Emma, looking relieved to have her out of his arms. He didn't even try to take his sunglasses off her, and he placed her lamb gently on her belly.

"What, you two are going to track him down and beat the truth out of him?" Ty asked.

"Sounds fun," Nick said as he looked away.

Zane raised an eyebrow at him, then met Ty's eyes. "Why don't you find Doc and you two go search Milton's and Nikki's rooms. O'Flaherty and I will *politely* question Burns."

Nick lifted his glass. "Always at the center of it, isn't he?"

"Burns has nothing to do with this," Ty snapped.

Nick just raised his eyebrows.

Ty looked between them, then stood reluctantly. "Promise you'll be civil."

Zane nodded, but Nick didn't answer. He narrowed his eyes at Ty instead, then shook his head and turned away to go off in search of Burns.

Ty pointed at him. "Keep him under control," he hissed. "Don't let him get his hands around Dick's neck."

"Are we talking figuratively or literally?"

"Both," Ty spat. He glanced over Zane's shoulder again. "Nick blames Burns for Sanchez's death."

"Oh God," Zane groaned, and he turned to jog after Nick.

Ty caught Kelly coming back down the steps with his canvas medical bag over his shoulder. Ty held up his hand. "He bolted, no drugs for him."

"What? That bastard." Kelly stopped on the staircase. "Where'd he go?"

"He and Zane went to question Burns about the dead guy's watch. It was the same as the one I used to wear, so they think Milton was one of Burns's operators."

Kelly just blinked rapidly.

Ty didn't bother trying to explain further. He climbed the steps toward him. "Anyway, we're supposed to go search over Milton's and Nikki's rooms, see what we can find."

"This is the worst vacation ever," Kelly said as he turned and followed Ty up the steps.

"Yeah, we don't use that word."

They hit the landing and made the turn down their hall. Milton's room was in the same wing as theirs were, but closer to the stairs. Kelly leaned against the wall as Ty fished the key he'd gotten from Stanton out of his pocket. "What are we looking for when we get in there?"

Ty shrugged. "Motive. Anything worth killing over."

"You realize I'm not a cop, right?"

Ty glanced at him and smiled. "No, but you're fucking one."

Kelly's cheeks reddened and he bit his lip to hide a massive grin. He failed miserably. "Thanks for being cool with it, bud. Nick stressed a lot about telling you and the guys."

"Seems Nick's stressed about a lot of things," Ty said with another sideways glance at Kelly. "Is he okay?"

"You'll have to ask him about that."

The nonanswer hit Ty harder than he'd expected. He lowered his head and jammed the ancient key into the door, wriggling it to get it to catch.

Kelly cleared his throat. "He's still terrified to tell the others. He's watching your reaction closer than you might think he is. I think he was afraid everyone would assume he'd taken advantage of me being hurt and drugged."

"Did he?" Ty asked neutrally.

"No. In fact I pretty much had to beg him to—"

"Stop. The deal is I don't freak out, and you don't share sex stories." Kelly snickered. "Okay."

They stepped into the room and Ty flicked on the lights. He'd been half-expecting to find the room turned upside down, trashed and searched. But everything seemed to be in its place.

"Huh," Kelly offered as he took a few steps inside and surveyed the room. "They cut his guts open but didn't try his room?"

"That, or they searched it neat."

This room was a little more Spartan than theirs, with a double bed and a small vanity. It had no balcony. It didn't even have windows. The bed hadn't been slept it. Nothing seemed out of place.

Kelly pointed toward the small desk against the far wall. "Laptop."

"See if you can get it up and running," Ty said. He headed for the bedside table and went through the small drawers, checked under the pillows and the mattress, got down and peered under the bed. He checked under all the tables and tried the bottoms of each drawer for anything taped there. He kicked aside the rugs and lifted them up to search under them. Then he went to the wardrobe that held Milton's luggage. He dragged everything out and put it on the bed.

"Jesus, he's got some heavy shit in here," Ty said as he hefted the third suitcase out of the wardrobe.

"This thing is password protected," Kelly finally said. "I can't get into it."

Ty nodded. "We'll take it to Zane, see if he can get past it."

Kelly came over to help Ty go through the suitcases. "He brought an awful lot of stuff for a week."

Ty nodded, frowning at the three large suitcases full of clothing, shoes, toiletries, and electronics. "It's almost like he wasn't planning on going back home," he said. He and Kelly shared a glance.

Kelly pulled out a Dopp kit and unzipped it. It was brimming with toiletries and medicine bottles. "Why would this all be packed up? He had six more days, why not take it into the bathroom, lay everything out?"

Ty's frown deepened. He turned to the large wardrobe. It was empty. No suits hanging, nothing folded into the drawers. All of Milton's things were neatly packed. "He either never unpacked, or he was planning on leaving last night."

Kelly was scowling when Ty met his eyes. "This guy's starting to feel shady, man."

Ty grunted in agreement. "We need to get into that laptop. Gather it up, we'll take it with us."

"What about his phone? Did he have it on him?"

"Yeah, but it got wet. It's useless."

Kelly shrugged. "Let's go put it in some rice."

"Rice?"

"Yeah, it soaks up the water." Kelly bundled up the laptop and stuck it under his arm. "I dropped mine in the toilet once. A little rice, a little Clorox. Good as new!"

Ty swiped a hand over his face as they left the room. "That is so gross."

Zane approached the table where Burns and Earl were sitting, drinking coffee and playing some sort of card game. He could feel Nick behind him. He was a very physical presence, and Zane now completely understood why Ty had always trusted the man to have his back.

"Earl. Director Burns," Zane said with a nod at each man.

"Hey, Zane, Nick. Take a load off," Earl invited with a jerk of his head to the empty chairs at the table. "We heard there was another murder."

"Yes, sir," Nick said softly. "I'm afraid we didn't come to play cards. Director Burns, we'd like to speak with you about a few things."

Zane glanced at him, surprised he'd gone the direct route. His jaw was tight and his green eyes were hard and sparkling. Zane groaned internally. Ty had been right. Zane was going to have to pry Nick's fingers from Burns's neck, he knew he was.

Burns and Earl exchanged frowns, then Burns placed his cards on the table and nodded. "What do you need to discuss?"

Nick's hard stare remained on Burns, but Zane looked between the two older men pointedly. "It has to do with work. It's probably best we speak in private."

Burns pursed his lips and stood. "I'll be back," he said to Earl. He came around the table, watching Nick with an almost curious expression.

Zane turned to lead them both into one of the unoccupied rooms that lined the great hall. They settled in the parlor. Burns sat in one of the chairs near the large stone fireplace, and Zane and Nick sat opposite him on a small sofa.

"What's going on, boys?"

"Was Milton one of your men?" Nick asked, his voice hard.

Burns's only reaction was a rapid series of blinks.

"The watch he wore," Zane said. "It was just like Ty's, the one you gave him with the GPS in it."

"He's also dead, just like most of your recruits," Nick practically snarled.

Burns cleared his throat. "This is going to be unproductive with him present. Unless he intends to use his alternative interrogation skills," he said with a point at Nick. He stood to go.

Nick was on his feet so fast Zane didn't even have a chance to grab for him. He blocked Burns's path, and the two men stood eyeing each other, trapped in the space between the chair and the coffee table.

"Son, you don't want to make a mistake here," Burns said almost kindly. "You need to get out of the way."

"I don't take orders from you. *Sir*. Sit down."

Burns narrowed his eyes and jutted his chin out, but he must have seen just as plainly as Zane could that Nick wasn't going to let him leave this room. He gave a curt nod and returned to the chair by the fireplace.

Nick remained standing, his arms crossed over his chest like a bouncer at a club.

Zane gave him a wary once-over before turning his attention back to Burns. "Was he one of your men?"

Burns cleared his throat and nodded. "He was."

"Was he planted with the Stanton company?"

"He was already part of the Stanton company," Burns said. "They're developing highly classified equipment for the military, we needed a watchdog. We recruited him."

"Why the hell didn't you come out and say that when we found his body?" Nick demanded.

"Because Stanton can't know. I don't have to tell you what a mess it would be if it got out that a government agent had infiltrated a private company like that. You can imagine how that would make Stanton and his board of directors react if they found out."

"Did you put him up to introducing Deuce and Livi?" Nick asked.

"What? No, why would I do that?"

Zane rubbed his fingers over one temple. "So, his sole job was to guard this technology being developed?"

"For me, yes."

"That means whoever killed him probably did it for the information he was protecting," Nick said to Zane.

"You should have told us this," Zane said to Burns.

Burns shook his head. "It's need-to-know, Garrett."

"That woman's life, the cook? Her blood is on your hands," Nick growled. "All your cloak-and-dagger bullshit, all it does is get people killed."

Burns didn't answer. He sat staring at Nick, his expression unreadable.

"O'Flaherty," Zane said gently. "Why don't you go find Grady and Abbott, see what they found?"

Nick continued to glare at Burns, his nostrils flaring and his jaw jumping as he clenched his teeth. He finally nodded and turned to leave. The door slammed shut behind him.

When Zane returned his attention to Burns, the man was still watching the door. His face had softened, and he seemed almost melancholy. He sighed heavily when he met Zane's eyes. "I admire his loyalty. And his fire. That was why I tried to recruit him."

"Director Burns," Zane said, continuing with his questioning despite the surprise of learning that Burns had actively sought Nick out as well as Ty and Elias Sanchez. "Why would someone take the watch off one of your operatives? Is information stored in it?"

Burns frowned deeply. "No. No, all it has is the GPS. And that's all a live feed; it doesn't store information. For that, you'd need the accompanying software system."

"And where is that?" Zane asked.

Burns shrugged. "My office."

"Is there any way to reach it remotely?"

"I suppose you could go through my tablet or laptop. Neither of which I have here. I've honestly never tried."

Zane nodded, even more confused than he had been. "Would breaking the watch corrupt the GPS?"

"Not the information that's already been sent. Why crack the watch open?" Burns asked.

"We have no idea. The watch makes no sense right now, and it's gone, so . . ." Zane ran a finger over his nose. "Who would even know it was special?"

"The watch?"

"Yeah."

"Anyone who knew it had GPS. Another operator. Anyone who's done black ops or dark ops and used a similar system, including Grady and O'Flaherty. I would suspect even you would have known to do that, had you recognized the watch for what it was."

Zane narrowed his eyes. "So, whoever knew the watch was a tracking device is who we're after."

"I would suppose, yes."

"And you didn't think that was need-to-know?" Zane asked through gritted teeth.

Burns sat forward. "Zane, you've always been a big-picture kind of guy. That's a unique ability. You shouldn't lose it."

Zane couldn't find his voice to respond.

"Is that all?"

Zane met his eyes. There were so many things he wanted to say to this man, and most of them would probably end with a punch being thrown. He almost wished he'd unleashed Nick just so he could witness it. He had to remind himself, though, that Burns was also the reason he and Ty were together at all. The reason they had remained partners long enough to solidify their relationship, even if it had been for ulterior motives. Burns was the one who'd given Zane his second chance. He couldn't find it in himself to truly hate the man even though he wanted to for the underhanded things Burns had done.

He swallowed hard and nodded. "That's it."

Nick practically pounced on Ty and Kelly as they were making their way through the great hall toward the kitchen stairs. His sudden appearance damn near kicked Ty's instakill into action.

"What'd you find?" Nick demanded.

Ty examined him with a growing hint of apprehension. He was as taut as a bowstring, and Ty could tell the next person to pass in front of Nick's target area was going to seriously take one for the team. "Did you do violence to anyone?"

"Only in my mind," Nick growled. "What did you find?"

Kelly held up the laptop. "It's password protected. We're going to let Zane take a stab at it."

Nick stared at him incredulously. "Take a *stab* at it? Really?"

Kelly blinked. "Oh. Oh, that was an unintentional pun. That was bad form, I'm sorry."

Nick just shook his head.

Ty snorted, though, feeling guilty for doing it. "We were heading for the meat locker to get Milton's phone, see what we could pull off it," he told Nick. "What'd Burns have to say?"

"Milton was one of his."

Ty's blood seemed to run a little colder. "Seriously?"

Nick nodded curtly. "Garrett made me leave before I heard anything else."

Ty could imagine why Zane had kicked Nick out if he'd been half as wound up in there as he was now. "Okay," he said carefully. He and

Kelly shared a glance. Ty's eyes drifted down to Kelly's little bag of medical tricks, still slung over his shoulder. Kelly gave him an almost imperceptible nod. "You two go see what you can do with the phone, I'll take the laptop to Zane, see if he can get past the security on it."

"That really the best use of our time right now?" Nick asked.

Ty came up short, frowning at Nick. "You got something better to do?"

Nick snorted and turned to stalk off toward the kitchen stairs. Ty hissed at Kelly and pointed to his bag as Kelly handed off the laptop. "Sedate the fuck out of him if he goes off the rails."

Kelly snorted and gave him a smart salute, then jogged after Nick.

"Holy shit," Ty whispered to himself before turning and going off to find Zane.

"Ty."

Ty skidded to a halt on the slick marble floor. He'd walked right past Zane, coming out of the parlor door. Ty turned on him, eyes wide. "Milton was one of Dick's guys?"

Zane nodded grimly.

"What'd he tell you?"

"Okay, so Burns says Milton was guarding some sort of new technology or information, he isn't sure which."

"That's what they cut him open to find, huh? Thinking he swallowed it? Has to be a memory chip or . . . a flash drive wouldn't go down easy."

"Likely not. Abbott's convinced they didn't find it, though. That's why they took the watch."

"For the GPS?" Ty guessed.

"Yep."

"Because he probably stashed it somewhere, and the watch can tell you where he's been."

"Yep."

"But they can't read it without the proper equipment. Why would they take it? And why fucking smash it?"

Zane shrugged. "They might not know any of that. Thought it was a transmitting chip. I don't know. What's with the laptop?"

Ty held it up for Zane. "It's Milton's. Password protected. You think you can get into it?"

"Yep," Zane said again without hesitation. He took it from Ty and glanced around the great hall. "Let's go find somewhere quiet."

Ty trailed after him, a smile playing on his lips. "You're kind of sexy when you take charge like that."

"Shut up, Ty," Zane said, but his voice trembled with laughter.

The kitchen had mostly been cleaned up by the time Nick and Kelly got back down there, but Nick still hesitated, just as he'd done that morning at breakfast. It was embarrassing as hell to completely lose it like he had, even if it had happened before in front of Ty and Kelly, even if he had pulled both of them through similar episodes of their own. Nick didn't like not being in control of himself, and he definitely didn't like the idea that he'd taken a swing at Kelly without even realizing what he was doing.

Kelly placed a hand at the small of his back in silent support before he made his way over to the freezer where all three bodies were being stored. There was no guard down here, but why would there be? Milton's body had already been picked clean of everything the perpetrators wanted, the cook had merely been collateral damage, and Nikki had just been placed in there. Who would have thought to guard the dead bodies in the first place?

For that matter, who would have expected dead bodies at a wedding? Ty and Zane, that's fucking who.

Nick wandered into the pantry, scanning the shelves. He grabbed a glass canister of white rice and stuffed it under one arm, then went off in search of a mixing bowl.

"I wonder why they didn't take his phone, too," Kelly called from the freezer. "I mean, they take a broken watch and slice him up on a guess that he'd swallowed whatever it is, but they don't take his phone just 'cause it's waterlogged?"

"We're obviously looking for someone who's never dropped his phone in a toilet," Nick said. He poured the rice out into a stainless steel mixing bowl.

"Ha. Ha ha." Kelly came up to stand beside Nick at the counter and placed the phone beside the bowl. "Considering you're the one who told me to put it in the rice, you shouldn't make jokes."

"I live on a boat; I can get water out of anything." Nick absently reached across the counter for a small glass jar of toothpicks and plucked one out to put in his mouth. He began taking the cell phone apart and shoving each piece into the rice separately.

Kelly leaned over the counter to rest his chin on his hand. Nick glanced at Kelly as he shoved the SIM card and battery deep into the rice.

Kelly was watching his face instead of his hands. "Are you okay?" he asked, voice gone soft and intimate.

Nick swallowed hard. "I don't know. If Garrett hadn't been up there with me, I would have taken Richard Burns's head off."

"Whether he deserves it or not, that's not like you."

"I know."

Kelly straightened, then pushed himself up to sit on the edge of the counter. "It'll take a while for that rice to do its thing. Why don't you tell me what's going on with you, Lucky? Maybe I can help."

Nick stared at the counter, at Kelly's hand resting against the white tile, his eyes tracing the lines of Kelly's long fingers. Kelly tapped them against the tile, and Nick met his eyes.

"My dad," he started, but he lost his voice before he could go further. He shook his head in frustration.

"Because he's sick?" Kelly guessed.

Nick nodded.

"What did he say to you when he called for you to come see him? You haven't been right since."

Nick didn't answer, chewing on the toothpick as he stared at the rice.

Kelly was silent for a few moments, then took in a deep breath. "When I was going through the foster system, I saw a lot of kids who were there because they'd been abused. This one kid, he was a few years older than me. Close to aging out of the system. He got word his mom had died of an overdose. He was all torn up about it, and I just couldn't understand why. His scars were still healing. So I asked him. And he told me he was glad she was dead. He was mourning the mother he could have had. Should have had."

Nick was silent, his eyes on Kelly the entire time.

Kelly patted his cheek and smiled sadly. "It's okay to mourn. You do it for you, not him."

Nick nodded and forced himself to swallow past the knot in his throat. "We're not at the mourning stage just yet. He needs a new liver. He wants me to get tested to see if I'm a match."

Kelly's expression changed from one of gentle sympathy to something else entirely. His eyes sparked, and the lines around his mouth grew hard as he squared his shoulders. "He wants you to donate a piece of your liver?"

Nick nodded, unable to speak.

"Are you going to do it?"

"I don't know," Nick whispered. "I don't want to. I want to let him die."

Kelly nodded, frowning in sympathy. But then he shook his head. "You'd never forgive yourself. Even if everyone knows he deserves it."

Nick lowered his head. "I know."

Kelly grabbed at his shirt front and pulled him sideways until Nick was standing right in front of him, between his legs. Kelly hugged him fiercely, and Nick buried his face in Kelly's neck.

"The decision you make, you make it for you. Not him," Kelly whispered into his ear. "You make it for you. And I'll be there."

Nick gripped him hard, hugging him for dear life.

Kelly sniffed and smiled against his neck. "You do you, boo boo," he said, his voice shaking with laughter.

Nick pushed away from him, fighting back tears with a surprised snort. "There's something so wrong with you."

"That's why you love me."

Ty couldn't sit still. He bounced his knees, he tapped his toes, he cracked his knuckles. He finally picked up a pen and began twirling it around his fingers just to give his hands something else to do as he watched Zane fiddle with the laptop.

"Okay, I got around the basic password protection, but there's a little extra encryption on this thing," Zane finally told him. "I would call him paranoid if he hadn't ended up dead."

"I can't believe he was one of Burns's guys," Ty said, shaking his head. "Was he recruited before or after Deuce and Livi started dating?"

"I don't know, Ty," Zane said without taking his eyes off the laptop screen.

"Would Dick really put a spy into Deacon's future in-laws?"

Zane glanced at him. "I don't know, Ty."

"I mean, that seems like a stretch even for Dick. I wonder if Deuce dating her was what brought Dick's attention to the Stanton company, or if Milton really did plant that seed?"

"I don't know, Ty," Zane repeated obediently. "Why don't you go ask him? Maybe he'll tell you more than he told me."

Ty sighed heavily, shaking his head. "He won't tell me anything, he'll just glare at me like he used to when I was little and make me feel like I'm ten. You know who *should* talk to him? Dad. It'd be just as uncomfortable as it was when Irish was interrogating me; I bet he'd tell Dad anything. Are you listening to me?"

"No, Ty."

Ty snorted and cocked his head at Zane. His brow was furrowed and his curly hair was a bit awry from running his fingers through it so many times. He had his tongue stuck between his lips and probably didn't even realize it. Ty stood, stepping behind Zane to massage his tense shoulders. "I'm sorry, I'm distracting you. Carry on."

Zane rolled his neck, leaning into Ty's hands. Ty was silent, letting him work. He still didn't understand what Zane was doing, but finally Zane sat back and put both hands in the air triumphantly. "Eat that, DOD!"

"You got through?"

Zane nodded and clicked one more button that turned the blue screen of the laptop into the normal desktop screen Ty was used to seeing. Dozens of files littered the screen, most of them labeled in some sort of numerical code.

Ty rested his chin on Zane's shoulder, dejected. "This is going to take a while, huh?"

Zane nodded. "Might want to take a seat."

Nick sifted through the bowl of rice with great care, placing each piece of the cell phone on a microfiber towel he had found in a drawer. Kelly watched over Nick's shoulder. When they had all the pieces, Nick began putting it back together.

He held the reassembled phone in his palm, and he and Kelly both scowled at it.

"Let's hope it's charged," Kelly said.

Nick turned it on and held his breath. The sound was garbled and the screen was a digitized mess as the phone powered on, but they could sort of make out what they were seeing on it. Nick first went to the list of recent calls. Kelly scrambled to get his own phone out and take pictures of the screen. They got partial lists of Milton's last calls, then moved on to the text messages. Some of them were beyond comprehension, but others were clear enough to make out. Kelly took photos of all of them.

The phone began to make a metallic whirring sound.

"Oh, that's a bad sound," Kelly said.

"No, it's not."

"Yes, it is."

"Just shut up and keep taking pictures."

"That's an 'I'm going to blow up' sound," Kelly insisted.

"I know, but we only have one chance to get this shit."

The phone popped, and they both jumped. The smell of burning electronics accompanied a sizzling sound, and after the first threat of fire, Nick dropped the phone into the bowl of rice. It sparked and fizzled, and the smell of burning rice mingled with the lingering aroma of industrial-strength cleanser in the kitchen.

Kelly huffed and sniffed at the bowl of rice. "Told you."

Nick glared at his profile. "What did we get?"

Kelly flipped through the photos of the text messages on his phone. "It looks like he was setting up a meeting, maybe. These times are from the other night. How the hell was he getting service to send these texts?"

Nick leaned over and squinted at the photos. They were basically poor copies of a rough original, and some of the words were unintelligible. But reading through the last dozen or so texts painted a pretty clear picture, and it wasn't hard to fill in the blanks. "He was setting up a buy."

"A buy? Like, what, he was selling something?"

Nick nodded and pointed at the text message. "It's shorthand. He was meeting a buyer at eleven last night, and he wanted money wired. Apparently his buyer had cash instead and they were arguing over payment. I can't tell more, it's too fuzzy."

"You think he was selling the defense contract technology Stanton's company is developing?"

Nick nodded grimly. "Yeah, I do. Odds are he either tried to cheat them, or he changed his mind, so his buyer killed him. I'm guessing they thought he had the information on him, but he didn't. That's why they came back for his body."

"So, what are we talking here? A flash drive? A memory chip? It has to be something small enough to swallow if that's where they were looking. And his room hadn't been tossed."

Nick shrugged. "I'm not a techie. We'll take it to Garrett, see if he knows. See what they've got off that laptop."

Kelly nodded and stuffed his phone back into his pocket. They left the mess they'd made. There was no one to complain about it now anyway.

Kelly glanced at the freezer as they headed for the steps. "Hey, maybe one of them will donate a liver to your dad."

Nick looked over his shoulder at Kelly, his eyes wide.

"I'm just saying. Three perfectly good livers sitting in there," Kelly said, completely deadpan. "Nobody's using them. I'll go get one for you."

Nick gaped at him. "How the hell did you ever pass your psych evals?"

"I cheated off your papers."

Nick rolled his eyes and started up the stairs.

"The Navy gives bubble tests. When in doubt, go with C."

"Kelly."

"Get it? Navy? The sea?"

"Kels, shut up."

"Oh, come on! You love puns."

Nick laughed, unable to stop himself.

Kelly plucked at his shirt as they headed up the steps, stopping him. Nick looked back at him, one eyebrow raised, expecting another joke. But Kelly was turning to head into the kitchen again. "You know, the cook hadn't been dead but for a few minutes when we came down here yesterday."

Nick nodded, his eyes darting toward the bottom of the steps. It dawned on him where Kelly was going with that. "How'd the killer get out?"

"Yeah." Kelly glanced up at Nick. "The steps are the only way in or out, we would have seen them leaving from the hall upstairs. Or hell, maybe even passed them on the steps."

Nick waited a breath, then stepped to stand beside Kelly.

"You think it's possible they hid well enough for Ty to miss them?"

"No," Nick said immediately. They descended the stairs again, standing at the bottom to look around the massive kitchen. It was mostly open. The cabinets had glass faces, and the counters and islands all had open shelves beneath. "There's nowhere to hide down here, not unless you get into one of the ovens."

Kelly grunted. "And there was definitely no one in the freezer; I went in there."

Nick paced a few steps into the kitchen, craning his head to seek out impromptu hiding spots. "I mean, you could do it, I guess. There's . . . I don't know. You'd have to be really slick."

"Or small," Kelly added. "I bet a woman could have hid down here."

"But someone that small wouldn't have been able to pick Milton up and hang him on that meat hook. There were *two* people. No way they could have hid, not from Ty."

"True," Kelly said, his shoulders slumping.

Nick's attention turned from the shiny appliances and bright white counters to the stone walls of the room. He peered upward, noticing the architecture for the first time, the way the room itself was laid out. "This was a chapel," he said in surprise.

Kelly glanced up, pursing his lips. "So?"

"Well, a Scottish church built in the late nineteenth century, there would have been a pulpit on the right side of the chancel. Sometimes the pulpit had a space beneath it or behind it."

"How do you know that?" Kelly asked.

"I think I saw it in one of those house makeover shows," Nick admitted, shrugging. He retained all kinds of normally useless information from books, podcasts, and TV shows he kept on as background noise when he was working. He'd never lost a trivia game.

"Okay, which side was the right side?"

Nick pointed toward the wall that abutted the rest of the house. They scanned over the stone carvings, the same angels they'd seen on the fireplace in their bedroom. Nick didn't see anything that looked like a hidden or raised space where the pulpit would have stood, but he saw something else he recognized.

"Ball and chain," he said, smacking Kelly's arm.

"You can't call me that unless we're married."

Nick smirked and stepped closer to the wall, running his hand over an angel with a chain through its wing. "Ball and chain," he repeated. "Like in our room."

Kelly came closer and took the gun from the small of Nick's back, stepping away and raising it, at the ready. Nick gave him a nod, then pulled the wing of the angel and flattened himself against the wall as something inside the stone clicked. It grated across the floor, making both Nick and Kelly cringe from the sound. Kelly kept the gun up, though, aimed at the darkness revealed inside the wall.

When it became obvious that it was empty, Kelly lowered the gun and they shared a glance. "Great," Kelly huffed. "Our killers know the place."

CHAPTER 9

Ty let his head hang, rubbing at his eyes. He looked up at a heavy sigh from Zane.

"More dead ends?"

"There's just too much chaff, here," Zane said in frustration. "Without something to go on—a number, a keyword—there's no way to find anything."

He gave up on the folders and instead pulled up Milton's email. They were scanning through it when something heavy clanked behind them. Ty whirled, reaching for a gun that wasn't there. Zane stood as well, but neither of them was armed. They tensed, preparing for whatever came out of the wall.

The leather-covered panel beside the fireplace swung open, and Kelly stepped out, gun in hand, sweeping the room before he pointed it at Ty and Zane. He straightened quickly, lowering the gun.

"Hi," he said.

Nick stepped out behind him a moment later, brushing cobwebs off his shoulders.

"What the hell?" Ty shouted. He looked around, searching for something, *anything*, to throw at them. "You scared the shit out of us, what if we'd been carrying? We could have shot you!"

"Yeah, but you didn't," Kelly said.

"How did you two end up in the walls again?" Zane asked, sounding like a weary mother scolding her children.

"Doc realized we should have seen the killer when we went down to the kitchen. So we started looking for places he could have been hidden."

Kelly grinned widely. "We found another entrance instead."

"How?" Ty demanded.

"The carvings of angels with a ball and chain," Nick said. He glanced over the fireplace beside him, then pointed to one of the carvings. "They're the way in."

"I've seen about half a dozen of those in the house." Zane sounded scandalized. "I even saw one on the exterior, at the corner wall near the patio."

"Escape route," Nick guessed.

"Wait, wait," Ty finally said. "So you two found these passages by accident. How do our killers know they're there?"

Nick shrugged and scratched idly at his forearm. "Family? Staff?"

"I wonder if they'd be in any public plans of the place," Zane added. "A little research could have exposed them."

"That's unlikely," Nick said. "These were basically a maze of panic rooms. They were built to protect the family from war, invasion, revolt. They would have been secret."

"We're going to have to sit the family down and see who knows about them," Kelly surmised. He checked the gun and then stuffed it back into Nick's jeans.

"What about the phone?" Ty asked.

"It kind of . . . blew up," Kelly answered.

"But we did get photos of some things before it went. From what we can tell, he used texts to set up a meeting last night. He either had a signal booster or he was the one blocking everyone else's signal. He was selling something to someone on the island."

"That's why he was all packed up," Ty said. Kelly nodded. "He was getting his money and getting out. So how'd he end up dead instead?"

"Deal gone bad," Nick said with another careless shrug. "Change of heart. Who knows?"

"No indication of what he was selling?" Zane asked.

"We were hoping you could tell us."

Zane nodded. "Let me get back to this, then."

Nick and Kelly came closer as Zane sat once more, and they all watched the screen as Zane pulled up the list of emails again. Ty scanned the subjects and the occasional first line of each. They all seemed to be rather innocuous work-related missives, except for the few that looked like online shopping receipts.

Finally, Ty patted Zane's shoulder and pointed at one of the emails. "See what that one says."

"A shipping confirmation from Brookstone?"

Ty rolled his eyes. "Just . . . humor me."

Zane shrugged and pulled up the email. But as they looked at the shipping confirmation, they realized it wasn't actually confirming the purchase or shipping of any goods. It was merely a time, date, and address from which the package had supposedly been shipped.

"It's a fake," Kelly said in surprise.

"I've seen this," Nick told them. He tapped the screen. "I've seen this with call-girl rings from Vice. You place an order, and they send you a receipt that looks like you were shopping online. Then to set up time and place, they use a shipping confirmation. It hides the paper trail, allows people to pay in different ways, and keeps your records looking clean if anyone gets into them."

"So, what, he was ordering call girls?" Kelly asked.

Ty frowned harder, reading over the email again. "That's Deacon's address in Philly," he realized. His breath left him in a rush. The date was for two days from now. "He ordered a hit on my brother."

"You don't know that, Ty." Zane's voice was even, but Ty could hear the anger in it.

Kelly touched Ty's arm, and when Ty met his eyes, Kelly was frowning hard. "No one has any interest in killing your brother. Amelia's the one who's valuable, right? This probably wasn't a hit."

"A kidnapping?" Zane asked.

Ty gritted his teeth. His entire body began to shake, and he had to take a deep breath to keep himself calm. "I'll kill him."

"He's already dead, Ty," Nick reminded him.

Ty stalked back and forth, fuming as he thought about the innocent little girl upstairs being stolen from her bed, taken by strangers, all so someone somewhere could make a buck.

"I'll kill him again, then!" Ty shouted.

"Yeah, someone already did that too," Kelly pointed out. "You want to go step on his intestines? They're still in a bag on the freezer floor."

"Dude," Nick muttered.

Kelly shrugged, unapologetic.

Nick stepped in front of Ty, blocking his path. "You want some real answers, Ty?"

Ty gritted his teeth, balling his hands into fists.

Nick raised both eyebrows. "Then how about you go talk to Richard Burns and ask him some hard questions for once?"

"Sure, Irish, why not just point a loaded gun at the man," Kelly said wryly. He stepped up behind Ty and put both hands on his shoulders, turning him until he could force him to sit. "Let's get a little more information before we go off storming the castle, okay?"

"I second that," Zane said.

Ty was shaking his head, still fuming even as Kelly put pressure on both shoulders to keep him sitting. "Dick never would have let it get that far if he knew. He wouldn't put Deuce or Amelia at risk for anything."

"Really?" Nick asked.

Ty glared at him, but he wasn't so far out of control that he didn't realize he was looking for a target, any target, to vent his anger on. Nick had always recognized when Ty needed someone to aim at, and he usually found Ty a suitable target, even if it was himself. But this time Nick didn't. His jaw was tight and his green eyes were hard, and Ty didn't understand why.

"What is wrong with you?" Ty asked him, standing to square his shoulders against Nick's. "You've been questioning me at every turn ever since we got deployed. You want to talk to me about this, Irish? Or should we keep going around in circles while people are dying?"

Nick flattened his lips into a thin line and nodded. "We've known each other for a long time, Tyler."

"That's why I don't understand why you won't fucking talk to me," Ty blurted. "When have we ever let something hang between us like this? When have you ever kept secrets from me as big as him?" He waved his hand at Kelly. "And he sure as hell isn't the only thing you're keeping close to the vest. What's going on?"

"We've told a lot of lies over the years," Nick said, his voice low and hard.

Ty's body went cold, tingling with the rush of realization. The things he had said and done, he'd been able to validate them all to himself at the time: He was protecting Zane by not telling him that Burns had ordered him to keep an eye on his partner. He was following orders and keeping his teammates safe when he didn't tell them why they were being discharged. Nick, though . . . his definitions of truth and honor were more black-and-white than Ty's ever had been.

"We've even told some of those lies to each other, but *damn it*, Ty," Nick hissed, finally letting the anger break through his cool façade. "You looked me in the eye and you lied to me. You lied to me when it mattered. You lied to *us*, and then you kept asking us to stand beside you like those lies wouldn't matter."

"Nick."

"I tried to go on like I still trusted you, Ty, but I don't. *I don't*. And I don't know if I will again. This is me faking it 'til I make it, and I guess I'm not very good at it when the shit starts hitting the fan."

Ty wanted to throw up. It was like being caught red-handed by someone you idolized and getting looked at like you were trash. Ty couldn't handle that kind of look from Nick.

"Why didn't you say something?"

"When?" Nick was barely controlling his temper, Ty could hear it in his voice. "Should I have raised my hand and said 'me too' when you and Zane were throwing down in New Orleans? Should I have done it in the hospital with Kelly lying there with a hole in his chest because *your* past came back to bite us? Or maybe on the ship. In front of all those men who were calling you captain. Should I have done it then?"

Ty blinked hard, nodding in understanding. Nick had always put the good of the collective above his own desires and needs. He would let an issue tear him to shreds inside before he caused a ripple amongst a team. The only reason he was saying it now was because Ty had pushed him to.

"You're right."

"I don't care about being right," Nick snapped. "I care about looking at my best friend and knowing he's telling me the truth. And I can't do that anymore!"

Ty couldn't swallow. He couldn't breathe. He couldn't make a sound. He couldn't do anything but stare at Nick and search desperately for a reason for Nick to trust him again. "I was following orders, Irish," he finally managed to whisper. "If anyone will understand that, it's you."

"Oh, I understand." Nick tapped a finger at his forehead. "I understand if you were given the order to put one between my eyes, you'd feel bad at my funeral."

He turned and paced away, leaving Ty with his mind reeling, his heart in his throat.

"Guys," Kelly said softly. "I understand this has to happen, but we need to shelve this for a few more days. Can we do that?"

Nick didn't turn around. Ty took a deep breath and nodded, though, trying to regain his voice. He met Zane's eyes, surprised to find his lover watching him sadly. "Okay," Ty rasped. "Let's see what else we can find. We know *Amelia* wasn't what Milton was trying to sell last night. So there's something else here."

"Department of Defense technology," Zane offered. "That has to be what he was selling."

"We find out who the buyer is, we find the killer," Nick said. His voice was still low and angry.

Kelly snorted. "How do we do that?"

"Okay," Ty said with a nod. "Zane and Kelly stay here, go through that laptop for anything even remotely related to this. Nick and I will go talk to Burns and Stanton."

Zane gave him a raised eyebrow, his eyes darting to Nick. "Is that a good idea?"

"It's the first good one he's had," Nick grunted.

Ty glared at him, torn between hurt and angry. "Why not? We're professionals here."

Zane snorted. "Because . . . well, sending you two out there together is like giving a toddler a lit match and telling it to go play in the sagebrush."

Nick and Ty shared a frown. "We'll be fine," Ty insisted. He shook himself out, squaring his shoulders. "Nick's calm. I'm calm. Everybody's calm. Murderers to find, kidnappers to kill."

It was Zane and Kelly's turn to exchange frowns. They both shook their heads.

"Nick can stay here with me and go through the emails; we'll discuss the interviews from yesterday," Zane proposed. "You and Kelly go question Stanton and Burns."

Ty snorted but nodded. "Fine. Irish, let me have that gun."

"Nope," Nick said, and he sat in the chair beside Zane and crossed his arms.

Kelly grabbed Ty's elbow and dragged him toward the door.

The constant press of Nick's presence beside Zane was beginning to make him edgy. He didn't know if it was simply because of how worked up Nick was, or if it was something about Nick's current mien that made sitting beside him almost physically painful. Zane had always known Nick to be a calming presence in a room, not the epicenter of something that felt like it was about to explode. That was usually Ty's role.

"You okay?" Zane finally asked him.

Nick turned his head but didn't quite look at Zane. He nodded, but his jaw was tight. "He plucks people up and puts them out there, tells them they're doing good. But he leaves them hanging in the wind. Just out there hanging and . . . dying. And for what? Their country?" He shook his head. "It's bullshit."

Zane didn't even have to ask who Nick was talking about. "Burns tried to recruit you when he did Ty and Sanchez, didn't he?"

Nick nodded curtly.

"Why didn't you go in with them?"

Nick leaned back in his chair, rubbing his hands over his face. "It felt wrong. Everything he told us, it just felt . . . it's hard to explain. It felt like maybe he wasn't the good guy."

Nick glanced at Zane quickly, probably to judge his reaction. Zane tried hard to keep his face neutral.

"I tried to tell Ty and Eli why I didn't like it, why I hadn't agreed to do it. But I couldn't explain the feeling, and there wasn't a fucking thing I could point to to back me up. Ty had already made up his mind, and you know how he is when he thinks he's right."

Zane smiled. "Yeah, I do."

"And Jesus Christ, you add in making his dad proud and he's a brick wall. I gave up on Ty, but I begged Eli to come to Boston with me instead of signing up for Burns." He trailed off, eyes on the desktop. His eyes were no longer focused on anything but the past.

Zane couldn't help but stare at him. "What happened?"

Nick shook himself and met Zane's eyes again. "Eli stuck with Ty. He said he'd rather go out with his boots on than be a civilian. And Ty told me I was a coward for refusing the offer and going back home to Boston."

"Really?" Zane asked, dumbfounded by that disclosure. He'd always imagined Ty and Nick so tight they had to be untied to take a piss. To discover they'd ever shared a harsh word was a revelation. And to hear that Ty had gone so far as to call Nick a coward, well . . . it gave Zane serious pause, especially after what he'd just witnessed. That Nick had been harboring the same feelings of betrayal Zane had felt . . . how the hell had he done it without letting it tear him apart?

Nick was nodding. "I didn't hear from him for a solid year. And I didn't try contacting him either. After ten years of going with gut feelings, it hurt like hell that neither of them would just *trust* me."

"How'd you two get right again?" Zane asked.

Nick was silent, staring at the desk, and Zane realized he already knew the answer. Ty and Nick never had gotten right again. Not really. And then New Orleans had happened, with all those secrets and lies spilling over.

"I'm sorry," Zane whispered.

"You remember on my boat, when you asked why I kissed Ty when I did?" Nick asked.

Zane nodded, not keen to relive those memories and emotions. "You said you knew you'd already lost him. I thought you meant . . . to me. That wasn't what you meant, though, was it?"

Nick was nodding, not seeming to realize that he was doing it. The issues between the two men went deeper than even Ty or Nick knew. They'd both simply been playing the parts they were familiar with, loyal to the very painful core, without questioning why it felt different.

Something about it made Zane inexplicably sad. Ty and Nick had the most pure friendship Zane had ever witnessed; to see that it had crumbling foundations hurt his heart.

"Burns took a handful of the best Marines in the Corps and turned them into six pieces of nothing. And all the bullshit his little side jobs put them both through? Eli being shot down like a fucking dog in some hotel room." Nick met Zane's eyes. "So yeah, I'm having a hard time controlling the urge to punch Richard Burns in the face. Or Ty, for that matter."

Zane snorted. "Understandable." He waited a beat, glancing at Nick again. "I'll hold him down for you if you decide to go for it."

Nick barked a laugh and smiled wryly. He jutted his chin out toward the laptop, scratching idly at his arm. "Okay, so what are we looking for here?"

Zane turned his attention back to the computer. "We're . . . we still need a place to start. We'll go through the other emails, see if we can make a timeline, see if there are any keywords or numbers that repeat. Did you come up with anything like that in your interviews?"

"Keywords or special numbers?" Nick asked.

Zane nodded.

"Not really. Only number I got out of it was the time on the watch. Goddamn, why am I itchy again?" Nick rolled his sleeve up and frowned at his arm. He'd scratched it almost to the point of bleeding. He glanced over his shoulder at the wall where he and Kelly had emerged. "It's got to be something in those walls, man."

"Kelly's not itchy. I wonder why you are."

"Curse of the red hair, I guess," Nick said wryly. He stopped scratching, staring at the desk and his notepad for a second before looking up at Zane with wide eyes. "I'm not the only one on the island who's been itching."

Ty and Kelly made their way to the dining room, where a sort of buffet lunch had been set up. With the cook dead, the head of the house still sedated, and the staff all frightened and grieving, everyone else was just doing whatever could be done to make life easier. The buffet was being cleared up already, though. Ty checked his watch.

"I didn't realize it was so late," Kelly said under his breath.

"Yeah, time flies when you're in a freezer playing with someone's intestines."

Kelly snorted. "Tell me about it. Every time."

Ty glanced at him, but Kelly was maintaining a straight face. He met Ty's eyes and grinned impishly.

"I think almost dying did something weird to you; you're like the beginning of a horror movie," Ty told him. He returned his attention to the large dining room, searching for Stanton or Burns. He didn't see either man, but he did spot Deuce and Earl, sitting in a corner eating.

He tapped Kelly's chest and gestured for him to follow as he wound his way toward their table.

Deuce saw them coming and gave them a halfhearted smile. Ty and Kelly both pulled up chairs and sat down.

"How's the investigation going?" Deuce asked.

Ty shook his head. "Not too good."

"What have you found?" Earl asked.

Ty shifted uncomfortably. How the hell should he even get into this with his dad, who had known Burns since they were teenagers? It would be like someone telling him that Nick had been doing all the things Burns had been doing for years, using his son to do it. He licked his lips, stalling until he could come up with something.

"Milton was a spy," Kelly told them before Ty could speak. Ty gaped at him. Kelly reached out and plucked a cucumber from Earl's plate. He pointed it at Earl. "For your buddy, Burns."

Ty stared at him as he crunched down on the cucumber. Deuce and Earl were both wide-eyed, mouths hanging open.

Earl finally turned to Ty. "What?"

"I . . . basically, yeah." Ty glared at Kelly, and Kelly shrugged. "Burns runs certain operators for jobs that . . . aren't really aboveboard."

"You're talking about black ops," Deuce said. "Uncle Dick runs black ops for the FBI? It's not just you?"

Ty cleared his throat, wondering why it had suddenly gotten so damn hot in this place. "Yes. And the dead man was one of his."

"And you're one of his?" Earl asked in a stunned voice.

Ty met his father's eyes and nodded.

Earl sat back, exhaling slowly. "That rat bastard."

Ty put up a hand, trying to calm himself more than anyone else. "Let's just focus, here. Do you know where Dick is right now?"

"I haven't seen him since Zane and Nick came to talk to him," Earl said through gritted teeth. "He came back to the table, said he had to get something from his room. Haven't seen him since."

Ty shook his head, glancing at his brother. Should he tell Deuce what they'd found on the laptop? One more glance at his father's angry face and Ty decided he'd lit a fire under enough of the Grady family for now. He pushed back in his chair. "If you see him, tell him we need to talk to him, okay?"

"Oh, I'll tell him all right," Earl growled.

Ty nodded, retreating with Kelly toward the great hall. Once they rounded the corner, Ty turned and smacked Kelly in the arm. "What the hell was that, Doc?" he hissed.

Kelly rubbed at his arm, scowling. "What? You were going to take a fucking week before you got around to telling them. Wasn't it more painless my way?"

Ty rolled his eyes. "Nick is going to strangle you in your sleep in the first six months, I guarantee it."

Kelly shrugged. "He tries that every night."

Ty squeezed his eyes closed, holding his head. "I told you, no sex stories and I won't freak out. That was our deal!"

Kelly was laughing, an evil little giggle that Ty knew well.

"I have a very graphic imagination, okay? Do you want me to freak out?"

"It's kind of fun to watch you freak out. Reminds me of the old days."

"I hate you so much right now," Ty grumbled.

They made their way toward the back patio in search of Burns or Stanton, but it was deserted. It seemed people were staying inside, sticking close to where they felt safe.

"Everyone must be locked in their bedrooms or something," Kelly observed wryly. He and Ty shared a frown. "What if they're rooming with a killer?"

Ty snorted and surveyed the patio one last time. Then Kelly's words truly sank in, and a cold dread began to settle in his stomach. He turned to Kelly. "Locked doors don't mean shit in this place, not with the passages in the walls. Even if they're not rooming with a killer, they're still in danger."

Kelly nodded and shrugged. "Hasn't that been true from the beginning?"

He and Ty stared at each other, then Kelly began to nod when he saw the look dawning in Ty's eyes.

"Difference is, we know they're in danger now," Kelly said.

"Shit." Ty turned to head back inside, striding for the dining room and Deuce. There were still a few people perusing the buffet, but for the most part the house felt deserted. Ty placed both hands down on the table where Deuce and Earl still sat and sighed heavily. "We have to get everyone in one room."

"What? Why? What's going on?" Deuce demanded as he took to his feet.

Ty shook his head. "Don't panic. Will you just help us gather everyone for me, get everyone together in that big sunroom? I promise I'll explain."

"Wait, the sunroom?" Kelly asked. "That doesn't sound safe at all."

"You can see through the walls, Doc," Ty whispered.

"Oh, good point," Kelly huffed, then patted Ty's shoulder and jogged away.

Deuce stared at Ty for another moment, then nodded. "Okay."

Ty left them there without further explanation, running after Kelly to head back to Zane and Nick. Finding the killer amongst them wasn't the priority right now. Making sure no one else wound up in that freezer, that was Ty's goal.

They met Nick and Zane emerging from the study, both men looking like they'd discovered something important.

"We need to get everyone together," Ty called to them.

"We need to get to the freezer," Zane told Ty as he and Nick brushed past them. Ty and Kelly shared a confused frown, then turned and followed.

They were almost to the kitchen steps when the lights flickered around them and went out.

The entire house was thrown into near darkness. The great hall had no windows, nothing to let light in except for the patio doors at the very far end, which were still covered with the massive tent. The storm was darkening the horizon, and the winter light was waning. Zane couldn't see a goddamn thing. He turned and reached out, cracking his knuckles against someone's hard muscles and earning a surprised whoof in return.

"Sorry!" he whispered, grabbing at the man he'd hit.

"You better know it's me if you're grabbing me there," Ty responded wryly.

Zane snorted and pulled him closer, hugging him tight.

"What the shit is this?" Kelly asked.

"Goddamn it!" Nick shouted. Something banged in the darkness as they all remained still to let their eyes adjust. "Unfuck your shit, Scotland!"

"Storm hit the generators?" Ty asked hopefully.

"Or someone hit them," Zane said softly.

"This place is run off a single power generator?" Kelly asked incredulously.

"It's run off wind, solar, and hydro power, just like all the other island communities in the Hebrides."

"How do you know so fucking much about these islands?" Ty shouted at him.

"I watch Discovery Channel when I can't sleep!" Nick shouted back.

"I . . . I did not know that," Ty said, sounding both angry and apologetic at the same time.

Zane grunted. "Okay, everyone calm down. The power being out isn't a big deal. We need to get to the freezer to check that body. We have a theory."

"And we still need to gather everyone in the sunroom," Ty added.

"Why?"

"No one's safe in this house alone. And right now everyone is separate and alone. Hell, it's the only place with light now. Why are we going to the freezer?"

Nick flicked his phone on, shining the light of the flash on the floor.

"Just . . . you two head for the generators, see what's going on out there," Zane said as he trailed after Nick and his light. "We'll meet you in the sunroom and help gather everyone."

"Hold on," Ty hissed, following and grabbing Zane's elbow. "Are either of you even armed?"

"O'Flaherty has his gun." Zane squeezed Ty's arm. "We'll be fine."

When Nick disappeared down the steps, the light went with him, and Ty's face was enveloped by shadow. "Well that's great, Zane, but Doc and I aren't armed so I'd rather not go out into the stormy night to check the generators that some psycho with an ax probably just killed, not without at least a sharp stick or something."

Zane nearly laughed. "We'll stay together then. Come on."

The flashlight reflected off the stainless steel of the kitchen, and Nick moved carefully toward the freezer, checking any blind spots and making certain they were alone down there. Kelly pulled the freezer door open, and Nick shined the light inside.

"What the hell are we doing down here, anyway?" Ty asked again.

Zane glanced at his shadowed face. "Nick is itchy."

"Again?" Kelly asked.

"It's the walls," Nick said. He had his knife out, cutting through the thick plastic bag they'd wrapped Nikki Webb's body in. He and Zane moved closer, handing their phones off to Ty and Kelly.

They examined the girl's arms and legs, finding several scratches. The skin was reddened and torn in some places, just like Nick's forearm.

Nick was nodding as he looked her over. "She mentioned being itchy when I interviewed her. I didn't think anything of it. But whatever's making me itch, it got to her too. She's been inside the walls."

"Wait a minute, so she's one of our doers?" Ty asked. "Son of a bitch."

"Looks like," Zane said. "She could be the woman we saw on the beach. Means her partner killed her. He's tying up loose ends."

"Allies being killed means the endgame," Ty pointed out. "And we don't even fucking know what game we're playing yet."

"Hide and seek?" Kelly suggested.

"Shut up," Ty huffed.

"Watch it," Nick growled. He sounded truly angry. He and Ty stared at each other in the light of Kelly's phone.

Zane could sense something coming to a head. He just hoped it waited until they were off this island.

Kelly subtly moved to stand between them. "We could be after just one person now. That's good, right?"

"We shouldn't assume that," Zane told him. He took his phone back from Ty. "Let's get back upstairs, check the power, and get some questions answered."

They vacated the freezer, closing it carefully behind them. Zane took Ty's arm and held him back as Nick and Kelly went up the stairs. "What's going on with you two? What set him off?"

"What do you mean?" Ty asked, though he sounded a little too nonchalant to truly be clueless.

"I mean why does O'Flaherty look like he wants to deck you? And why's it all coming out now?"

Ty shrugged, glancing up the steps. "Stress, I guess."

"You didn't say anything to him about him and Kelly, did you?"

Ty seemed offended that Zane would even imply that. He huffed in answer. "No. What's bothering him, it's our issue. Him and me." He pulled his arm away and started up the steps. "And I don't know how to fix it."

When they reached the great hall, Kelly was trying to explain to Nick why they needed to go to the sunroom, but Nick had planted himself in the middle of the hall, arguing that he needed to get into Nikki Webb's room and search her things.

"It might already be too late, but we need to see what she had up there. She might have answers."

"We need to arm ourselves is what we need to do," Ty countered. "Who cares who's doing this or why if we're all dead by morning?"

Nick glanced at him, then he and Kelly shared a look. Kelly nodded, but Nick's jaw tightened.

"Gun room? Or our rooms?" Kelly asked.

"Both," Ty said with a nod at Nick and Kelly. He tossed Kelly the key to their room. "Gather everything we've got from our rooms. You know where I stash my shit. We'll head for the hunting stuff. Meet in the sunroom."

Before they could separate, though, Stanton stalked out of the sunroom, two of his Snake Eater bodyguards trailing after him with lanterns.

"I hope you have a good reason for causing this sort of alarm, young man," he said to Ty. His normally placid voice echoed off the walls of the great hall.

Ty took a few steps to meet them. "Sir, we'll explain everything, but right now you and everyone else are safer together in the sunroom."

"Then join me, won't you? And explain now before there's a panic." Stanton waved a hand toward the sunroom doors, and Ty had little choice but to do as he was asked. The request wasn't exactly unreasonable, after all.

Ty gestured for the others to come with him. Zane would rather have them there as backup if things got out of hand, so he was glad Ty was at least on the same page with him. The Snake Eaters took up their posts on either side of the doors, and they wouldn't let Ty follow Stanton in until he submitted to a search.

"Are you fucking serious right now?" Ty asked.

English put a meaty hand on Ty's chest and pushed him a step back. "You're doing your jobs. We're doing ours. Hands up."

Ty did an impressive job of keeping a tight rein on his temper, doing as he was asked. English ran the wand over him, then let him in the room. The others each went through the same routine, with Nick's hip setting the wand off again. Frost patted him down just as he'd done the first night, quietly joking about his shrapnel being inconvenient, then let Nick through. Nothing else pinged, though. Where and when had Nick stashed his gun?

"Gentlemen, you have the room," Stanton announced once the glass doors were closed.

Ty glanced over the small crowd. He looked to Stanton again, narrowing his eyes at the man. "That's good, Mr. Stanton," he said, his tone changing to one that made Zane groan internally. He was about to do something ill-advised, Zane knew that much.

Out of the corner of his eyes, Zane saw Nick and Kelly share a glance and then subtly move farther apart, spreading out. They knew that tone of voice too.

"We've determined one of the victims is actually a culprit. One of the victims was trying to sell your company's technology. And one of the victims was trying to buy it," Ty announced, keeping his voice bland and almost amused. "Care to guess who is who?"

"Is this some sort of a joke?" Stanton asked.

"Ty, what the hell is going on?" Deuce asked from one of the sitting areas.

"Did Ernest Milton have access to the DOD tech you were developing?" Zane asked Stanton.

Stanton looked briefly shell-shocked before recovering his wits and nodding. "But only pieces of it. He was trying to *sell* it?"

"To someone on this island," Ty provided.

"It's kind of obvious it wasn't the cook," Kelly added drily.

Stanton rubbed at the bridge of his nose, shaking his head. "This makes no sense. Ernest would never sell that technology. He knew how sensitive it was, and he was a patriot."

"Aren't we all," Nick murmured.

"He also didn't have all the pieces. Without all three sets, it's useless to any buyer. Is that what got Ernest killed?"

Zane glanced at Ty, earning a raised eyebrow in return. Three sets? That meant it was possible Milton had gone through with the sale of his information, hoping his buyer wouldn't be wise to how many pieces there were.

"Who has the other pieces?" Nick asked.

"I control one," Stanton answered. "It remains with me at all times. The other remains with the head of security. He is currently in Philadelphia."

"Milton wasn't just selling his piece of the technology," Ty told Stanton. His eyes darted to Deuce and Livi. When he spoke again, it was through gritted teeth. "We found a confirmation on his laptop. He'd hired someone to kidnap Amelia from their home in two days' time. Probably as leverage for your piece of the information."

Deuce lurched to his feet, protesting wordlessly. Stanton put a hand to his mouth, turning to look at Deuce and Livi before meeting Ty's eyes again. "That . . . I told Milton to do that."

"You what?" Livi cried.

"It wasn't a kidnapping," Stanton said, raising his voice as more people protested. "It was a test of your security, to see if someone could get to her."

"And you didn't think to *tell* us this?" Deuce shouted.

"Once the wedding date was moved, the point was moot."

Ty took a step back and turned to Zane, frowning as the Stantons and Gradys began to argue. The shouting and accusations bounced off the walls, wild gesticulations and posturing mirrored by candlelight in the darkened glass. The scene quickly devolved into chaos, but Ty and Zane ignored the feuding families.

"Something's not adding up, right?" Zane asked. Ty nodded. "If Milton was running a check on Amelia's protection, it's possible he was doing the same thing the night he was killed."

Ty nodded again, covering his mouth with his hand as he spoke. "He could have been baiting the buyers, trying to find out who they were. If they killed him, it means he recognized them, and they knew him well enough to know he wouldn't be selling this shit."

"So our bad dead guy is now a good dead guy?" Kelly whispered. He'd come up behind Zane, so quiet in the confusion Zane hadn't realized he was there.

Zane glanced over his shoulder. Kelly stood with his arms crossed, scowling. Nick hung back, edging farther from the three of them. Zane did a double take when he saw the look in Nick's eyes, like he was staring into the distance, no longer truly with them.

"Oh shit," Zane whispered.

Ty and Kelly both turned to investigate, both of them stiffening when they noticed Nick edging closer to the door like he might be trying to escape. But Nick didn't look for an escape when he suffered his flashbacks. He went on the attack.

The Snake Eaters had waded into the fray, trying to separate Stanton from the rest of the angry group. Stanton, though, had Livi by both arms, apparently trying to explain his actions to his daughter as she shouted at him. One of the Snake Eaters, the woman named Avery Kline, came up beside Stanton and pried his hands from Livi. Then, in the confusion, she wrapped her arm around his neck and yanked him backward, pulling her gun and using him to shield her body from the other Snake Eaters. Then she fired into the air before Zane could move to stop her.

The shot echoed, like fire bouncing off their eardrums. The glass ceiling shattered and rained shards down on the occupants of the room. Ty and Kelly both hit the ground, covering their heads. Neither man had seen what Zane had seen; they'd merely heard the shot and reacted. Screams of terror and pain followed. People dove to the ground, shielding their loved ones or covering their ears. Rain poured in through the shattered panes. Ty and Kelly clambered to their feet again.

"Anyone makes a move and I put one in his ear!" Kline shouted. She directed her words to her fellow Snake Eaters, who all looked stunned by her betrayal. She knew they were the only ones in the room who were armed because they'd wanded everyone as they came in. "Guns down, now!"

English pulled his lapel aside, showing her his weapon. He glanced at Frost and Park, nodding for them to do the same. All three men set their guns on the floor with great care.

"I came here for one reason, and I'm getting off this fucking island. Now," Kline said to Stanton. She pointed her gun at Livi's head. "Take me to that memory drive or I kill her."

Stanton nodded furtively. She began to back toward the doors, dragging him backward with her. She aimed the gun at Zane and the others, eyeing them suspiciously as they stood with their hands in the air. She sneered at them. "Fucking Recon, my ass."

Another gunshot tore through the sound of the torrential rain, and then the bullet tore through Avery Kline's head, dropping her as Stanton cringed away from the splatter of blood and brain matter. He stumbled away, leaving Nick standing behind the body of the woman he'd just shot, gun still drawn.

"That's *Force* fucking Recon to you," Nick said to the dead woman. "Bitch."

y and the others stood in stunned silence. The only sound in the room was the rain pouring in through the ruined roof. Ty looked from the bleeding body to Nick and back. He didn't dare move, and he was glad the rest of the room seemed too stunned to make any sudden motions that might set Nick off. He didn't know if they were losing Nick to the past, or if the man had been paying closer attention to the Snake Eaters than Ty and the others had and had simply anticipated a move.

Either way, it paid to be careful around him.

Nick turned his weapon on the other Snake Eaters when English made a move toward his gun. "Leave them," Nick ordered. "Backups too, on the ground."

English, Park, and Frost all complied without complaint. They were all hardened veterans; they recognized a man on the edge when they saw one. They kicked their guns toward Nick and backed away from them, hands held above their heads.

Nick glanced at Ty and the others, nodding his head toward the weapons. Kelly jumped when he realized Nick wanted him to move, and he bent to gather the guns and extra clips, handing the spares over to Ty and Zane and checking them before shoving two of them into his pants. He gave Nick a curt nod, never speaking a word. They reminded Ty of Bonnie and Clyde knocking over a bank.

Nick surveyed the people in the sunroom. Ty glanced over them as well, wondering what Nick was looking for. Several people were drenched from the rain, including Deuce and Livi. More were bleeding from cuts caused by falling glass. Mara's cheek was bleeding, and Earl was cupping her chin to examine it, paying Nick and his gun no attention whatsoever.

Everyone else was staring at Nick, not sure if he was a hero or a new villain.

"Next person who wastes my time with a lie is losing a kneecap," Nick announced.

Villain, then.

Ty moved slowly, coming up behind Kelly to whisper in his ear. "Can we take him out without hurting him?"

Kelly shook his head. "Don't need to. Just watch."

"Three pieces of tech. Three targets," Nick said, addressing Stanton. "What are they contained on?"

"Computers. Secure files. You don't need the gun," Stanton said, trying to sound calm and failing.

"It seems more effective than being pleasant and trustworthy," Nick countered. "How are the files accessed?"

"A key code. A six-digit code. I only know mine. And then an override code must be entered. I'm the only one who knows that as well."

"Well, at least they won't have to cut out your eyeballs for the security or anything. Next time, don't make yourself the key," Nick said wryly. He lowered the gun, stuffing it in the small of his back. He glanced at Kelly, then Ty and Zane, and shrugged. "We're running short on time here."

Ty gaped at him. He finally snapped out of it and turned to Stanton, feeling the need to both apologize and yell at the man. The Snake Eaters were all glaring at them, looking mutinous.

"Where's your other man?" Ty asked English.

"Kid duty."

Ty walked over to him and handed him his gun back. He held up the backup. "I'm keeping this 'til I can find a better one."

English nodded reluctantly.

"Get all these people into a room and keep them there. Preferably one without a carving on the wall of an angel attached to a ball and chain."

"Pardon?" English asked, his tone flat and tired.

"Just . . . roll with it." Ty checked his clip, then shoved the gun into his belt. "We'll be back with more weapons. Keep everyone calm."

Ty turned to his men, casting a stray glance at Nick to make sure he hadn't truly snapped. Nick was smiling crookedly at him, though. Ty had to fight against his own smile. Nick had obviously enjoyed that a little too much.

He gave orders as they left the sunroom and emerged into the darkened great hall. "Round up all the weapons, and any stray guests or staff you run across. The kids are in the nursery on the third floor, get them down here."

Nick and Kelly both gave him curt nods and jogged off toward the grand staircase. Ty and Zane followed the light of Zane's phone toward the room they'd seen on their tour the first day, where stag heads and stuffed birds mingled with hunting rifles and antique weaponry.

"What the hell?" Ty said as they walked. "Why would she go bonkers now? No one was onto her."

"I don't know. Maybe she thought we had more than we did, took the offensive route."

"Pft."

"Not everyone can handle the cloak-and-dagger shit like you can, Ty."

"No, but if Nikki Webb was the woman who killed Milton on the beach and the cook in the kitchen, she had a man with her. How the hell does Kline fit in? That means we have three killers on the island. And the Snake Eaters can't fucking be trusted."

"Right."

"As soon as we get armed, we're taking Amelia and keeping her with us."

"Agreed."

They took a wrong turn and had to backtrack, getting confused with all the lights out. Zane insisted he knew where they were, though, and Ty trusted his mental maps to get them there.

"Okay, so was that crazy or savvy?" Zane finally asked.

"What?"

"Nick. Is he pretending to be crazy to scare people into telling him the truth? Or is he actually crazy and scary?"

Ty winced, shrugging. "Sometimes I don't know."

Zane snorted. "That was ruthless. It was kind of hot."

"Don't fucking start with me, Zane. I'm not even kidding."

Zane laughed, but went quiet when they found the door to the room ajar. A sense of impending doom began to settle in Ty's stomach.

Zane turned his light off, and Ty toed the door open. There was just enough light still coming through the windows for him to see the broken glass of the empty gun cabinet.

"Well, that can't be good," Zane whispered.

Nick let Kelly lead them to their rooms to gather all the weapons they'd packed. Nick trailed to a stop in front of Nikki Webb's door.

Kelly turned and gave Nick a questioning shrug. "What are you doing?"

"I'm going to search her room."

"But Six told us to—"

"Fuck what he told us, Kels," Nick growled. "He's not our Six anymore, and he's wrong this time."

Kelly looked stunned for a moment before nodding. He strode closer and grabbed Nick by his shirt, yanking him closer to kiss him. "I'll meet you back here in five."

Nick nodded, breathless as Kelly pulled away. He watched Kelly fade into the darkness, then turned to the room Nikki Webb and what's her face, the Sun Tzu fan, had shared.

He knocked first, wishing he could remember the other woman's name. She'd fucking spelled it for him, for Christ's sake. There was no answer to his knock.

He knocked again, then waited a beat before trying the doorknob.

A sound from the stairwell halted him. He went still, cocking his head to listen. There was a thump upstairs, then a grunt and a quiet click. He crept toward the stairs, listening intently. The only sound he could discern was the soft whimpering of a small child. It was so distant he couldn't tell if it was coming from upstairs, or from his memory of the past.

With a last look back at the hallway, he started up the dark steps to investigate.

When Ty did a head count of the people milling about in the dining room, he was alarmed to find only half the people on the island were present, and neither Nick nor Kelly were among them yet.

"Where the hell is everyone else?" he asked Deuce in a whisper that seemed to echo in the large room.

Deuce shrugged. He was still drenched from the rain in the sunroom. "Everyone refuses to come out of their bedrooms until the ferry gets here. And frankly, Ty, with all the good guy shooting going on here, I don't blame them. Why do you want all of us down here?"

"Will you bring Livi over here, please?" Ty requested, trying to keep his tone soothing.

Deuce went to retrieve her, murmuring to her as they rejoined Ty near the doorway.

"What's going on?" she asked.

"Do you know about the passages inside the walls of the house?" Ty asked her, deciding that easing into things was no longer an option.

She blinked rapidly at him, shaking her head. "The what?"

"Ty," Deuce said disapprovingly.

"I'm not joking. Nick and Kelly found an entrance in their bedroom. There are passages that go through the entire house. That's how the killers got into the kitchen and killed the cook. That's how they've been moving around without being seen. Deacon, all the rifles and small arms used for hunting have disappeared. Someone is either armed to the fucking teeth, or they're making sure none of us can be. No one is safe locked in their rooms. We need to get everyone down here, make sure we have safety in numbers. And we need to find every carved angel with a ball and chain in its wing. Those are the entrances. I also need to know every single fucking person on this island who knew about those passages."

Deuce was nodding urgently, but Livi seemed stunned. Even when Deuce moved away, she remained rooted to the spot, her mouth ajar. Ty put a gentle hand on her shoulder. "Are you okay?"

"The ball and chain wings," she said, her voice dazed. "There's one in the nursery."

Ty's heart dropped. "The one on the third floor?"

"The kids are all up there," Livi whispered. "We thought they'd be safe with the nanny and a bodyguard at the door. Ty . . . Amelia is up there."

Nick climbed the winding stairs, his mind a swirl of emotions he didn't normally find himself hindered by. He was grieving over the life he'd been forced to take. He was conflicted over the combination of guilt and nonchalance he was feeling over the decision to take that shot instead of the admittedly more risky option of trying to restrain her. And he was angry. He was furious, in fact, and no amount of trying to walk it off seemed to be able to cool him down.

That in and of itself told him that he was closer to cracking than he had been in a very long time. It had gotten beyond his normally impressive level of control, and with nowhere to go and lick his wounds, it would continue to spiral unless he could find a way to block it all out until he had a chance to decompress.

He and Ty had been through many fires together. They'd had a few fights. After the year they'd spent not communicating at all, Ty had been the one to reach out to Nick, first saying that he missed him and then adding that he needed help from someone he could trust. Nick hadn't hesitated. He never did. Ty was his best friend, and no matter what they did to each other, they would always be brothers. His loyalty was reciprocated too, with Ty jumping to his side whenever Nick needed him.

Nick wasn't sure he could forgive Ty for all the lies he'd uncovered in the past year, though. He hadn't been able to get over it even while they'd been deployed, and now that they were here, embroiled in someone else's problems again, Nick couldn't reconcile the anger and betrayal. Not this time.

He came to the last riser of the staircase, and his thoughts were interrupted by another thump and a quiet whimper. Something about the sound—a sound he heard in his dreams, a sound he'd *made* hundreds of times as a boy—made the hairs on the back of his neck stand up. He took the last few steps two at a time. He moved quickly and silently in the dark, taking care the floorboards beneath his feet didn't creak. He got to the nursery door and nearly tripped over the body of the Snake Eater on the ground. It was Hardin. Blood was streaming from a wound on the man's forehead. Nick checked his pulse and found nothing. He put his palm over Hardin's staring eyes and closed them.

"Hooah, soldier," he whispered. He patted the dead Snake Eater down, but his weapon was gone. Nick reached for his own gun and raised it toward the door.

He hesitated only another second before he pushed the door open. The nanny was standing near the massive fireplace with her back to the door. The five Grady cousins were all cowering in the corner, the oldest boy trying to shield the younger ones with his small body. He was no more than ten.

"You can't take her!" he shouted at the nanny.

Maisie backhanded the boy so hard he stumbled to the side. He quickly recovered and put himself back in front of his cousins with a determined snarl, blood dripping from his lip.

Nick saw red and shoved into the room. The woman turned when she heard him, startling and taking a quick step back. Nick stalked toward her, not slowing when she pulled a gun with a silencer from the folds of her dress and pointed it at him. She wasn't even holding the damn thing the right way. He flinched when she pulled the trigger, but nothing happened. She'd forgotten to take the safety off.

She fumbled with the weapon, still backing away from him, her face contorting in terror. She screamed for help, the shrill cry enough to pierce eardrums. She finally managed to get the safety off, and she fired rapidly, a frightened spray of bullets from a person who'd obviously never handled a gun before. One of the shots burned as it went past Nick's ribs. She nearly stumbled over her own feet when the shot didn't even slow Nick down, and Nick was on her before she could even think about reloading the gun. She tried smacking at him and kneeing him in the groin, both moves he easily deflected. He held her gun hand by the wrist and wrapped his fingers around her throat, picking her up by her neck until her toes were barely able to touch the ground.

She fought to bring the gun up, choking and sputtering. The way she fought, she certainly wasn't the one who'd taken out the Green

Beret at the door. She wasn't alone. Just as he thought it, Nick heard the heavy footsteps of someone coming down the hallway. Her partner must have been doing a perimeter check, leaving her to retrieve Amelia alone.

"How many?" Nick asked, letting her toes graze the floor so she could breathe to answer.

"They'll get what they want no matter what you do," she managed to say. "Half a million pounds for one little girl. I couldn't say no. No one could."

Nick loosened his grip, setting her back down. He yanked the gun from her hands and tossed it away, still glaring at her with murderous intent. He waved a hand at the children. "Fireplace," he snarled.

They hustled to obey. Nick told them how to open the secret door. Then he raised his gun.

Maisie took a halting step back and stumbled over a toy on the floor. "You're not a killer. Not like them. I can see that!"

"Is that right?" Nick asked with a slow smile. He began backing toward the fireplace. The footsteps grew slower and quieter as they approached. He couldn't risk a gunfight with an unknown number of assailants and five children in the room. He'd have to retreat.

"Maisie?" a man whispered from behind the half-open door. The accent was Scottish.

Nick waited a breath, until he could feel the wall behind him, until one of the kids reached up and took his hand. Then he raised his gun and fired at the man in the doorway.

Ty had to fight the urge to dive to the ground when the anguished screams and booming gunfire echoed through the house. Everyone froze, struck momentarily dumb by the unexpected sound of battle. Ty's eyes met Zane's for a brief moment before they both lunged out of their chairs and sprinted out of the dining room for the stairway. They met Kelly on his way down, out of breath and panicked.

One look at him and Ty knew something was horribly wrong. "What is it, is it Nick?"

Kelly shook his head jerkily, his eyes straying to the people in the foyer. "Not Nick."

"The kids?" Deuce blurted.

A tray of coffee crashed in the foyer. Concerned cries echoed off the marble of the great hall. There were gasps and murmurs as the panic and confusion became contagious.

"What do you mean, what happened?" Deuce demanded. His limp was almost absent as he rushed up the steps.

"They're gone," Kelly whispered. "Nick and I split up. When I came back he was gone, and when I heard the shots I went up to the third floor, but the room's empty. There's no one there but two dead bodies."

"Where's Nick?" Ty asked again.

Kelly opened his mouth, but no words came out. He managed to shake his head and spread his hands wide. "He's not up there, he's not down here. He's gone too. Maybe he went after whoever took the kids."

Zane cursed under his breath, the sound sending shivers down Ty's spine. "Do you think Nick got lost in a flashback?" Zane asked.

Deuce grabbed Ty by his shirtfront. "You said we could trust him!" he shouted.

Ty gripped his arms and shook him violently. "Stop! We'll find them. Come with me and keep your mouth shut."

Ty and the others followed Kelly to the third floor playroom where the kids had been stashed for safekeeping. The nanny who'd been assigned to watch them was laid out on the floor, bleeding from several gunshot wounds. Her face was bloody. A windowpane was shattered, and the wind whipped into the room, tugging at their clothing and hair. Bullet holes littered the rock walls behind her, and more had lodged into the door of the nursery, like she had fired back at an assailant shooting from the doorway.

The room itself was a shambles, with toys tossed about and furniture turned over.

"Is this . . . normal for a kid's room?" Zane asked carefully as they stood and surveyed the scene.

"Aside from the dead nanny and the bullet holes . . . sometimes," Deuce answered helplessly. He caught sight of something and pounced on it, picking up Amelia's ratty gray lamb and holding it up for Livi to see.

Livi covered her mouth with her fingers as tears began to stream down her face.

"We'll find them," Ty assured her. "Someone get in those fucking walls and start looking."

"Could Nick have done this?" Deuce shouted. "Someone took out that guard, and he was a Green Beret!"

Ty met Kelly's eyes, at a loss. They both knew Nick would never, ever hurt a child, no matter how lost in his memories he became. But would he hurt the Snake Eater who'd been guarding the door? Or the nanny? If they stood between him and someone he thought he needed to rescue? Yeah. Definitely.

Zane cleared his throat and stepped closer to Kelly, speaking so low Ty could hardly hear. "Would the, um . . . the medication he's on, would it cause behavior like this?"

Kelly shook his head vehemently.

"What medication?" Ty asked.

Kelly rubbed at his eyes and shook his head again. "He takes propranolol for a tremor in his hand."

"Tremor," Ty echoed. "What the fuck, since when?"

"Propranolol?" Deuce said as he came closer. "That's sometimes prescribed for PTSD."

"That's not Nick's issue," Kelly said.

"The hell it's not," Zane grumbled. "Every member of your team has PTSD."

"What are you, a shrink now?" Ty snapped. Zane shrugged.

"It can be hidden well, especially by people like *you*," Deuce insisted with a wave of his hand at Ty. "Could he have snapped and done this? Or run off?"

"What do you mean, people like me?" Ty took a step that put him face-to-face with his fuming brother.

Zane stepped between them and put a hand on both their chests.

"Something would've had to have triggered him," Kelly said.

"And Nick sure as hell wouldn't hurt those kids," Ty added with a pointed look at Deuce.

"Then find them, Ty!" Deuce shouted.

Zane took Deuce's shoulder and held him even when he tried to shove away. "You need to calm down," he said quietly.

Livi was still crying, but she gripped Deuce's elbow. "They're right. We're not helping by panicking."

Deuce took a deep breath and stepped away, running his hands through his hair. Ty gave Livi a nod of thanks, then noticed several more people in the doorway, watching and waiting. He hesitated, momentarily indecisive.

"You're sure no one came by you, Doc?" Zane asked Kelly.

"Positive. I was right there at the stairs when the shooting started. By the time I got up here, it looked like this. No one got by me."

"Means they went through the walls," Ty murmured.

"Okay, we need to find the kids," Zane announced, taking control when Ty still hesitated. "Split up into groups of four or five, no one goes anywhere alone. Check every room top to bottom and then lock it behind you as you leave. Start at the wings and work inward to the center of the house."

Zane divided them into groups and then assigned each group a wing and level of the house. The groups split off and headed for their assigned areas. Ty was already fidgeting, trying to map out the directions Nick could have gone as Zane gestured to Emma, who was still standing at the doorway. "You come with us. We'll circle the house, see if we can pick up anything outside. If Nick's in the walls, he would have headed for that escape door at the corner of the patio. Deacon, Livi, you two stay here in this room in case the kids ran for it and try to come back. Got it?"

Deuce's jaw tightened, but he nodded. "Find my baby."

"We will."

They collected flashlights, then Ty led Zane, Kelly, and Emma down to the front door and outside. There had been a break in the storm, but Ty didn't know if they'd be able to find anything out there, or how long the rain would hold off. They spread out and began scouring the grounds, Ty and Zane moving one way, Kelly and Emma the other, searching in a circle around the mansion for tracks or signs of a struggle. It took them too many minutes to reach the gardens in the back of the house where the inner passages would have led someone to exit.

Ty was too worried to talk, too worried to question Zane about how he'd known Nick was taking medication, or why Nick hadn't told Ty about any of these things that were going on in his life. What the hell kind of friend had Ty been to him that he felt he couldn't share? And now Nick was missing, God knew if he was okay, and the last real words Ty had exchanged with him were in contempt and anger.

It made Ty physically ill. His hand holding the flashlight began to tremble.

"He's okay, Ty," Zane said.

"We can't know that."

"Got something!" Kelly called out in the darkness. He and Emma were waving their flashlights, and Ty and Zane hurried through the inky night to find them. When they reached the spot, they could see deep prints in the muddy grass. The strides were long and the footprints were obscured by motion and mud.

"Someone was running," Ty said. He played his light over the path, peering back at the house. The tracks didn't come from the patio, but rather the corner of the wall. The same corner where Zane had seen the carved angel with its ball and chain. That proved their theory correct, but it didn't make Ty feel any better.

They followed the tracks for several yards, realizing there had been no attempt at covering them.

"If this was Nick, it's sloppy as hell," Kelly finally said. "It can't be him."

Ty didn't comment. Normally he would have agreed with Kelly; he'd never seen Nick leave a trail this obvious. But if Nick really had suffered a full-blown flashback or panic attack, who knew what state of mind he was in? The children all knew and trusted him. They would have followed him if they believed he was protecting them.

"Got blood here," Ty called. They were losing evidence to the rain quickly, and almost as soon as he'd spotted it, the blood had been washed away. The ball in Ty's stomach grew heavier when he realized the tracks were leading them directly to the cliff's edge. He picked up the pace, no longer trying to read the story the tracks were telling them. Kelly stopped and picked up something that glinted in the light of his flashlight.

"Oh God," he whispered. He held up a gold claddagh ring that Nick rarely took off. "This is his."

Ty broke into a jog, following the obvious path in the grass until they took a sharp left. Ty momentarily lost the trail, then picked it up again. The cliff's edge opened up at his side like the gaping maw of some primeval monster, angry waves crashing far below. Nick had run along the edge of the cliff.

"Was he going for the cliff?" Zane asked, sounding just as confused as Ty was.

"It's possible, I don't know."

"Could he have survived that fall?" Emma asked, sounding stunned and horrified.

"The fall, yes, if he cleared the rocks," Kelly answered. "The water, no. Not for long."

"Could he have cleared the rocks?" Zane asked.

Ty gave a helpless shrug. "I . . . I don't know. I know I couldn't."

"Why . . . why would he do this?" Emma asked.

Ty had no answer. He backtracked, trying to find some clue in the trail. He finally saw one in a patch of mud, and he bent to look closer. "There was someone else out here."

Zane came to look over his shoulder, offering the light of his flashlight as well. Ty showed them Nick's track, light and barely there in the grass. There was another, heavier print in the mud. It overlapped Nick's footprint, meaning whoever had made it had come after.

"Someone was chasing him," Emma surmised. "There was someone else up there with them."

"It's just one pair, though," Ty told them. "Nick was *running* from one guy? That doesn't seem right."

"I don't care if it's the fucking hounds of the Baskervilles!" Kelly shouted. "Nick would have stood and fought! Nothing scares Nick enough to make him run, to try to jump off a fucking cliff! Nothing!"

Ty reached out to take Kelly's arm, but the man shoved him away and pointed a finger in his face. "He came here for you, Ty! He came here because you're his brother, and he'd do anything for you!"

"I know, Doc," Ty managed to say, his voice breaking.

"You know damn well he wouldn't have left those kids unprotected, I don't care what kind of flashback he was having! And he wouldn't have run! He wouldn't have run away! He would have stood and he would have fought! You know he would have fought!"

Ty held up both hands, wanting to comfort Kelly but too confused and heartbroken to try. He didn't understand what the tracks were telling him. Everything he knew about Nick screamed the evidence was lying, because damn right Nick would have fought. Ty had seen him stand his ground in situations where even Ty wanted to duck and cover. Nick would have fought to his very last breath no matter what he was facing.

"Maybe he *would* run," Zane said after a few moments of silence.

Kelly turned on him, eyes blazing in the light of the flashlights. Thunder crashed right over them, and the skies opened up again. Zane held up a hand to avoid Kelly's angry words.

"He *would* run from someone," Zane said again. "If he was leading them *away* from something else. Something he was protecting."

Kelly stared at him for a beat, then he and Ty locked eyes as they both realized what Zane was saying.

"Nick's the one who moved the kids," Ty said quickly. "He's not pursuing someone. He took the kids. He must have been there before the shooting started."

Kelly swiped a hand over his mouth, looking down at the tracks and then to the cliff. "He must have gotten wind of something coming and didn't have time to call for help. He hid the kids, then took off running, left a trail an idiot could follow."

"Hey, *I* found that trail," Emma grunted.

Somewhere in the darkness ahead of them came three gunshots in rapid succession, then a garbled shout through the pouring rain.

"Oh Jesus," Ty breathed as he shined the weak light of his flashlight into the night.

Kelly jammed the ring onto his finger, then cupped his hands around his mouth and yelled, "Nick!"

His voice was swallowed by the pounding surf below and the downpour from above. They all waited, holding their breaths, desperate for a return call. Ty couldn't tell the difference between the beat of his heart, the sound of the surf and rain, and his desperate desire to hear his best friend's voice. All the sounds of that moment were, to his ears, Nick crying out for help.

The touch of Zane's hand to his shoulder spurred him on, and they followed the sound of the gunshots, holding to the swiftly dissolving trail, watching it zigzag like Nick had been dodging something. It came nauseatingly close to the edge at times.

The wind and rain whipped at Ty's thin shirt, whistling in his ears, stinging his eyes until they teared. He had no doubt those gunshots hadn't been heard inside the thick walls of the mansion.

They climbed the incline that led to the crumbling ruin of the lighthouse on the hill. When they hit the top of the hill, the scene before them kicked Ty's instincts into gear, and he and Kelly both threw themselves to the ground. Zane followed suit, and Kelly pulled Emma down so they wouldn't be seen.

A man stood at the very edge of the jagged cliff, holding something bundled in a white blanket that practically glowed in the moonlight. Ty could tell it was Nick merely by the set of his shoulders. Another man stood with his back to them, pointing a gun at Nick.

"Give me the kid, and no one gets hurt," the man with the gun shouted into the wind. His accent was Scottish.

Ty's breath left him in a rush. "Amelia," he gasped. Nick was holding Amelia, clutching her to his chest to protect her.

If Nick said anything, his response was lost in the wind.

"I don't need her alive!" the gunman shouted. "I just need pieces of her to send to her granddaddy!"

Zane grabbed at Ty's arm and back, trying to keep him from getting up, but Zane wasn't fast enough. Ty lunged to his feet and charged the man. He hit him from behind. The gun went off as Ty and the gunman tumbled to the ground.

Ty rolled several feet away, flattening out in time to see Nick, his side bloodied by the stray shot, lose his balance and fall over the edge of the cliff with Amelia in his arms. Ty scrambled to his feet and dove toward the edge of the cliff, grasping desperately. His fingers found Nick's, and their hands clasped together, the momentum dragging Ty several feet in the wet grass and ripping something apart inside his shoulder. He dug his toes in, managing to stop their slide. He wound up with his chest at the edge of the cliff, his shoulders and head hanging over, and his fingers wrapped around Nick's forearm.

Nick hung from one arm, grasping Ty's wrist in an iron grip. He swung freely over the jagged rocks and the frigid ocean below. A teddy bear fell away from his other hand, the white blanket fluttering after it. Nick watched them fall, then grimaced up at Ty.

"Give me your other hand!" Ty shouted.

Nick reached up and fumbled for Ty's other hand, but when he moved and his weight shifted, Ty began to slide again. The earth beneath him was soft and muddy, the grass wet.

Nick cried out in pain and dropped his hand, shaking his head. "Let go, Ty!"

"Fuck you! Find a foothold until we get help!"

Nick tried to reach out for the cliff's inverted face, but as soon as he moved, Ty slid yet again. The cliff was too far away for him to touch it, much less grab for anything solid.

"Ty!" Nick shouted. "We'll both fall if you don't let go!"

Ty shook his head, flat out refusing to accept that. He tried to pull Nick up, but his separated shoulder screamed even when he flexed his muscles in preparation for moving. He felt a hand at his belt, heard Emma shouting at him.

Ty opened his eyes again, meeting Nick's. "I can't lift you, you're going to have to climb."

"I can't climb," Nick said through gritted teeth. Even hanging by a thread over certain death, he sounded annoyed with Ty for being an idiot.

"Try!" Ty shouted.

"I can't climb if you're the thing I'm climbing because you're not attached to anything! Fucker!"

"Try it anyway, Jesus Christ!"

Nick made one more attempt to reach for Ty with his other hand, but it merely pulled Ty closer to the edge. Gravity tugged at him, taunting him, beckoning him toward the sea as the top half of his body slid over the sloped edge. The earth beneath him began to crumble, falling into Nick's face and hair.

Nick shook it away. He looked back up, meeting Ty's eyes. He sounded calm when he spoke. "Let go, Ty."

"I'm not letting go," Ty told him. "I'm not."

"Don't make me be the reason you die," Nick growled. He relaxed his fingers, leaving Ty to cling to him alone.

Ty let out a whimper as he tightened his hold. "Don't do this to me, Nick, please don't."

"Let go."

Ty shook his head.

"Let go!"

"No! I have help, they're coming! Just hold on!" Even as he spoke, though, he could feel himself slipping. Where the fuck were Zane and Kelly? He shouted over the roar of the ocean, "Help!"

Nick reached down, fumbling for his belt.

"What are you doing?" Ty asked.

He pulled a knife from a sheath, looking up at Ty with a grim smile.

"Don't you do it," Ty said. "Don't you stab me, you fucker!"

Nick flicked the knife over his fingers, the blade catching the reflection of a streak of lightning.

"Zane! Doc!" Ty shouted. He shook his head at Nick. "Don't you fucking dare stab me with that knife!" He tried to slither backward, desperate to get more purchase in the ground, to hold Nick there until more of the others came to their aid. Emma didn't weigh enough to keep them from going over the edge.

Nick's green eyes were unreadable, the knife in his hand. Ty shook his head. "I gave you that knife for your birthday, you motherfucker!"

Nick made one last lunge, swiping the knife through the air, aiming for Ty's forearm, aiming to create a scar that Ty would carry in his nightmares for the rest of his life. The motion of his body pulled Ty even closer to the edge, and Ty squeezed his eyes closed because he would be damned if he let go when that knife sank in.

He wasn't letting go.

Zane heard a sickening crunch when Ty made contact with the man. He didn't know if it was Ty's bones breaking or the other man's, but the way the man sprawled told Zane those cracked bones probably belonged to him. The gun went off when Ty hit him, then again when he hit the ground. Zane felt a bullet whiz between himself and Kelly, narrowly missing both of them. Neither man took cover, though. They both bolted forward to attack.

Zane grabbed the gun as it skidded across the wet grass and backed away to train it on the mystery attacker. He needn't have bothered because Kelly pounced on the man, hitting him over and over until his knuckles were bloody and raw and the man was nearly unrecognizable.

"Kelly!" Zane shouted, moving closer as Kelly continued the thrashing.

"You mess with my fucking team!" Kelly shouted. He grabbed the man's shirt and pulled him off the ground, throwing himself into the next punch. "Chase him off a fucking cliff and think that can kill him!" He threw another brutal punch, then pulled him up and put their faces close together. There was no way the man was conscious. He gurgled as he breathed. His eyes rolled into the back of his head.

"Doc!" Zane shouted.

Kelly sneered at the killer, and he hissed when he spoke. "I'll show you how we deal with your kind, you sniveling little son of a bitch."

Zane stuffed the gun in the back of his belt and went to pull Kelly off the man before he could beat him to death. Kelly tried to break from Zane's grasp, but Zane shouted at him. "We have to help Ty and Nick!"

Kelly stopped struggling immediately, and his head whipped around. It was then that Zane noticed Ty stretched out, hanging over the edge of the cliff. Emma had Ty's belt in her hands, pulling with all her might. Zane could see her boots creating furrows in the grass as they slid over.

Zane and Kelly both scrambled to the cliff. Zane threw himself over Ty's back, hoping his weight would slow the inexorable pull of gravity. They got there just in time to see Nick draw his knife. Kelly reached over the edge, catching Nick's forearm with his hand before Nick could strike.

Kelly yanked the knife out of his hand and tossed it into the night. He grabbed his arm with both hands. Ty screamed in pain when he tried to help, but neither man let go. Zane slid his arms under Ty's and used him as if he were a rope. The three of them worked together to pull Ty and Nick from the brink.

Once Ty was on solid ground, Zane let go of him and grabbed at Nick's shirt, then his belt, helping Kelly haul him over. Nick scrabbled at the wet grass, looking for purchase, but he never found it. He and Ty both would have gone over for sure.

When they got far enough away from the cliff, Nick sprawled on his back, breathing hard. Kelly fell onto his ass and put a hand on Nick's stomach, laughing in relief. But Zane crawled toward the edge, his panic enough to override his fear of heights. "Did Amelia fall?" he cried.

"It wasn't her," Ty groaned. He was rolling around in the grass, holding his right arm. "It was a decoy." He sat up, wincing. Some of those cracking bones had obviously belonged to him. He glared over at Nick, who was on his back, a hand held to his stomach. "Asshole!"

Nick responded with a weak laugh. Kelly knelt next to him and shined his flashlight on his torso. His shirt was bloodied and torn.

"Is he okay?" Zane asked.

Kelly shook his head and shoved his flashlight into Zane's hands. "He'll be fine. We need to get him inside though."

Ty crawled closer. "Is he conscious?"

Kelly tapped his fingers against Nick's cheek.

"Quit it, Jesus Christ." Nick swatted at Kelly's hand.

"Yeah, he's conscious," Kelly answered.

Ty leaned over him. "Where are the kids, Irish?"

"I found a place to stash them," Nick answered. His words were a little slurred. "Gave the oldest one a gun and told him to shoot the next person who came around the corner."

"What happened?" Zane asked.

Nick lifted his head, looking at the man Kelly had beaten half to death. "Guy took out the Snake Eater at the door, sent the nanny in for Amelia. The oldest boy wouldn't let her get to her; that's when I walked in." Kelly took Nick's arm and helped him to his feet. They all clambered off the wet ground and moved further away from the treacherous edge of the cliff, going to stand over the groaning form of Nick's attacker.

"It's Jockie Fraser," Ty said, eyes wide.

"Who the hell is that?" Emma asked.

"The groundskeeper."

"Wait, so the groundskeeper and the nanny?" Kelly asked. "This is an island thing and not a Snake Eater thing? Damn it!"

"You owe me twenty bucks," Nick told him.

"Fucker!" Ty shouted as he tore his eyes away from Fraser to look at Nick again. Zane could see the warning signs coming. Ty grabbed Nick's shirt, heedless of either of their injuries, and shook him. "You tried to stab me so I'd let you go!"

"I would have taken you with me, Ty!"

"Stab me so I'd let you fall!" Ty shouted, not appearing to hear anything anyone else was saying as Kelly and Emma both tried to calm them. Zane moved forward, putting a hand on Ty's shoulder that Ty didn't even notice. "Don't you fucking remember the last time?"

"Yeah, I remember shoving a friend off a cliff to save your life!" Nick cried. He pushed away from Ty, holding his bloody side.

"Stupid, selfish fucking son of a bitch!" Ty took a swing before Zane could stop him, catching Nick under the chin.

Nick staggered backward into Kelly, who barely managed to catch him and keep him on his feet.

Zane lunged, wrapping his arms around Ty before it could turn messier. Ty was breathing hard, almost gasping for every breath, and he was very nearly sobbing. Zane placed himself between the two of them. Ty rested his chin on Zane's shoulder, then lowered his head, and Zane hugged him close, not sure what else to do for him but make sure he didn't try to hit anyone else.

Nick had his hands on his knees, apparently trying to shake the cobwebs after Ty's punch. Zane knew what a sucker punch from Ty felt like. Not many men could come back from one, certainly not quickly. Nick's angry face was highlighted by a streak of lightning that hit too close for comfort. The rain was still torrential, obscuring their vision, making it hard to hear.

"Do you have any idea what it would do to us if you fell?" Ty shouted at Nick, his voice breaking. "What it would do to me?"

Nick shook his head, looking wobbly. He hadn't tried to straighten up yet. He fell to his knees, and before Kelly could grab him, he tumbled face-first into the grass.

Kelly knelt beside him, a hand on his cheek. "Well, that's just fucking great, Ty!"

Zane held Ty tighter. His entire body was trembling. It was like trying to hold on to a bolt of pure energy.

"What about the kids?" Emma shouted over the sound of the storm and the crashing waves below.

"Those kids could be anywhere. How the hell are we going to find them before someone else does?" Zane snarled. He pointed at Fraser. "We all know there are more people on the island working with that asshole."

"Oh God," Ty whispered. He was apparently just realizing that he'd knocked unconscious the only man on the island who might know where the kids were hidden.

Amelia might not have been Zane's blood, but he still considered her his niece. She was somewhere in danger, being hunted by ruthless people who'd already killed to get to her, and they were all helpless to find her.

"Ty," Zane grunted. "We have to go find Amelia. Doc and Emma will take care of Nick. Come on."

Ty met his eyes, nodding dazedly. He turned his attention back to Kelly. "Where would Nick stash them?"

"He said he didn't know," Kelly snapped. "Maybe if he was conscious he could lead us there!"

"If he was going on instinct, where would he have gone?"

"I . . . I don't know," Kelly stammered. "There's so many places inside those walls he'd . . . it has to be the basement. He always took his sisters to the basement when his dad was drunk. He'd have gone down until he couldn't go anymore, then he would have hid them. Anything underground. Look underground."

Ty gave a curt nod. "Okay. It's a start." He looked down at Nick one last time, hesitating. "Tell him I'm sorry when he wakes."

Kelly glanced up, glaring briefly. "Tell him yourself."

Zane pulled Ty away before he could respond. They turned to hurry back to the mansion, but Kelly called after them.

"He always booby-trapped the stairs! Be careful! Think like Nick!"

Ty groaned. "Think like Nick. I'm going to fucking die in Scotland."

CHAPTER 11

When they approached the front door of the mansion, the feeling of foreboding once again crept into Zane and settled in his stomach. This time, though, he was pretty sure he had a good reason for it.

They slowed as they came to the door, left ajar to reveal the gaping black hole of the interior. Both of them took out the weapons they'd stolen from the Snake Eaters, checking that they were loaded, making sure the safeties were off. It was something they'd done a hundred times before, maybe a thousand times: readying themselves to head into danger, taking that last moment to prepare. As partners. Sometimes side by side, sometimes with only a voice on an earpiece to let Zane know Ty was with him.

Zane glanced at Ty, who was shoving the clip back into his gun. They would never be partners again. The realization hit Zane hard. Ty met his eyes.

"I love you," Zane said quietly.

Ty stared at him for a few breaths. "Should I ask you to marry me now?"

Zane couldn't stop himself from grinning, but he shook his head. "Ask me after we live through this."

Ty stepped closer and placed a gentle hand on the back of Zane's neck as he kissed him. "I love you too," he whispered.

"You find Amelia," Zane said, his voice hoarse when Ty moved away. "I'll go for Stanton, make sure he's safe. He's probably the next target."

Ty nodded, and they headed into the house.

In a few steps, Ty was gone, vanished into the darkness. It was a not-so-gentle reminder of what his lover was capable of, but it comforted Zane in ways he didn't want to examine too closely.

He made his way to the dining room, where he could see the flickering light of the fireplace, candles, and hurricane lamps. He lowered his gun when he stepped into the room.

Earl was sitting in a dining chair facing the doorway, a rifle aimed at Zane. He lowered it and nodded to him, setting the weapon across his legs again.

Zane gave the room a quick glance.

Mara sat with her arm around Susan Stanton, who was crying quietly. Mara's cheek had been roughly bandaged. Several others appeared to have been wounded by the falling glass. They needed to get Kelly in here to tend to them.

Stanton sat with his son, Theo, their heads bowed over a table as they spoke quietly. They were examining a map or blueprint, making marks on it. A dozen other guests were huddled around dining tables, some with blankets or coats wrapped over their shoulders, others conversing quietly or simply staring at Zane.

The Snake Eaters were gone.

"Where's English and his boys?" Zane asked Earl.

"Did you find the kids?" Earl asked.

"No."

Earl's shoulders slumped. He looked older than he usually did, but the shadows from the fire did odd things to people's appearances. "Stanton ordered them to search the house for Amelia. He told them her safety was more important to him than his own, so they went out."

"Shit," Zane hissed. "Ty's off looking too; if they run into each other there's going to be some—"

"Blood," Earl provided wryly.

Zane grunted.

"I figure if Stanton's a target, then you're looking at last line of defense," Earl said with a tap to his chest. "We found this rifle on the wall above the fireplace. It's loaded, but I don't even know if it'll fire."

"You have a knife?" Zane asked. Earl nodded and patted his hip.

Stanton had noticed Zane there and was making his way to them. "Did you find Nick?" Earl asked.

Zane nodded, waiting until Stanton and Theo joined them. "He interrupted the nanny and the groundskeeper trying to kidnap Amelia. He stopped them, and sent the kids into the passages within the walls. He hid them somewhere inside the walls and then ran as a decoy for Fraser." He met Stanton's eyes. "Did you know those passages were there?"

"Yes, we used to play in them when I was a boy," Stanton answered. He was nearly mumbling, frowning so hard his eyebrows were touching. "Jockie Fraser? I've known him since he was little. He was Theo's playmate on the island during the summers when we'd visit."

"Jockie did this?" Theo asked, looking horrified. It was the first time Zane had seen the man with any sort of expression. "I don't believe it."

"We caught him with a gun, threatening to send *pieces* of Amelia to your father. Believe it," Zane growled.

Theo and Stanton both blanched. Zane could hear Earl growling, and he took a deep breath, sorely tempted to go off the rails with them and rage about the threat to the little girl. Others had drifted closer, listening in, probably wanting to know if they were safe now, if it was all over. Zane looked over them and raised his voice to be heard.

"Nick couldn't tell us where he stashed the kids, so it's simply a matter of finding them before anyone else does now. Who else knew about the walls?"

"My wife. Some of the older staff. We never told the kids when they were little, we were afraid they'd play in them and get hurt or lost. Frankly, I'd forgotten about them. What about Jockie? Did he talk? Tell you who else is involved?" Stanton asked.

"He's not capable of much of anything right now," Zane admitted. "But when he is, we'll get everything we need out of him, I can guarantee you that."

Hamish Boyd, the butler Zane had only met the day he arrived, forced his way through the crowd. He used a cane to do it, shoving at people with it to clear his path. "Did I hear you say Jockie and Maisie are responsible for this?"

Zane met the old man's eyes. He'd lost his wife to this ordeal, possibly the greatest loss of anyone on the island. Zane wasn't sure how to answer him.

"How were two locals connected to the bodyguard lady?" Earl asked. "Or the maid of honor?"

"We don't know yet," Zane answered, mirroring their growing frustration with his own. "All we know is the target, and that is the information Mr. Stanton is protecting."

There was a ruckus from several of the people standing in front of Zane, and when Zane looked over his shoulder, Kelly, Nick, and Emma were there, Jockie Fraser supported between Nick and Kelly. He was unconscious. And very, very bloody. Kelly had really worked him over. Zane was beginning to see the doc in a new light.

"Has he said anything?" Zane demanded.

Kelly shook his head. Nick didn't much look like he should be supporting anyone's weight at this point, not even his own, and Emma was having a hard time helping him. They cleared off one of the dining tables, and Zane helped Kelly heft Fraser onto it as Emma and Earl guided Nick to a chair.

Earl came up beside Zane and looked down at the unconscious Scot on the table, then around at the people gathered and gawking. "Someone get some rope."

Ty took the steps two at a time, racing up to the third-floor nursery. Every step jarred his shoulder, but he knew putting the damn thing back in by himself would just risk permanent damage. He was out of breath and his arm was on fire by the time he reached the door. Deuce and Livi both stood when they heard him coming, their eyes wide and hopeful. They clung to each other as Ty stepped into the room.

"Anything?" Deuce asked.

"We found Nick. He's the one who took the kids. He hid them to keep them safe."

"Why?" Livi asked.

"He heard the nanny here trying to take Amelia. She was working with the groundskeeper."

"Jockie?" Livi asked in horror. "But Maisie and Jockie have lived on this island all their lives! Her mother was my nanny, and his father was the groundskeeper before him. We played with them when we were little."

"I don't know the whys," Ty said impatiently. "I don't have any answers yet. All I know is Nick couldn't tell us where he hid the kids, just that he did, and then he went running to lead Fraser away from them. I need to get into the walls and find them."

Livi glanced at the entryway, gaping open beside the fireplace. "Daddy's men went in there ten minutes ago to look. They said my dad insisted."

Ty jerked toward the opening, alarm streaking through him. One Snake Eater had already been proven to be a traitor. And one Snake Eater was dead. How the hell could they trust any of the ones left?

"What's that look, Ty?" Deuce asked.

Ty met his brother's eyes. "I don't know who the fuck to trust out here. I'm at the 'shoot first and feel bad later' stage."

Deuce nodded, then brought Livi's hand up to his lips and kissed it. "I'm coming with you."

Ty thought about arguing, but he knew from the look in Deuce's eyes that he'd never keep him out of those passages. His baby girl was in there. Ty nodded. "You take the flashlight. I'll take the gun."

Livi held on to Deuce's hand when he took a step toward the fireplace. "I'm coming too!"

Ty stopped and watched them, eyebrows raised.

Deuce opened his mouth to protest, but Livi pointed her finger in his face. "Don't you tell me I can't come 'cause I'm a girl. I'm smaller and more mobile than either of you; you might need me in those passages."

"I wasn't going to say you can't come because you're a girl," Deuce said soothingly. He reached into the passage and grabbed a handful of spiderwebs, complete with desiccated bugs and one very pissed-off spider. He held it up to her face. "I was going to say you can't come because of this."

Livi barely restrained a scream, but she did manage to smack Deuce in the face before hopping away and doing a little "get it off me" dance. "Fine!" she cried.

"Head downstairs so you're not alone," Deuce told her, then followed Ty as he ducked into the passage, aiming his powerful flashlight toward the curving stone steps near the exterior wall of the house.

Ty could already feel himself panicking a little over the closeness of the walls.

"You going to be okay in here?" Deuce asked softly.

Ty nodded. "If a bunch of kids can follow a crazy guy with a Boston accent and a gun down here, I can do this."

Deuce chuckled almost desperately. When they got to the stairs and Deuce pointed the light down, Ty's breath left him in a rush. It was so narrow they would both have to turn sideways to get down it. Ty's shoulders might not even fit. He certainly couldn't lead with his gun. "You've got to be five-finger fucking me," Ty muttered.

Deuce patted him encouragingly. If his brother could be calm and supportive when his toddler was down here, in danger, with nothing but a ten-year-old with a gun and this maze of darkness to protect her, then Ty could deal with his claustrophobia.

He started down the steps, cussing the entire way, scraping rock and dust off the walls with his shoulders, wondering if it would be easier just to miss a step and ride down the damn things like a slide at a waterpark. It was certainly steep enough. The walls were so tight Deuce didn't even have trouble with his bad leg. All he had to do was flex his arms and the walls held him in place as he took each torturous step.

It seemed like an eternity until they reached the next floor. The passages went off in three directions. They followed the outer walls, but also went into the heart of the house, probably between two bedrooms.

Deuce shone the light down each passage, cursing under his breath.

"He'd have kept going down until they couldn't go anymore," Ty said, echoing Kelly's advice.

"Why do you think that?"

"Because it's Nick. Nick always took his sisters to the basement to protect them from his dad. Then he'd go back up and push his dad's buttons so he'd be the target instead of them. It's the way he works."

Deuce was silent, nodding sadly. They continued down the winding stairs. Ty had to take deep breaths to keep himself calm, but whenever he did, he'd get mouthfuls of dust, cobwebs, and musty air. He had to fight not to start coughing and alert anyone to their presence. Concentrating on the struggle was the only thing keeping him from panicking.

Eventually they'd have to start making noise, calling out for the kids, risking unfriendlies being drawn to them. The Snake Eaters were down here somewhere, and friend or foe, if they startled those men, blood would be spilled. Ty wanted to go under the radar for as long as possible.

When they finally reached the bottom of the staircase, there were only two passages to choose from: right or left. Ty should have been able to breathe a sigh of relief, but there wasn't enough room in the subterranean hallways to even puff out his chest. He closed his eyes, bringing his gun up to rest the cool barrel against the bridge of his nose.

"You okay?" Deuce asked, his whisper harsh in Ty's ear.

Ty nodded and swallowed past the knot of panic in his throat. "Okay, Nick would have been leading them, acting on instinct," he muttered, trying to put himself into the mind-set Nick must have been in. He'd rather be in Nick's mind-set than his own right now anyway.

"Is he a lefty or a righty?" Deuce asked.

"Lefty, why?"

"Given no time to think it through, he'd go with his dominant side. He'd choose left."

Ty raised an eyebrow, and Deuce shined the light toward his chest so they could see each other.

Deuce nodded. "Trust me. Go left."

Ty picked the left passage and they hurried down it, trying to be silent and listen. Water dripped, and some unidentifiable banging sound echoed in the distance. It could have been the pipes of the old house, or someone moving on the main level above them, or even the Snake Eaters down here searching.

When they reached another intersection, the space opened up. It looked as if they were nearing an older part of the house, or maybe even tunnels that predated the mansion. Ty instructed Deuce to shine a light on the stone, and when he did, they stared at it with matching frowns. There was a jagged line of mismatched masonry. The bottom half was smooth, gray stone, worn with time and put together with such precision and skill that no mortar had been used. The top was a mixture of darker rock and brick and mortar.

"This looks like ruins from that castle," Deuce said, running his hand over the bottom half of the stone.

"Oh God. If this was part of the castle complex, these tunnels could go all over the island. Livi said there were lava tubes and caves. They would have used those to connect these things."

Deuce put a hand over his mouth, shaking his head.

A wave of desperation and fury swept over Ty. He was completely powerless to do anything to help his brother, or any of the people he loved, right now. He had rarely experienced that kind of helplessness, and he didn't know how to deal with it. "Nick couldn't have taken them far in the time he was down here; they have to be close."

"What if they got tired or impatient? What if something scared them and they moved?"

"I'll get her back, Deacon. I swear to you."

Deuce just nodded, still covering his mouth.

A voice echoed off the damp walls, and Ty grabbed Deuce's shoulder and pushed him against the wall, flattening himself beside his brother at the corner of the intersection.

"Should have been marking these fucking walls!" someone was saying.

"We're never getting out of here," another voice commented, sounding calm and collected despite his prophecy of doom.

The echoes made it impossible to tell, but Ty thought it sounded like English and Frost.

He whistled low to get their attention. Their shuffling footsteps halted, and everything went silent. A light played over the walls.

"Identify yourself," English finally called.

"It's Grady." Ty didn't step into sight, though. He handed his gun to Deuce and put his finger to his lips. Deuce nodded. "Did you find her?"

"No. We didn't realize how fucking big these tunnels were down here," English answered. "Thank Christ you're here, though, do you know where we are?"

"Yeah, I can lead you out." Ty put one hand out into the passage to let them know where he was, then carefully stepped out into the light of their flashlights. The three remaining Snake Eaters all looked relieved to see him. None of them made an untoward move, but then, he hadn't told them where they were yet so it didn't ease Ty's suspicions.

"We'll help you keep looking for her," Frost offered.

Ty nodded, both grateful and still wary. He pointed the way he'd come. "We're a straight shot from the stairs up. That way. If you need to get out. Small spaces, man." He patted his chest, then held his breath, waiting to see if they'd make a move or if they were on the up-and-up.

English came forward, his light aimed toward the ground. "Got anything to mark it with when we come back this way?"

Ty breathed a sigh of relief. He wasn't going to be turning his back on these men anytime soon, especially not with one arm out of commission, but at least for now they'd passed his test. He bent and picked up a small rock, marking on the wall with it. It made a faint chalky line on the stone. Ty did it again harder, trying to make sure they'd see it.

"I can't go back up those stairs," English said to Frost and Park. He indicated his massive shoulders and arms. "I damn near got stuck coming down them. Maybe we can find an exit on this level."

"The kitchen has an exit," Deuce said. He turned his flashlight back on and handed Ty his gun. English and Frost both jumped when he spoke, then calmed immediately when they realized it was him. Riddle Park didn't seem surprised, though. He was hanging back, probably for the same reasons Deuce had been. Ty met English's eyes, shrugging.

"I hear you, man," English said. "Can't be too careful."

"Especially since Kline . . ." Frost glanced from Ty to Deuce.

"This was her first run with the company," Park told them. "She wasn't us."

English was nodding. "She's on me and I'll take responsibility for that. If you don't want to trust us, I don't blame you. But these fuckers killed Hardin, and he was our brother. We want this. We've got your back on this, Sidewinder."

Ty stared into his eyes and saw nothing but truth and anger and pain. "I'm sorry for your loss. He died protecting five young lives. Man's a hero."

"Yes he is."

Ty filled them in on what they'd learned, and where they should be searching for Amelia and the other children.

"What about bringing O'Flaherty down here?" Frost asked. "Can't he lead us to them? Is he okay?"

Ty winced, hesitant to admit he had knocked their only solid lead unconscious during a fit of anger. "He was wounded, but when he wakes he'll be the first one down here searching. The problem is he said he was going so fast, he's not sure he knows where they are. He also said he gave the oldest boy a gun, so we need to be careful."

"Are there any more Tangos to be worried about here?" Frost asked.

"We don't know. Fraser's alive," Ty answered. "So we'll get it out of him. But we have to assume someone else was leading this thing. To be able to reach your girl and turn her, it couldn't be a local in charge."

"Guys," Deuce said, his voice shaking. "Can we please find my baby girl?"

Ty gripped Deuce's shoulder and squeezed. "We'll stick together, when we come to a split, we'll divide into groups. Cover more ground that way."

"Why not just call to them if they're down here?" Frost asked.

"If someone's down here looking for them and they answer our calls, there's no guarantee we get to them first," English answered before Ty could respond. "We should look first."

Ty nodded and glanced at Deuce again. "That's your call, bud."

"That's my baby girl out there. I'm not letting anyone get to her before I do. We'll look for them."

Ty gave him a curt nod. He hadn't expected any other answer. He turned to English and the others. "What did you see the way you came from?"

"There are storage rooms," Frost answered. "Some of them look like they were once jail cells."

Ty and Deuce shared a look. "Definitely part of the castle complex," Deuce grumbled.

"Castle?" English asked. "It's on the other side of the island."

Ty nodded. "You see our problem."

"Son of a bitch," English snarled.

"What information do we need right now?" Kelly asked Zane. When Fraser had regained consciousness, they'd tied him to a dining chair, and Earl was now standing with a shotgun aimed at his face.

"We need to know how many, and who. The whys and hows can come later," Zane whispered. He was watching Kelly work, fascinated. Kelly was patching Nick's side up, with Nick laid out on a table, his face turned away from them. The bullet had grazed him, skipping off a rib. It had been just enough to knock him over the edge of the cliff and draw blood, but it hadn't done any permanent damage. Kelly had cleaned it and was using some sort of skin glue from his medical kit to close it up.

"As soon as we get what we need from him, I'm going into the walls to find Ty," Zane told them. "He's been gone too long, something's wrong."

"The passages open up when you go down a level," Nick said, his voice having returned to his usual soothing, sedate tone. "It's a maze down there, natural caves and lava tubes mixed with man-made tunnels and rooms. They probably go all the way over to the castle ruins."

Zane felt the blood draining from his face. That was a lot of territory to cover. "Can you find those kids, O'Flaherty?" Zane asked, his voice coming out rougher and more accusatory than he'd intended.

Nick turned his head and met Zane's eyes. "Yes."

He sat up when Kelly was done. Kelly had cut his tattered shirt off him, so there was nothing for him to put back on. His green eyes were hard when they landed on Jockie Fraser, and his jaw was set. "Give me five minutes with him first."

Zane looked from Nick to their prisoner, who was staring at them with wide eyes. Earl glanced over his shoulder when he heard Nick's words. He met Zane's eyes, then nodded. They'd already tried asking him questions. It hadn't been very effective, with Fraser repeatedly refusing to answer and demanding legal counsel. It was time for a new tack.

Earl and Zane picked Fraser's chair up, carrying him between them into the game room next door, where the billiards table took up most of the space. Nick followed them, still shirtless. He grabbed a towel from behind the bar and threw it over his shoulder, then he sat to unlace his shoes and pull them off.

"What's he doing?" Fraser asked when they set his chair down, eyes still wide. Earl checked his bonds, refusing to answer.

Nick took one of his socks off, then stood and strolled over to the billiard table. He glanced over at Fraser as he reached into one of the pockets, then pulled one of the billiard balls out and dropped it into his sock. His expression stayed completely blank the entire time.

Fraser began to shake his head. "You're insane. You can't do this!"

"This can be avoided if you tell us what we need to know," Zane said. "Who paid you?"

Fraser glared at Zane. His hawklike nose was badly broken and his eyes were swelling shut from the beating Kelly had given him.

"Start talking, Fraser, or I let him at you," Zane said with a jerk of his head at Nick.

"You're bluffing," Fraser spat.

Zane shrugged. "I may be." He glanced over his shoulder at Nick, who was standing and staring at Fraser with the same dead-eyed expression he'd awoken with. "But he's not."

Earl patted Zane on the shoulder and headed for the door. Zane lingered, giving Fraser a last chance to talk and watching Nick with a sinking feeling in his stomach. Nick met his eyes, letting the heavy billiard ball swing in its sock, demonstrating just how effective it would be as a weapon.

Fraser jutted his abused chin out, refusing to speak again.

Zane didn't say anything more before retreating through the door. When he turned to pull it shut, he got a glimpse of Nick standing in front of Jockie Fraser, his feet shoulder-width apart, his bare back covered with a Celtic cross tattoo that followed his spine from the base of his neck to the small of his back. Three whiplike scars crisscrossed his muscular back and shoulders. The makeshift ball and chain hung from his hand, swaying as Nick wrapped the end around his fingers.

Zane lowered his head and pulled the door shut before the first scream could tear through the great hall.

Ty turned the corner and almost smacked into a brick wall before Deuce could follow with the flashlight. He held his arm, trying to keep it from throbbing as they stood in the dead end of the corridor, fuming and desperate.

"Backtrack," Ty murmured, and they made their way back to the last intersecting corridor. Ty made a large X on the wall, and they continued to retrace their steps.

"Will you let me at least tie your arm down?" Deuce asked.

"I need it. It's fine," Ty insisted, and he slid his hand into his waistband as a makeshift sling.

They met up with the other three at what Ty had deemed the crossroads, a large section of tunnel that appeared to have been cut from a natural cavern.

"Anything?" Deuce asked the others. They all answered with negatives, and they all looked sympathetic to Deuce's increasing desperation.

"We'll find her," Frost assured him. He even put a hand on Deuce's arm to offer him a little comfort.

Ty ran his hand through his hair, sucking in a ragged breath as the walls edged closer and closer to him. The weight of the earth pressed down from above. Even though he knew they were no longer under the mansion, they were still under tons and tons of dirt. What if they were under the hill? What if the lighthouse ruins were up there, weighing down, crumbling, threatening the integrity of the stonework?

"Oh God," he whispered, grasping at his chest.

"Ty?"

"I can't breathe, man. We need to double-time this."

"What's going on?" English asked.

"He's claustrophobic," Deuce told the others.

"So let's fucking call for them and get out of here."

Ty shook his head, but he looked at Deuce almost desperately.

Deuce met his eyes in the light of the flashlights, his jaw jumping. "You promise me you'll get to them first."

Ty took a deep breath. "We'll get to them, Deacon, I swear to you. I swear."

Deuce handed Ty his flashlight and stepped toward one of the tunnels, cupping his hands around his mouth and calling out for the kids. His voice shook as it echoed through the tunnels.

Each man held his breath, waiting. The blood was beginning to roar in Ty's ears when a small voice echoed along the corridor. Deuce gasped.

"Go!" Ty whispered harshly. He pointed at English. "Go, go!"

The three men started down the corridor in pursuit of the child's call. Ty took a moment from his panic to admire their precision. He really hoped none of them turned out to be bad guys, because he liked all three men, and he hated killing people he liked.

Deuce tugged Ty's good arm. "Come on, Ty, hold on a little longer."

Ty ran with him, helping Deuce on his bad leg and relying on his brother to lead him through the obscure, cramped spaces.

A silenced gunshot boomed through the passages ahead of them, followed by shouts and cries that seemed to echo and multiply. Deuce cursed and quickened their pace. Ty had no idea how his leg was keeping up. He supposed the concern of a parent overrode everything else. Their flashlight bounced off beams from the Snake Eaters' lights, and they came upon all three men taking cover at an intersecting passage. The muffled wailing of a baby came from around the corner.

"Who's shooting?" Ty called.

"Kid shot at us when we tried to open the door," Frost answered. "They're locked up in a room, looks like an old root cellar."

Ty glanced at Deuce and nodded for him to go around the corner. "Call out, tell them who you are."

"Cooper! It's Deacon, buddy, we're here to take you back. Open the door, okay?"

Ty heard the boy's muffled response through the hole he'd shot in the thick door. "Nick told me not to open the door unless someone gave us the password! You might be with someone who's making you say it's okay!"

Deuce looked back at Ty, eyebrows raised.

"Goddamn it, Nick," Ty grunted. He closed his eyes against the thought of the narrow passages pressing down on him. "Fucking password."

"Smart kid," English said. He was still crouching against the wall, his gun and flashlight in his hands, his large body stooped and hunched to fit into the narrow corridor.

Ty closed his eyes. He was beginning to hyperventilate, struggling for the breath to stay calm, to keep his mind clear. He'd never make it out of these fucking tunnels if he didn't leave soon. Now. They had to get those kids out and moving right now. "Cooper, open the door!" he shouted. "It's Ty and Deacon, kid, we need to get you back to your parents!"

"What's the password?" Cooper shouted back.

"Damn it," Ty hissed.

"That's not it!"

Frost and Park both covered their mouths to muffle their laughter.

Deuce took Ty's good arm. "Come on, Ty, you know Nick better than anyone. What fucking password would he give these kids?"

Ty shook his head, gasping for breath. He groped at the stone walls, searching for something solid. Cool and solid and immovable. Something strong enough to hold up the thousands of pounds of dirt and rock above them. "Oh God."

Deuce grabbed him and pulled him toward the door, grasping Ty's face in both hands. "Breathe, brother, come on. Calm your mind. Think. *Please*, Ty, my baby is in there."

They could hear Amelia wailing inside the room. The gunshot had come from the silenced weapon Nick had taken off the nanny, but it had still probably been incredibly loud and frightening in that enclosed rock room.

Enclosed and locked.

Enclosed, locked, and under tons and tons of rock.

Ty rested his forehead against the thick wooden door and fought the urge to be sick. Deuce's hand was on his shoulder, squeezing, keeping him grounded, but his head was swirling with panic and terror.

What word would Nick give them? One word to let them know they were safe. One word he would trust someone else to say to them in his absence, since he'd fully expected to be killed or at least maimed by Fraser when he left them. One word. One word that, in Nick's mind, meant everything.

Ty took in a deep breath. "Oohrah."

Zane and Kelly sat together on a bench seat in the great hall, watching the door to the game room in silence. The walls were so thick, they couldn't really hear anything from inside. Zane was thankful for that much.

"I should be down there helping look for Amelia," Zane insisted.

"You should be right here," Kelly said. "When Nick gets answers, we'll need you here. Ty's a big boy, he can handle himself."

Zane glanced at him, trying to convince himself Kelly was right. If Fraser gave them information, Zane was the only one who had enough pieces of the puzzle to do anything with it.

He cleared his throat. "*When* Nick gets answers. You really think he'll be able to?"

"Nick has extensive experience with, uh . . . enhanced interrogation techniques," Kelly said, his voice flat.

"What?"

"The alternative set of procedures?" Kelly said, turning his head to meet Zane's eyes. He wasn't smiling.

"What the fuck are you talking about?"

"Torture. Nick was trained to torture." Kelly returned his gaze to the door, his expression unchanging.

Zane stared at his profile for several seconds before turning his attention back to the door.

Darkness had fully set in, but they'd lit every fireplace, candle, hurricane lamp, and lantern they could gather. It made the mansion feel truly gothic, with flames flickering everywhere, shadows being cast in all directions, and the fireplaces crackling and giving off enough warmth to make walking into a room feel like coming in out of the cold.

Zane would have really enjoyed a blackout like this, in a place like this, if it weren't for all the dead bodies piling up in the freezer.

There was a bang and crash from the kitchen, and voices began to echo up the steps. Zane and Kelly both stood and started toward the stairwell, shining flashlights down and holding their guns at the ready.

The first person to come into sight was John English, a frightened child in each of his massive arms, clinging to his neck. He raised his head when the lights hit him.

"You found them, they're all safe?" Zane blurted, lowering his weapon.

English nodded and continued up the steps. Frost and Park followed behind him, the two older boys between them. The kids were all smudged with dirt and spiderwebs, their clothes dusty and covered in some sort of white rock dust. But they were all safe.

English and his Snake Eaters headed for the dining hall, where they could reunite the children with their parents. Deuce and Ty were having a harder time mounting the stairs, mostly because Deuce was clinging to Amelia and refusing to use the hand railing to help him up the steps, and Zane instantly recognized Ty in the throes of a very real panic attack.

He and Kelly darted down the stairs to assist.

Deuce refused to let his little girl out of his arms, so Kelly helped him up the steps, taking his weight.

Once Deuce and Amelia were in safe hands, Ty slid down the stairwell wall and refused to move. Zane knelt in front of him, setting his light on the step above them.

"You're okay, doll," he whispered. He gently touched Ty's cheek.

Ty gasped in breath after breath, shaking his head. He wouldn't open his eyes, so Zane simply leaned in and kissed him. Ty wrapped his arms around Zane's neck, clinging to him, unable to even speak.

Zane didn't know how he'd made it out of those walls without breaking down completely. He slipped his arm around Ty's waist and hefted him to his feet. "Come on. Big and open upstairs."

Ty's fingers dug into Zane's shoulder as Zane helped him up the steps. As soon as they made it out of the stairwell, Ty let go of him and awkwardly lowered himself to the ground with one hand, flattening out on the cool marble. He pressed his cheek to the floor and stroked his fingers over the tile. "I thought I'd never see you again," he cooed to it.

Zane barked a laugh before he could stop himself. "Nice to see I was missed." He bent and put a hand on Ty's head. "Are you okay?"

Ty nodded jerkily, finally opening his eyes. "We found her."

"I noticed. Come on." Zane helped him off the ground and headed for the bench where Kelly was once again sitting. Ty's steps were wobbly, but he seemed to be shaking the panic off. He always did.

Zane sat next to Kelly, and Ty stood for a second, his brow knitted in confusion. "What are we doing?" he asked.

"Waiting for Nick," Kelly answered. He pointed at the door.

"Is he okay?"

Kelly shrugged. "He is. I wouldn't put bets on Jockie Fraser, though."

Ty looked from him to the door again. "Nick's in there with him?"

"Getting information," Kelly provided.

"Oh no. No, no," Ty murmured. He started for the door.

"Ty, we gave the man a chance to talk," Zane called after him.

"It's not Fraser I'm worried about!" Ty shot over his shoulder.

The door opened before Ty could reach it. He stumbled to a halt in front of Nick. Zane and Kelly both lurched to their feet. Nick stepped out, glancing around the hall and at Ty. He met Kelly's eyes, then Zane's, and beckoned them in with a jerk of his head.

"We need Earl, too," he said quietly.

Zane frowned in confusion, but turned and called for Earl to join them. They followed Kelly into the room, closing the heavy door behind them.

Jockie Fraser was slumped in the chair. His face didn't look any worse than it had when they'd left him in here, but since it had already looked like he'd gone a round with an MMA fighter, that wasn't saying much.

His hands, still tied to the arms of the chair, were quite obviously broken. Zane had no doubt there were other injuries they couldn't see.

Nick walked up to stand beside and a little behind Fraser's chair, and Fraser winced away from him with a whimper. Zane stared at him in morbid fascination.

"Tell them what you told me," Nick ordered.

"The man who hired us," Fraser gasped. He licked his lips and took shallow, rasping breaths like he couldn't get enough air. "His name was Burns. Richard Burns."

CHAPTER 12

Nick had known the name would cause a shock wave, but he was so eager to get the hell out of that room and away from the man he'd been questioning, he hadn't cared about what sort of responses to expect.

Ty remained motionless, staring at Fraser with the sort of blank expression that said he was rapidly playing through all the possible reactions in his head to find the most appropriate one. Zane and Kelly both made noises of confusion and disbelief. And Earl turned on his heel, storming out of the room under a cloud of curses.

"Bullshit," Ty finally whispered.

Nick lowered his head and started for the door, brushing past Ty as he went. He didn't intend to be here for the second round of questioning.

Ty grabbed his elbow and frowned. "Are you okay?"

Nick glared at him. "Next time you need help, you call Digger." He stalked out of the room before Ty could respond, and sought out the darkest, most remote corner he could find, treading into territory of the house he hadn't explored. He didn't care, though; he just needed to get away from that room and get the blood off his hands. His back hit the wall of the alcove he'd found, and he slid to the ground, pressing the heels of his hands into his eyes and curling his fingers through his hair.

The captain who'd strolled through camp one day fifteen years ago had plucked Nick from the canteen and told him he had extra duty for him. When Nick had learned they wanted him to train with CIA interrogators, he'd flat out refused, insisting he wasn't cut out for that sort of thing. They'd told him *that* was the very reason they'd chosen him.

Well, fuck them. Nick had been right. He wasn't cut out for it.

The scuff of a bootheel alerted him to someone near, and he raised his head. His night vision was still ruined, but it didn't matter. The beam of a flashlight swept across his bare feet.

"Nick?" Kelly whispered. He came closer, the flashlight remaining on Nick's feet instead of climbing higher. All Nick could make out was Kelly's silhouette. He knelt and handed Nick a bundle. "I got you a change of clothes. Are you okay?"

Nick nodded and took the shirt. He leaned forward and slipped it on, realizing that he'd been freezing and hadn't even noticed. His fingers were shaking when he tried to button it up.

Kelly covered them with his own, lowering Nick's hands into his lap. "It's okay," he whispered. Then he took both sides of the shirt and pulled Nick toward him. He buttoned the shirt in silence, only meeting Nick's eyes when he was done. "We have another night on this island. And there are still a lot of lives in danger. You did what you had to do."

Nick stared at him. "We'll keep telling ourselves that, huh?"

Kelly nodded. Then he took Nick's hand and helped him off the ground. "Get out of those pants."

Nick managed to huff a laugh.

"Because they're wet! Pervert."

Nick shed the remainder of his wet clothing and changed into the dry garments Kelly had brought him. He hated to admit it, but it felt better just being dry and warm. Kelly took the cuff of Nick's soaked jeans and wiped at his hands for him, holding the flashlight between his cheek and shoulder so he could see the dirt and blood.

Nick remained quiet, even when Kelly held his hand and watched his fingers trembling for a few seconds. There was nothing further to say about any of it.

"Come on," Kelly murmured. "Zane had an idea about the computer files. He said he wanted your help."

When they reached the study, they found a fire blazing and giving off enough light to see the darker corners of the room. Zane was seated behind Milton's laptop. He and Ty were having a heated discussion, one that cut off sharply when Nick and Kelly entered the room.

"You found something?" Kelly asked.

"Fraser's still talking," Zane told them. "He said he met with a man in a pub on the mainland a month ago who offered him a million US dollars to do this. He was to recruit Maisie as well. Neither could turn down that kind of money for something they thought would end with a ransom job and everyone returned safely."

Nick sat in a chair by the fire, beginning to shiver. Kelly hovered near him, the fire casting odd shadows over the lines of his frown.

Ty was watching both of them, his expression unreadable. "He said he didn't know who killed Milton, just that it wasn't either of them. They had nothing to do with buying his information; their sole purpose was to get to either Stanton or Amelia."

"That's where Nikki comes in?" Nick guessed. "Milton was her mark?"

"We can only assume."

"What about Kline?" Kelly asked.

Nick glanced up at him. "Who?"

"The hot, kickass lady you shot in the face," Kelly provided.

"The back of the head, really," Zane added.

"Yes, thank you!" Nick snapped.

"She was a backup to make sure the others got the job done," Ty said. "I guess. I don't know. She thought she was the last man standing and panicked."

"Burns does like his backups," Nick said.

Ty narrowed his eyes.

"But!" Zane said loudly. "Fraser said that the morning Milton's body was discovered, he did stumble over Maisie and the body. But Maisie told him she'd been slipped a handwritten note under her door in the middle of the night. It told her to go find the body, break the watch, and change the time. If that failed, she was to take it and dispose of it."

Nick scowled hard enough that the bruises on his face hurt. "Why?"

"Presumably to destroy what they thought was stored info about his past movements. Jockie didn't know, and he didn't ask. But he said that before Maisie could change the time, they were interrupted by other staff."

"Wow," Kelly whispered. "That means if Nikki was in the walls and Maisie was the one who wanted the watch, they were probably the ones who cut Milton open. Dude, talk about nightmare nannies."

"Focus. You have no proof of any of that," Nick said.

"Oh, excuse me Mr. I'm Not a Cop Anymore."

Nick rolled his eyes. "So if Maisie just broke the watch but didn't change the time, why is it wrong? Did Milton do it?"

"We can only assume the time on Milton's watch is something he wanted us to know," Zane said. "The question is what does it mean?"

"It's the file number," Nick realized.

Zane grinned and nodded. "That's what I was thinking. Milton left it as a hint in case he didn't make it. He knew that watch was special, something connected to Burns and even Ty. He knew they'd know that type of watch wouldn't show the wrong time unless it was set wrong. The only reason it didn't ping was because Maisie broke it."

"Speaking of Burns, where the fuck is he?" Kelly asked.

"Dad has the villagers out with their pitchforks looking for him," Ty said.

"It wasn't the killers who left that note for Maisie, or they'd have just done it themselves. That was the big kahuna. Burns would sure as shit know to tell Maisie to get rid of that watch, though."

"Burns isn't masterminding these murders, Irish," Ty snapped.

"Our job is to get into that file," Zane said with a pointed look at Ty. He turned his attention to Nick. "I think the file number he used for this information was also the code to his part of the DOD info. What was the time?"

"3:48," Nick answered.

"They're six-digit file names."

Nick's eyes widened. "You want me to remember the seconds?"

"Do you have your iPad with the pictures?"

"I . . . I don't know what happened to it."

"Then yeah, I want you to remember the seconds," Zane said.

Nick glanced at Kelly, incredulous. Kelly shrugged and tapped his temple. "You were obsessing about it. You know what time it said."

Nick snapped his mouth closed and leaned forward, resting his chin on his hand. "It looked like a smiley face," he finally said. He stood and took a clock off the mantle. "Ten, maybe. Give or take five seconds."

"That, I can work with." Zane turned back to the computer, stretching his shoulders before beginning to type. He was at it for almost ten minutes, long enough for Ty to get twitchy and start pacing, for Kelly to lay himself out on the couch, and for Nick's mind to travel back to the sound of a billiard ball cracking ribs and a man begging for mercy.

"Found it," Zane finally announced. "It was military time. Fifteen, not three."

They crowded around his seat, all of them trying to see the computer screen. Dozens and dozens of files were contained in the password-protected folder. As Zane clicked from one to the next, they began to tell the story of what Milton had been involved in, and what he'd been trying to do on the island.

There was evidence and documentation of all the threats Stanton had received. Evidence that Amelia was indeed a target. Evidence that someone intended to hit them at Livi and Deuce's wedding. There were photos of Nikki Webb and her true identity, her fake passports, and several jobs she'd been suspected of being involved with. She was a professional hitter.

"This says she always works alone, never with a partner. Why'd she change up her MO?" Nick asked.

"A million-dollar payday will do that," Ty reasoned.

The files had nothing listed on her partner, though. Whomever she had been spotted on the beach with was still a ghost. Still on the island. Still a threat.

Milton related in a document that he intended to engage Nikki by agreeing to sell her the information she was after, and then take her out. Obviously, things hadn't gone to plan. Milton hadn't been expecting a second person at their meeting.

"Explains the crack to the back of his head," Kelly said.

There were communications from Richard Burns, labeled with shorthand that Nick recognized as meaning a third party had provided the information. They detailed three of Stanton's island staff who were involved and warned that the two groups might be controlled by the same people, and therefore aware of each other and able to join forces if need be.

"Burns knew all this was coming," Nick said through gritted teeth. He turned and shoved at Ty. "Why the hell didn't he tell Deacon to cancel this shit?"

Ty was speechless, still staring at the screen in disbelief. "Burns isn't responsible for this."

Nick turned away, shaking his head. Kelly moved with him, patting his stomach like he was trying to keep him calm. Nick knew, though, that Kelly had determined over years of practice that the best way to keep Nick from attacking was to grab him right around the hips and upend him before he could get going. Kelly wasn't comforting him, necessarily, he was just preparing to put him on his ass if he lost it.

And he was damn well about to lose it.

Zane could see the warning signs, he just didn't know what the hell to do about them. Before coming here and spending more time with Nick and Kelly, he hadn't even known Nick was capable of losing his temper, much less the many and sundry things he'd demonstrated tonight. He really was more like Ty than Zane had ever guessed. Looking between the two of them, at the two friends squaring off against each other, at the rock and the hurricane, Zane couldn't guess who would win the coming fight. He didn't want to find out, either.

"Something bigger's going on here, Ty, something it sure as hell looks like Dick Burns knew was coming. If he didn't plan it all to begin with!" Nick hissed. He pointed toward the staircase. "Now either you go up there, find him, and find out what the hell it is, or I will!"

Instead of bellowing back at him, Ty put his hands up in appeasement.

"Don't," Nick snarled.

Ty closed his eyes and nodded. "Okay, just calm down."

"I'm tired of being calm," Nick said, his voice dropping to a measured murmur. "I'm tired of being used. This ends tonight, whether by your hand or mine."

Zane was of the opinion that Nick was far more threatening when he was cool and composed than when he was shouting. Kelly seemed to agree; he took a careful step away from them, moving to stand beside Zane.

"Just give it the night, okay?" Ty tried. "Everyone is safe right now. The ferry comes tomorrow, and then we'll have time to deal with everything, figure this shit out. Just one night of peace for everyone before we go demanding answers and stirring shit up."

"One night of peace?" Nick repeated incredulously. "Six people are dead! We're investigating this bullshit on an island in the middle of fucking nowhere because we're trapped here! There are people panicking all over the fucking place, all the weapons are *still* missing, and we are one pig's head on a stick away from *Lord of the Flies*! A night of peace went out the fucking window when we landed, Beaumont!"

Zane was pretty sure Nick was going to have a stroke if Ty opened his mouth one more time. He and Kelly both moved closer, prepared to break up yet another argument between them.

"Burns may still have you like a puppy on a leash, Ty, but I'm not his fucking golden retriever. National security or not, *family* or not, we have to get answers from him. We fucking deserve answers from him, everyone on the island does."

Ty's nostrils flared and he pointed a finger in Nick's face. "Don't even pretend this is about closure for these people, that this isn't about your beef with Burns," he snapped.

"I'm not. I'd gladly lock that bastard up and throw away the key. Far as I'm concerned, if it weren't for him, Eli would still be alive and I wouldn't have a box of his things sitting on my boat that I'm still afraid to go through!"

Ty took a step toward him. Nick put a hand on his chest, pushing him back. He held up his finger like a parent scolding a small child, daring Ty to come at him again.

"Eli was loyal!" Ty shouted. "If you hadn't left us, if you'd stuck with us instead of crawling home with your tail between your legs, maybe he'd have had someone watching his back and he'd still be here!"

"Oh," Kelly said. He grabbed Zane's sleeve to stop him from moving to interfere. "Nope. He's going to get what he deserves now."

Nick grabbed Ty's jacket and pulled until they were almost nose to nose. "Did you ever stop and think, Ty, if you had *listened* to what I was saying then, listened to what I was trying to tell you about Burns and his fucking job offers, none of it would have gone down the way it did?"

Ty's jaw tightened. He began to shake his head, and Nick let him go, shoving him away.

"Of course you didn't," Nick snarled. "It's never on you, Ty."

Ty still looked furious, but Zane could see something else creeping into his expression: the realization that Nick might be right.

"Eli *was* loyal. He could have taught you a thing or two about it," Nick said tiredly.

"Fuck you, O'Flaherty!" Ty shouted. "I know what loyalty is, and that man is like a father to me! If you had a father you gave a shit about, you'd be doing the same thing!"

Nick's jaw clenched and he took a step back, putting himself out of Ty's reach. Or perhaps putting Ty out of *his* reach. His next words were whispered. "I'm tired of risking my life for you, Ty."

Ty staggered back as if Nick had shoved him. He couldn't form a response even as Nick turned and stalked out of the room, slamming the door behind him and rattling the ancient glass panes in the windows. They watched him go, all of them stunned into silence.

Kelly shifted his weight, and the floorboard creaked under his boot. Ty tore his eyes away from the doorway to blink at Kelly and then Zane.

"Oh God, did I really just say that?" Ty asked, voice hushed.

Kelly cleared his throat, looking indecisive. He finally took a step for the door. "I'll go after him."

"No," Ty held out a hand. "No, I . . . I'll go talk to him."

He stood rooted to the spot for a few more seconds before he seemed to work up the courage to head for the door. He closed it gently behind him, leaving Zane and Kelly in the uncomfortable silence left behind.

Kelly glanced at Zane and smiled weakly. "Good times, huh?"

Zane shook his head. "I hope Nick kicks his ass."

"Me too." Kelly frowned. "Maybe we should . . ."

"Follow them?" Zane provided. "Yeah, definitely."

Ty found Nick sitting on the very edge of the cliff, perched on a rocky outcropping that didn't threaten to shoot him over the edge like the grassy parts did, his feet dangling over the side. Ty hesitated to move closer, finally fighting past his innate fear of falling in order to edge up to the cliff and sit. He settled down beside Nick, gravity pulling at his legs, the cold rock beneath him threatening to pitch him over the edge to the rocky sea below.

"I don't guess we could have a heart-to-heart somewhere less likely to end in you pushing me off a cliff, could we?" he asked wryly.

Nick didn't answer. He was gazing past his own feet at the whitecaps glowing in the moonlight.

Ty was finding it hard to breathe against the tightness in his chest. They'd had their fights over the years, some of them just as nasty as the words they'd exchanged minutes ago. Nick always gave as good as he got, though, so him just walking away scared Ty. Truly scared him. Everything about Nick had felt different since they're returned home from deployment, and Ty didn't know what to do about it.

"As soon as it came out of my mouth, I tried to take it back," he whispered.

Nick lifted his head and sighed.

"Your father doesn't deserve for you to care. I know that, Nick. I know that. And you've always been there for me, even when you probably should have told me to go fuck myself."

Nick didn't respond. He ducked his head again and swiped his hand over his chin.

"I was wrong," Ty tried. "I know what you've done. I know what you are. I was . . . are you even listening to me?"

"You're an asshole, Tyler," Nick said. "But I've known that from the start. That's the reason we've stayed friends."

"Because we're both assholes?"

"Yep. You really think anything you say can hurt my feelings?"

"Well . . ."

Nick huffed and shook his head.

"I haven't been a very good friend to you," Ty said, almost choking on the sentiment. "Not nearly as good as you deserve."

Nick finally looked at him. "You earned my loyalty when you sat beside me on that bus to Parris Island. And every day after. So the times you want to be a complete cockholster like tonight, I tend to overlook it."

Ty tried hard not smile. He snorted quietly, then bit his lip so he wouldn't laugh. "I appreciate that."

"Shut up."

"Okay."

They sat in silence, both staring out at the water, both knowing the conversation wasn't done. When Nick spoke again, he didn't preface it with anything, not even an audible inhalation.

"You need to stop drinking in front of Zane."

Ty nodded slowly. "I realized that the other night. Did he say something to you?"

"No. But it's hard for him regardless, and you're a sloppy drunk."

Ty nodded again. It wasn't anything he didn't already know or hadn't told himself. He'd needed to hear it from someone else, though. Nick had always been good at that.

The silence threatened to return when Nick chose not to expound on his advice. When he spoke again, he changed tacks faster than Ty usually did.

"My dad is dying."

Ty glanced at him, struggling with his immediate reaction to the news. Finally, he just went with it. "Good."

Nick nodded. "That was my first thought, too."

Understanding finally dawned on Ty. "And you been feeling guilty ever since, right?"

Nick shrugged. "I'll always feel guilty."

"Is that what's been going on with you? I know you have Kelly now, but . . . if you need to talk about it, I'm still here. I'm still here."

"He needs a new liver," Nick said, still staring off into the water. "And I'm the only one in the family who might be a match to his blood type and size."

"He wants a part of your liver?" Ty blurted. "Well, fuck him!"

Nick laughed.

Ty wavered between outrage and fear. "Are you going to do it?"

"I don't know."

"Nick . . ."

"If I don't do it," Nick started, his voice low and calm like it almost always was, "I might as well be putting a gun to his head and pulling the trigger. That'll be on me, not him."

"No one would blame you."

Nick didn't answer. He stared off into the night for several minutes. Both of them were silent. Then Nick lowered his head and brought his hand up to his eyes. His broad shoulders slumped like he was finally bending under a huge weight, and he gasped for air.

Ty scrambled closer to him, the cliff's edge always in the back of his mind, and put his arm around Nick. Nick collapsed into him, and Ty cradled his head against his chest, beginning the rocking motion that always brought him comfort when he needed it.

It wasn't the first time one of them had held the other when he broke down like this, and it probably wouldn't be the last.

Ty patted Nick's hair and rested his chin on top of his head. Nick had stood like a rock in a tempest his entire life, rain beating at him, the tides trying to carve away his soul, the relentless howl of the wind always at his shores. But Nick was the first to smile, the first to laugh, the first to joke. He was the first to put his shoulder to yours when the storm came calling.

He deserved more than a family who turned their backs on him. More than a lifetime of second best. And he damn well deserved more from Ty than to be merely an afterthought when Ty needed help.

The more Ty thought of it, of the way Nick's smile could light an entire room despite how broken he had always been, the angrier he became. His body began to tremble and he held Nick tighter. Tears came unbidden to his eyes and he hung his head, ashamed to realize he wasn't worthy of the loyalty Nick had always given him. He would never be worthy.

"I'm sorry," he gasped. He ignored the tears and kept talking. "I'm sorry I've been a shitty friend. And I'm sorry about Eli. If we'd listened to you, then he'd still be alive. You were right, and I'm so goddamned sorry he's gone."

"Damn you, Ty," Nick said, his voice muffled by his own tears and Ty's chest.

"You were right then, and you're right now about talking to Burns. I'll go with you, okay? We'll talk to him together."

Nick huffed a breath and sniffed. "You better not be getting snot in my hair," he finally said.

Their laughter was a pitiful mixture of sniffles and snickers. It was the only way either of them knew to combat the pain and sadness.

"Listen, your dad . . . I don't want you to do it because you're my brother, and I love you, and you deserve to live your own life." Ty cupped Nick's face between both hands. His voice was stronger when he spoke again. "You've spent your whole life trying to prove to yourself that you're a good man. Well, you are. I may not be one, but I know one when I see him, and you're the best there is. So don't you dare go off and risk yourself for him if you're just trying to prove that to yourself again, you understand? I don't want you to do it. But if you do, I'll be right there with you. I promise."

Nick gave a single nod.

"I'll be there." Ty met his eyes for a few more seconds, then released him and sat straighter. He wiped at his face, still sniffing. "Damn you."

"Ty," Nick grunted, smacking Ty's chest with the back of his hand. "Is that a boat?"

Ty wiped his eyes again. "I don't know, I can't see anything 'cause I'm crying like a little bitch!"

"It's a boat," Nick insisted.

Ty squinted out over the water. He heard footsteps coming up behind them and turned to see Zane and Kelly approaching carefully. Nick scrambled to his feet and put his hand under his nose, shielding his night vision from the reflection of the moon off the waves.

"I think it's one of the bigger launches. The tides are pushing it back in."

Ty finally made out the flashing, bobbing emergency beacon of the boat Nick had spotted. "That's a long way out, dude."

"Can you swim that?" Zane asked as he came to stand beside Ty.

"We sure as fuck can. We'll need wet suits," Nick answered.

"Oh, hell no," Kelly said. Nick peered at him. Kelly crossed his arms. "*Fuck* no. You wait until daylight to swim that shit or I'm not patching you up from the hypothermia."

"Less than thirty hours before the ferry's due," Zane reminded them. "No need for drastic measures yet, okay?"

They all nodded, though Nick seemed reluctant. He stared off at the blinking lights until Kelly grabbed his arm and pulled him away. "Come on. They'll be getting dinner together soon. We need to eat or we might start getting pissy with each other. We wouldn't want that."

Nick snorted and let Kelly pull him. Ty and Zane watched them walk away. They both had their heads down, watching their footing, and Kelly soon snaked his hand around Nick's waist. Nick threw an arm over his shoulders, and it was like the most natural thing in the world for both of them. Ty still wasn't quite processing the two of them as a couple, but nothing about them felt wrong when he watched them like this.

Zane tapped his shoulder. "Can we please move the fuck away from this cliff?"

Ty scooted backward, then crawled until he felt he was a safe distance away before taking to his feet. Zane laughed at him the whole time.

"Bastard knows I'm scared of heights," Ty mumbled. He brushed at his knees and then his ass, but the wet grass had soaked through his jeans. They started off toward the gardens and the mansion beyond.

"What did he mean when he said you earned his loyalty on the bus to Parris Island?" Zane asked quietly.

Ty sighed in the darkness. "You heard the whole thing?"

Zane shrugged apologetically. "We were afraid someone would get tossed off the cliff."

"Valid." They walked in silence for a few seconds before Ty cleared his throat. "When we were loaded onto the bus for Basic, we were all pretty much young and stupid and scared, you know? Kids from all different places, all different backgrounds. Some of them were nervous and chatty, some of them were too scared to talk. There were a couple loners who we all kind of pegged as guys who wouldn't make the psych cut."

Zane snorted.

"I remember the first time I saw Nick. Big kid, you know? I mean he's a big guy now, but he was already almost that size to start with. Most of us at seventeen or eighteen, we could fit three to a fucking bus seat. The red hair and the green eyes, he was kind of hard to miss. He was sitting on a bench, ramrod straight. A couple guys were kind of poking fun at him for trying to pretend he was already a Marine with the posture. And a bunch of us had noticed he had a black eye, but his knuckles weren't bruised. They were on him because he'd obviously been in a fight but hadn't fought back or even defended himself."

Ty had to stop and shake the memory a little before he could continue. It still made him angry. Zane was silent, letting him gather his thoughts.

"Through all that shit they were talking, Nick never said a word. He just sat there and watched them. He didn't look angry. He didn't look amused. He was just . . . sitting there, blank. And for some reason I was fascinated by it, so I watched him. I mean, one look at him and you could tell Nick was a hardass. I remember thinking, this is someone with restraint. This is someone who'll take a punch to the face and walk away instead of brawling. This is someone I need to know, because I knew I'd never be that kind of person. And the more shit he took, the angrier I got for him. So when we loaded onto the bus, I made sure I sat beside him." He began to laugh with the memory. "I had to shove a kid and tell him to keep moving to get to the seat, and I just plopped my happy ass next to him."

Zane smirked. "I can imagine what that looked like."

"I remember the look he gave me when I sat, like, 'Oh my God, who is this idiot and why is he smiling?' I introduced myself, shook his hand. And I realized, the way he reached for my hand, that the reason he'd been sitting like he had was because his ribs were hurt."

"Jesus Christ." Zane sounded as angry as Ty had been back then. "His dad?"

Ty nodded. "A parting gift for abandoning the family to go play hero when he should have been going to work and earning money."

"I hope Nick lets him rot," Zane said under his breath.

Ty nodded his agreement. He knew it probably wouldn't happen, though, because Nick wouldn't be able to live with himself if he didn't do what he could to save someone, even someone as evil as his own father.

"Anyway. One of the guys sitting in front of us turned around to say something and I told him to shut the fuck up and turn back around before he got a handful of something he wasn't ready for. Nick told me later it was the first time someone had stood up for him just because they could. Ever. First time in his life."

"And that's why he says you earned his loyalty when you sat down."

"That's right. When I asked him who'd broken his rib, he said his father. When I pointed at his knuckles and asked why he hadn't hit back, he told me he had. But he'd used a baseball bat." Ty smiled when he remembered the silence that had come over the kids sitting around them, eavesdropping. There had been no mistaking Nick's tone for a joke, but Ty had laughed his ass off at the time. "I just told him I liked his style, and we were inseparable after that. When I got news that Deuce had been in his wreck, I was . . . Nick was the one who kept me from going AWOL. We looked out for each other, had each other's six."

"You two going to be okay now?"

"Yeah," Ty said without giving it even a second of thought. "I need to do better by him."

When they reached the patio of the mansion, they found a lot of activity going on, much more than could be justified by the tail end of dinner or the fact that someone had partially repaired the generators. As they stepped into the circle of light cast by the landscape lighting, Nick came jogging out to them, Kelly on his heels.

"What's going on?" Zane asked.

Nick grimaced, trying to catch his breath. "Richard Burns is dead."

CHAPTER 13

hey tried to keep Ty out of the room, but he bulled his way past all three of them, so they just followed him in, hanging back. Earl was there, refusing to leave. Richard Burns was sprawled on the floor. There was no blood, no obvious injuries or signs of violence on his body. The room, however, hadn't come through unscathed. Tables were overturned, pictures and lamps had been knocked to the floor, even a small chaise lounge had been tumbled over and crashed into a wall.

The stone walls were so thick throughout the mansion that no one had heard what seemed to have been a pretty epic battle.

The electricity was working again in parts of the mansion, including this room. Ty didn't know how, and he didn't ask.

"His neck's been broke," Earl told Ty. His voice was gruff. He knelt beside Burns's body, holding the man's hand.

"Dad . . ." Ty took a few halting steps and stopped again. His knees went weak, and he would have sunk to the floor if a strong arm hadn't wrapped around him.

He gripped Zane's shirt, clinging to him.

"I'm sorry," Zane whispered.

Earl's eyes traveled over all four men. "Look around this room," he said, his voice full of gravel and anger. "Tell me what happened. And then find out who did this."

Ty nodded, his breath coming harder, his focus narrowing down to nothing but the body on the ground.

Kelly knelt by the body. "May I, sir?" he said to Earl.

Earl refused to let go of Burns's hand, but he nodded. Kelly began to check the body over. Zane left Ty where he stood, moving to search the room along with Nick. Ty finally tore his attention away from the body of his adopted uncle and began to scour the room too.

Burns had obviously fought against his attacker. He'd fought with all the skill and knowledge he'd acquired in his years. Someone had still managed to take him out, and for that they'd either been very good, caught Burns when his guard was down, or both.

Anger and grief boiled deep in Ty's gut. He could barely concentrate on the crime scene. Zane and Nick had made a round of the room and returned to the body, hovering over Kelly as they waited for his report. Ty could find nothing but the obvious signs of a struggle in the room. If they had actual crime scene equipment, they might be able to do something with this, but no visual evidence had been left behind. In a fight like this, *something* should have been left behind.

Ty swallowed hard. "It was a pro."

Kelly sat back on his heels, sighing and glancing up at Nick and Zane. "He's been dead for hours. Probably right after he left your interview with him."

Ty was still moving around the periphery of the room, unable to look back at them. He couldn't see Richard Burns on the ground like that.

"Could it have been Kline?" Nick asked.

Kelly shrugged. "She certainly had the capability."

"We know there's at least one more out there, a guy. The man we saw on the beach," Zane reminded them.

"Could that have been Fraser?" Kelly asked.

"He said it wasn't and . . . I believe him," Nick said.

"Did you ever tell the truth when it was us?" Ty asked him.

Nick gave him a negligent shrug. "A man like Fraser hasn't exactly been trained for what I put him through."

"I'm not a medical examiner," Kelly announced, trying to cut the tension, "but I'm pretty sure his neck was snapped."

He pointed to Burns's chin, refraining from lifting it off the floor. They had to get down on the ground to see what he was talking about. Ty moved closer, looking almost sideways in an attempt to see but not see. There were bruises where Kelly was indicating, like someone had taken his chin and jerked it.

"The positioning's all wrong," Nick murmured. He was on his hands and knees beside Kelly, tilting his head to see.

Kelly nodded. "Either it wasn't someone with training, or Burns fought like hell and fucked up their hold."

"Or the person was injured," Zane pointed out.

"Burns was a large man," Nick added. "Avery Kline would've had a time of this too, no matter how skilled she was. Trying to snap someone's neck when they're a foot taller than you isn't exactly easy."

"That would explain why she panicked and made that move on Stanton," Zane whispered.

Earl was glaring at both men. "I ain't hearing any answers from you two, just a bunch of maybes."

Nick and Zane both glanced at him guiltily before going back to their examination. Earl got to his feet and paced a few steps, his eyes meeting Ty's. He stopped in front of him, then put his arm around Ty's shoulders, releasing him quickly when Ty winced away, holding his dislocated shoulder. Earl took his good arm again, and Ty was forced to look at the body of Richard Burns.

Earl pointed at him. "Look at that man, son."

Ty stared at his father for a few moments, then turned his eyes to the floor.

"I met him on a helicopter going into the jungle, Ty. You know what that is?" Earl grabbed Ty's shirt front, pulling him closer to whisper in his ear. "That's Nick on the ground, Beaumont. You go fucking find who did this, and you kill him."

Ty stared at the men kneeling. At the body on the floor. His stomach turned at the thought of any of these men in Burns's place, lying dead on the floor, murdered. He remembered the anguish of standing at Elias Sanchez's funeral, of carrying that casket. He remembered the desperate need for revenge.

"Yes, sir."

Earl stormed out of the room. He had to go somewhere and grieve, somewhere to be away from the body of his oldest and dearest friend. And to deal with guilt, because he'd spent the past several hours enraged over the things he'd learned about Burns.

The Grady family would never be the same after this loss.

Zane clambered to his feet and came to Ty, taking him by his good arm. "Come on," he said into Ty's ear.

Ty shook his head, his nostrils flaring and his focus narrowing to a pinpoint. "Someone else was behind this, Zane. Someone else was orchestrating this."

"Come on, Ty, let's get out of here."

"It wasn't him."

"Ty."

"Someone else did all this!" Ty shouted, jabbing his finger at Burns's body.

"Tyler," Nick barked. "Get your ass in gear and go!"

Ty nodded woodenly, moving to obey that tone of voice almost automatically. Zane stayed with him, fingers digging into his arm.

"Are you okay?" Zane asked as soon as they were on the stairs.

"They killed him, Zane."

Zane stopped halfway down the steps and pulled him closer. "I know." He turned Ty to him, making sure he met his eyes. "You've taken a lot of hits in the last few days, Ty. Let me take this last one for you."

Ty stared at him, struck breathless, struck speechless. He snaked his arm around Zane's neck and hugged him tight. He nodded, still unable to speak.

"We'll round up everyone physically capable of doing this," Zane murmured against Ty's hair, "and we'll find out who it is even if we have to take Nick's ball and chain to every one of them."

There were a great deal of complaints when Ty and Zane gathered every able-bodied person in the dining room and frog-marched them into the study, but the weapons they wielded and the look in Ty's eyes were enough motivation to get everyone moving and keep them cooperating.

There were two groomsmen: Christian and Matthew. Three bridesmaids: Catalina, Miyoko, and Ashlee. Livi's brother, Theo, and Emma's cameraman, Marley. Mackie and Hamish Boyd were the only two staff members who remained, since Fraser was still tied up in the game room. And Ty had somehow convinced the three Snake Eaters to come peacefully. Zane didn't know how he'd built that rapport, but he was grateful he didn't have to wrestle John English through a door he didn't want to go through.

Twelve suspects.

Several others joined them to help keep order, and to help parse the evidence. Stanton, Earl, Mara, and Chester were there, as was Emma, who was still protesting Marley's inclusion in the suspect pool. Deuce and Livi had left Amelia with Livi's mother, Susan, and come to be part of the meeting. Nick and Kelly soon came into the room as well. Several of the people who'd heard Jockie Fraser's screams shied away from Nick when he entered the room.

Zane moved toward the corner, nodding for Nick to join him. "Got anything we can cull the herd with?"

Nick stared at him for a few seconds. "I never realized how disturbing your accent is until you use cow analogies."

Zane fought hard to keep his face as deadpan as Nick's. "Yeah okay, say car."

"Shut up. Kelly narrowed down time of death to a six-hour window, but he wants to make sure everyone knows he's essentially guessing. Considering the last time Burns was seen was six hours ago, I'm going to back him on his assessment."

"Great," Zane huffed.

"He told me that when he and Ty went looking for Burns, Earl said he hadn't seen him since his talk with you and me. So . . . it's probably safe to say he went to his room and someone was waiting there for him."

Zane nodded. "No one could have knocked on Burns's door and surprised him. You're right, they would have had to've been lying in wait. Okay, let's see what we can shake loose." He gave Nick's shoulder a pat and stepped away.

"What the hell is going on?" Ashlee Knight demanded. Zane knew her only as the bombshell from Nick's notes. She certainly looked the part.

"There's been one last murder," Zane announced.

There was a murmur of shock and alarm, but at least half the people in the room looked like they just wanted to go to bed. Death was no longer traumatic for the island.

Zane glanced at Nick and Ty, holding his breath. They had so little to go on, he was going to have to bluff his way through this. He hoped they would play along.

"We've captured or killed all the people responsible for this massacre, all but one," he said to the people crowded into the room. "The ladies in the room can relax, the killer we're looking for is a man."

The three bridesmaids shared relieved, frightened glances before going to sit on a chaise near the far wall, holding each other's hands and leaning on each other in a huddle.

"Are you saying the killer you're looking for is in this room right now?" Christian Orr asked. He'd been introduced to Zane as Deuce's best friend from Philadelphia.

"I sure as hell hope so," Zane drawled.

"Jesus Christ," Mathew Ferguson shouted. He glanced to the wall, where Deuce stood amongst the other observers. "Deacon, are you serious right now? You've known me since we were freshmen in undergrad!"

"Just roll with it, Matt," Deuce told him. "They're good, they'll find out who did this. You got nothing to worry about. Unless you killed someone."

"Like hell!" Matthew shouted, but he remained seated.

Zane stepped into the corner for another refrain, beckoning Ty, Nick, and Kelly with him. A buzz of nervous conversation started up behind them. "Who the hell do we like for this?" Zane whispered.

Kelly shook his head. "I want to see if I'm right, man."

"You want to take bets, don't you?" Nick asked, voice flat.

Ty rolled his eyes and rubbed his hand over his face.

"What we really need is a confession," Nick said to Zane. "We don't have anything but hunches here. We need someone to stand up and say they did it."

"Oh, is that all?" Zane glared at Nick as he moved away again. The other three remained in the corner, watching him.

Zane considered the remaining suspects. Nine now. Three military men trained in the art of combat. Two old men who'd worked on the island all their lives, one who'd lost his wife to this mess. Three privileged, well-educated males from Pennsylvania, one of whom had everything to gain from his father's death or downfall. And then there was Marley, the adventuring cameraman Emma Grady was willing to vouch for.

"Nick, how long ago was Fraser contacted?" Zane asked.

"He said three weeks."

"Three weeks. And Livi, you met Nikki Webb when?"

"Two months ago."

Zane glanced at Emma, narrowing his eyes. "When did your team get shelved?"

"A month ago. Why?"

"When did Deuce ask you to bring your cameraman?"

"Last week, when he invited me to the wedding."

Zane nodded, narrowing his eyes at Marley King.

The man's eyes grew wider and he pointed to himself. "I'm a vegetarian," he said. "I don't kill things. Hell, I don't even like cutting my grass, man. That fresh-cut grass smell? That's plants in distress!"

Kelly moved closer to Zane, lowering his head and crossing his arms. "Burns's knuckles were fucked up, man. Whoever he fought with would have bruises starting to show. See if any of them are wearing makeup."

Zane peered at him. "Makeup?"

Kelly nodded, completely serious.

"What if it was Kline?"

Kelly shrugged. "Got to start somewhere, right?"

Zane took a deep breath. "Anyone got any makeup remover on them?"

Catalina Cruz raised her hand, as did Ashlee, who was sitting beside her. They dug in their purses and produced several disposable wipes. Kelly collected them with murmured thank-yous, then turned to Marley as he took one of the wipes out of its packet.

"I'm not wearing makeup," Marley told them, chuckling nervously. He waved a hand at his face. "Nobody on this island can match this perfect skin tone."

Kelly was smiling, but he still gave Marley's face a few swipes. He examined the wipe, then showed it to Zane.

"Looks like you're free to go, Mr. King," Zane said. He was pleased, because he really liked Emma's cameraman.

"Are you fucking serious with this?" Theo Stanton asked. "Makeup remover?"

"Anyone want to confess and make this go faster?" Nick asked. He was leaning against a side table near the door, arms crossed over his chest.

John English stepped forward. "No, but I'll volunteer to get my damn face wiped off next."

"Me too," Matthew and Christian said in unison.

Zane caught English throwing Ty a wink and a smirk. He knew what needed to happen here, and it seemed he was helping out. Ty appeared to trust the man, so Zane would as well. For now. If he threw Ty another wink they'd be having problems, though.

Kelly went to each man, wiping their faces with the makeup remover wipes. When he approached Theo, the man stood and glared at him.

"You're not touching me with that."

Kelly cocked his head, and a slow smile developed on his face.

"Why is that?" Ty asked Theo. "Allergies?"

"No, it's called civil rights, and I have them. I haven't killed anyone, Jesus Christ." He waved imploringly to his father and sister. "This is ridiculous, you both know I'd never do this to our family!"

Nick cleared his throat. "Kelly, put him down."

Kelly moved with shocking speed, wrapping Theo up and pinning his arm. Then he stepped between Theo's legs, turned, and dropped to his knees, letting gravity hurl Theo over his shoulder and flatten him on the floor.

Theo lay gasping for breath, shocked into immobility. Livi screamed, and Stanton shouted a wordless protest, but no one else moved.

Zane stepped forward and pulled his gun, pointing it at Theo's face. "How about you answer some questions the easy way, hmm?"

Theo nodded, still gasping for breath.

"If company secrets were sold, what would happen to the company?"

"We'd lose the DOD contracts. Shareholders would start selling off left and right. We'd be forced to liquidate everything in the following year. In eighteen months, we'd be bankrupt."

Zane glanced over his shoulder at Stanton.

"He's right."

"If I were part of this, I would be digging my own financial grave. The company's worth billions of dollars; no rival could offer me enough money to give that up, much less betray my family," Theo said through gritted teeth.

Zane relaxed and stuffed the gun back into his pants. He and Kelly helped Theo up. "Next time just let him wipe your damn face," Zane said. He gave Theo a shove toward his family and turned to the remaining suspects.

Hamish Boyd pushed to his feet, using his cane to make his way toward Zane. "If you are truly considering me or Mackie as suspects over these hired thugs, you must be a sad example of a Yank policeman."

"No, that's me," Nick broke in. He'd drawn his weapon and had it pointed at Hamish's head.

"Nick," Zane whispered.

"His cane is a gun, Garrett."

Zane's eyes darted to Hamish's cane.

"Are you serious right now?"

"I've seen them before," Nick assured Zane. "It's a gun."

"That's preposterous!" Hamish shouted. He raised the cane to wave it around, and Ty hit Zane from the side, tackling him to the ground and covering his body with his. There was a sound like someone opening a biscuit can, and then the room devolved into madness. Zane rolled to his feet, drawing his weapon.

Solomon Frost, the blond Snake Eater who seemed to have made friends with everyone, had tackled Nick to the ground, and they were now wrestling over the gun in their hands. It went off, punching a hole through the wood paneling near Deuce and Livi's heads. Livi screamed and Deuce lunged in front of her, shielding her and forcing her low to the ground. He reached out for the woman next to him, Miyoko Mason, who was holding her bloody arm and screaming that she'd been shot. The bullet fired from Hamish's cane gun had hit her instead of Zane.

Hamish was frantically groping for something on the handle of his cane, and just as Kelly was about to take a run at the old man, he found the switch and a short knife flipped out of the bottom of the cane. Kelly skidded to a halt and took a step back.

"What the fuck kind of butler are you?" he shouted.

Hamish grinned and pointed his cane at Kelly's face. "A bitter one."

Zane didn't know which way to turn or who to help first. Ty hadn't gotten off the round yet. He was curled on his side, holding his arm, but it wasn't clear if he'd been shot or if he'd merely aggravated his already hurt shoulder.

Nick hadn't yet gained the upper hand against Frost, but he had managed to land an elbow or two to the man's face and wrap his legs around Frost's waist so he couldn't roll off and get away.

Kelly had his gun out, pointing it at Hamish and ordering him to stand down. But he didn't seem like he wanted to pull the trigger, and the old butler could see that.

"You had your own wife murdered," Kelly said to him.

"You've obviously never been married."

Kelly pursed his lips thoughtfully, shrugging like he might understand that reasoning.

English and Park pounced on Frost, burying Nick under yet another dog pile of limbs. Zane turned his gun on Hamish, only to fire off to the right at the last second when he saw a man standing directly behind Hamish, shovel raised high.

Chester took a mighty swing and whacked Hamish in the back of the head. The butler collapsed to the ground, his cane falling harmlessly at his side. English managed to subdue Frost, holding him in a headlock as Nick scratched and clawed his way out from under their weight.

Zane still stood in the middle of the chaos, every sense alert to every movement, every fiber of his being telling him there was still danger.

"What the fuck just happened?" Deuce shouted.

Chester laid his shovel over his shoulder and grinned at Zane. English and Park finally got Frost on his face, holding him down with a knee to his back. Kelly was helping Ty off the ground, looking at his shoulder and nodding. Nick was still sprawled on the floor, staring at the ceiling.

"Anyone have any rope?" English called out.

Kelly pulled out a pair of handcuffs and thrust them at Park.

"Why the hell do you have those?" Ty asked.

Kelly shrugged and grinned. "They're Nick's."

"Oh God, no," Ty blurted, covering his eyes.

Nick laughed. He rolled over and pushed himself to his hands and knees, but he remained there, either unable or unwilling to stand. He glanced up at Ty and Zane. "He likes the uniform, too."

"No no no!" Ty cried.

"Well, that's just unnecessary," Earl said from the doorway. He had grabbed Mara and the two uninjured bridesmaids when the shooting had started and shoved them out of the room to safety. He also had the antique rifle from the dining room in his hands.

Hamish moaned and began to move. Zane shoved him to his back with the toe of his boot and pointed his gun in the old man's face. "Start from the beginning."

"I don't know who paid us," Hamish said groggily. His head was bleeding freely, but no one cared. "And you know the rest."

"Humor me."

"Jockie came to me with this plan. He said a man in a tavern had approached him. This island belonged to our families for centuries, and look at us! We're servants on our own home!"

"Who else was involved?"

"No one! My wife had second thoughts and said she was going to tell Stanton, so we voted to get rid of her. That woman Nikki killed Aileen, then she and Maisie cut open Milton's body to make you think Aileen was in the wrong place at the wrong time."

"Gross," Ty grunted.

"It worked," Kelly added.

"Who killed Milton and why?" Zane demanded.

"I think we have that answer over here," English called. He had his gun in Frost's mouth, and he took it out and pressed it to Frost's cheek. "Talk."

"Nikki figured out Milton was working for the government. She told me she needed backup for their meet," Frost told them. He sounded both ashamed and sorrowful, like the entire thing had been something he'd been convinced to do rather than wanted to do. "I'm sorry, boss."

"Shut up," English snarled. "Lenny's dead because of you. You're dead to me too, for all you're worth."

Frost blinked up at him, his jaw tightening.

"Keep going," Park ordered. They were the first words Zane had heard the man speak.

"Milton gave Nikki a flash drive. She gave him a suitcase of money. Then I hit him in the head and we left him there. We didn't realize until later that the flash drive was corrupted. It put a virus on the computer we uploaded it to and erased everything."

"Did you put that flash drive on my laptop?" Zane asked, remembering the inexplicable failure of his brand-new laptop.

Frost nodded.

"Did you kill Nikki?" Zane asked him.

"Yes. That was my job, to clear her after she'd done hers. I thought I was the last man standing, so when people kept dying I started freaking out too. And I didn't even fucking know Kline was with us until she went crazy and put a gun to Stanton's head. I swear to God I didn't kill the guy upstairs!"

Park stood and walked away from him. He took his sunglasses off and rubbed his hand over his eyes, revealing one that was milky white and another that was dark as obsidian. Then he put the glasses back on.

English shoved the gun harder into Frost's face. "What else?"

"That's all I know!"

"Who hired you?" Zane shouted at him. "Was it Richard Burns?"

"No! That was the name we were instructed to give, to cause chaos because he was on the island. The locals all thought he was the guy, okay? He was being set up. We were supposed to take him out at the end, but I swear I didn't do it! It had to have been Kline or that fucking gardener!"

"Give us a name!" English demanded, digging the gun under Frost's cheekbone.

"He was South American! The guy who hired me. De la Vega, okay? I never saw his face!"

Zane's entire body flooded with ice. He lowered his weapon, blinking as the edges of his vision began to darken. De la Vega. The head of the Vega cartel, the man who'd tried to kill them in New Orleans. He'd come after Zane through Ty, and when that hadn't worked, he'd come through Deuce's in-laws.

Zane turned to meet Ty's eyes. Ty shook his head.

"Is that the guy from NOLA?" Kelly asked.

"Yes," Ty whispered.

"The guy who got Kelly shot?" Nick asked through gritted teeth. He had finally climbed to his feet.

"The locals, they all thought this was about money, about getting their island back. But that was just because we needed a smoke screen. It wasn't even about the stuff on the flash drive! Our job was to retrieve the information, then plant it in Garrett's computer so he'd go down for the theft," Frost admitted. "All de la Vega wanted was for Garrett to go down. That's it. I asked him, why not just kill the guy? And he said he wanted Garrett to suffer. That's all he said."

Nick and Kelly were both staring at Zane, but Zane's world was narrowing as he listened. Ty's hand came to rest on his back.

Frost's voice was going higher, pleading as he explained. "But when the flash drive scrambled his laptop, the mission should have been aborted. I swear to God, Boss, that's when I retreated. These fucking island hicks don't know when to stop or we'd have just walked away!"

Zane sat heavily, his heart and head throbbing. "This was never really about Stanton's company. This was about *me*."

CHAPTER 14

hey stood on the edge of the cliff, staring out at the moon sparkling on the waves.

The boat bobbed in the distance, its emergency beacon blinking and reflecting on the water like Christmas lights. It made Nick miss his boat. He always lined the vessel with strings of lights for Christmas.

"Do we try for it?" English asked.

"I want to go home," Kelly grunted. "I say we swim for that bitch, fuck waiting for the ferry."

Ty, Nick, and Zane murmured in agreement. Park merely nodded.

"Who's physically capable of making that swim?" Nick asked, looking down the line at all of them.

Ty shook his head. Kelly had put his shoulder back in joint, to the tune of much squabbling and name-calling and Ty screaming in the end.

Zane wasn't injured at all, but he looked dubious. "I can try for it," he said, "but I'm not a very strong swimmer."

"I'm good for it," English said with a nod.

Nick looked him up and down. "Dude, is there a wet suit that will fit you?"

English laughed. "Probably not on this island."

Nick shook his head. The sea was far too cold to swim without a wet suit. He'd die before he got halfway there.

"I can swim," Park said. His arms were crossed, and he was still wearing his sunglasses even in the dark of night. "But perhaps we should use that canoe on the beach instead."

"The what?" Ty and Zane blurted at the same time.

Park nodded toward the beach below. None of them could see what he was seeing, so Nick lay out on the edge of the cliff and shined his light down there. A battered red canoe reflected back at them.

"How the hell?" Nick asked over his shoulder.

"His sunglasses have night vision," English answered, deadpan.

"Seriously?" Ty and Kelly both said.

"No."

Both their shoulders slumped in disappointment, and Nick laughed. He wasn't sure if it was really that funny or if he was just at the end of his sanity. He didn't really care either. He stood and brushed himself off, then patted English on the chest and jerked his thumb over his shoulder at the beach below. "It's all you, buddy."

English nodded, gesturing to Park.

"Wait, we can't send them alone. What if they leave us here?" Kelly asked.

Nick raised an eyebrow at his lover, but it was a valid question. He glanced at English, who was nodding.

"Fair enough. Who wants to go with me?"

"I will," Zane offered. He and Ty exchanged a glance, communicating silently for a few seconds. Then Zane checked the ammunition in his gun. Nick handed him his knife with a nod.

They turned to English to see if he'd object. The big man shook his head. "He's already told me he can't swim. If I want to kill him, I'll just tip the canoe." He gave them all a cheeky grin, then turned to make his way down to the beach.

"Oh," Ty said. "Oh, hell no."

Zane laughed and patted him on the shoulder. "It'll be okay." He followed after English, leaving the four of them up top to watch their progress through the real set of night vision goggles they'd found in the stash of weapons Frost had cleared from the mansion's stalking room.

Park turned to them, frowning. "Garrett know how to drive a boat like that?"

"No, why?" Ty answered.

Park shrugged. "Neither does John."

Nick rolled his eyes and shoved the night vision goggles at Kelly, then began to strip himself of any unnecessary accessories.

"What kind of Green Beret doesn't know how to handle a boat?" Ty asked.

"He thinks he does," Park said, beginning to grin. "That's the problem."

"Wait up!" Nick called to the two men, jogging to catch up to them on the beach path.

The sun was rising when the boat neared the shoreline. The dock was the only place even remotely capable of taking a vessel the size of the craft they'd retrieved, but there was too much damage and debris to get close. They had to ferry people two and three at a time, using the canoe and the lifeboat they'd found on board. Ty wasn't even able to help do that because of his throbbing shoulder. He sat aside and watched despondently.

They left the house as it was, the bodies where they'd been lying, save for Burns, who they'd wrapped in canvas and taken with them. Earl had been adamant he wouldn't leave Burns behind. Luggage was left in the rooms, only the necessities taken with them back to the mainland. Hamish, Fraser, and Frost were all tied down, tied up, and gagged so none of them could speak for the entirety of the two-hour boat ride back to the mainland. Mackie had been left to his cottage and his destroyed dock.

Nick worked on the radio, trying to raise assistance. He finally picked someone up, but they couldn't understand his accent and he couldn't understand theirs. He wound up cursing into the radio and giving up on trying to raise anyone else.

Ty stood beside him at the helm, feeling as if they still had so much left to say but not sure where to even start. He was still having trouble pushing past the shock of Richard Burns's death. He couldn't imagine going through that loss without Nick to help him.

Nick finally looked him up and down. "You look like hell, Ty, go sit down."

Ty remained for several more seconds. When Nick glanced at him again, Ty said, "I love you like my own brother. You know that, right?"

Nick stared at him.

"I know you've got to be mad at me for a while. But remember that, okay?"

Nick gave him a curt nod, swallowing hard. Ty turned away from him, heading out of the pilothouse. Deuce met him in the doorway, Livi on his arm.

"You two okay?" Ty asked them.

"Today was our wedding day," Livi said, her voice choked. She covered her mouth, fighting back tears. Then she took a deep breath. "We wanted to thank you for what you did. We were coming to thank Nick."

Nick still had his back to them, but his head was turned, listening and watching out of his peripheral vision.

Livi moved past Ty and went up to Nick, not saying a word, merely hugging him. He was forced to take one arm off the wheel to return the hug, his big hand gentle on her slim frame.

Livi was crying quietly when she released him. She moved back to Ty and Deuce, tears streaming down her face.

"Are you okay?" Ty asked again, unsure of what to do for them.

She laughed shakily and nodded, wiping at her face. "After everything that happened, I feel so stupid. I just . . . I thought we'd be married when we got back to the mainland. It wasn't even official, it was just a . . . stupid ceremony on a stupid island!"

Deuce pulled her into a hug, resting his chin on her head. He met Ty's eyes, smiling weakly.

Ty nodded in understanding. Then an idea hit him. He turned to Nick again, narrowing his eyes.

Nick stiffened when he saw the look. "What?"

"You're the captain of this ship."

Nick's eyes darted from Ty to Deuce and Livi, who were both frowning at Ty in confusion.

"You can marry them."

Nick stared, his mouth hanging open. "That's a horrible idea."

"He can marry us?" Livi asked.

Ty shrugged. "It's just as official as a ceremony on a stupid island."

Livi's blue eyes grew wide and hopeful.

Nick pointed a finger at her. "I'm immune to those looks."

"Five minutes, Irish, you can marry them."

"I don't know how to perform a marriage ceremony, Ty!"

"Please," Deuce said quietly. "Everyone we love is on this boat. That's all that matters. Just say man and wife for us in front of our families."

It seemed like Nick was going to protest, but he finally cursed under his breath and turned to slow the boat.

As soon as he turned back, Livi darted toward him and hugged him around the neck. "Thank you," she whispered. Then she left the pilothouse to get everyone together.

Deuce gave Nick a smile and a nod before going off after her. Ty couldn't keep from grinning as Nick glared at him.

"I'll make you regret this," Nick warned, walking past.

Fifteen minutes later, they'd gathered everyone, and Nick was at the bow of the ship, Livi and Deuce standing before him. No one was with them, no best man or maid of honor, no father of the bride giving her away. Livi had put her wedding dress on, sans all the accessories, to leave her in a beautiful white sheath gown that spread out in a train behind her. Amelia sat on the train, gnawing on the expensive silk.

Nick took a deep breath. Ty could tell he was nervous. Probably close to just throwing himself overboard rather than doing this. He finally looked at Deuce and Livi and gave them a signature O'Flaherty grin.

"Deacon Grady," he started. "Do you intend to spend the rest of your life with this woman? Love her, cherish her, let her pick out the curtains, and shield her body from any future bullets?"

Deuce chuckled and gazed at Livi, reaching to take her hand in his. "I do," he said softly. He slid a ring onto her finger, never taking his eyes off her face.

Nick turned to Livi.

"Olivia Stanton," he said.

"I do," she said before he could continue. She wrapped her arms around Deuce's neck and kissed him. The boat erupted in cheers and applause, and Deuce took Livi in his arms and turned her, dipping her for a kiss. Amelia grabbed onto Livi's train and slid across the deck as it moved, laughing gleefully.

Nick stood with his hands spread, incredulous. "Why am I even up here?" he demanded.

Livi and Deuce laughed merrily, kissing again before Deuce set her on her feet once more.

"Only other part of this thing I know is 'you may now kiss the bride!'" Nick told them, clearly offended that he hadn't been able to at least do that part.

Livi laughed again and stepped forward to give him a kiss on the cheek, and then she and Deuce turned to their family and loved ones and raised their joined hands. Everyone clapped for them, some people giving off whistles and howls. Deuce bent to pick Amelia up, and he wrapped his arm around his wife, walking into the crowd with his family. Ty stood to the side, still clapping, watching his brother with a smile on his face. Zane was next to him, brushing against him as he clapped.

He glanced up at the bow of the boat only to find Nick watching them.

"Anyone else want to get hitched while I'm up here?" Nick asked, staring at Ty and Zane pointedly.

Ty swallowed past the sudden knot in his throat and turned to Zane, warmth spreading through him. Zane's eyes had widened, his mouth parted but no words coming out. Ty grasped his hand and kissed his fingers. "Will you marry me, Zane?" he whispered.

Zane looked from him to Nick and back, a grin spreading across his lips. Then he shook his head. "No," he answered, laughing.

Ty huffed and fought not to smile.

Nick walked past them, shaking his head. "Damn, son."

"That's cold," Kelly added before they were gone.

Ty and Zane both watched them go, then turned back to each other, both of them smiling. Ty pulled Zane to him and kissed him, holding him by a handful of his hair so he couldn't get away. "I'll get you eventually, my pretty," he whispered.

"And I look forward to it," Zane mumbled against his lips.

CHAPTER 15

Ty, Nick, and Kelly were still in their dress blues. Zane had loosened his tie and removed his suit coat because he refused to be in a funeral suit longer than he had to be. They'd retreated from the graveyard and taken up residence in a local tavern, one Ty had apparently frequented when he'd been based in Washington, DC.

Zane was drinking Coke. Ty had ordered a scotch to toast Richard Burns, but after that he'd stuck to Dr Pepper. Zane had caught a glance between Ty and Nick that spoke clearly to the fact that Nick had read Ty the riot act at some point about drinking in Zane's presence.

Nick and Kelly were drinking water. Zane didn't know whether to be grateful to them or to be pleased that these men, men who reportedly had always been hard-drinking, hard-partying hooligans, would refrain for him.

Either way, he'd given them each a nod in recognition of what they were doing.

"I can't believe all this shit circles back to me," Zane said, staring at the tabletop.

"If you pull one of those 'everyone I love dies, let me disappear' moves on me, I'll hunt you down," Ty told him.

Zane laughed sadly. "Noted."

"This is the mole," Ty told him, almost growling. "He knew Burns was closing in on him. He's the only one could have known enough information to feed to de la Vega and pull this shit off."

"This the same mole who made the mess in New Orleans?" Kelly asked.

Zane nodded, still staring. "This isn't going to end until the cartel is gone. Or I am."

The table fell silent, and the sounds of the noisy tavern began to fade until Zane was sitting in the silence of his own head, staring at the wood grain of the table.

"So this de la Vega guy," Nick finally said. Zane raised his head, blinking away the deep reverie he'd been lost in. Nick was lounging in the corner of their booth, his arm around Kelly's shoulder, his other hand on the table like he was accustomed to sitting with people he didn't hide his hands from. He tapped his fingers and met Zane's eyes. "How do we take him out?"

Zane smiled. "That'll just have to wait until after your little surgery, now won't it?"

Nick rolled his eyes and took a sip of water. He was donating his liver to a father who had terrorized him all his life. He was a better person than Zane, that was for sure. Zane would've sat back and watched the man die.

"We'll investigate from our end," Ty said, sounding determined and a little scary. Zane liked it. "To get to de la Vega, we have to get to the mole. That's our first move."

They all nodded, glancing around at each other.

"Does that mean you're coming back to the FBI?" Zane asked Ty.

Ty shook his head. "We both know I can't. I think what you call me now would be the Wild Card."

Zane met his lover's eyes, thrilled to see the life back in them. Whatever had happened to Ty and Sidewinder out there, it had sapped the joy out of all of them, taken the very thing that made them capable of walking through Hell and doused it. But now, looking at these three men, with a purpose given to them once more, with a mission, Zane could see that fire returning.

De la Vega had poked the wrong hornet's nest this time.

Nick fought to open his eyes when he heard voices. He finally managed to make his head fall to the side and peered through his eyelashes to see who was in the room. The motion must have drawn attention, because the voices stopped and the room fell silent.

Nick closed his eyes again.

A moment later a cool hand was on his forehead. "Nick?" the voice whispered. "Wake up, babe." When Nick finally got both eyes open, Kelly was smiling down at him. He grazed his fingers along

Nick's cheek and bent to whisper in his ear. "Lots of people here to see you."

A separator curtain screeched as it was pulled across the room to give them a little more privacy. He was still groggy as hell, and it took him a long time to focus, and an even longer time to understand what was going on. He'd given a piece of his liver, one he'd managed to keep healthy by some miracle, to his father. It hadn't even really been a choice for him. As soon as the tests came back saying he was a good match, he knew he had to do it.

His father would live on, whether he deserved to or not. Nick's conscience was clear, and the missing piece of his liver would eventually grow back. He hoped.

Almost a dozen people were crowded around, all holding some form of "special delivery" baby presents.

He started to laugh but had to stop when pain threatened. "Assholes."

Ty and Zane were both there, as were Owen and Digger. Nick had known they would be, though, because they'd flown in last night to be with him before the operation. Digger stood at the foot of the bed, and Owen was sitting in the corner holding a huge teddy bear that hid most of his body. When he realized Nick was awake, he stood and placed the bear in the chair to move closer.

"How you feeling, O?" Digger asked.

"Like less of a man," Nick said, drawing laughs from the others.

"You look it," Digger told him, and held up a jar filled with liquid and some sort of . . . stuff.

Ty quickly grabbed the jar and hid it from sight. "Dude, no."

"Gator livers!"

"No."

"They'll help his grow back faster!"

"Definitely no."

Nick groaned and tossed his head to the side, trying to purge that visual from his mind before that visual purged his stomach.

"So gross," Ty muttered, and he left the room with the jar under his arm.

The rest of them were still laughing when Ty returned, and Nick finally managed to look back to the foot of the bed without feeling the need to throw up.

Kat and Erin were standing there, both of them with bouquets filled out with baby's breath, little pink daisies, and balloons. They giggled as they placed the dainty arrangements on the table near the wall. Even Nick's oldest nephew, Patrick, had come with them. He was snickering gleefully when he handed Nick a card that everyone had signed. It read, "Congratulations on your special delivery."

"What'd you guys do, send out a memo?" Nick asked, still trying to avoid laughing.

"It seemed appropriate," Ty said. He held up a bouquet of cookies on sticks, all of them in the shape of baby bottles, shoes, and bonnets, then set it down on the table next to Nick. The vase read "For the Little One."

Owen tapped Nick's foot, then gestured between him and Kelly. "You two got some 'splainin' to do, Lucy."

Nick's stomach dropped. "Who told you?"

"Doc couldn't stop pacing in the waiting room. Finally, he just blurted out that he needed a hug because he loved you and he was freaking out."

Nick managed a warm smile. "You okay with it?"

Owen nodded, pursing his lips. "Okay enough to provide hugs in waiting rooms, I guess. I'll reserve my final judgment for the whole story. Assuming I'm going to get it?"

Nick nodded. Digger wrapped an arm around Owen's shoulders and patted his chest like he was proud of him.

Kelly chuckled. He held to Nick's hand tighter. "When Nick can have a beer again, we'll sit you down and explain all you want."

Owen seemed satisfied with that. Nick found his throat getting tighter. He no longer had any secrets from any of them. His conscience was clear again, and it was a massive weight off his mind and soul. All he could do was nod and blink back tears of relief.

The only thing that didn't fit the theme was the gift Zane had brought him. It was a box of shotgun shells, the right kind for Nick's Ithaca 37 pump action. They were green-tipped, though, with little radioactive symbols etched on them.

"Zombie rounds," Zane told him, tongue in cheek. "In case you came out of the surgery mostly dead."

This time Nick laughed even though it hurt. He held to his side gingerly, trying to keep from laughing harder. "These should come in handy, Garrett. Thanks."

"I also brought you season one of *The Walking Dead*. We'll sit and watch while you recover."

"Is this . . . zombie bonding?" Ty asked.

Nick grinned up at Zane, nodding. "A man after my own heart."

"I thought zombies were after brains," Kelly said wryly. He pointed at Zane. "You stay away from his heart, that's mine."

The group chuckled. Nick rolled his eyes and closed them again, still smiling. And while he could hear the others shuffling around and murmuring quietly, he couldn't force his eyes back open. "Thanks for coming guys. I'm sorry I can't . . . stay."

Kelly's hand came to rest on his forehead again, then slipped down to cover his eyes so he'd stop struggling to try to open them. "They'll be back when you're not out of it, okay? Sleep."

Each visitor came up to the bed and gave Nick some sort of touch before leaving, whether it was a kiss on the forehead from his sisters, a squeeze of the shoulder from Owen, or a gentle fist bump from his nephew. They all seemed to know what the contact would mean to him regardless of whether he could drag his eyes open to see them again. Ty leaned over him and hugged him tightly, pressing his cheek to Nick's and calling him brother, telling him he loved him. Zane petted his head affectionately.

He heard them file out until the room felt empty.

Kelly's fingers drifted down his arm, making Nick smile. "The surgery went well," Kelly told him. "Your dad's in ICU, but he's doing fine. They'll be bringing him in here later on, so don't be surprised if he shows up."

Nick nodded. He could honestly say that he didn't care how his dad was doing. He'd done everything in his power to give him a fighting chance, and the man was on his own from now on. Nick was done with him. He squeezed Kelly's hand and took a deep, painful breath.

"Did you really mean it when you said you were done carrying a gun?" Kelly whispered.

Nick forced one eye open. A frown marred Kelly's features, and his eyes were sad and sympathetic. He leaned closer to Nick.

"I don't want you to give up something you love because of me. And I'm worried that's what you're doing."

Nick forced both tired eyes open and blinked hard, trying to keep them from watering. "Kelly."

"Is that what you're doing?" Kelly asked. "Because in a few months you'll be mostly healed up. In a year you'll be whole again. The Boston PD would take you back in a heartbeat, and you're one hell of a detective. You're a better detective than you were a Marine, and Nick, that's saying something because you were one hell of a fucking Marine."

"Doc."

"That's saying a hell of a thing, you know? And you don't just give up on something you're that good at, Nick, you don't."

"Kels."

"You've always liked your job. And you love a mystery. You're not happy without a mystery to solve."

"*You're* a mystery," Nick said. He reached up to trail his fingertips down Kelly's face. "I'd have you."

Kelly snorted.

"I want us to start something, Kels. You and me. Something we'll live through. Something we'll grow old doing. We can't do that if I'm a cop."

Kelly bit his lip, and his eyes were just as misty as Nick's. "Are you sure?"

Nick didn't answer. He was staring at Kelly, completely smitten, wondering why it had taken him so fucking long to realize he loved the man.

"I'd do anything with you, Kels. Anything you wanted."

Kelly grasped Nick's face in his hands. "I've been trying to figure something out. You see, I can tell you I love you, and it's the same words I've always said to you from the first day I realized you'd have my back in a firefight. I love you, brother. Those are the same words I say to Six and Digger and Ozone. You know? They were the same words I said to Eli the last time he called. They were the same words my parents said the night they left and died in the rain."

"Kelly," Nick managed to say as tears began to fall for some reason. He pressed his hand to Kelly's cheek. A tear hit his thumb and he realized they were both crying.

"But I don't understand why those are the same words I have to use for a feeling that's not the same anymore," Kelly continued, his voice lower, more intimate and more confused. "I . . . I *need* you. I adore you. I want to wake up every morning and make you fix me breakfast so I can watch you cook. I want to . . . I want to spend the rest of my life with you doing things that make life worth living. I want to make you smile. I want you to take me to every baseball stadium out there and teach me every single little thing you know about the game because I love the way your eyes light up when you talk about it. I want to . . . what words do I use for this feeling if 'I love you' has already been used?"

Nick tried to swallow against the lump in his throat and couldn't. He shook his head, at a loss. He stared into Kelly's eyes for long moments before finally attempting to speak. "How about . . . marry me?"

Kelly smiled and wiped at his eyes. "Okay."

Kelly bent to kiss him, his lips barely grazing Nick's. Then he kissed him harder, stopping only to sniffle and wipe his cheeks again, using Nick's hospital gown to do it. He rested his head on Nick's shoulder, and Nick wrapped a clumsy arm around his neck.

"I love you, Nick," Kelly whispered. "No matter what those words meant before, we know what they mean now. They're ours now. Just ours."

Nick whispered the words in Kelly's ear, feeling a new weight to them. Instead of a sense of panic like he'd half expected, he felt nothing but calm. He could marry Kelly tomorrow and never look back, never regret the decision. He and Kelly could spend their lives together—as boyfriends, as husbands, as partners-in-crime, as any damn thing they wanted—and there wasn't a thing about that prospect that made him nervous. He buried his nose in Kelly's messy hair and closed his eyes, unable to keep them open any longer with Kelly's scent engulfing him and lulling him to sleep.

Kelly kissed him gently one more time, then placed something in Nick's hand and positioned his thumb over a button. "Rest, babe.

Here's your morphine drip. Enjoy it for me. I'm going to go get food with the others, okay?"

Nick managed a smile, and Kelly kissed him once more, but he still couldn't drag his eyes open as Kelly left the room.

Marry me. It made him smile as he drifted off to sleep.

He floated in and out of awareness for a while. He wasn't really in pain, but it wasn't a restful sleep either. The beeps and shuffling footsteps and whispered words of the hospital were soothing in a way, and eventually even the steady breathing of his father in the next bed after they moved him into the room was something that eased Nick's mind.

He wasn't sure what it was that disturbed him, but his eyes were open before he realized he was awake. A male nurse stood next to his bed, checking his vitals and messing with the machines. Nick looked him up and down, moving nothing but his eyes to do it. Then, for some reason, his mind began casting around for something, *anything*, that could be used as a weapon.

He tossed his head like he was suffering through a restless sleep and then rolled, edging toward the table where Ty's heavy crystal vase of joke cookies sat. A hand shot out and gripped his wrist, wrenching his arm until he whimpered. Another hand landed on his incision, making him cry out and curl into a protective ball. He grabbed at the man's arm, trying to push it away, trying to get away from the agony.

He glared up into the eyes of the nurse, recognition dawning as he tried to gasp for air.

"Almost got the drop on me, O'Flaherty," Liam Bell drawled. "Impressive."

The bed on the other side of the curtain creaked as Nick's father moved. "What's going on over there?"

Liam glanced over his shoulder, letting up on the pressure on Nick's arm and incision. He reached out to the screaming machines and silenced them somehow, then pulled the green mask down his chin. A smirk curled his lips.

Nick pressed his hand to his incision, feeling blood seeping through the stitches. He curled up and rocked, unable to stop himself. "What are you doing here?" he gritted out.

"I heard you were under the weather," Liam said, his tone entirely conversational. He pulled up a chair and sat, then gently took Nick's hand in his, cradling the morphine clicker in Nick's palm. He wrapped Nick's fingers around it and pressed his thumb against Nick's, making him push the button a few times. "Let's just up this a little, shall we? Can't have you in pain."

"You okay over there, boy?" Nick's dad asked.

"Dad, it's fine," Nick managed. "It's fine. Go back to sleep."

Liam rolled his eyes and stood. "I'll be right back." He yanked the curtain aside, standing in the middle of the room to look down at Brian O'Flaherty's bed. "You have some fucking nerve, don't you?" he said as he examined the equipment around Brian's bed.

"Who the hell are you?"

"Just a friend of your son's, don't mind me," Liam murmured distractedly.

"Bell, leave him alone," Nick tried to say, though his voice was weak and his words were slurring and panicked. He tried to reach the call button, which had been moved out of the way to make room for the box of zombie shells.

Liam plucked Brian's IV line between two of his fingers, then pulled a syringe from his pocket. He whistled as he injected whatever was in it into the IV.

"Liam!" Nick shouted. He reached for his own IV to yank it out, intending to get out of bed, but his movements were sluggish and his mind was growing foggier. He couldn't manage it. His hand landed on the shotgun shells, prepared to hurl the box at Liam's head.

"Relax, he'll be fine. He'll just go to sleep." Liam tossed the syringe in a receptacle and then leaned over Brian. "I ever see you with a drink in your hand again, I'll put a hole through your fucking skull. Understand? You don't deserve this man as a son."

Nick saw the anger and fear in his father's eyes before the medicine Liam had injected him with put him to sleep.

"Wanker," Liam added. He pulled the curtain closed again and sat down beside Nick. He batted Nick's hands away from the heavy box of shells, then from the IV line and the nurse's call button. His movements were extremely gentle considering he'd just jabbed the heel of his palm into Nick's incision several minutes before. He patted Nick's chest. "All right, then."

Nick groaned and tried to shove him away, but couldn't. "Why can't you just slink off to somewhere and die like you were supposed to?"

"Well, that's not very nice."

"What the fuck are you doing here?"

"I knew now would be the best time to see you, since when you're healthy you tend to punch first and discuss after you've tied me to something that's not very fun."

Nick grunted.

"To get right down to it, I need your help."

"Go fuck yourself," Nick growled. He tossed his head and writhed on the bed, fighting through the pain.

Liam took his hand in his, pushing Nick's thumb to hit the morphine drip again. He held on to him this time, as if he were offering comfort.

Nick glared at him. "How could you convince yourself I'd help you do anything?"

Liam glanced at the doorway. "Because I finally have leverage over you."

Nick's eyes darted toward the door.

"You and the Doc, yeah? Never saw that coming."

"You hurt him and you're a dead man. I'll hunt you down and make you suffer, I promise you that."

"I accept those terms. And . . . I am suitably intimidated by the violent declarations of an otherwise gentle man. The thing is, I'm going to need your help. The details are a bit fuzzy yet, but rest assured it is something you and only you can assist me in doing. And when the time comes, I'm going to need you to mobilize without questions and without your nasty habit of being morally opposed to . . . things."

"Things?"

"You know. Stuff."

Nick's breathing was growing more labored, and it was harder to fight past the morphine to keep his eyes open. The only reason he was even still conscious was pure hatred.

Liam smiled kindly at him. "You help me on one simple task, and then you and the Doc sail off into the sunset together. You refuse, and I finish the job New Orleans started with that hole in Doc's chest."

Nick squeezed his eyes closed, gritting his teeth against the mere notion. He thought he might throw up.

"Do we have a deal?"

Nick shook his head.

"Say no to me, O'Flaherty, and I go downstairs right now and off him. He's in the cafeteria sitting beside a window. Perfect head shot from across the street. Can you imagine Tyler's face with the doc's brains spattered all over it? I imagine he'd be quite devastated."

Nick curled onto his side and covered his eyes with his hand. He hated himself for doing it, but he clutched at Liam's hand harder as pain and grief wracked his body. "Okay," he whispered.

"We have a deal?"

"None of them come to harm," Nick said. He looked up at Liam, desperate. "I do whatever you want and you leave them all alone. Give me your word."

Liam smiled fondly. "I always liked that about you, O'Flaherty. You were the one Sidewinder who actually meant it when you said, 'I promise.' You have my word. Do I have yours?"

Nick glared at him, the molten hatred threatening to burn right through his heart. He managed to get the word out anyway. "Yes."

Liam smiled brilliantly and patted him on the cheek. "There's my white knight. Now, surely I mustn't remind you that anyone you tell about our little arrangement will come to a sticky end."

Nick could do nothing but grit his teeth and glare up into Liam's ice-blue eyes.

"I'll be in touch. Speedy recovery and all that," Liam drawled, smirking like it was some private joke. Then he pulled another syringe from his pocket and put Nick out of his misery.

Zane tossed his badge and keys on the counter and shoved the door shut behind him. The days at work seemed to be getting longer, the responsibilities weighing heavier. He wasn't sure how much longer he had the will to stick this through. The only thing keeping him there was the very real threat that still hovered over everyone and everything he loved. He had one more battle to fight.

And then he was ready to sleep in with his lover, to curl up on a Sunday and watch football, to read a fucking book without wondering when he'd be called into work.

"Ty?" he tried. The house was still and quiet. The Mustang hadn't been parked in the back, so Zane was pretty confident Ty wasn't home. The disappointment was striking.

He shrugged out of his jacket and began thumbing through the stack of mail on the counter, but a small box sitting there caught his attention. He set the mail aside and picked up the box. It was black with a simple white ribbon on it. A notecard tucked into the ribbon read, "Open Me Now."

Zane smirked. It had almost become a joke between them, Ty's many and varied ways of asking Zane to marry him. Zane almost dreaded the day he was convinced to say yes because then the attempts and the fun of saying no would stop.

He slid the ribbon off the box, still smiling and shaking his head. Inside was a purple velvet bag, and when Zane peered inside he found a wide silver band. His stomach flipped as he shook it into his palm. It wasn't shiny or new, and it had obviously been handmade. Etched into the side were numbers Zane quickly recognized as latitude and longitude coordinates.

"Oh God, Ty," he whispered. He was chuckling as he pulled out his phone and punched the coordinates into his GPS. It gave him directions, telling him the location was less than half a mile away. At least it was close.

Zane grabbed his coat and slid the ring onto his right ring finger. It was a perfect fit. He walked several blocks toward Fell's Point, then turned where his phone indicated and began searching for somewhere that looked like it was supposed to be his goal.

When he found his destination, it was not what he was expecting. The only reason he even knew he was there was because Ty was sitting on the front stoop, waiting for him.

Zane peered up at the three-story building. It was brick, with white trim that was flaking and falling off to reveal green underneath.

The front door was covered with stickers and graffiti, and the glass had been covered up with paper grocery bags. A torn black and orange For Sale sign was taped to it.

The windows all boasted corbels and hand-carved wood, but they were visibly rotting. The basement steps on the sidewalk led to a dark hole that may or may not have been home to vagrants at night. The only thing that could be said for the building was that it probably had an incredible view of the harbor from the back, and that Zane's lover was sitting on its concrete steps.

Zane snorted as Ty stood to meet him. He held up the ring and wiggled his finger. "I can't say this is your best attempt."

Ty grinned. He turned and tapped the For Sale sign. "I bought it."

Zane's smile fell, and he glanced up at the dilapidated building again. "You what?"

Ty pulled the door open. It was unlocked. "Come on."

"Ty, you *bought* this building?" Zane stuttered as he followed Ty inside. "With what, Monopoly money?"

Ty's laugh echoed off the empty interior. Inside, the building didn't look much better. There was an old bar that stretched the length of the narrow front room, and in the back were steps going up and what may have been a storeroom with a rear exit.

Ty lifted his hands and turned to Zane, smiling almost shyly.

Zane gaped at his surroundings. "I'm . . . confused."

Ty patted the bar. "It used to be a bar."

"I see that."

"It has two stories upstairs. It needs complete renovation, so we can gut it and do whatever we want to it."

Zane glanced up again, imagining all the work that would take. Ty without a job and without any leads on the mole was beginning to be a scary prospect.

He turned back to Ty, still waiting for when this would turn into a good idea.

Ty was still smiling gently. "You see, no matter what we do to the row house, we'll always know it was mine first. We can't cleanse it of that and make it truly ours. But here we can start fresh. Build whatever we want."

Zane bit his lip, nodding. "Okay. What about this level, though? It's still a commercial district."

"I realized the one thing Fell's Point didn't really have," Ty said, his voice sincere and hopeful, "was a bookstore."

Zane's stomach flipped. He loved old book stores. Loved the smell of them, loved to walk through them, loved sitting in them and reading in a ratty old chair. Ty had known that from the beginning, from the day in New York City when he'd gamely followed Zane into a bookstore and sat there as Zane browsed.

Ty's lips twitched. "And we could sell black market orchids from the back."

Zane's breath left him. He was standing in the middle of the craphole building Ty had bought him, and suddenly he could see what Ty was truly proposing. A life where neither of them carried a gun. A life where Zane could sit in a bookstore all day, could know that Ty would be there when he went home, right upstairs. A life for them, together. A future. Ty wanted them to cut and run.

Zane thought he had experienced love before. Thought he had known what it felt like to be the center of someone's world.

He had been wrong, because it had never felt like this.

Ty squared his shoulders and straightened himself. He cut quite the figure, his steady presence overpowering the dusty surroundings. His voice was quiet and clear. "Will you marry me, Zane?"

"Yes."

Ty laughed, and his shoulders slumped with relief. He moved toward Zane, reaching out to hook his finger through the bullet hole in Zane's jacket and pull him close. "Thank Christ, 'cause I was out of ideas after this."

Zane laughed with him, the sound echoing off the bones of their future home, ringing in a new chapter in their lives like the bells of a cathedral. Their laughter was still echoing off the walls when Ty took Zane's face in both hands and kissed him for all he was worth. They wrapped around each other, clinging to the promise of the life they could have.

Explore more of the *Cut & Run* Universe at:
riptidepublishing.com/titles/universe/cut-run

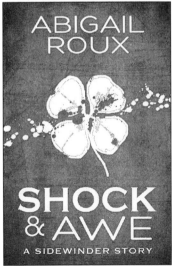

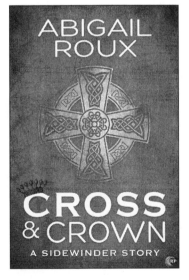

To learn more about the first five titles in the *Cut & Run*
series, please visit: abigailroux.com/books/default.html

Dear Reader,

Thank you for reading Abigail Roux's *Ball & Chain*!

We know your time is precious and you have many, many entertainment options, so it means a lot that you've chosen to spend your time reading. We really hope you enjoyed it.

We'd be honored if you'd consider posting a review—good or bad—on sites like **Amazon, Barnes & Noble, Goodreads, Twitter, Facebook, Tumblr,** and your blog or website. We'd also be honored if you told your friends and family about this book. Word of mouth is a book's lifeblood!

For more information on upcoming releases, author interviews, blog tours, contests, giveaways, and more, please sign up for our weekly, spam-free newsletter and visit us around the web:

Newsletter: tinyurl.com/RiptideSignup
Twitter: twitter.com/RiptideBooks
Facebook: facebook.com/RiptidePublishing
Goodreads: tinyurl.com/RiptideOnGoodreads
Tumblr: riptidepublishing.tumblr.com

Thank you so much for Reading the Rainbow!

RiptidePublishing.com

ALSO BY
ABIGAIL ROUX

ABOUT THE AUTHOR

Abigail Roux was born and raised in North Carolina. A past volleyball star who specializes in sarcasm and painful historical accuracy, she currently spends her time coaching high school volleyball and investigating the mysteries of single motherhood. Any spare time is spent living and dying with every Atlanta Braves and Carolina Panthers game of the year. Abigail has a daughter, Little Roux, who is the light of her life, a boxer, four rescued cats who play an ongoing live-action variation of Call of Duty throughout the house, one evil Ragdoll, a certifiable extended family down the road, and a cast of thousands in her head.

Visit Abigail's website for more info: www.abigailroux.com.

Enjoyed this book? Visit RiptidePublishing.com to find more romantic suspense!

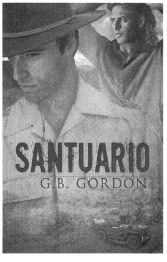

| Catch a Ghost | Santuario |
| ISBN: 978-1-62649-039-0 | ISBN: 978-1-937551-65-0 |

Earn Bonus Bucks!

Earn 1 Bonus Buck for each dollar you spend. Find out how at RiptidePublishing.com/news/bonus-bucks.

Win Free Ebooks for a Year!

Pre-order coming soon titles directly through our site and you'll receive one entry into a drawing to win free books for a year! Get the details at RiptidePublishing.com/contests.